P9-DWW-714

FOLLOW
ME
DOWN

SHERRI SMITH

A TOM DOHERTY ASSOCIATES BOOK • NEW YORK

This is a work of fiction. All of the characters, organizations, and events portrayed in this novel are either products of the author's imagination or are used fictitiously.

FOLLOW ME DOWN

A Forge Book
Published by Tom Doherty Associates
175 Fifth Avenue
New York, NY 10010

www.tor-forge.com

Forge® is a registered trademark of Macmillan Publishing Group, LLC.

The Library of Congress Cataloging-in-Publication Data is available upon request.

ISBN 978-0-7653-8670-0 (hardcover)
ISBN 978-0-7653-8672-4 (e-book)

Our books may be purchased in bulk for promotional, educational, or business use. Please contact your local bookseller or the Macmillan Corporate and Premium Sales Department at 1-800-221-7945, extension 5442, or by e-mail at MacmillanSpecialMarkets@macmillan.com.

First Edition: March 2017

Printed in the United States of America

0 9 8 7 6 5 4 3 2 1

For Tara

FOLLOW
ME
DOWN

1

DAY 1

WEDNESDAY, EARLY MORNING

My first thought was my mother had started another fire. Or maybe she did something nasty to a fellow patient again. Last year she stabbed a woman sitting next to her in the dining room with a fork because, she said, the woman tried to steal her dessert. Both times I had to cover the costs (the woman needed four stitches, one for each tine), which I couldn't help but suspect the care home had inflated. I always pictured the nurses clanging their after-work mai tais together, telling each other they deserved this little something extra for having to deal with *that* woman.

I almost didn't answer. I'd just spent the last slow hour helping a prostitute pick out hair dye (Midnight Vixen by L'Oréal seemed a professionally sound choice) after refilling her Valtrex prescription and was taking my second break of the overnight shift. But it was the strangeness of the hour. My phone never rang at 6 A.M.

"Mia Haas?" A gruff voice.

"Yes." I was sitting with two front cashiers, sipping weak coffee and eating powdery donuts for a cheap rush to carry me through the next two hours.

"This is Wayoata Police Chief John Pruden."

"What did Mimi do now?" I offered up a theatrical sigh for the benefit of my co-workers who had never heard me mention Mimi before now and locked myself in the bathroom for privacy.

"I'm calling about Lucas."

"Sorry, what?"

"Your brother, Lucas. Have you heard from him?" He sounded irritated he had to repeat himself.

"Why?" My teeth sunk into my lower lip. Visions of accidents sucked me into a panic, of bloody highway collisions and motorboats crashed into rocky lakeshores with beer bottles still rolling back and forth on deck. A school shooting. Wayoata was the kind of crappy town where angry, awkward outcasts went on shooting rampages. "What happened?"

Pruden evaded my question. "So you're telling me you haven't heard from him in the last seventy-two hours?"

I tried to think when I last talked to my twin brother. He called me a couple of weeks ago but didn't leave a message, which meant it wasn't important. Just one of those catch-up calls and a full report on Mimi. The twenty-four-hour chain pharmacy where I worked in Chicago had opened yet another location two blocks away, and I was doubling up on shifts until another pharmacist was hired.

"No, I haven't. What is this about?"

Pruden muttered something I didn't catch, then followed up with "We can't find your brother."

"What do you mean, you can't find him?" The better question would have been to ask why they were looking for him, but of course I didn't think to ask that yet. I was too blindsided. "He's probably at work." It was June. Exam time. Lucas wouldn't be anywhere but in his classroom. If he'd suddenly decided to quit, he wouldn't have done it during exam time. Plus, he would have told me.

"At work?" Pruden parroted. I'd insulted him; obviously it's too early for Lucas to be at the school. "He's not at work. You need to come in. When can you get here? Sooner the better." Someone jiggled the handle on the bathroom door.

I pushed for more details—really, really pushed—but Pruden insisted we talk in person.

Immediately after hanging up, I tried calling Lucas twenty times in a row. Each time I expected him to pick up so we could laugh at this whole absurd situation. He'd have a funny story about some woman he'd met and half moved in with for the last week and would be stunned that the police got involved over a few unwarranted sick days.

But Lucas wasn't picking up his phone. The ringing, the pause as the call rolled over to voice mail was all dashed hope and building dread. The heat from my phone burrowed deep into my ear, turned into an electric buzz that stayed long after I stopped trying. No answer.

Still sitting on the toilet lid, I went to my brother's Facebook, thinking there'd be a selfie of him doing whatever and I'd know he was fine, but his account had been deleted.

I Googled the *Wayoata Sun*. My ears started to hum; my windpipe twisted. It looked like a novelty newspaper. Pure bogus. The kind you get from some mall parking lot carnival with the words "WANTED AKA [INSERT YOUR COOL NICKNAME HERE]" above your laser-printed face. Yearbook photos, side by side. One staff, one student. My brother and a teenage girl. The breaking news headline, LOCAL TEACHER PERSON OF INTEREST IN STUDENT'S MURDER. It was dated yesterday.

I scrolled down to the comments section, and here was a litany of abuse against my brother. Cap-locked words, among them "MURDERER" and "RAPIST" mottled the screen like bullet holes. Even our miserable old neighbor who liked to plant plastic roses in his front flower bed, their startling, colorful heads peeking through the North Dakotan snowdrifts like the earth below was oozing blood, had managed to get in on the verbal stoning: *Rot in hEll sick muther-fucker!!#!* It struck me as especially serious that Paul Bergman felt no need to hide behind a username.

Earlier articles depicted the disappearance and search for a sixteen-year-old girl named Joanna Wilkes. She'd been missing for three weeks before her body was discovered in Dickson Park two days ago.

It didn't take me long to pack. I flung an armful of clothes into my suitcase, fistfuls of underwear and socks; I noticed the red makeup bag at the back of my underwear drawer. Put it in my suitcase, took it out, put it back again. I couldn't imagine going to Wayoata without it. Zipped up the suitcase. It didn't take me long to do anything because I couldn't stop moving. I lived alone in a loft-style apartment in Wicker Park. I'd filled it with all the right things to coordinate with its industrial look of brick walls and exposed ductwork, but somehow it still looked uninspired.

With what I paid in rent each month, I could have afforded a mini-mansion in Wayoata. This was something Lucas had kept reminding me of in the first few months after he went back home. As if all that stood between me and Wayoata was a prime piece of real estate; as if prime real estate existed anywhere at all in Wayoata.

On the plane I ordered a whiskey and water to keep my teeth from sinking into my bottom lip. There was no one to call. Not really. No one to tell me, *Oh, that thing about Lucas and a student was just a big misunderstanding, another snafu our Wayoata finest are known for. It'll be straightened out by the time you get here—in fact don't even waste your time coming in.* We did not have an extended family. Our mother had fled Omaha after a falling-out with her parents when she was nineteen and never talked to them again. Supposedly, they died sometime when Lucas and I were children. She'd told us this very matter-of-factly: "Your grandparents are dead, so stop asking about them." We had an aunt, but I had no idea how to get in touch with her. She had called us every second Christmas for a while, but for whatever reason, that had ended. Mimi would go around, ice clinking in her glass, saying she was estranged from her family, drawing out the word "estranged" like it was a sophisticated, glittery term.

Wayoata does not have its own airport. The earliest flight landed in Bismarck. I had to drive another three hours northeast to get there. I'd reserved a silver sedan online, but the car rental clerk handed me keys for a candy-red PT Cruiser and tried to up-sell the insurance coverage. I asked for something else, anything else. The color didn't matter—it could be a beige or black sedan, the kind of car that didn't draw any attention (negative or positive)—but the clerk just shrugged helplessly.

The drive was claustrophobic, with open fields so lacking in depth and dimension the view could have been a canvas backdrop. The sun lit up the greasy bug spatters on the windshield; they looked like a demented child's finger painting. After leaving for college, I'd returned once a year for Thanksgiving and would sit in my mother's room, plate in lap, silently picking away at the pinkish turkey the care home provided. Once Lucas moved back, nearly five years ago, I no longer felt obligated to make an annual visit, telling myself that Mimi now had Lucas to visit her anytime she wanted and that was important to me, that Mimi had someone. Equally important was that the someone wasn't me.

I knew I was getting close when I saw the same old anti-abortion billboard: a photo of some four-year-old forever stuck in the late nineties with her neon sweater and ribboned hair with ABORTION KILLS CHILDREN scrawled across her. Thirty seconds later, I was passing Wayoata's welcome sign. WAYOATA: HOME OF THE CORN AND APPLE FESTIVAL produced the usual knot in my throat. Just seeing it made me feel sticky and heavy. Someone had spray-painted an "S" in front of "Corn," and the smiling cartoon corn below had been given a penis tip shooting three ejaculating dashes onto the heavily lashed apple. It said something about the town that the welcome sign was always in some state of defacement while the antiabortion sign remained unscathed.

Then came the two competing gas stations lit up like casinos. The houses got closer together. Labyrinthine residential streets followed; the backyards offered views of rusted grain elevators, and the roads looped around and back out to Main Street to avoid dead end signs;

no one wanted to look out their window and see a dead end. A number of storefront businesses had shut down. Wayoata was too far northeast to have benefited from the state's Bakken oil boom, and so, like at prom, where one side of the gym was full of ugly girls who wouldn't put out, all the able-bodied men migrated to the other side, where the getting was good. Faded purple ribbons hung from trees and streetlamps like half-opened gifts.

I went directly to Lucas's apartment and leaned on the buzzer for what seemed like hours. Buzzed the caretaker—no answer there either. The building was built in the early seventies before the farm crisis, when Wayoata was at its peak. Even the name, "The Terrace," in curlicue font over the front entrance, was hopeful for eight stories of plain beige brick. A high-rise by Wayoata standards. A permanent SUITES AVAILABLE sign was bolted to the brick beside the glass doors. I walked over to the parking lot and looked for Lucas's truck, but the parking spot was empty.

I got back into the car and made the heavyhearted drive to the police station. There was only one. I pictured my brother there, clad in an orange jumpsuit, pleading his innocence through prison bars while a self-satisfied Pruden, his legs up on his desk, wiped squirts of jelly donut off his chin. We'd figure it out. Hire a lawyer. Make bail. Sue the Wayoata police for unlawful imprisonment. On the way out, Lucas would say, *Well, that was a bit of a Sticky Ricky.*

Sticky Ricky. Hadn't thought about that for years. Mimi had a boyfriend for a while she called Ricky instead of Rick, like he was some sort of ostentatious pool boy because he was three years younger than her. I was fourteen, doing the dishes when Ricky started to grind up against me. Lucas saw, and without saying a word, he grabbed his hockey stick and whacked Ricky in the small of his back, hard. That's the kind of brother Lucas was. Ricky ditched Mimi, told her he didn't need the bullshit kids she came with. Along the way, this incident got abbreviated to Sticky Ricky and became a long-running inside joke that we applied to assholes and awkward life situations for the remainder of our teen years. *What a giant fucking Sticky Ricky.*

I didn't know why I was thinking about this, other than somehow trying to deflate what I read in the newspaper, deflate the fact that I was even here in Wayoata and that my brother wasn't answering the door.

The station had undergone a serious renovation since I'd last been there. Gone was the mix of wood paneling and forest-green walls that had given it the feel of some backwoods hunting lodge. Now it was open concept and off-white. The front desk had the arc of a hotel check-in desk, two flat screens shared warnings on speeding, texting while driving, and the perils of the zebra mussel.

The receptionist jumped up when I asked for information on Lucas Haas. She gave me a stunned look, her lips curled up, buckteeth on full display before leading me to a door with a plastic plaque that read INTERVIEW ROOM #1 (though there was no second interview room down this, the only hallway). "Chief Pruden will be right with you," she said with a librarian's whisper.

I sat down in a molded plastic chair. A second passed, and Pruden opened the door. He was followed by a younger officer with a brown crew cut, clean-shaven. Blue eyes and cleft chin. Milk-fed. Wholesome. He looked like a trainee. If he was about to introduce himself, he didn't get to, because Pruden sat down and just started talking.

"Miss Haas. Or is it Mrs. something now?" Pruden asked. It was considered bad etiquette in Wayoata to get a woman's marital status wrong. I'd known Pruden most of my life. He'd "escort" Mimi home from time to time, for whatever reason, usually because some Good Samaritan had called to report that a drunk woman was about to drive or was already driving. Sometimes he'd attempt some kind of cringeworthy humor at the door to ease the situation—"Your mom's a bit of a troublemaker, kids"—but we knew better. Mimi had to have something on offer for Pruden to let her DUIs slide by.

Mostly he'd stand there a minute, red-cheeked, as Mimi blathered away, before giving us an embarrassed nod good-bye. I wondered how many times this man's cock has been in my mother's mouth.

"It's Miss," I answered. My voice sounded funny. Tinny and fake. Pruden awkwardly extended a damp hand. He smelled faintly of the outdoors and mosquito repellent. He was well past sixty with fluffy silver hair and a meaty nose. His light blue button-down was wrinkled, and a paternal paunch gathered over his leather belt. You could easily picture him spending his Sundays parked in a recliner, muttering angrily at the television while his mousy wife flitted about, handing him beers and pleading with him to take his heart medication. He probably should have retired a year or two ago.

"Thanks for coming in." Pruden said this, all casual, like he hadn't been hanging the specifics of my missing brother over my head, like the Internet had yet to be invented. "I really wish we were meeting under different circumstances. Can I get you some water? Coffee?"

Pruden's hospitability was making me edgy. "No thanks. I just want to know what's going on. Why is my brother being associated with this . . ." I couldn't bring myself to say murder. "Of being involved with this girl?"

"Joanna Wilkes. Her name is Joanna Wilkes." Pruden's voice tipped toward moral outrage, as if I was trying to dehumanize the murder victim by not saying her name (which I was, but only because my brother had been declared a person of interest).

"Joanna Wilkes," I repeated, looking him in the eye. "Have you found my brother?"

"So you know about Joanna Wilkes, then? What did your brother tell you about her?" Pruden answered, sounding nice and encouraging, like he was trying to coax out a victim impact statement.

"Lucas didn't tell me anything. I read about it online. Why is this happening? Why would the *Wayoata Sun* call my brother a person of interest?"

Pruden let out a heavy sigh, like he'd been holding his breath.

"OK, let's just take a step back for a second. First things first. Can you tell us about the call you received from your brother at 10:17 A.M. this past Friday?"

I had no idea what he was talking about. "What call?"

"The call lasted thirty-two seconds. On Friday," the trainee added.

"Oh, that." I remembered now. Lucas had called me Friday morning, but it was just a pocket dial. A bunch of rustling, some breathing. Not good that they already had my brother's phone records. "We didn't actually talk. He just called me by accident."

"Huh." Pruden looked at the trainee, then back at me, skeptical. "Why didn't you just hang up, then?"

"I did."

"After thirty-two seconds. A lot can be said in that time." The room was getting small. Hostile. So this explained Pruden's reticence on the phone. He'd wanted to ambush me when I got here. Catch me off guard so I'd panic and spill whatever supposed escape plan Lucas had revealed to me in thirty-two seconds.

"Look, I'm here because I want to know where my brother is. I want to know what's going on. You're telling me my brother's missing, but you're interrogating me over a pocket dial?"

For the first time, it occurred to me that if there was some crazed killer on the loose, something bad could have happened to Lucas too. Maybe he'd come across his student in the middle of being murdered, tried to intervene . . . left something behind that made him the person of interest, and really he was . . . I couldn't even think it. That didn't make sense anyway, because this girl had been murdered three weeks ago and Lucas had just called me on Friday. Still, I was scared. I'd been scared since I left Chicago.

"You don't know where my brother is, do you? Where is my brother? How do I know if he's OK? I need to see him." I felt an urge to grab on to Pruden like I was suddenly drowning. Pruden's lips went thin.

"Like I said, we don't know where your brother is. We don't believe Lucas is in Wayoata. On Friday, we asked him to come in for an interview on Monday. He didn't show. It looks like he left in a hurry. His phone, clothes, and wallet were at his apartment, but his ATM card is missing." I strained to catch up to what he was telling me, to find a good reason why Lucas would skip out on a police interview and leave with only a bank card. Pruden leaned in even closer to ensure eye contact. "On Friday he called you."

My chin dropped toward my chest, my shoulders went so tight it hurt to cross my arms. I was bundling myself in, taking on some form of a seated fetal position, my frantic anger shifting to defense mode. I shook my head. It was almost involuntary, how much I was shaking my head no, like a Parkinson's tremor. I looked like I was a step away from plugging my ears and going *Lalala, I can't hear you*. "Well, maybe with all of these insane accusations swarming around him, he needed a break." I tried countering, feeling flush with desperation. My tongue sticking to the roof of my mouth. "Maybe he just went for a drive to clear his head before facing all of this bullshit head-on."

Yes. Perfectly reasonable. Just drive away until everyone in this town returned to their senses. But was it reasonable to take a road trip when everyone thought you were guilty? Even Lucas, who didn't always think things through, had to have considered it would look like he was fleeing.

"He needed a break? That's it? Huh. Guess I'd need a break too in his circumstance." Pruden gave a false chuckle, his lips sputtering on air.

"I didn't mean it to sound like that—"

Pruden cut me off. "Anyway, no, he didn't go for a drive. His truck was vandalized in the school parking lot a few days ago, someone even set the engine on fire. It's now sitting in a junkyard. So no, he didn't take his truck on any vacation."

"Who would've done that?" I asked this with an almost comical measure of outrage, all things considered. Like a vandalized truck was the most barbaric thing I'd heard so far, but the thought that everyone had turned against my brother was taking hold, and my sisterly protectiveness had kicked in. Everyone in Wayoata loved Lucas. It was just the way it was. Even his students called him Haas, no Mr. required.

Pruden gave me a weak smile, leaned his chin on his cocked fist. "To narrow the search, I'd likely have to start with who wouldn't have done it. But right now, we're focused on actual urgent matters. Now, Miss Haas, I'm going to be asking the questions for a little while, OK? Then you can ask yours." He paused to make sure I was following. "Aside from this pocket dial"—the way he said it, he might as well have used finger quotations around "pocket dial"—"has Lucas been in touch with you? E-mail, text from another number, a call, in the last seventy-two hours?"

"No."

"So, when was the last time you were in contact with him?" He dropped his hand from his chin, a let's-get-down-to-business gesture.

"He called a couple of weeks ago, but didn't leave a message. I tried calling him back, but it was during the day and he was probably teaching, so I didn't get ahold of him." Maybe he hadn't been teaching. Maybe he'd looked at my name flash on his screen and pressed Ignore. "I've been on the night shift at my pharmacy. We've been working opposite hours, so it's been difficult to get in touch. To actually talk."

"Yep, I get it," the trainee piped up. "People are so busy nowadays, it's hard to stay connected." He was nodding with so much false enthusiasm that I got the feeling he was playing good cop to Pruden's bluster. "So you really haven't talked much lately?"

"No. We've just missed each other over the last little while."

"All right. Moving on," Pruden grumbled. "Could you write out a list of people that Lucas might've contacted if he were trying to lay low?" He pushed a pen and pad of paper toward me.

I ignored it.

"I mean, is there anyone you're aware of that your brother might go to if he was in trouble? A family member?" Pruden pushed the pad of paper closer. "A good friend? Someone who would help him out."

"No, there isn't." Did he really think I was going to start listing names while he cruelly played coy? Was this some kind of test—if I didn't list names, I was helping Lucas get away?

"Can you just tell me why exactly my brother is a person of interest in this? Please? I'm worried sick right now, and I want to know where he is. What have you been doing to find him?"

Pruden bristled. This was not a man who liked to be questioned. "This police department has been doing everything it can, *Miss Haas*. We have alerts out at every bus station, airport, and border crossing. We're knocking on doors and talking to everyone in this town. We want to know where your brother is too. He's in a lot of trouble, and I think you know that. By helping us, you're helping him."

"Listen, whatever you think he's done, it isn't true. This is a mistake."

"Did Lucas ever mention Joanna Wilkes to you?"

"You've asked me that already. No. I'd never heard of her before today." Pruden rested back into his chair.

"Huh, I find that interesting. Since you've been reading the *papers,* then I guess you know that Joanna was a student of Mr. Haas's. She was only sixteen." He kept looking at me, expecting a reaction. I had none. "She'd been missing since the end of May. Her body was found Monday morning in Dickson Park. She was murdered. Bludgeoned with a rock and strangled with her own fashion scarf." Pruden said "fashion scarf" delicately, like it was something normally bought in the feminine hygiene aisle. "You should know, as a prior Wayoatan, that we don't get a lot of murders around here. You'd think Lucas would have brought it up with you. That one of his students had gone missing."

"And you think my brother was involved with her murder. But why? What evidence do you even have? He would never hurt one of his students." Lucas always spoke about his students with animated interest. He really did care that they did well.

"Was Lucas seeing anyone lately? Did he have a girlfriend that he talked about?"

I had to fight the rage jetting up inside of me. I didn't want to answer any more questions. I wanted to leave, I wanted them searching for my brother so he could straighten this all out. "I get why you're asking me that, but seriously?" I let out an angry laugh that bounced hard off the wall and died fast. My teeth re-clenched. "If my brother is missing, it isn't because he ran away. It isn't because he was involved with this student. The only reason why my brother would be gone, is because someone wants him gone. He could be hurt. You need to be out looking for him, not wasting your time with me, asking me about his dating life like there's a clue there."

Pruden sniffed, played up his restored calmness. "Please just answer the question. It's in your brother's best interest."

"You're not listening to me. Maybe Lucas knows something, maybe he knows who did this" My voice was tipping too far toward hopefulness for my own good. I sounded like I was trying to convince them of the existence of unicorns.

"And you're not listening to me. Answer the question," Pruden snapped back.

I raised my hands, a you-gotta-be-kidding-me gesture. "Fine. Fine. No. Not lately. He wasn't seeing anyone serious, as far as I know." He was never seeing anyone serious. Lucas and I were inherently disabled when it came to forming long-term relationships.

"Did he confide in you at all about his work? Does he like being a teacher?"

"He does." He coached hockey and played things like Pictionary in the English classes he taught. What was not to like?

"What else can you tell me about your brother's lifestyle?"

"Lifestyle" was a bad word in Wayoata. It stood for all kinds of deviancy. Lifestyle was short skirts and promiscuity that made the rape victim partly culpable. What did they think I was going to tell them? That Lucas liked to choke his sexual partners with fashion scarves? This wasn't happening. I was in the middle of a sweaty, hypervivid nightmare. My stomach lurched. Another nervous guffaw rolled up my throat.

"You can't be serious?" I swallowed audibly.

"You have a real strange sense of humor. I doubt many people would find a dead teenage girl funny." His eyes narrowed. The air went out of the room. "You keep asking me if this serious? Your brother is a person of interest. You know what that means? We'll probably have an arrest warrant ready for him within the week, and when we find him—and we will find him—he'll pay for what he's done. This, missy, is very serious business."

"What proof do you have?" My face was getting hot, my mouth tasted like acid. I promised myself that whatever Pruden said next, I wouldn't believe him. I would refuse to think for one second that this wasn't just some big misunderstanding; my twin would show up an hour from now and explain it all away.

"Unfortunately I can't discuss an open investigation with you in any detail." I let out an exasperated burst of air that Pruden continued to talk over. "What I can tell you is that there is evidence that Lucas was romantically involved with Joanna. We needed to talk to him, he knew that we needed to talk to him, and now, when we find Joanna's body, he's suddenly gone."

"Lucas wasn't involved with his student. He wouldn't. You don't know what you're talking about. Lucas would never kill anyone." Lucas hated the sight of blood. He'd come out of the bathroom, chalk-faced and in full swoon, if he saw a bloated tampon that didn't flush. Even on the ice, if a fight produced the slightest spritz of blood, my brother skated in the other direction. People called him a finesse player, but really I knew, it was his aversion to blood that made him avoid the mindless, glove-dropping fights. He'd be too squeamish to bludgeon.

"You would know if your brother murdered someone? That's what you're saying? You think Lucas would just call you up and tell you? Is that what he did in that thirty-two second call? Cause if that's what you're saying—"

"No, I'm not saying anything like that."

"Well, then. Me, I think it's far more revealing that he didn't say anything to you at all. Joanna Wilkes was missing for over three weeks. One of his students. He was put on an administrative leave last week, and he didn't tell you about that either, did he? He didn't call you up and say, 'I've been put on a leave because I'm suspected of having sexual relations with one of my students'? No, he didn't."

I couldn't take a breath. Pruden had a point. My tongue was stuck to the edge of my teeth; my heart flapped in my chest. The clock on the wall was ticking fast and loud, urgent as a time bomb. I made my face go rigid. Poker-faced. I couldn't let Pruden see me rattled. "This is fucking ridiculous. Maybe I should get a lawyer." I said this with much more gumption than I felt.

Pruden grunted. "You can do whatever you want, Miss Haas, but right there, you wanting a lawyer makes me think you might have some reservations about your brother's innocence."

"You're wrong. You have the wrong person." I knew how these things worked. The police got an idea of how something happened; they set their sights on something and stopped looking anywhere else. At anyone else. I knew this firsthand, and while this had worked out for me once, it was like some karmic debt had come due, only Lucas was the one paying it out instead of me.

Pruden folded his arms and looked at me like he was a human lie detector test. He let out a sniffle of a laugh and cocked his head in a taunting way. "It's pretty telling that he's not here."

"He didn't do this." There was no way. The earth was round, and the sky was blue, and my twin wasn't a murderer. These were fundamental truths.

"It's also telling, in my opinion, that your brother did not partake in any of Joanna's search parties when all the other able-bodied teachers at Westfield did. What do you make of that? I think maybe it was because he already knew she was dead."

I didn't answer. Just kept shaking my head no. Blood rushed to my ears.

Pruden sighed, handed me a folded piece of paper and his card. "It is imperative you call us immediately if Lucas contacts you. This is a criminal investigation." He stood and left. The pneumatic door made a gentle *whoosh* behind him.

I unfolded the paper. It was the missing poster for Joanna Wilkes. Same yearbook photo that was in the newspaper. Homecoming-queen pretty, she stared out from her mane of ginger-red spiral curls that cascaded over each shoulder, two dimples, her mouth fixed into a wide, bright smile.

"Would you like some water?" the younger officer asked. I'd practically forgotten he was there. I really couldn't stop shaking my head. I needed something to calm down. He took this as a no to his offer and made a quiet exit. *Whoosh.*

I turned the missing poster over on the table. I felt like I was in a trance.

Several minutes passed before I could stand up.

Outside the station it was hot and windy. Parking lot dust gathered in angry little funnels. I'd forgotten how windy it was there. Focused on my jelly legs, I put one foot in front of the other. I just needed to make it to the car. Getting inside the car, feeling hermetically sealed off from the station, would let me think.

"Mia?" The younger officer had followed me into the parking lot. I ignored him. Unless he was about to tell me that he'd just tracked Lucas down and everything had been cleared up, then I had nothing more to say. *Leave me alone, leave me alone.* I just wanted to get inside the shitty car and think. Process. I wanted to go back to Lucas's apartment and find him strolling down the front steps on his way to the police station.

I tried to unlock the car using the keyless remote but accidentally set off the alarm. Of course. The trainee was suddenly next to me. The car bleated. "A rental," I explained. I pushed Lock, Unlock, the red button, repeated the sequence. Hands shaking, I couldn't do it, I couldn't even turn off the alarm. I cursed, hot tears leaked from my eyes and ran down my cheeks. I fumbled the keys, picked them up. Tried again to turn off the earsplitting alarm.

"Here, let me." The officer took the keys from my hands, a careful extraction, pressed something, and the car went silent.

I gained some composure and muttered, "Thanks."

He opened the driver's door, leaned in, and handed me a tissue from the complimentary box of Kleenex that came with the car. "You don't remember me, do you? It's Garrett. Garrett Burke." The moment he said his name, I immediately recognized him.

"Skinny G?" I knew Skinny G very well; he'd been in the grade below me. We were both the only lasting members of computer club in middle school, where we spent lunch hours mastering *The Oregon Trail* and splitting bags of Doritos, hard-core breaking the no-food-or-drink policy. We shared one Cool Ranch–infused kiss in the stairwell before I moved up to high school. I hadn't thought about him in years.

"No one calls me that anymore." He squinted into the sun. He still had the same mouth, lips that looked like they were always leaning toward a smile.

"What are you doing here?" It was a stupid question. I didn't know why I was so surprised that the other officer had to be a middle school crush. The past was crammed down your throat everywhere you turned here; you could never escape it.

"I work here." With a gentle lift of an eyebrow, he nodded in the direction of the station. "Look, I'm sorry about Pruden in there. He was coming at you pretty hard. It was insensitive."

I made a *pfffsh* sound. "Like you were doing anything to stop him."

"Well, he is the police chief." He gave me a palms-up shrug. "He's a little old school, I know, but, Mia, I'm working this case too, so if you need anything, have any questions, or just want someone to talk to other than Pruden, you can give me a shout. Anytime. I mean that." He wrote down his number on the box of Kleenex.

"I do have a question."

Garrett nodded, his posture hunched, and I flashed to when we were equal heights.

"Can I go there? Is Lucas's apartment free to go into?" I had to go back there, get inside and see it. See that he was there. See that he wasn't there. I kept picturing yellow police tape and some part-time cop sky-high on self-importance gleefully pushing me out.

"We finished up there last night. So yes, you can go there."

I nodded, took back my Kleenex box, and drove off.

2

Back at Lucas's apartment, I buzzed the caretaker again and again. No answer. I stood there, waited for someone to come out or go in, but no one did. I walked around to the back door, passed the dingy-looking pool enclosed by a chain-link fence. Two boys, in clear defiance of the no-horseplay rule, were hitting each other with Styrofoam noodles as their mother yelled at them from one of the plastic patio chairs to stop. A girl, early teens, was the only one in the pool. She floated on an air mattress, perky breasts pointed skyward, her blond hair splayed around her head in waves, wearing a white bikini and oversized sunglasses. She lifted up the strap of her bikini bottoms to check her tan. A man old enough to know better, definitely in his thirties, with a substantial enough chin-puff that I could see it from there, shamelessly leered from his balcony. The boys stopped running to peek. Their mother yelled at them again. The girl smiled.

Through the glass door I could see a woman vacuuming a grimy paisley carpet peppered with cigarette burns. I knocked, loud. She didn't hear. I kept knocking, but it wasn't until she turned around to suction up something next to the staircase that she noticed me, turned off the vacuum, pulled one earbud out, and opened the door.

"I'm looking for the caretaker?"

"My dad's not in right now." Music pulsed just above one of her heavy breasts. Her dad. I could see now that she was one of those unfortunate girls who looked middle-aged until seen close up. She was exceptionally tall, almost six feet, with broad rounded shoulders and a very bad Blondissima dye job that was almost blue, making her dark inky eyebrows pop like a punch line.

"I need to get into my . . . into Lucas Haas's apartment. I'm his sister, Mia Haas."

She flicked her T-shirt, sticky with sweat, and jutted her chin out at me. "You got ID?"

"I do." I pulled my driver's license from my wallet. She stared at it with the intense scrutiny of a traffic cop before handing it back. "I'll get the key."

"Thanks." I followed her down the hallway to a door with a plate that read PROPERTY MANAGER.

As she opened the door to the caretaker suite, I caught a whiff of stale cigarette smoke and saw the caretaker sprawled on the couch, shirtless, his belly large enough to block his face. An empty six-pack of tall boys was scattered over the coffee table. I looked away. The door closed.

I stood there for what seemed far too long just to get a key. I overheard the girl trying to wake her dad. Then she was back. I expected the key, but instead she said she had to open his place up. "Policy. Only the leasing agency can give you a key."

"That's fine."

The ring of keys jingled as she led me to the elevator and pushed the Up button several times in quick succession, as if an elevator's speed was based on some equation dependent on button presses. It took a couple of uneasy minutes to arrive; stairs would have been much faster. The doors opened to an abandoned dolly. She rolled the dolly out and pushed it into the lobby, where it came to a slow stop in front of the floor-to-ceiling marbled mirrors. Once on the elevator, she pressed 4 three times. She looked over at me, then away quick as peekaboo, her low voice shy and quiet. "I'm Bailey, by the way." I couldn't tell how old she was. Eighteen? At least eighteen.

The elevator was painfully slow. "Thanks, Bailey, for getting the key."

She nodded. "No problem. Mr. Haas was my English teacher. I'm in grade nine."

Never would have guessed fourteen or fifteen years old, but now I was interested. "He is?" I emphasized the present tense.

"I hate the sub we have now. I really miss Mr. Haas. He was hilarious." She snorted, as if at the onslaught of fond memories his name conjured up.

It wasn't exactly the reaction of a pupil who was worried her teacher was a murderer. "I'm sure he'll be back teaching your class soon."

She turned and looked at me with a doubtful expression. "You really think so?"

"Of course. Yeah." The doors opened slowly, and I squeezed through them at first chance. Suddenly, I wanted to get away from her, from any student of Lucas's. "I'm glad to hear my brother is so well-liked by his students."

"Yeah, totally. Once he had a rule that anyone who was late because they were buying a coffee had to buy him one too. It was just really funny—once he had, like, four coffees on his desk."

There was one Starbucks in the Target near the school. It had opened after I left, but I could imagine the girls at Westfield running around feeling so metro with low-foam triple grande skinny hazelnut macchiatos, the white and green accessory of their celebrity idols.

"That's funny. Sounds like Lucas." It didn't sound like him at all. Lucas didn't even like coffee.

"Yeah, he was, like, all jittery for the rest of the day." She did a quick, jerky body roll like she was being electrocuted to demonstrate. The shyness was slipping, and her voice was suddenly too loud, too cheerful; it was jarring. She was about to say something else, some other anecdote, and I couldn't bear to listen to it, so I complimented her bracelet. Bailey nodded, as if the compliment had been expected, and looked down at the chevron twiney bracelet tied snug around her wrist. Friendship bracelets must be so retro now; they were retro when I was fourteen.

She slipped the key into apartment 44, and I sucked in a hopeful breath that Lucas would come lumbering toward the door, looking like he'd just woken up from an epic five-day nap, wanting to know who the hell was coming in uninvited.

Bailey pushed the door open. "So where is Mr. Haas, anyway? I haven't seen him around."

I ignored her question. Thanked her again for letting me in and went around her as she stood with her back to the door to hold it open.

Of course he wasn't there. Blinds drawn, the apartment had the lonely, silent feeling of a sealed tomb. The first thing I noticed was the smell, the rotten stench of something decaying. The living room was full of cardboard pizza boxes and unwashed glasses with amber adhered to the bottom. A mostly empty bottle of Canadian whisky sat in the middle of the table. Fingerprint dust was everywhere, on every light switch, the doorknobs, the glasses on the table.

The furniture—what I could see of it, his clothes were all over the place—was all bachelor pad. An overstuffed leather couch and a ratty-looking brown recliner with a well-stocked IKEA liquor cart wheeled up next to it. Such variety within arm's reach. A flat screen on a stand, thrift-store brass and smoky glass coffee table. A faux cowhide in the middle of the room like a cow had dropped and spattered. A poster with different brands of beer.

Lucas had always been a slob, even as an adult, but then he'd never had to pick up after himself. Our mother's fault. She made his bed right through high school, lovingly drawing the sheets, plumping up his pillow. She was obsessive about it, so he never learned to do it. It would not occur to him that whatever spill or mess he was responsible for wouldn't just disappear on its own after he left the room. But this was beyond that. This place was a total disaster. I could see him sitting there on the couch slowly getting drunk as the sun crept across the sky behind tightly drawn curtains. Shut out from his job, coaching, from his long-standing status as the good guy.

A loud sniff. Bailey was still there, poking her head inside, her ankle anchoring the door, her face scrunched with curiosity like she was finally getting a good peek into the teachers' staff room.

I shooed her out and bolted the door.

I opened the front closet door first. From wire hangers dangled Lucas's leather jackets, a Michelin-man parka, a few Windbreakers with the Bulldogs sports logo on the back and the chest and COACH written on the arm. Found an extra set of keys hanging on a nail. Here too was his sneaker collection, a lingering phase from his early twenties and the only thing he kept tidy. There were about nine pairs of pristine sneakers, carefully arranged on two wire shelves. Still in the box on the top shelf were his most prized "kicks," flashy red LeBrons. He'd bought them for a ludicrous amount of money when he lived with me in Chicago, off a very sketchy guy he found on the Internet.

Aren't you going to try them on at least? I had asked in the cab afterward.

Are you kidding? You can't wear these! He clutched the box, opened it, and looked in at those bright cherry-red high-tops like he was glaring into a SAD light box.

I pulled the box out. It was empty. So what? He finally donned them for his fast getaway?

Back in the living room, I flicked open one of the pizza boxes and saw crusts peppered with mold gathered on wax paper that had turned to a plasmic consistency. In a corner of the room was a stack of Mimi's water paintings. Mainly setting suns, loons on lakes, and swirly flowers on cheap canvas. I could imagine Lucas's face each time our mother gave him a new one, his locked-jaw grimace followed by a thank-you through clenched teeth. There was one, though, he had made a point to hang. The painting was of a sunset. A pink-yellow sun disappearing behind the trees across a greenish body of water. What made this one special enough to hang, I couldn't tell.

The kitchen was a small alcove with a stubby breakfast bar. His school bag was on top of the counter. An old leather satchel of the kind associated with college professors with patches sewn on their elbows. It looked like the police had already rummaged through it. There were several granola bar wrappers, his keys, and a red folder with "Late" written in permanent marker on the front. The file had a few unmarked essays on *The Great Gatsby*. His school planner was also there; I flipped through it. A blur of reminders for hockey practice and assignment due dates. A phone number, with the name Tom next to it.

At the back of the planner, on a few blank pages, were a series of numbers written like he was trying to work out some elaborate math problem. I wondered if he'd started gambling again. For a while, after college, Lucas got into sports betting. I'd had to lend him money a few times, to help him pay off losses. He was guarded about the amounts he lost. He swore off it after that, psychoanalyzed himself, said something like maybe he was just living vicariously and the gambling rush was as close as he was going to get again to the rush on the ice. He'd ended up paying me back only half of what he owed me, but a few years had passed, and I'd sort of written it off, unless we were having some kind of disagreement—then I'd bring it up. I kind of liked that I had that to hang over him.

In the corner, next to Lucas's geometric doodling (always a bunch of stacked squares like a perfect game of *Tetris*) something was written and partially scratched out. I could only make out the first part, "Gent." Did the rest spell "gentleman"? Was that what he was trying to be, with whom? I looked back at the numbers, wondered again if he was in debt. A gentleman always pays his debts?

I called the number, got a voice mail that simply stated I had reached Tom. I left an awkward message explaining that I was Lucas's sister and I had come across his number and wanted to talk.

On Lucas's fridge door was a clipped stack of bills, minimum payments up to date, and a picture of us at Christmas. My mother's arm was draped around both our necks, pulling Lucas in a little tighter than me. Lucas and my mother were smiling, and I looked like I usually do in childhood photos, gazing slightly off to one side as if constantly devising an exit plan. Behind us was a Christmas tree. I could not think of what would have made this Christmas memorable enough for Lucas to put it on his fridge. There was probably some joke that went with it, something that Mimi bought us that was so off base it ended up being hilarious, like the year she bought a pair of goldfish that were floating belly-up by Christmas morning or the bottle of hair mousse, wrapped up candy-wrapper style, for Lucas when his head was shaved.

Lucas was already showing signs of how annoyingly good-looking he was going to be. He took after Mimi. Blond, startling blue eyes, and movie-star bone structure. He inherited her supposed Scandinavian ancestry, so much that Lucas only ever needed a giant Styrofoam hammer to go as Thor on Halloween. We had to take her word on that one, since there was no one else to ask. I had no idea where I got my dark hair.

As an adult, I'd actually witnessed women going slack-jawed over him, like, unable to speak for a few seconds as they took him in. I wished I could say I had the female version of my brother's face, but I didn't. For twins, we didn't look much alike at all. Lucas was still *GQ* prettier than me. I was dark and broody. My eyes a steely gray. Not plain. Maybe even striking at times. But a face you had to look at a bit longer to see its appeal. The one thing we shared was tough skin. Mimi had to stay out of the sun, or else she would burn up, her chest a freckly mess of peeling skin, her shoulders scorching hot, while Lucas and I turned golden brown, sun-kissed.

Suddenly a loud, ugly belching noise shot through the apartment and made my bones jump. The Polaroid fluttered from my hand and landed on the kitchen floor. There was an old-school Mirtone wall intercom, the shade of nicotine, across from the front closet. Someone was there. I pressed the Talk button. "Hello? Hello?" Thrust my finger on Listen. Waited for someone to speak, but all I could hear was whistly white noise.

I sprinted out of the apartment, didn't even consider the sluggish elevator, and ran down the stairs. Skipping every second step while hanging hard on to the copper-smelling, chipped-paint railing. Beelined across the lobby and into the front vestibule. No one was there. I stepped farther out, keeping my hand on the door because I'd forgotten the keys. Wanting so desperately to see my brother strolling across the parking lot. Instead there was just a plastic bag skittering around like tumbleweed. Downtrodden, I made my way back upstairs. Feeling victim to the intercom equivalent of knock-knock ginger. Probably the wrong number.

Back inside, I picked up the photo and slid it back under the palm tree magnet. Opened my brother's fridge. It was nearly empty. A carton of eggs, the usual condiments, and three cans of beer still yoked by the plastic rings, a small pile of six-pack rings next to it. I took one of the cans, opened it, took long swallows, then pressed it to my cheek and wandered down the hallway.

The bathroom light was on. The door half closed. I wanted to hear a shower running, an electric razor buzzing, but nothing. I pushed the door open. There was his toothbrush, fully pasted and ready to go, sitting on the side of the sink. It was like he was standing over the sink, looking into the mirror, about to brush his teeth when he decided, fuck it, and walked out on his life. But that didn't make sense. Wouldn't he at least brush his teeth before becoming a fugitive on the run? Wouldn't he take his toothbrush with him? Or his expensive electric razor so he could maintain his neatly edged two-day beard and the look of a European soccer player? Or his hair gel or his cologne? Lucas was vain; he would still want to look good.

Even if, and I couldn't believe he'd risk such a very public fall from grace, but even if he were to have become sexually involved with one of his students who, just through sheer bad luck, happened to be murdered, he would stay and fight the charges. He wouldn't be able to stand that people thought he did it. His need to be known as a good guy was almost pathological. We were the approval-seeking by-products of our histrionic alcoholic mother; we just went about it differently. I cared less about being likable than being considered impressive, whereas Lucas really wanted to be liked, the guy everyone wanted around, and that was who he'd always been.

Unless.

Unless he's dead too. I wasn't just posturing for Pruden. This was a real fear. Some yahoo, maybe the same yahoo who lit his truck on fire, went after him. The kind of red-necked guy who'd want bragging rights at every bar that he took care of that sicko teacher preying on teenage girls. I could come up with half a dozen names right now, on the spot. Guys who'd at least claim that if they were alone in a room with Haas they'd cut his dick off, but not necessarily go through with it. Guys who'd trash his truck, go after him online, but only grumble something under their breath to him in person.

I couldn't think this. It was too hard. If some vigilante spent the last few days bragging about giving Lucas the beating of his life (that ended his life), wouldn't Pruden have heard about it by now? I wouldn't put it past Pruden to cover it up, but would he really keep up with a bogus hunt for Lucas? Would he have even called me here?

Fuck. Stop.

Lucas called me Friday. Pocket dial or not, he called me and that meant he was alive. I knew this was some loose reasoning, but what else could I do? Thinking my brother was dead was last-resort thinking.

I went into his bedroom. Again it was a mess, but I knew there was a method to his madness. The last time we lived together was only five years ago. Lucas came to stay with me with big plans to live in Chicago. He was dabbling in acting and modeling. It was his first attempt at something after accepting he was not going to be a professional hockey player. After the initial excitement of getting some extra work playing a firefighter on a soapy TV drama wore off, he mostly loitered around my tiny apartment between sporadic shifts as a waiter, charming my off-limits roommates, watching *SportsCenter,* and eating cereal from a mixing bowl. With no real direction, he claimed to be having a serious quarter-life crisis while I'd just finished my pharmacy degree and was leafing through MBA programs at different Ivy Leagues. I had dazzling visions of myself in a top hat and tails, twirling a gratuitous walking stick as I climbed the pharma corporate ladder. I'd have nicknames like Conglomerate or Powerhouse or just Moneybags.

Then, just like that, Lucas decided to move back to Wayoata and get a teaching certificate.

I pressured him to stay, pointed out he had given the whole acting thing only eight months, and even if he decided to do something different with his life, there were more and better opportunities in Chicago, but I couldn't convince him. He invoked our mother as an excuse to run home, tail firmly between legs. *She's all alone. No one goes to visit her most of the year.*

There was nothing I could say to that, even if we both knew he was bullshitting. He hadn't been that worried about Mimi before things got a little hard and aimless, so I backed off, thinking he'd quickly get bored in Wayoata anyway. Obviously, that didn't happen.

I opened drawers, came across a leather glove at the back of his sock drawer that I guessed was the one from Mimi's car. The sight of it gave way to the skin-crawly seasickness I always got when I thought of Mimi, her "accident." I slammed the drawer shut. Sunk down, hugged my knees. I couldn't decide why he would have kept it all these years. I took a few nausea-battling breaths, then reminded myself it wouldn't be the first time we were on the receiving end of the Wayoata police department's incompetence.

We were seventeen when our mother had her car accident. Her injuries were severe (her sodden brain hit the inside of her skull like wet toilet paper on ceiling tiles, *splot*). But when Lucas and I were given the go-ahead to clean out her beige-gold LeSabre (Lucas insisted we do this ourselves, like it was some kind of pseudo funeral rite), he noticed that our mother's change was still stacked in its holder, her sunglasses still clipped to the visor. The dent on the front of the bumper where she'd smacked into a tree was underwhelming. There was even a man's leather glove. Just one. It didn't add up. At least not in Lucas's opinion. I knew better. I'd tried to point out Mimi's car was a total sty and it wasn't really that odd that we'd find a stray glove under the heap of store receipts, flattened cigarette packets, torn panty hose, stubby lipsticks. Lucas wanted to pursue it anyway. He was fixated on the glove.

Reluctantly, heart pounding in my chest, I had gone along with him to urge the police to investigate what he thought might be a staged accident, but luckily, Pruden was no Marge Gunderson. Before Lucas could even finish what he'd been referring to as his opening argument, before he could wave the black glove around, Chief Pruden cut him off. "The roads were icy. Your mother was drunk and wasn't wearing a seat belt. Let's not pretend she didn't ever drive in that sort of condition. Just be happy she hit a tree and didn't kill some *nice* family."

Case closed.

Except, during those months before leaving for college, if we saw Pruden around town, my brother would eye him up and down. Make menacing but harmless gestures, like rubbing his middle finger on the bridge of his nose or, once, the pow of a finger gun. He'd tell anyone who'd listen that Pruden was an incompetent asshole. He was seventeen and angry and felt he'd been ignored. Now I couldn't help but wonder if Pruden hadn't held a grudge and was taking pleasure in pinning something on my brother.

I stood up again, opened his closet, and looked for an empty space from which a suitcase had been taken, where he'd packed his spare toothbrush and spare razor. Nothing was missing but Lucas.

And his ATM card. The reminder was a gut-punch. He could technically just buy it all, toothbrush, T-shirt, jeans. He could empty his account in one fell swoop after crossing the Canadian border and then really disappear. He would go to Canada, wouldn't he? I mean it's right there. Only if he was guilty, but he wasn't.

I sunk down into his bed. What the fuck was happening? I was reeling. I truly understood what it meant to reel now. I felt cold and feverish. The dim ceiling light pulsed. I rolled over and cried into the pillow that still smelled like my brother's hair gel.

3

DAY 2

THURSDAY

I woke up after a chattering, flimsy sleep with a coiled stomach. I made Lucas's bed, pulled the sheets tight, plumped up the pillow. I called in to work and began using the sick days I had hoarded up. I bagged up the pizza boxes and cans of beer, let the stained glasses soak. Picked up his oily Bulldogs ball cap off the coffee table, then put it back. It looked like it belonged there. I was focused now. Lucas was only a person of interest in Joanna's murder. They had given him the weekend to mosey on in for an interview, so whatever evidence they did have had to be relatively weak (then again, this was before her body was found, before my brother did a magic disappearing trick). Still, Pruden said they didn't even have an arrest warrant yet.

Someone else had killed this Joanna girl, but whatever feeble connections Pruden had managed to rustle up, they were enough for him to home in on Lucas and not bother looking for anyone else.

I needed information. I needed to find someone else to sic Pruden on. Another suspect.

I called Wyatt again, Lucas's best friend since Little League and currently his assistant hockey coach for the Westfield Bulldogs. He was a goofy spiky-haired kid who laughed at everything Lucas said and called me Mia Diarrhea. Sometimes Mia Gonorrhea, but that wasn't until high school. He was a bit of a try-hard. At one point he carried around two cell phones and told everyone one was for the "bros" and one was for the "hos," but I never heard either phone ring.

We'd stayed vaguely familiar with one another through Facebook. I had messaged him before leaving home, and when I didn't hear back fast enough, I rummaged through my drawer of old cell phones that I had always intended to recycle and found an old phone number for Wyatt. Luckily, Wyatt hadn't changed his number much since his bro and ho days. I'd left a voice mail asking him to call me. Followed that up with a text:

IT'S MIA. WTF IS GOING ON THERE? HAVE YOU TALKED TO LUCAS???

Never got a response. I could see that he'd been online since my message. He'd retweeted something and wished someone happy birthday on Facebook. It was as if he was hiding behind a glass door pretending not to be home while I rang the doorbell. *But I can see you, asshole!!*

This time his phone went straight to a full voice mail.

I did remember where his parents lived; maybe they could give me Wyatt's address. I took it for granted that they hadn't moved, because people here didn't tend to move around a lot.

I pulled up to the sprawling brick bungalow. Wyatt's parents, the Thompsons, owned a landscaping company, Eden Green, that did quite well. I knew that because, before her accident, Mimi worked as a bank teller at the Wayoata Credit Union and she loved to talk about other people's money. Who had what in their accounts. Their debts or lack of. Just being near money, even if she never had enough of her own, set off some kind of buzz inside her.

The house was far less immaculate than I remembered. Nothing was planted in the raised flower bed, the grass was too long, and the driveway, between the parked SUV and silver pickup, was littered with bikes and toys and chalk drawings. The archway over the front stone path was gone. Not exactly endorsement material for a landscaping company.

A little boy with such white-blond hair he was ghostly looking, stood in the bay window and pointed at me. The curtains flapped around his head, a girl shouldered her way in next to the boy. Same blond hair. I could see her scream something over her shoulder. Then another small face showed up in the window, then another.

A sign, PRECIOUS TREASURES DAY CARE.

So the Thompsons had moved. I'd started to retreat down the driveway when the front door opened. "Hi, Mia."

It was Wyatt all casual, like I dropped in all the time and he'd been expecting me. He was wearing sweatpants and a Vikings T-shirt. His hairline was making a fast getaway from his forehead, but he had the same two-day-trimmed-beard look as Lucas. In high school, Wyatt was always emulating Lucas's fashion tics. When Lucas noticed, he'd switch it up, do a fauxhawk or buzz cut, and without fail, a couple of weeks later, Wyatt had the same haircut, or same sneakers in a different color. I didn't know how Lucas put up with it.

Wyatt came down to meet me in the driveway barefoot. Behind him, two more kids had pressed up against the glass and started making faces at me.

"Sorry to drop in like this, but I tried calling. Why haven't you called me back? Didn't you get any of my messages?"

"It's OK. My son dropped my phone in the toilet yesterday. I should really check the messages." A contrived chuckle. "Those aren't all my kids, by the way." His lips continued to curl, one part smile, one part grimace, like he'd said the joke a thousand times before and even he couldn't stomach repeating it. "We just have two. My wife runs a day care. We bought the house from my parents. They're in Arizona now."

A series of statements I wasn't sure how to respond to. I frowned.

It was a lame excuse for not getting back to me. This wasn't how I expected to be greeted. I'd thought he would rush toward me when he saw me walking up. That we'd immediately start hustling about like two stranded islanders with a cruise ship in the distance passing us by.

"Have you heard from Lucas at all?"

One of the white-haired kids opened the door. "Da-daa-dee." Another kid was pushing out from behind her and then another, and Wyatt took several minutes to corral them back inside. "I'll be in the garage," he hollered, fast, I guessed to his wife.

"In here." He pressed whatever configuration into a security keypad on the garage, and the door rolled open.

There wasn't a car in the garage, only a couple of lawn chairs and an elaborate workbench and a fridge. He hit the button and the garage door came down and the light turned gray. Unventilated, it smelled strongly of gasoline and grass clippings from the mower, but it had to be one of the tidiest garages I'd ever been in. This was a guy who hid out in his garage a lot.

He motioned to one of the chairs. I sat down. "No, I haven't heard from him at all. The police were already here asking that."

"I'm trying really hard to understand what happened. I just don't get it. The police think he took off because he was involved with that student. Lucas, murder. Like, it's just all so fucking unbelievable. It really is so ridiculous I would laugh if I didn't feel like crying."

Wyatt gave me a twitchy look. He wasn't joining me in my tirade on the incompetent police or the whole absurdity of the accusation. Something was wrong. Why wasn't he more upset? Why was he making me pull information out of him like this? I swallowed, felt like shit for asking, but I had to. "Was Lucas involved with that student? And please don't give me some silent bro-code bullshit."

Wyatt stroked his fuzzy cheeks. "Most people around here think so. If he was, he certainly didn't say anything about it to me, but then I don't really know what Lucas has been up to lately."

"What do you mean?"

"Just that we didn't talk all that much lately."

"But you're coaching together."

The world just kept spinning off its axis. I realized I'd had this snow-globe version of my brother in the town where nothing ever changed. Lucas mentioned Wyatt all the time when we talked. They were always friends. Best friends.

"Well, yeah, we'd talk about hockey during the season, but that's about as deep as our conversations went."

"Something happen between you guys? Was Lucas gambling again?" Maybe Lucas had borrowed money and hadn't paid him back. They'd had a little spat. Something Wyatt was blowing out of proportion. Something Lucas would never mention to me if it had to do with gambling.

"Nothing like that. I mean, I think he was gambling again, but that had nothing to do with anything. We just kind of, I don't know, life happened, I guess. Different schedules, whatever. I'm married with kids, Lucas isn't. Different priorities. I'm running the family business, so I'm really busy." I was about to point out that a landscaping business in ND allowed for a lot of downtime, but Wyatt started in about his winter hours and snow removal. "We really haven't been close friends for a while." It sounded rehearsed. He stared straight ahead, same smug look he'd always had because he never had to worry about money or college or what to do next, because his future was safe.

"Lucas made it sound like you were still good friends." I tried to think of something specific. "You guys went to that Minnesota Wild game." There was a picture on Facebook, both of them in red-and-green jerseys, clutching beers.

"That was two years ago."

"What happened between then and now?" I pressed.

"I just . . . nothing." Wyatt brushed at his sweatpants, his ears turning red. A tell he still had from childhood that he was getting angry.

"Nothing? Just like that, all those years of friendship fell to the wayside over nothing?"

"I know you're thinking I just ditched him like everyone else when people started to talk, but it's not like that, Mia, really. Lucas wanted to go out, go drinking, hit on chicks, go fishing all day on Saturdays, shit we've always done, but I've got kids now. I can't party it up like I did before, and you know what? If the tables were turned, I know Lucas would have distanced himself from me."

Wyatt had a point, but I wasn't going to admit it. I felt a little sorry for my brother that he'd been demoted in Wyatt's life from hotshot to that buddy who couldn't let go of the good old days.

"Well, if you do hear from him, please, please call me. Tell him to call me." I stood to leave, feeling wilted and a little oxygen-deprived from the smell of gas.

"Wyatt? Wyatt? Whose car is that?" A nasal voice, sharp and badgering and instantly familiar cut through the garage door. My skin prickled. The door started to lift, letting in a hard burst of sunlight. Standing there was a tall blonde holding a coffee mug with LIVE, LAUGH, LOVE scrawled across it. I always thought that accessorizing oneself with trite, mass-produced platitudes was the cheapest way possible to seem like a good person. I couldn't help but believe someone had to be hiding a dark side to need that sort of prop. (I nearly dropped a friend in college after noticing her keychain read FAMILY: THE BEST THINGS IN LIFE AREN'T THINGS.) The fact that *she* was holding said mug just added major credence to my theory.

"Hi, Carolyn." That's right, Wyatt had married Carolyn. I mean I *knew* that; I just tried to block it out. Carolyn Reidy, or I guessed Carolyn Thompson now, had been Lucas's first serious girlfriend. She'd pretended to be my friend for a whole month before I finally realized why she was so insistent on coming over even when I pushed to go to her polished house (turned out she didn't love weeknight teen dramas as much as I did). After she and Lucas started dating, I told him that Carolyn had used me. She retaliated by telling everyone that I *like* liked my brother in an unhealthy way. She stayed sugar sweet to my face when Lucas was in the room, so my twin decided to stay out of it. One of the rare times he'd acted like an outright dick.

They broke up shortly after graduation. Lucas dumped her the first week into college. In total they went out for fourteen months, and the whole time I had to listen to Carolyn's attention-seeking eating disorder. She'd eat like a pig, then disappear to the upstairs bathroom and pretend to vomit, loud and theatrical grunts followed by sensual moans. I really couldn't tell if she was puking or masturbating, but when Lucas heard and came banging on the door, she'd stumble out of the bathroom into his concerned arms with a little triumphant smile. What she didn't realize was that the household position of bathroom vomiter was already filled by our mother. Her second mistake was thinking that Lucas would want to hold her hair back past senior year (the Haases were not genetically wired to be caretakers).

"Oh." Carolyn startled when she saw me. "It's you. I hardly recognized you." She fake-gasped and gave me a once-over that would've at one time made me go puddly with paranoia.

She didn't clarify, but that was the point. The queen of vague statements or unfinished sentences prefaced with sounds you'd make for a puppy, Carolyn meant to plant seeds of self-doubt for you to obsess over (aw, you're wearing a V-neck/aw, you have sandals on/so cute, you like music). She probably wanted me to think I looked so old she couldn't tell who I was, but that didn't work on me anymore. If she really didn't recognize me, it was because I was twenty pounds lighter than I was in high school and had a two-hundred-dollar haircut instead of one of those rough kitchen cuts done by Mimi's tipsy girlfriend.

"Well, you look exactly the same." I was trying to be equally vague, hoping she'd think she was outdated. But it was true. She was still painfully thin, still so ice-blond pretty under those soccer-mom bangs. I'd always hoped Carolyn would get fat. I really, really wanted her to be fat—like, had-to-rent-a-crane-to-be-removed-from-her-house fat—and was truly disappointed to see that she wasn't. In yoga pants and a too-tight tank top, she had the same willowy frame. Her face, however, had the permanent wince of purging etched into it. Maybe she hadn't been faking it; that was something at least.

"Looking for Lucas, huh? Poor Mia. You must be a nervous

wreck." She crossed her stick arms, hugged herself as if she'd caught a chill. Wyatt came up beside her and rested an arm on her tiny shoulder. The slightest shudder passed over her face, like the weight of his hand was too much. "I never thought he was capable . . ." Carolyn wisely let her voice trail off.

"He isn't."

She frowned. Touched her Lululemon hairband. "Well, I guess family have to believe the best of one another. But his latest girlfriend was a former student of his. I think that says something about his taste."

Former student? My hands and feet went cold, but I put on my best poker face. I didn't want to give Carolyn the satisfaction of knowing something about Lucas that I didn't. "That's right. What's her name again? Where can I find her?"

Carolyn breathed in through her nose, slow. Basking in having information I wanted. "She works at Casey's. Her name's Zorro or Zarah? Something like that."

"It's Zoey," Wyatt interjected, then gave Carolyn a thought-I-was-helping shrug when she shot him a look.

"I hope Lucas comes to his senses and turns himself in. We're both worried about him. He's a very sick person." Carolyn looked up and down the street as if Lucas were creeping around nearby, wanting to peek in on her day care.

I turned around, too quickly, to leave and knocked over a bucket full of crayfish that wasn't there before, their pincers flicking open, shut. A boy screamed, and Carolyn rushed over and picked him up into a full cradle, though he was at least five years old. He was in a full tantrum—"She *hurrrrrted* them!"—by the time I reached my car.

I cranked the air-conditioning. I couldn't get the smell of grass out of my throat. So, Wyatt had finally graduated from sidekick status, to what? A lesser version of Lucas? He had his high school sweetheart, his job. Carolyn had someone enough like Lucas to keep her interested.

After my brother dumped her, Carolyn had displayed some very alarming behavior. She kept showing up on campus—no small feat, considering he went to school twelve hours away. She'd go to the pubs Lucas went to, grinding up on other guys to get his reaction. He'd find her slumped against his dorm room door in the morning, still drunk, makeup smeared all over her face. Finally she enrolled there, sitting in the last row of his classes staring at the back of his head. It freaked him out. I kept telling him to go to campus security and report her, but he said he didn't want to embarrass her. It finally culminated in Carolyn getting into his room by seducing his roommate, trashing his things, cutting up his clothes, and dumping his laptop in the toilet. She was suspended for a term. When she returned, she left him alone, joined a sorority, started dating other guys, then apparently moved home and married Wyatt. I pictured her going around town, ever the vengeful bitch, reminding everyone that she had once been Lucas's girlfriend and, in a frantic, mysterious whisper when Joanna's name came up, saying, *Let's just say a lot makes sense now. He lost interest in me right after high school.*

Casey's Bar didn't open until noon, so I had time to kill. I knew I should go and see my mother, squeeze her rigid hand and tell her Lucas was missing. After two loops around the care home, I couldn't bring myself to go in, so I drove aimlessly, stopping in front of the place we grew up in. A blocky black-and-white house in a third-rate neighborhood, with a postage-stamp-sized lot that Mimi always had trouble paying the mortgage on. The house where Lucas and I were partners in hiding our mom's car keys, watering down her liquor bottles, unclamping her hand from her glass when she passed out. We spent hours on the pullout couch watching late-night horror movies we were too young for and falling into nervous, twitchy sleeps when Mimi went out on her "long dates," the ones that meant she wouldn't be back until the following day. Whoever lived there now took better care of it. It'd been repainted. The Christmas lights and rosy-cheeked plastic Santa that was strapped to the chimney all year round had been taken down. The window that had been my room now had Hello Kitty decals covering it.

My mother lived in a group home called the LightHouse for Women. After the accident, she went into a coma for two weeks. When she woke up, she had a spotty memory and the intellect of a nine-year-old. From the street, it was a cheery yellow three-story house; closer up, it showed signs of neglect. An eave had come loose and was gently swaying in the wind. The paint was peeling, and the mailbox, overstuffed with flyers, had dropped from where it'd been fastened into the cedar siding next to the door and just left where it'd landed on the porch floor. Its dictum was *Semi-independent Living*. A third of my income went there.

I rang the bell, and a loud, deep chime sounded. I could feel the start of a migraine kneading its claws up my temples. I hadn't had a migraine in years. Not since I was a teenager. The inside door was open, and I could see into the main-floor living room, where a woman sat on an antique sofa with a blanket wrapped around her, picking her scalp and staring at the TV. She was not going to get up and let me in.

Finally a body waddled out of the dark, cavernous hallway.

"I'm here to see Miranda Haas," I said through the screen.

The nurse, short limbed and moonfaced, looked me over. "I haven't seen you here before."

It was an accusation. This must be their chance to shame family members who rarely visited, who needed to ask guiltily, what room their relative was in.

"I'm her daughter. I live out of town."

The nurse looked as if she were going to argue; I was sure my mother never mentioned me either. "We've had people from the media come by, and of course it was very upsetting for your mother."

"Media? What media?" *Please say that this was still confined to some reporter from the* Wayoata Sun. *That this hasn't reached the outside world.*

"Oh, there's been a few, but after the first one, we haven't let anyone try to interview your mother. Don't need a repeat of *that.*"

"So she knows, then, what my brother has been accused of?" I was relieved I wouldn't have to be the one to tell her. I didn't ask what "that" meant.

"We try to upset her as little as possible." She waved me inside, and we walked through the kitchen to the back door. "She's in the garden. Your brother, he was so good to his mother. He visited twice a week, every week. Like clockwork. I just don't know what went wrong with him."

I passed the scalp-picker, who had started heating up some microwave popcorn and stood watching it, fully transfixed.

"She is having a very good day. That's good for you." The nurse ushered me out the door.

The garden, it turned out, was a patch of overgrown weeds and brush at the end of the backyard. A woman, who had to be my mother because she was the only one in the garden, was dressed in a floral-printed nightgown despite the heat, high-necked and long-sleeved, puffy around the shoulders. Her hair was parted down the middle and braided, the color of bleached straw. She tilted her head to one side, then the other. She looked like a life-sized pioneer doll. I hadn't seen her in five years and felt paralyzed.

In the kitchen, the microwave beeped, and I could overhear the nurse arguing that more cooking time didn't need to be added. "Remember how it burns?" she kept repeating.

"Hello, Mimi. It's me, Mia." I took a shaky step forward. We only ever called her by her nickname, never Mom, and no, the cutesy similarity of our names was not lost on me. There are pictures of us in matching pastel dresses, her red-painted fingernails resting on my shoulder like a garden rake. A sort of half grimace, half smile on my face as Mimi beamed over me. I can say with certainty that she loved me most before the age of eight, when I could still be cajoled into being her prop and sitting through her primping sessions. She'd pull and curl my hair, paint my toes, all to match her. She'd tell me how much she loved to show me off, but I was naturally shy. I had trouble maintaining eye contact and hated attention. Even if I tried to be the extroverted, giggly little girl Mimi wanted, I somehow did it wrong. Lucas was the *easy one* because he brought her all the attention she craved. He wasn't difficult because she didn't expect him to be someone else. Hockey hero, outgoing, and popular. Or maybe this was too kind. Maybe it had nothing to do with who he was, he was easier simply because Mimi needed male attention so desperately, so persistently, that her son could fill in the dry spells. Something I could never do for her. Even when I tried to be the extroverted, giggly little girl Mimi wanted, I somehow did it wrong. "Well, that was embarrassing," she'd inevitably announce, as we drove home from lunch with her coworkers or from a friend's daughter's bridal shower. Once I figured out I'd never please her, I tried hard to stop trying. Still, there was always something in me that craved that one last appraising glance after she'd dressed me up and decided yes, I was adorable and lovable, and she'd lift me off the bathroom counter, hand me her tissue to kiss off my excess lipstick, our lip marks side by side, and we'd be on our way.

"Oh, good, you're here. Come see, come see." My mother's voice was still husky from years of booze and cigarettes, and as I got closer, she still had the same familiar scent of mint and cigarette smoke from my childhood. I was surprised she was allowed to smoke. It seemed wrong somehow, though it was perfectly legal.

"Very good." I wasn't lying. The picture she was painting was disturbingly good. A rougher, darker version of the cluster of wildflowers before her. I could see it hanging on the wall of a trendy restaurant. She'd definitely improved.

"It's inspired by nature." Her eyes were wide; she didn't blink.

"I can see that." Mimi only started painting after her accident. I remembered she'd taken art classes for a time in the evenings, but then she was always taking a class. Cooking, Spanish, woodworking—another way she trawled for men. The class was a success or a failure based on whether she "graduated" with a new love interest, not whether she could actually cook, speak Spanish, or cut a piece of plywood straight. She'd have been the perfect plucky, chick-lit kind of movie protagonist if she hadn't been so prone to leaving two children at home unattended. "Do you know who I am?"

She let out a laugh, which sounded suddenly adult. "Of course I do." She turned around and looked at me. Not looked, but examined. "Look how dry your hands are." I glanced down at my hands; they did have that chalky dryness to them that came with handling pills and paper. I had an aversion to lotion from years of watching Mimi lotion herself up after bathing, her skimpy robe falling open; the clapping moist sound was so porny. The fragrances, so cheap and off-putting. I'd say Mimi had developed an artist's eye for details to notice my semichapped hands, but she'd always spoken freely about my body as if I had no idea what I looked like unless she told me. "And your hair's different."

"It is. I've let it grow long again." It startled me. That she'd remember my hair was different. If she did really know who I was, and it seemed like she did, she didn't come over and hug me or even give me a chilly shoulder pat. Mimi was never affectionate with me, not sober, at least, and when she was drunk, it was a suffocating, simpering sort of affection. I'd go all steely until she got off me.

"You should see Nurse Shelly's hair. It's so pretty."

How easily my mother could undo me. Even now. I should have been able to dismiss this, yet I still felt cut at my knees, and I didn't even know what Nurse Shelly's hair looked like. "I'll be sure to take a look." That was Mimi too. Always comparing me to others, better little girls and, I guess, women now. She'd bait you that way, get you to ask, *But what's wrong with my hair Mimi?* and never give you an answer. The point wasn't for me to fix my hair, but to understand that the world was full of people I was less than. Less pretty, smart, outgoing, bubbly, nice to be around. All cloaked as general statements. I'd bring her a math quiz with a shiny A-plus, and her response would be *Oh, you should see so-and-so's daughter. She's so creative.*

She nodded. Turned back to her painting.

I sat down on a wrought-iron bench covered with leafy detritus and watched my mother swirl her brush into a Styrofoam plate with blobs of different paints (the LightHouse only permitted acrylic or water paint, never oil due to a resident solvent sniffer.)

Mimi made a dab here and there on the canvas, then cleaned her brush in a plastic cup of water.

So this was a good day. I watched her tilt her head, side to side. Quick, hummingbird movements. I felt a surge of pity, all spiky and tender, toward her. I decided I wasn't going to say anything about Lucas. It seemed pointless. There had been a time I loved to tattle on him, tell her anything that could tip the scales toward me a little bit. Nothing had ever worked.

I wanted to leave, but worried what the nurse might think of me.

"When's Lucas coming?"

"I'm not sure."

"Well, I hope he gets here soon. I hate being alone."

"You're not alone. I'm here with you, Mimi."

"Why are you here? You're never here."

"I'm sorry about that. I would come more, but I live in Chicago now."

"Chicago? With your husband?" She said "husband" with a little giggle, like it was a slightly scandalous word.

"I don't have a husband." I'd just broken it off with a blue-blooded finance lawyer who spent his childhood "summering" in swanky East Coast towns and whose smug smile just got smugger when he asked when he was going to get to visit my "neck of the woods." I could tell he was envisioning pictures with kitschy monuments and ironically wearing mallard sweatshirts, while he sipped hot chocolate with my wholesome Minnesotan parents. (He could never keep North Dakota and Minnesota straight.) Lucas would have wanted to punch him out.

I could have told my mother about my job. About my group of friends, other pharmacists who liked to get drinks on Friday nights and bitch about the number of people who firmly believe they're allergic to generics and certain colored pills. Or how nice my apartment was in Chicago, all about the stainless-steel appliances. Or how I was still thumbing through MBA programs. How I started jogging. I could have told her how easy it was for me to be alone. Something she could never do.

I could have given her answers to questions she'd never ask, now or before the accident. I could have forced a one-sided mother-daughter interaction, but I could never stomach trying to endear myself to her, the hopefulness in my own voice.

"Why not? Why don't you have a husband?" Her voice went high into a schoolyard taunt, but was too rough to pull it off, so she sounded like a seven-year-old with bronchitis.

"Haven't met the right one yet."

She turned away from her canvas and faced me. "Maybe if you dressed nicer." She started jabbing her paintbrush hard into the Styrofoam plate and walked toward me. The plate balanced on her fingertips. "I think you would look good in ruby red."

She bent in close, poised over me, so that I was nose to nose with her. Cracker dust dotted her lower lip. For a second I thought she was going to kiss me, and I tried hard not to shrink back. Her eyes narrowed, she made an *uh-huh* sound like she'd answered some question she'd posed in her mind, and reflexively my lips curled up. *She knows. She knows that I did this to her.* The truth was somewhere in her mind, scurrying around inside one of her brain's many hollows, and one day she'd catch it. I was sure of it.

Then Mimi's hand snapped back fast, her eyes went dark, and she wielded the paintbrush like a maestro's baton, bringing it down in a spatter of rusty-red slashes. Running the brush all over the front of my white V-neck.

"Mimi, stop." I stood up, forcing her to step back.

"But you look so much better in red." I caught her by the wrist as gently as I could, but this turned out to be wrong thing to do. She dropped her plate of paint upside down in the grass, pulled free, shrieked loud enough the birds scattered, and started to stab her brush over and over into her painting, tearing up the canvas. "Look at what you've made me do."

The nurse came running out. "Are you hurt?" She looked at my chest in horror.

"I'm fine. I'm fine. It's just paint."

The nurse turned her focus to Mimi, trying to calm her as I made a run for it back to my car.

Before I could even slip the key into the ignition, I ripped the red makeup bag out of the glove compartment. Unzipped it, turned it upside down, scattered the orange pill bottles on the passenger seat, and read the labels, quick as a savant. There was a little of everything, Xanax, Ativan, Valium, Adderall, Ambien, Percocet. *Don't think about it! Don't think!* Mouth watering, I uncapped the bottle that would best blur the edges. Closed my eyes and enjoyed the chalky, bitter taste rolling down my throat.

I was a pill popper. Lately, a recovered pill popper. Though maybe "recovered" was a little too hopeful; I did bring the stash I could never force myself to flush. It started in college. A BZP at a party, and I was smooth-talking my way into a crowd much cooler than myself. A social crutch that self-perpetuated, and soon I needed an Adderall study buddy or an Ambien for a much-needed marathon sleep. More BZP.

I became fluent in doctor shopping, knew all the symptoms for whatever ailment would get me my desired prescription. I pillaged medicine cabinets at parties. From there, it seemed a natural progression to a degree in pharmaceuticals.

My first job was a residency at Northwestern Memorial (one of the top-ten highest-ranking hospitals in the US—impressed yet?). I did rounds, taking medication lists from patients. Tried to soothe them in their worst moments. I loved elderly patients the most. I was their purveyor of goods that had, up to this point, kept them alive. "You'll get your heart medication right here at the hospital, OK? Be right back." I had to think under pressure. Use my degree. Analyze dosage and interactions. I made recommendations to the physicians! I was trained in Code Blue!

But of course a busy, overworked hospital dispensary was too tempting. A pill popper's Shangri-la. I started double-dipping, just a pill here and there. The chief pharmacist, a cheery woman with big hair and a troubled son (code for drug addict), who referred to herself as my mentor, began to suspect what I was up to. She called me into her office one afternoon, a cubby of a room wallpapered with order forms, and asked me point-blank if I was stealing.

"No, of course not!"

"Can I check your pockets?"

"No."

We spent a few minutes playing stare-down. If she checked my lab pocket, she'd find two tablets of Oxycontin. If she didn't, she wouldn't have a scandal on her hands. She wouldn't be questioned on her own ability to run things. "Why, Mia? You have so much promise. Why are you doing this to yourself?"

The way she looked at me, with such stinging parental disappointment, I could feel myself shrink down to figurine size. I couldn't answer. How did I describe the gnawing feeling that thrummed underneath everything I did? How pills made it easier to live with myself, with the secret I was keeping? An offer was made that we both pretended was born solely out of her goodwill: if I went into a program and got help, she wouldn't report me to the state licensing board. I agreed, and she shuffled me out of the hospital like a broken IV pole.

I finished the program. Moved into my new apartment. Found a new job as a glorified cashier with relentless, terrible hours. I started jogging, a hamster-wheel endeavor for that runner's high that kept eluding me beyond a few fleeting gasps of well-being.

So it had been two years since I'd pulled out my little red makeup bag. Two long years that I'd fought against my plentiful triggers.

I should really throw the pill up before it starts to dissolve in my hungry stomach acid and works its way into my bloodstream. Before it makes my neurons fizz. I should zip the bag back up and toss it in the next Dumpster. I eyed the bag like it was a baited animal trap. Like the bag itself was the bad influence. I stuffed the pill bottles back inside. Ordered myself again to throw up.

But I didn't. I was looking forward to the fizz too much. Instead I put the makeup bag back inside the glove compartment. Flopped back against the headrest, closed my eyes for a second or two, then started to drive.

Two long years.

And now there I was.

Casey's sports bar hadn't changed. The sign was off, but at night it blinked neon red with the letter "Y" shaped like a long tongue licking the preceding letters. Inside was still the same old weathered wood, grungy, with an unreasonable number of flat-screen TVs. It was post lunchtime, but still fairly busy. The men looked bored; they ogled their phones as much as the waitresses, who wore knock-off Hooters uniforms. Green and gold, like oversized, sexed-up leprechauns.

I sat in a booth, hoping to avoid seeing anyone I might know. A bulgy-eyed waitress named Brandy came to take my order, her green shorts pulled up too high over her bony hips. "Anyone else joining you?" She looked worried. Nice women don't go to bars in Wayoata to drink alone. I had to be either slutty or a lesbian. Slutty was the far more acceptable option. I was glad I'd left three buttons undone on the Neiman Marcus denim top I'd changed into, just to throw them off. "Should I leave menus?"

"No thanks. Is Zoey here?"

"Zoey starts at three, but she's always late."

I ordered a tomato juice the shade of Mimi's paint job on my shirt. A near-adequate meal replacement.

"OK, well, I'll just leave these. Just in case." She left two greasy menus.

I chewed the soggy celery and looked out the window into the parking lot, trying to shut out the whispery drone of an announcer covering a golf tournament and the smacking sound of hot sauce being licked from fingers. The warm, relaxed feeling of the Valium started to radiate from the back of my neck and spread outward, wrapping itself around my shoulders like an old friend's embrace.

Across the street was the strip mall with a Chinese buffet restaurant, a used women's clothing store called Encores, and a "full-service" beauty salon with a sign out front that read CONGRADULATIONS TANNIS.

I put the word "Gent" into Google on my phone. "Gent+Wayoata," "Gent+Lucas Haas." The actor came up. I scrolled farther down to see a list of search results for news sites with headlines like HIGH SCHOOL TEACHER SUSPECT IN STUDENT'S MURDER, STUDENT-TEACHER AFFAIR GONE WRONG, MISSING STUDENT TURNS UP DEAD—TEACHER DISAPPEARS. My brother's name was next to words like "suspect," "murderer," "vicious," "slaying," and "missing," and pictures of Joanna Wilkes's beaming teenage face. The story was gaining traction. It was trickling out of Wayoata, out of North Dakota to newspapers and five o'clock news channels in Nebraska, Minnesota, and Manitoba. It was like a bad rash that spread each time it was scratched. I couldn't bring myself to click on any of them.

I typed in "Gent+Debt" . . . then remembered that whenever anyone in Wayoata wanted to keep something private, hair plugs, gastric bypass surgery, an abortion, etc., they would drive sixty miles east to St. Roche. A site came up. GenTech in St. Roche. A paternity testing center.

Oh my God. Lucas got his girlfriend pregnant! His promiscuous girlfriend. Why else would he need the test? He was trying to work out how much he would have to pay in child support, so it had to be his. He would never have left if he knew he was going to have a baby.

Not willingly.

My muscles spiked with adrenaline. My mouth went furry, the tangy juice curdled on my tongue.

I was struck with a howling vision of a midnight mob with hands still covered with nicks and cuts from trashing his truck, yanking him out of his bed. Dragging him back to Dickson Park to deal out some Old Testament justice under the angry haze of torchlight. My heart started to beat faster, but then, just as quickly, it went spongy and soft on the Valium. *Calm down. Lucas just called on Friday.* Maybe he took off *because* he got his girlfriend pregnant.

We never knew who our father was. Mimi would dole out little bits of information here and there when she was drunk enough, details that were conflicting and nonsensical. She just liked getting Lucas's rapt attention. The description always added up to a pastiche of all her previous boyfriends. I gave up listening to her, trying to piece together some image of what he looked like, who he was. She could easily have had no idea who our father was anyway. The only consistency was that she had been very young (hardly twenty years old) and he was much older and married and had moved away before we were born.

For a while, Lucas was obsessed with finding out who he was. He felt that if Mimi lied all the time, then maybe she had lied about our father moving away. He became convinced that certain men around town bore a striking resemblance to me. He took after Mimi, while I had the wild-card features that could be our father's—dark hair, olive complexion, a Mediterranean nose. Maybe it was that guy who helped him with the chain on his bike at the end of our street or his Peewee coach. He would follow the guys around like a duckling until they got annoyed and wanted to know why. Lucas would make something up, because his father, his real father, would have known why.

Then one day he just dropped it, vowed he would never abandon his future children. "I don't even want to know someone who could run out on their kids."

Didn't childhood convictions like these often go limp in adulthood? I tried to picture Lucas tiptoeing out a back door, giving the whole just-going-out-for-a-pack-of-smokes shtick, then gunning it out of town. Too panicked to give a second thought to that whole, completely unfounded "person of interest" crap.

Nope. I couldn't see it. Couldn't see him skipping out on his future child's life. He was too scarred by being abandoned by our own father. And I get that patterns repeat, I do, but not with us. Lucas and I were too self-aware. We were not ruined by our mother. We were not. The Haas twins made it out of their miserable childhood just fine. I could say this with absolute, Valium-infused certainty.

Plus, why would he have been working out child support equations if he were planning to skip out? *Though maybe it will make perfect sense once I meet this ex-student/girlfriend.*

I ordered another juice, settled into the Valium, and watched the sky cloud over until light, hazy rain started to fall.

At quarter past three, a purple hatchback with a pink lei hanging from the rearview mirror came banging into the parking lot. A dark-haired girl got out and ran, looking damp and frazzled, across the lot. The other waitress was on her, pointing at me. Zoey nodded, went to the back of the restaurant, presumably to change into her uniform. Another fifteen minutes, and she reemerged in a cropped tank top that revealed a very toned stomach, her vampy black hair refluffed and resting like a silken stole on her shoulders.

"Mia?" Zoey plopped herself down across from me. "I knew it was you. Wow, you look so much like him. Like, your face shape. Honestly, I am getting chills right now." As proof, she held out her tawny, goose-pimpled arms.

"Thanks, I don't see it, but people automatically say that a lot once they find out we're twins."

Zoey nodded. Pursed her full, glossy lips. In her tiny uniform, it was easy to see why Lucas would find her attractive; she was built. All smooth muscle and large rounded breasts. A body like a high school student. One who had the time to play volleyball and basketball, and run track and field, and attend cheerleading practice. This looked very bad for him.

"I was so worried it was that bitch again from the *Sun.*"

"It's nice to meet you." All I could think about was a budding fetus inside this girl.

"Yeah, I know, huh? Finally. Lucas talked about you all the time." She touched her hair.

"You too," I lied. "Do you know where my brother is?"

"I don't. I've asked around. Thought he could be staying with the Sorenson cousins, but Bo, do you know Bo too?"

I nodded. The Sorenson cousins were a couple of years older. They had a reputation as enforcers on the ice, the kind of melon-headed thugs who chased other players into the corner and nailed them into concussions. Every third or fourth word out of their mouths was "pussy" and they could taunt other guys into doing stupid, dangerous shit for their entertainment. They were also well known for dropping their partial dentures into unattended Solo cups and would double over with laughter when the person felt the brush of false tooth against their lips and spewed out their mouthful of beer.

"So Bo even took me to his house to prove that Lucas wasn't hiding out there." I was sure Bo was also hoping for something a little more. How gullible was this girl? "Anyway the Sorenson cousins are keeping their eye out and if they hear anything about where Lucas is, they're gonna call me right away." She chirped resolutely, like the burly Sorenson cousins were professional mantrackers.

"So you have no idea where he is?"

"I wish I did. I'm so worried about him. He hated that people were talking shit about him. I think he's just taken off for a few days, until things cool over, y'know?"

"I am so relieved to hear you say that. It's exactly what I think." I wanted to hug her. Pull her in, my comrade, and start to plot exactly how we were going to get Lucas back here. My pricked, tensed muscles, for the first time since I got here, went lax and rubbery. Like I'd just finished a marathon.

"I know he didn't do this, he said he'd never cheat on me." And then she had to go and let out that bit of reasoning. I practically winced. Noooo. I wanted her to say she knew my brother couldn't do this because she knew it wasn't in him to do it. Not some fairy-tale trust in him that he wouldn't cheat on her.

"When did you last talk to him?"

"Not since he dumped me, via text message." She overenunciated "via," so it flung from her lips like a ninja star, and jutted out her chin as if expecting an explanation from me. I tried to look sympathetic. She sighed. "Anyway, the police say I'm the last one he had any contact with. He sent it to me Friday afternoon. They're using it to create a time line or something."

"What did the text say?" So Lucas pocket-dialed me in the morning, then dumped his girlfriend by the afternoon?

"It said something like 'I'm done with you.' Whatever. After the police took a look, I deleted it. I think he was snapping under the pressure. It just didn't sound like him. He was trying to protect me. I know people are making a big stink that I'd been his student, but I had mono my sophomore year. Bad. I was only in his class for, like, the first month. I'm twenty-one years old now." Inky tears started to spill onto her cheeks. "Shit," she grabbed a napkin and tried to sop up her mascara, gave up, and kept it scrunched in her fist. "It's just all been so awful. The cops kept grilling me about when and how the relationship started, like they thought he was pressing his hard-ons on me since freshman year. Telling me he was likely grooming me. Seriously? Grooming me for a relationship almost five years later? Like that makes any sense."

"How long were you together?"

"Four and half months." She looked hurt that I didn't already know that. Clawed her hair again. "Things were going so good. I felt like he was my soul mate. I know people say that a lot, but this was different. I could just talk to him. Look." As evidence, she took out her iPhone and showed me a picture of them together on Saint Patrick's Day. It was taken at Casey's, and their faces were pushed up together, Zoey with clovers painted onto her cheeks, green beer in front of them. He looked happy.

Zoey filled me in. They first met (technically it was the second time), predictably, when she started working at the bar. Lucas came in a lot after hockey games, "for the wings—they're really good—he wasn't all pervy and gross. Unlike his co-coach, or whatever."

"Wyatt?"

"Yeah. That guy is in here all the time. I don't think he likes going home. So, anyway—"

"And he hits on you?"

"Totally. He's so touchy. I mean, he never did it in front of Lucas, but whenever he's here just on his own, or with other friends, especially when he's with other dudes, he acts like we had something going on between us. He's all winks and dirty jokes and grabbing my ass. Once he pulled me into his lap; that pissed me off. Mostly it's annoying. But, whatever, he leaves good tips."

Typical Wyatt. It was like everything Lucas touched turned to gold in his eyes. If there were rumors circulating about Lucas and his student Joanna, did he try the same thing on her? Was that why he was acting so sketchy and trying to disassociate from Lucas? Was he worried that something he said or did to Joanna was going to come back to bite him?

"Aaaannnyway . . ." Zoey said it little more sternly this time. She wanted to talk about Lucas. About their "courtship." "I'm the one who came on to Lucas. Do you know how rare that is in a place like this? I practically had to beg him to have me over. In the morning I was thinking, all the girls at Westfield wanted Mr. Haas, and, wow, here I am, in his bed."

I kept waiting for her to tell me she was pregnant, but she only continued to gush about Lucas. "When Joanna Wilkes went missing, were you with my brother that day, did you talk to him?" I knew the police would have asked her this already, but I wanted to hear for myself.

"No. I wish I'd been, but I was working here until close, at two A.M." She leaned forward, lowered her voice to a whisper. "I even told him I would lie for him, say I was with him, but he wouldn't let me get involved. People turned on him so fast here. His truck was totally trashed, windows smashed, 'sicko' spray-painted on the side. I was there for him. That's why this text, it just came out of nowhere."

"It doesn't sound like him, to break up with someone through text." In fact I had no idea if this was something Lucas would do. I didn't think so. Still, maybe he wanted to avoid a face-to-face breakup with everything going on. He couldn't handle one of his ex-students looking so lovelorn and disappointed.

"I know, right? I don't believe Lucas would ever hurt anyone, but the thing is, the night that girl went missing, he didn't answer my texts for, like, three hours. He said he fell asleep. I didn't tell the police that, just so you know. That I texted him, and he didn't answer. Though I'm sure they know about it anyway."

I could see how the police interviews with Zoey went, her barely eighteen looks, sounding naive and brainwashed by Lucas, a master manipulator who'd been working on seducing her since she was just a bright-eyed high school student. Get 'em good and young, while they're still malleable.

A couple other waitresses had been throwing Zoey dirty looks for the last fifteen minutes, and I guessed one finally told on her, because an older woman from the back, with a MANAGER button pinned to the strap of her sequined top, was coming toward the table.

Zoey mumbled, "Shit, gotta go."

I reached out, grabbed her hand. "But you're OK, then?" I wanted her to tell me she was pregnant. I needed to know it was this girl, sitting right here in front of me, that my brother had impregnated. It had to be her.

She sniffed, her head drooped. "I will be, when he's back and we can talk. Really talk."

"What I mean is, is the baby fine?" I whispered gently, suddenly wondering if I'd spoken out of turn. Maybe she'd lost it, under the stress. Maybe she'd decided not to have it. I felt a sudden rush of excitement at the prospect of being an aunt. I could see a little girl who looked like Lucas, or even me, out shopping, at movies, over tea confiding in me things she couldn't tell her mother, or whatever aunts and nieces do.

"Baby? What baby?" She pulled her hand away, her voice suddenly loud, defensive. The manager did a U-turn back toward the kitchen.

"I just thought . . ." But I didn't know what else to say. I couldn't think fast enough to backpedal out of it. "You're not pregnant?"

"No, I'm not." Her nostrils started to flare, her eyes blinked rapidly, then her arms went tight around her stomach, pushing her breasts up so high they were spilling out of her bra. "So he got some other chick pregnant?"

I didn't say anything; my mind was blank.

"Huh, well, isn't that just fucking great. So he did cheat on me? With who? Was he with that girl Joanna? Someone else? I knew it. I gave four and a half months of my life to that pervert pedophile, and he got some slut pregnant and dumped me in a text?! Fucking asshole!"

I wanted to calm her down, but I was too slow-witted—fucking Valium—and before I could say anything, she had stormed off to the bathroom, sobbing.

4

Dickson Park was a short fifteen-minute drive south, a sprawling stretch of wilderness right on the edge of town. It was just after 4 P.M., and despite how exhausted I was feeling, something was drawing me to go looking in those woods. The woods that always felt like they were watching you back.

The park was named after James David Dickson, founding father of Wayoata, who cleared the land of Native Americans after finding out *Wayoata* meant "bountiful." Something like that. A plaque was mounted on a stony pillar not far from the public bathrooms detailing the final bloody battle that was fought next to the river, where Dickson waged a surprise attack. Stories that the park was haunted were common fare. An unmarked sacred burial ground was blamed for any strange happenings in the park. And there had been some: hikers getting lost on a trail they knew well, the drowning of a girl widely known to fear water, and in 1988 a husband who'd just snapped and murdered his wife and toddler midpicnic with a corkscrew. He was found covered in his family's blood, leaning against a tree, humming Tiffany's "I Think We're Alone Now" between swigs of wine. Or so goes the legend.

Then there were the stories about Chappy, a ratty-dressed sex offender, with a face that had been mangled by a frying oil incident in prison. He sold brooms on the street in the summer; no one knew where he went over the winter. He looked like a Depression-era hobo, right down to the torn plaid suit jacket and the flower sticking out of a buttonhole. If you got too close when you passed him on the sidewalk, he'd swoop in, flashing a rotten-toothed grin, his breath hot and boozy as he'd try to hand you the browning flower off of his jacket. Giving a sad-clown expression when the kids scattered. One summer, halfway through high school, Chappy gave up selling brooms and vanished.

Everyone said he lived in Dickson Park. That he leered in the shadows at little kids sucking on fast-melting Popsicles, at teenage skinny-dippers, while furiously jerking off into the bushes.

Mostly, at night, when the weather was warm, Dickson Park was a place for teenagers to get drunk and pair off into the woods.

As I drove up the winding dusty road into the parking lot, I still got the feeling it should be littered with warning signs to KEEP OUT, TURN BACK, LAST CHANCE. And then I did pass a sign. Written in red, drippy, spray paint: DICKSON PARK CLOSED AT 9 P.M. CURFEW IN EFFECT. Underneath that, in marker, someone had written HIDE YOUR DAUGHTERS.

It was sunny again by the time I parked, and the rain had turned everything blinding bright. I wasn't sure how long it would take me to find the spot where Joanna Wilkes's body was found, but when I looked at the park map, there was a heart drawn in permanent marker off one of the trails, near the river. I tensed up.

As I started across the open field toward the woods, I noticed the massive makeshift memorial that had been set up under the picnic shelter. Dozens of teddy bears, notes with "Miss you" in marker, roses still in their grocery store plastic wrap, and unlit candles that likely made the park ranger very nervous, gathered between and on top of all the picnic benches like a deserted Valentine's Day party. Shielded too from the rain. People here were thrifty, and there'd eventually be an awkward discussion of what to do with all of this stuff, because it'd be a "real shame" to just throw it out.

A purple foil balloon with a half-peeled dollar-store price tag was tied above Joanna Wilkes's obituary. Someone had taken the time to laminate and tape it to one of the shelter's pillars.

> *Joanna Wilkes will be deeply and eternally missed by her parents, Kathy and Ian Wilkes; big brother, Ben; and younger sister, Madison. In her short life, Joanna, known affectionately as Jo, had already accomplished so much. An honors student at Westfield High School, Jo was a gifted dancer and brought light and joy to everyone who watched her. She loved being a role model to her fourteen-year-old sister and adored watching her brother's football games. She was excited to see the world and was planning to move to New York City to pursue a career as a dancer after graduation.*

"You leaving something for Jo?"

I looked up. Two teenage boys and one pug-faced girl were sitting at one of the picnic benches outside the shelter, passing a joint between them. A Colt 45 malt beer in a sunken brown paper bag sat like a centerpiece in the middle of the table. The girl sounded and looked drunk—sad and drunk. She wore tight cut-off jeans and a severe V-neck T-shirt with the tatty lace of her pink bra peeking out. I could see her ten years from now with three kids, looking back to when she could hold the attention of two boys.

She called again, "You got something for Jo?"

I nodded.

"Hey," one of the boys in a low baseball cap and crisp white tank top whispered as I approached the table, "want some?" He held the joint up. The girl swatted at his arm, hissed that I could be a cop. He laughed, that obnoxious squeal of potheads.

"No thanks, and I'm not a cop." He easily accepted this.

"I left her that white bear," the girl continued, "the one with the checkered apron and floppy chef hat, because she was on student council and always organizing bake sales, so now I'm just trying to get myself fucked up enough to go in there and take it back." She held her hand out for the joint.

"Why do you want to take it back?" I asked.

"Oh, you haven't heard the latest? Josh Kolton has gone to the police and everything."

I waited, started to grind my teeth. Please be something feasible, a violent convict fresh out of prison who recently strolled into town or a long-whispered-about church pastor or creepy Chappy. Anyone to take the heat off of Lucas.

The girl sat up. "He was here the night Jo went missing. He's saying he saw her walking into the woods with the lunch lady. No one really believes him, but I had to go and give her a chef bear."

"Fuck up." White Tank Top grinned into the girl's face. She turned away.

"You mean Mrs. Davies?" I made a face. She was the lunch lady when I went to Westfield. She always gave me extra dollops of gravy on my french fries and a side of mayo to dip them in, without charge because I "didn't cause trouble and cleaned up my table." At the time I thought she was sweet. Now it was clear she'd been trying to kill me. The girl looked confused. Right. Mrs. Davies was ancient then; she had to have retired by now.

"No, Miss Babiak," the other boy piped up, "and she's way too fat to have hiked all that way. Josh Kolton is an idiot. He's just trying to get noticed."

"Like you're not?" Tank Top smirked. "Anyway, I believe Josh. I really do," he continued, solemn, then started laughing. "Where d'you think the lunch lady gets all the meat?"

"Ew, gross." The girl slapped his arm.

A lunch lady for a suspect with a mystery-meat motive was not helpful. "Did you know Joanna well?"

I was asking all of them, but the girl answered.

"I wasn't good friends with her, but I knew her since, like, grade two. She was a snob, not to speak ill of the dead or whatever."

"You just think that 'cause she wouldn't let you cheat off her in math." Tank Top poked her in the side. This kid was annoying.

"Whatever," the girl mumbled.

The other boy, speaking between gulps of the papered beer, said, "She was pretty cool. I did a history project with her."

"Yeah and you wanted to bang her the whole time. Bet you still tried to when you found her." Tank Top thrust once.

"Shut the fuck up." Beer Boy lunged across the table and punched Tank Top midtoke in the chest, hard enough that he started choking and dropped the joint.

"Fuck you, Liam! You almost pissed on her body." Tank Top stood, eyes all watery, and walked off. The girl followed.

I sat down. "You found her body?"

Liam nodded, tucked his greasy chin-length hair behind his ears, picked up the joint, and inhaled deeply, then flicked it into the grass. "Yeah, I can't get it out of my head. Seniors were let out early to join the search parties. A lot of people were just, like, happy to get out of school, but I really looked, y'know?" His bloodshot eyes flickered over me; he stroked the corner of a very wispy mustache with his thumb.

I pushed him to tell me more. It didn't take much. It was obvious Liam liked telling it since he'd parked himself here looking for new people to tell it to. Never once did he ask me who I was.

"That morning it was already really hot, and after a couple of hours, the guy I was with said he was getting heatstroke and had to take a break. Total pussy. So I kept going, and I ended up by the river. And yeah, I was gonna take a piss. I drank, like, four bottles of water at this point."

I nodded, tried to look impressed.

"I was close to the river, just behind the tree. I unzipped, and when I looked down, there was something next to the tree, tangled up in the leaves. It took, like, a second, y'know, for it to really sink in. I think my first thought was that it was, like, a dead animal or something. I kicked at it, saw it was no animal. I dug up a handful of leaves, and hanging from my hand was all this hair." He made a clawlike gesture, showing me which hand he used. "It was sick. I was totally freaking out at this point, but knew I had to keep going. The hair trailed down toward the river. You could only see it when you were looking for it—it was all mixed in the long grass and leaves and shit. And actually the whole place did smell like shit. That should've been my first clue but then I saw the body. She was weighed down by rocks and branches." He pulled out another beer from his school bagpack. Scratched at the back of his neck. "Her face." He let out an airy burp, shook his head. "Her face was so bloated. Her mouth was open. There was more hair, so much hair scattered all around the banks. I've been dreaming about it, the hair. I wake up thinking it's all over me, in my mouth, tickling my nose." He shuddered as if on cue.

This was a horrifying, sickening scene. My stomach dropped out. I jabbed my thumb against the jagged car key to stop the wooziness from gurgling up. No one should be left in the woods, alone and shorn and dead. Somehow I managed to say words like "couldn't imagine" and "terrible," my voice coming from a distance, bypassing the dread welling in my throat.

Liam swished some beer around in his mouth. "I found her and you know what I got in return from the cops? Shit for disturbing the crime scene. Can you believe that? Dickheads. Thought I'd get a reward or something. It's too bad, man. Joanna was that girl, you know, who talked to everyone. She wasn't into cliques or anything. She was above that shit, but no one ever bugged her about it either. Everyone knew she was planning to donate her hair to Wigs for Kids with cancer. Who knew Mr. Haas was such a sick fuck? You think he cut off her hair as some kind of trophy?" He sucked back the can of beer so fast it started to crumple.

Through gritted teeth, I murmured, "I don't know." I couldn't listen to this anymore. I couldn't. My brother was *not* a sick fuck. He didn't take *trophies*. I moved out of myself. Did the numbing thing the Wayoata me had always been so good at when confronted with ugly emotions. Looked toward the trail that would lead to where Joanna was killed. "Can you tell me exactly where you found her?"

"Ah, you're one of those, huh?" He eyed me. It was the first time he'd looked directly at me. "You're all into the gruesome shit, aren't you? Some dude actually drove here from Aberdeen, like it's a tourist attraction now. Freak. Take that trail"—he pointed with his beer can—"and you'll know it when you see it." He shook his head, another long draw on the beer can, his eyes still on me, a look that was intensifying into a leer. "You're pretty. You sure you don't want some? It's original green Kush." He said this with so much enthusiasm, like I'd be swayed by this particular strain, took another joint out of his shirt pocket and waved it back and forth.

"I have to go." I wanted to see the crime scene, the place my brother supposedly killed his student, before it got too dark. More kids were spilling in to hang around the picnic benches, carrying six-packs and blankets. The park had probably never been so popular. A group of boys bellowed, grabbing their groins, "Dicks in the Park," over and over, the same chant from when I was in high school, while girls shrieked with laughter.

The next couple of hours would probably be about power drinking and daring one another to go deeper into the woods. Come nine o'clock, I was betting, they'd all have to be chased out of the park.

It was a thirty-minute hike down a narrow pathway with tree roots snaking out of the ground. I tried to imagine Lucas walking this trail as a killer. Joanna would be in front of him because it was a single-file type of trail and it was the gentlemanly thing to do. She'd think they were just going on some aimless lover's stroll, blissfully clueless that he planned to bash her skull and choke her to death. And here my mind ran through a list of motives; he sensed her pulling away and if he couldn't have her, she deserved to die/she was extorting him to stay in the relationship by promising to tell everyone if he left her and he could lose his job/because maybe there was a baby growing inside of her that he didn't want/because he just wanted the thrill of watching her die? Joanna would glance playfully back at him, a tight bud of a spring flower tucked behind her ear. Her lovely red hair catching the light and Lucas would give her one of his big grins in return, while pressing his finger into the tip of a pair of scissors hidden in his pocket. The grin dropping from his face the moment she turned around, or maybe not. Maybe he wore a violent little grin the entire time. But I couldn't believe it. Even if he was having sex with Joanna and she threatened to tell or for any other reason, why the hair? Why would Lucas want to cut off her hair? So someone who had cancer wouldn't get it? That was a certain brand of spitefulness that just didn't exist in Lucas. More proof it wasn't him. I realized quickly this was a pretty fucked-up argument to defend Lucas with: couldn't be him—he wouldn't take a cancer patient's chance to have a wig.

Police tape fluttered loose from trees, just off the trail. I went down a narrow, seldom-used path. Mosquitos swarmed; I slapped at my neck. It was more heavily wooded here than other parts. The light was tricky, almost dark but with twinkling pockets of sunlight weaving in through branches that looked like they were never still. A good place to kill someone in relative privacy. I could glimpse the river though the brush, glinting like a serrated knife. So this was where she died. This was where my brother supposedly bludgeoned and choked the life out of a teenage girl, then dumped her in the river. Something lurched inside of me. My heart felt unsteady, and my skin jittered. I worried for a second that I'd faint and be discovered there. The other twisted Haas twin found dozing at the kill site. How damning would that be?

I made my way down the grassy riverbank. The forward momentum would have made it easy and quick to drag a body into the water. The river was deeper, more wild in the spring after the melt, but by May it was safe enough to wade into. By summer you could swim. The killer wouldn't have had to worry about a current sweeping her away. He could have taken his time anchoring her down with sticks and rocks, making her body blend into the riverbed.

I bent down, ran my hand over the stony shore as if scouring for some clue the cops had missed. What exactly, I had no idea. A driver's license with a picture and the address of the real killer would be ideal. But there was nothing, of course. Other than some fresh cigarette butts and beer can tabs, the area had been picked clean.

Back in the parking lot, my phone was flashing. My voice mail was full. One message was from my sinusitis-afflicted manager named Brad, who sniffed his way through a reminder that I needed to bring in a doctor's note if I planned to be away for more than three days. And if, *heavenforbid,* I needed more than four days, I better fill out a short-term disability form.

The second message was from Pruden. "Hello, Miss Haas, I'm calling to let you know that there will be a press conference at nine A.M. tomorrow morning at the station. It would be really helpful if you could be there and appeal directly to Lucas to come in and talk with us. See you tomorrow."

Another from my old guidance counselor, Mr. Lowe, although he introduced himself as Lucas's co-worker. He'd packed up some of Lucas's school things. If I was interested, I could pick them up after three thirty. Nothing important, just posters and books. (I imagined the throat-clearing awkwardness surrounding that final bullet point at the staff meeting: *So who wants to contact the sister?*) Before Mr. Lowe ended the call, he blurted, "Sorry." Sorry for picking the short straw, sorry for calling, sorry for packing his things, sorry that my brother was a suspected fugitive on the run, he didn't say.

The rest were from reporters wanting a comment. One was from the *Chicago Tribune.* I could picture the newspaper spread around the lunch room at work, splotches of mayo dripped over Lucas's face as my co-workers speculated if he was related to their truant pharmacist. I'd never told anyone I was from North Dakota, because the minute I did, I suddenly had an accent full of accentuated vowels and had to endure a spate of "you betchas" and "doncha knows."

I deleted them all.

I called Garrett back instead of Pruden, because I knew from experience that once Pruden made up his mind, he didn't change it. The good cop had to at least pretend he was on my side as he wheedled me for information. It didn't even ring. "Hello?"

"It's Mia Haas. Before I make a public plea that my brother turn himself in, I need to know more. What exactly do you even have on Lucas other than gossip, because we both know how quickly rumor becomes gospel in this town."

"I understand that. Let's talk. Can you meet?" He gave me the choice of a coffee place or an Italian restaurant, both close to the station. He was basically saying, *Hey, let's keep this informal, get friendly, get you relaxed and then, when you slip up and reveal the true nature of that thirty-two second call, we can dart across the street where I can force you into giving an official statement.*

I chose the restaurant because I needed a drink.

We met at Perry's, where the bread bowl never goes empty and the entrees are mammoth. Its trademark dish was pasta shells stuffed with taco chips. It was 8:40 p.m., twenty minutes before closing , and the place was completely empty. Back in the city, our arrival so close to closing would have annoyed the hell out of most waiting staff, but this waitress gave us a nice big North Dakotan smile. The air smelled of garlic and candle smoke. She led us to a table and relit our stubby candle on the checkered tablecloth. When I tried to tell her it wasn't necessary, her eyes popped, as if noooo, the candle was part of the dining ritual and we could not continue without it. I worried an accordion player was going to leap out at us any minute.

I ordered a gin and tonic, hoping alcohol would numb my building headache. I didn't really want to rummage through my bag for something better in front of Garrett. Not that I would. The Valium had been a one-time thing. I needed to keep my wits about me.

"You have to order something, or you can't get a drink. Sorry." Her bottom lip puckered out, as if she felt really bad about this rule.

"What are you going to have?" Garrett looked at me over the menu. "You should eat. Have you been eating?"

"No thanks. Nothing for me."

Garrett ordered a glass of the vinegary-smelling house wine and calamari (who orders calamari in landlocked ND?). "We can share," he said. He was wearing a fitted red plaid button-down and jeans. If he'd been lankier, he'd have looked like a hipster, but he was so broad-shouldered and barrel-chested he looked like a veritable lumberjack. My last boyfriend had had a three-thousand-dollar cappuccino maker and couldn't have put together an IKEA table, whereas you got the feeling if you were lost in the wilderness with Garrett, he'd know how to take care of you. He certainly hadn't looked like this in middle school.

I felt suddenly self-conscious as to what I looked like and glimpsed a fun-house version of myself in the napkin dispenser. Immediately feeling foolish and disloyal to my brother. Two minutes ago, Garrett had pulled my chair out for me like this was a high school date, and I was falling for it like some idiot.

"I went there, to where Joanna Wilkes's body was found. I talked to someone who said a kid named Josh Kolton saw her go into the woods with the lunch lady from Westfield High. Has this even been looked into, or are you just focused on Lucas?"

"That Kolton kid is usually so stoned he wouldn't know what he was looking at on a good day. He's just starved for attention; you know how teenagers are. Anyway, we checked that out, and the lunch lady, Maria Babiak, was at her second job as an elementary school janitor. She punched in at four fifteen P.M., punched out at one A.M., which more than covers the time Joanna went missing." My shoulders sagged. "Mia, I know how difficult this must be for you. Lucas was the last guy I would have thought would be in a situation like this. All we're trying to do is get answers, figure out why a sixteen-year-old girl, with a very bright future ahead of her, is dead."

"I understand that, but I can't see Lucas doing this. I can't. He didn't do it. There's just no way he would lure a student into Dickson Park, choke her to death, and cut off all her hair. No, there's no way. None of this is Lucas."

"Fucking Liam, we told him to keep that detail to himself. Now the whole town knows." He clenched a fist around the stem of the wineglass and took a teaspoon sip. Grimaced. "I swear this is balsamic. Look, all we want to do is have a conversation with Lucas, that's it. Surrender is his safest option."

"Surrender? Surrender doesn't sound like you just want to have a conversation."

He flashed a conciliatory smile. "You're right, Mia. 'Surrender' is a poor word choice, and I don't mean it like that exactly. It's just sometimes in these sorts of circumstances, people are driven to do drastic things."

"Are you telling me you think my brother might kill himself?" My body went soupy. Was Garrett not telling me something? Did Lucas leave a note? Some crazed ramblings that could be interpreted a hundred different ways?

"I'm sorry. I feel like I've led this conversation down a dark path. That's not my intention. Obviously I can't speak to Lucas's current state of mind, right?" Garrett ran his hand up the back of his buzzed head, his muscle popping through his shirt. "There's absolutely no reason to think Lucas has hurt himself *at this point.* He took his ATM card with him, remember? It's just a matter of time before he needs to use it." And here I remembered (or really, was slammed with a bout of denial-fatigue as hard and biting as swimmer's cramp) that Lucas did have a gambler's tendency to keep a good amount of cash on him especially if he was gambling again (poker tables in smoky back rooms don't take debit). Lucas could go days without needing to use his bank card. Maybe weeks. Of course I wasn't going to say this to Garrett. "What I'm saying, Mia, is that I think we'd all feel better with Lucas safe and sound, here in Wayoata."

He said this with so much sympathy I couldn't tell if he was planting fear to make me more compliant or if he believed Lucas committing suicide was a genuine possibility. Either way, both entailed me thinking my brother was guilty.

"Well, I can speak to his state of mind, and he wouldn't kill himself because he has no reason to." I gave him an angry smile back. Shrugged a little too loosely and reached for my drink. No. Only cowards killed themselves, that was something Lucas had said. I was sure of it. The Haases kept themselves alive, even if it made everyone else around them miserable.

"I just wanted to reiterate the importance of persuading him to come in and talk to us."

"So then tell me, already! What do you have on my brother that puts him at that park?"

"It's not just about putting him at Dickson, Mia. We have eyewitness accounts of a relationship that existed between him and Joanna, confirmed by a text message Joanna sent Lucas about a weekend getaway two weeks before she went missing. We think that was a blunder and all their other communication may have been done through burner cell phones; friends said they sometimes saw Joanna with a different phone. This might make sense, since Joanna had left her phone in her locker. Kids at school thought Lucas gave special attention to Joanna. They were seen together chatting it up in his classroom after school, in the hallways. They were even spotted in his car parked on a side street."

I couldn't speak for a second. Felt a rush of anger toward my stupid, stupid brother. I wanted him here so I could shake him, swat the back of his head. *What the fuck were you thinking?* "Evidence of a relationship is not evidence of murder." My voice had gone wet and sticky. It was a line straight out of a TV crime drama, and I immediately felt dunk-tank disoriented. It was not something that should be coming out of my mouth, not ever.

"You're right, but if Lucas isn't guilty, then where is he? We told Lucas not to leave town, and well, he did. That makes him look very guilty, doesn't it?"

"Maybe he felt threatened. His truck was vandalized—everyone in town already thought he did it. Pruden probably made sure of that. He couldn't investigate his way out of a paper bag, so he's just letting the court of public opinion do the legwork for him. Bringing him gossip like a cat dropping dead mice on a back step." Even I knew I was starting to sound like a delusional broken record.

"You don't really believe that?" Garrett looked at me with a mix of pity and skepticism. This conversation was really getting too similar to the one yesterday at the station.

"Well, there were a lot of suspicious circumstances surrounding my mother's accident that Pruden ignored." I was, I knew, veering off into dangerous territory, but I decided why not use it? Why not use something I was guilty of to help my brother.

"Yeah, the chief mentioned you might feel that way." Garrett nodded briskly.

"He did?" I felt a cross between irritation that I couldn't unsettle Garrett and slight paranoia that they were discussing me. For a second I held my breath. What if they did reopen Mimi's case? Would Lucas and I get side-by-side cells?"

"Yeah, he said you both felt your mother's car accident should've been handled as suspicious and this might make you reluctant to work with us." He eyed me like I was a petulant child. "But if it makes you feel any better, I looked over your mother's file, and there was nothing in it that suggested it was anything but an accident. Her blood alcohol level was three times over the limit."

"But there was a glove left behind in the car. A glove." I pressed my finger into the table like I'd just made a major point.

"I didn't read anything about that."

"Of course you didn't, because Pruden worked the case."

Garrett started to say something, stopped. He looked nervous about this awkward shift in the conversation. He was here to glean information about Lucas, not talk about my mother or his boss's incompetence. He was visibly grateful when the waitress showed up again and set down the platter of calamari. A gelatinous entanglement of appendages that jiggled like Jell-O. Garrett picked one out, dipped it, chewed for a long time, scrunched his face up, and pushed the plate away. "I would not even let you try this." He picked a breadstick out of the basket, took a bite. "Here, have a breadstick. It will make me feel better."

I hadn't eaten since yesterday. I took one from the basket, slick with oil, and passively let it slide down my throat. Garlic and baked cheese goodness. The breadsticks were the only reason this place was still open.

"Pruden already has his mind made up about Lucas; I don't. I'm still open to the possibility someone else could be responsible for this. We just need to talk to Lucas again. See if he can explain some things. Find out why he ran." He wagged his breadstick at me.

"So just small-town gossip and one text conversation, that's it? I mean, I think I've watched enough crime shows to know that's not a lot." The knot in my stomach had loosened. It was a witch hunt. They had no one else and needed someone to blame.

"We're still waiting on DNA results, Mia. So for now we're looking at patterns of behavior." Garrett's jaw flickered. "That's why you need to do the press conference. Maybe if Lucas sees you up there, he'll rethink his current strategy. You need to convince him to come back and face these accusations like a man. That's what he needs to do."

DNA.

Three letters that felt like three shots to the head from a nail gun. Of course they were waiting for DNA. I realized I'd been running on a civilian's misconception that DNA processing had an hour turnaround and that any DNA had already been analyzed and deemed inconclusive (because they wouldn't find Lucas's DNA on that girl—I had to believe that). I was tempted to snap back that Garrett didn't need to prove anything because Lucas didn't do it, but that hardly made sense in this context. So I nodded and agreed to do the press conference.

The waitress started the vacuum and ran across the restaurant like some manic housemaid in a passive-aggressive way to get us to leave. Garrett paid up, and the waitress gave us a big, warm have-a-nice-night wave good-bye. Outside, the OPEN sign flickered off. We stood in front of the restaurant in the pink June twilight.

"This alleged weekend getaway, where was it supposed to be?"

"St. Roche, but Joanna had to cancel because of a dance practice." Garrett stared at me, removed a toothpick from the corner of his mouth, and rolled it back and forth between his thumb and index finger. "Why?"

The knot in my stomach returned; the ground pitched forward. I was back dangling from a pendulum speed-swinging between hope and fear. I couldn't decide if I should ask whether Joanna was pregnant or not. I could hear Mimi's voice, clear as if she were standing right next to me, saying in my ear, *Don't be such a tattletale.*

"I was just curious. I'll see you tomorrow."

I couldn't ignore my headache any longer. It felt like something had unfurled its prickly body and was now slithering around, snapping vessels inside my head. Streetlights were going hazy along the edges of my vision.

I pulled in to a convenience store. Cupped my eyes and massaged my temples with my thumbs. A couple of kids on bikes circled the lot aimlessly, sipping enormous cups of pop, pausing every so often to stare into my car. There were other reasons Lucas could have been planning to go to St. Roche with Joanna; I was sure of it.

I just couldn't think of any.

The Valium was a distant memory. It surprised me how intact my tolerance felt after such a solid stint at sobriety. The painkillers were already calling out to me again. I had a little bit of everything, but no acetaminophen or ibuprofen. I zombie-walked inside the store, bought some Advil and a bottle of water. By the time I got back into the car, I'd convinced myself my headache was too dire for Advil, so I took a Percocet instead. Everything felt dire. I couldn't be handicapped by headaches while I was trying to both find and exonerate my brother.

As I exited the lot, a black big-wheeled tank of a truck pulled up close behind me. Headlights on high. Its front end was covered with one of those big, glinting metal guards. I slowed down to let it pass, my eyes watering from the pulsing light, but it kept riding my bumper.

My first thought was bored teenagers screwing around. I sped up, and it sped up. I slowed down again, and it slowed down. I opened the window to wave at it to pass me, and it strobed its lights back.

We drove like this for a few minutes, a synchronized cavalcade. I watched the truck in the side mirror. Tempted to hit my brakes hard, to force it to back off. I changed lanes, and the truck followed like my car was magnetically towing it. *Go away.* I wanted to give it the finger, but something told me not to, that whoever was in the truck was fucking with me and would like that too much.

I was getting nervous. Trickles of sweat slid down my back, and yet I felt cold. A chill inched across my neck. I remembered how Percocet could sometimes make me paranoid—was this even really happening? Was I just imagining how close they were? It wasn't like everyone didn't need to take Main Street to get somewhere in this town.

But Percocet did not work this fast. I wished it would.

Ignore them. Just ignore them until they get bored and go away.

I had just flicked my rearview up to decrease the glare of the truck's searing headlights when I felt a full-body sucker punch as the truck rammed into my back end. I flung forward, my head snapped toward the dash, the seat belt hugged my rib cage tight. I went breathless, like someone had sat down on my chest.

The truck came up behind me again, not as hard this time. Kissing my bumper and then pushing my PT forward.

The whole car started vibrating, heaving a death rattle, like it was about to snap. I braked, but nothing happened. I was being steered, ridden like a bike.

"What-the-fuck, what-the-fuck, what-the-fuck." The car was going to break apart, and I was going to be smeared across the road like its gooey center. Gripping the steering wheel, my jugular jumping, I brought my foot down hard on the gas, pressed it to the floor. Accelerated and broke away.

Suddenly the truck shot past me. Cut back in front of me, then hit its brakes so that I nearly rear-ended it. I swerved over onto the shoulder. A cloud of gravel dust kicked up around my car so that I only saw the fiery rear lights of the truck as it fishtailed away. I didn't even try to get the plate number.

My bone-white hands stayed on the wheel, like they'd been nailed there. *Who the hell was that?* A sickly feeling rushed hot across my chest. It could have been anyone. I'd been back for over twenty-four hours, it was likely common knowledge at this point that I was there. Without Lucas, I was the next best thing for the town to take its anger out on. I tried to release the brake, but couldn't. The dark flat landscape tilted back and forth. I flung open the car door and drew in quick, labored breaths. Half hanging out of the car, I could picture the truck returning and sideswiping me. I got back into the car. Foot shaking, I started to drive.

Welcome home.

5

DAY 3

FRIDAY

I fell asleep in my clothes on Lucas's couch. I dreamt that Lucas and I were looking for Mimi in the backyard of our childhood home. We'd buried her, and now we couldn't find her. It was raining heavily, but we just kept digging all these little holes until the ground looked pockmarked. Lucas paused his grating whistling of Orbison's "Here Comes the Rain, Baby," only to say, "Huh, I thought we put her right here. Right here." He shook his head, moved half a foot over, and brought his mud-caked shovel up and started hitting the ground again and again.

I jolted awake, skin blazing. Ran to the bathroom and retched into the toilet. Slapped my face with cold water.

The night of my mother's accident, Lucas was having a party. Mostly his hockey team and a few lucky girls were there. It was February, and one of a handful of parties he'd started having as graduation approached. I guess he'd stopped caring what his friends thought of Mimi because we would soon be leaving her behind. It also didn't hurt that Mimi was permissive of teen drinking.

Up until then, we'd both avoided bringing friends around, because our mother was an attention-seeking drunk. She would poke her head into our bedrooms, under the pretense of looking for something, like hairspray (she went through hairspray like crazy; sometimes I seriously thought she must drink the stuff), and the next minute, she would infiltrate our conversations, spread out on the bed like "one of the girls" or peek under the fort built in the living room for the umpteenth time—"Oh, there you are."

That night, Mimi fluttered in and out of the basement, an unfinished concrete dungeon that Lucas had recently claimed as his own with beat-up couches and a busted foosball table held together with duct tape. Mimi refilled chip bowls, then lingered long enough to insert herself into conversations. Laughing too loudly. She kept her hands on Lucas's friends too long, on their backs or shoulders, until they moved away first. I wasn't at the party but upstairs at the kitchen table half studying and half eavesdropping; still I knew exactly what Mimi was up to. I could hear the sudden stops in conversations, the awkward hushed laughter that followed Mimi's breathy voice. Eventually she didn't bother with the chip bowls or ice or straws or whatever it was and just stayed downstairs like another party guest.

Lucas poked his head into the kitchen. "Keep her upstairs—fuck, Mia, help me out." He was pissed.

"You keep her upstairs," I snarled back. He should have known better than to have that many people over and expect Mimi to act like a normal human being. Plus, I was feeling left out. Carolyn was there, and I didn't want to make it any easier for Lucas.

Mimi came back up to refill her drink (she knew enough to keep her own bottle of gin out of the reach of the guzzling teens). Her cheeks flushed like she was the belle of the ball. She swayed at the kitchen counter to the music pumping through the floor. The way she was moving, all hips, I could tell her buzz had taken her back to when she was seventeen and unencumbered and could have the choice of any boy. She'd even dressed for the occasion in a lacy camisole top and tight pants.

Then a skinny-armed boy came upstairs to use the bathroom. My mother followed him, licking her lips like he was a piece of tender meat. I didn't know what was happening there, but I could imagine. Not that I wanted to imagine. I went downstairs, tried to get Lucas's attention so I didn't have to walk all the way in, but he was busy with Carolyn.

"Lucas, Mom's in the bathroom with your friend." I hadn't meant to say it so loudly, but everyone froze. Lucas's face shifted, went dark and angry. His friends laughed. "MILF" was tossed around. Lucas fled the basement, taking two steps at a time. Upstairs, Mimi was just exiting the bathroom, dabbing her relipsticked mouth, with the boy now flush-faced and smiling. Lucas stood there, looked at Mimi with hard contempt. His mouth set in a razor-sharp line. "You're disgusting." Lucas fled the house with his posse of friends, slamming the door so hard the house rattled.

Mimi waved at them, ridiculously, like nothing had happened, like she was about to hand out goodie bags at a birthday party. She hummed as she fixed herself another drink. I pictured the thoughts cruising through her head. *Guess those tight-bodied high school girls got nothing on me. You still got it, Mimi.*

I must have lingered too long, because when the last ice cube clinked against her glass, she spun around. "Oh, what are you looking at? You tattletale. Tattletale, tattletale, tattletale." Her hair had come loose and had fallen over her left eye. Her lipstick was smudged, and her bra strap had slackened and fell down her exposed arm. "Always competing with me, aren't you? That boy would never be interested in you anyway."

I didn't say anything. I didn't need to.

"Jealousy is unbecoming, Mia, especially when it's directed at your own mother." She clutched her chest, did her Betty Boop blinking thing that she did when she got this sloppy. She was a couple of hours away from passing out.

I continued to ignore her. She always wanted to provoke when she was like this, and the only satisfying retaliation was to not let her. Let her writhe. I mumbled, "Whatever," and tried to pass her in the kitchen, but a soused Mimi meant a moody Mimi, and suddenly she was on top of me, trying to hug me. "Oh, sweetheart, I just hate when we fight." I could smell the guy on her, felt her fingernails claw into my back. It was a vicious kind of hug, like she was trying to squeeze something out of me that wasn't there.

I couldn't breathe. I pushed her off, harder than I meant to, and it was like she was made of air, her bird bones flung back and she lost her footing and toppled. Her head cracked against the corner of the kitchen counter. Her eyes fluttered shut, a couple of seconds passed, and they flicked open again. A wide, stunned look on her face. She touched the side of her head, under her hair, held her hand out. Blood. I moved to help her but she was already scrambling to stand.

"I never should have had you. I was only supposed to have one." Her bloodstained finger pointed upward—one. Only one.

"You're a nasty drunk, and I wish you'd never had me either."

Mimi grabbed her purse and keys and left. I didn't try to stop her. I had no idea where she was going, I didn't care. She always took off like this at all hours of the night. I scooped out some ice cream as soon as her car pulled away and watched TV, happy to be home alone. Lucas stomped in an hour later and went to bed. We didn't talk.

It was four in the morning when the police arrived to tell us that Mimi had been in a car accident. It looked like she had passed out at the wheel, driven off the road, and hit a tree. Her injuries were severe enough to put her in a coma. Four days later, a neurologist from Minneapolis informed us that our mother might not make it, and if she did, it was unlikely she would be the same person. When Mimi finally roused, it was apparent that she wouldn't be coming home.

Of course I knew that it was me who caused Mimi's head injury. Not her car's slow roll into a tree. When Lucas brought it up to the neurologist that Mimi wasn't driving all that fast, the doctor simply answered, "Head injuries can be funny like that."

Some of Lucas's friends and their parents helped us out financially. (These same people who were probably now damning themselves for having ever given us a cent.) There was a fund-raiser with a silent auction that let us stay in the house until we left for college, then it was put up for sale.

I never told Lucas anything. I didn't want him to know. I was afraid

I would lose him, the last remaining fully functioning member of my family. I was afraid he would hate me for making us near orphans. For making Mimi a lifetime burden. It was why I lied to Lucas about the cost of her care; he had to feel he was paying his half, because he'd feel bad if he wasn't.

I have a hundred choose-your-own-adventure moments that made for a different outcome: Lucas and I sprang an intervention on Mimi that night. She stopped drinking, she worked hard at winning us over (she knew she had to work harder with me), and we'd gone on to have an adult relationship with her that was deep and meaningful and self-aware. Or else, again I didn't push her and she continued drinking, her liver festered, her face pickled, and I got to hate her. I got to live a life without hauling around this guilt. On her deathbed, a death hastened by booze and an undiagnosed STI, I'd find it in my heart to forgive her and finally have closure.

But I did push her.

A sleeveless gray tunic, black slacks. It was the only outfit I'd brought with me that was remotely suitable for a press conference. I laid it out on Lucas's couch, showered, and spent another twenty minutes cursing at myself for not packing a hair dryer. As I pulled my hair up into a severe knobby bun, last night's headache pulsed a few last dying twangs. Classy diamond stud earrings. Nothing flashy. I powdered on some makeup, glazed my eyes with waterproof mascara and matte eye shadow until I looked like a well-rested, reasonable person. I glossed my lips to cover their redness from chewing them, a nervous habit. I checked myself in the mirror. You'd have to take someone this polished-looking seriously. Some small prideful part of me whispered, *Look at me, I've made it. I'm not decked out in Kmart. I did not get pregnant and stuck here.* A fever that struck down how many Wayoatan girls? Like my mother.

Like Joanna would have been.

I tried a stunned headshake. *No, no, no. He didn't.*

Flicked off the light.

The sky was an innocent blue as I drove to the press conference. Something was rattling somewhere in my rental car. I should probably file a police report about being run off the road, but then I pictured the inevitable paperwork and insurance forms and I knew I wouldn't be able to deal with it. Not now. So I turned the radio up and went over what I would say to make Lucas come back. When I saw the media vans crowded around the police station, my hands went clammy and I had to fight a violent urge to turn the car around. The sheer number of them. I'd been expecting a handful of reporters to make the trek all the way here for a press conference, the most exotic being from Minneapolis (I'd even comforted myself with the thought that someone from the *Chicago Tribune* had only called me; they hadn't actually sent a reporter for such a flimsy story). Nothing like this. It had broken out of the Midwest and gone national. Of course it would. Lucas was photogenic and on the run. Joanna was an NYC-bound ballerina. The golden boy from Wayoata, circa 2002, had killed the golden girl of Wayoata, circa now. Pruden was already standing on top of a temporary stage, behind a lectern that looked like it had been borrowed from a restaurant. The PLEASE WAIT TO BE SEATED sign was covered up with a printout of the Wayoata Police Department insignia. Garrett, in full blues, saw me and jogged over, opened my door, and ushered me past the throng of cameras, microphones, and iPhones. He led me by the arm into the station, like I was frail, or maybe he was worried I would back out.

"Sorry, Mia. I had no idea it was going to be this big. Do you need anything, bottle of water? We have about five minutes."

"No, I'm fine. I mean, I'm not fine. Not at all."

Garrett nodded like he knew what I meant, but clearly he didn't. Or else he wasn't listening because he was watching Pruden through the window as he delivered the official police statement. The same blah-blah vague person-of-interest bullshit, who just became a whole lot more interesting due to his absence. I glimpsed thwarted ambition on Garrett's face. He was stuck behind a guy who refused to retire.

He probably had visions of himself cracking this case and making police chief before he was thirty. He looked back at me, tried to give me a pleasant smile like he was about to sell me a new car.

"OK, so just a quick primer. Don't offer your opinion about whether Lucas is guilty or not. It'll just confuse the point of this conference. It will upset the family, who are here. All we want is for you to talk directly to Lucas. Offer your support. Appeal to him that turning himself in is the best thing he can do."

"If I knew I wasn't going to be able to say what I wanted, I wouldn't be here right now," I snapped. As if he was trying to censor me like some authoritarian thought-cop.

"I told you this last night." He gave me a surprised look.

"No, you did not say I couldn't offer an opinion about his guilt. Why would I have agreed to do this?"

"Mia." His voice went into placate mode. "This really isn't the place for that. I get why you want to say Lucas is innocent. I get that. I do. And you will have lots of other opportunities to do that, once Lucas is back. But this whole town is on high alert with your brother still out there. People are scared, and if you could for a minute see it from the family's point of view—"

"But Lucas is my family." *Fuck you. I'll say whatever I want.*

"You know what I mean." He thumbed the corner of his mouth. Squeezed my shoulder in a way that I didn't like. It was too pitiful. "Just remember, talk directly to Lucas. Say whatever you need to say to get him to come in. All that matters right now is that Lucas turns himself in." A woman came up to us and said something to Garrett. "Ready?" He looked at me. Put his police cap on his head, pulling it down low, making his blue eyes go steely gray. For a second I wanted to feel the weight of his arm around my shoulders again. Wanted to feel weighed down because I was so sure I was at any second going to deflate like a balloon and disappear.

I shook my head no, but I followed him outside. Took two steps up onto the platform. The crowd looked so much bigger from up here. So many eyes were aimed at me, I thought I would crumple under the weight of them. My cheeks started to burn up.

Pruden glanced over his shoulder at me, his eyes narrowed to hyphens, then wrapped up his statement. "The police service is requesting the assistance of the public to find Lucas Haas. If you have any information, please call immediately."

Garrett nodded at me. "Your turn," he whispered like we were back in computer club.

The Wilkes clan were standing out in front, the four of them. Each in white T-shirts with JUSTICE FOR JOANNA printed above Joanna's picture, same as the one from her missing poster. A cruel thought jumped into my mind: Well, they certainly had time to get new T-shirts made up; they can't be that *aggrieved*. (I knew they were new because others in the crowd were still wearing the BRING JOANNA HOME T-shirt, like they were souvenirs of hope.) The family was holding hands and may have been praying. The eldest son was leaning into his father, who looked as if he would topple over from the extra weight. His eyes hidden behind the glare on his glasses. The daughter, Madison, was staring down at her feet. A high blond ponytail dangled in front of her face. My gaze moved to the mother and . . . THAT was the mother?! My heart dropped.

Kathy Wilkes (née Russo). She still had that pageant beauty glint but was now round as an M&M's candy and coated with an orangey spray tan.

I knew her, or really knew of her. She was about a decade older than me. Every year at the Corn and Apple Festival parade until I was nine or ten, Kathy was the topper on the Harold's Grocers float. She'd stand in the middle of a Styrofoam fruit platter, wearing a tiara and a gown that looked like it was made of cotton candy. She'd wave at the curbside crowd like the Wayoata princess she was. Her grandfather owned Harold's Grocers. He'd opened it in the forties, and it was now a Midwest chain and Wayoata's claim to fame. Harold's Grocers and its processing plant employed nearly a quarter of Wayoatans. Lucas was fucked.

I had to look away from the mics dangling from boom poles and bobbing cameras with lights that were suddenly hitting my eyes like spritzes of bleach making everything go white and stinging. Aware that my mouth had fallen open with surprise, I pressed my lips together. *Kathy Russo* was Joanna's mother. It had thrown me off. Lucas *really* needed me to say something good about him. Of course I wasn't going to say what Garrett wanted me to. I wasn't going to coax my brother home like a cat out of a tree. No. Lucas would sense a trap. He'd know I drank the Kool-Aid, and wherever he was, he'd be farther gone. He had to know, really know, that I was on his side. He needed me, more than ever, if he was up against Harold's Grocers. Jesus. This just kept getting worse.

I couldn't talk for a second. My tongue sat thick and useless in my mouth, and when I did speak, my voice sounded strange and very far away. "I would like to state first that my brother, Lucas Haas, is not responsible for Joanna Wilkes's murder. Lucas is a kind and gentle person, incapable of violence. Whoever did this is still out there and needs to be brought to justice. Lucas, if you're watching right now, please come home. I promise you, this will all be sorted out." The mic squealed. I flinched. The Haases' bad habit of feigning coolness when the world was ending had crept in (years of dealing with an alcoholic parent will do that to you). Immediately I knew my voice had gone too lilted and casual at *this will all be sorted out.* I cleared my throat, leaned toward the mic again. "Just come home and help find the person who really did this by clearing your name. I love you, I believe in you."

I stood there a second, immobilized by the stone-cold quiet that followed. A second passed, then a rush of questions were pelted at me. *Is your brother guilty? Why did he do it? Where do you think he's hiding? Did you know he was having an inappropriate relationship with a child? Did you notice anything growing up that indicated he could be guilty of such a horrendous act? Did he sexually abuse you as a girl? Don't you think your terminology, "all sorted out," reflects a blasé attitude to the murder of a young girl?*

"I didn't mean to sound blasé." Garrett's hand was on my shoulder, directing me away from the microphone. His lips pressed into my ear.

"I warned you. Don't answer them. Let's get you out of here. Follow me."

As I stepped down behind Garrett, Kathy Wilkes cut me off. It was like she had teleported from the front of the platform to there, *poof.* Her head was cocked slightly to the side, her eyebrows up in a quizzical expression. A hush fell, and I could hear the air fizz. The earth rippled underneath my feet. An awkward second passed. It looked like she was trying to put together the right words but couldn't. I took a breath, decided to say something first. I wasn't going to outright apologize, because that was an admission, but I guessed something equally asinine for a mother who'd lost her daughter would be *I'm sorry you think my brother is responsible for your horrible tragedy.* When she saw I was about to speak, Kathy's face morphed into something wild. The cameras buzzed around my eyes. Her hand, the hand that had waved in the parade all those years, came up and connected against my cheek. My head snapped to the side, a keening whistle sounded in my ear.

"How dare you? My daughter is dead," she wailed.

I stumbled back, a flash of pain and a sort of schoolyard embarrassment at having my ass handed to me in front of so many people. Kathy's husband made a grab for his wife, but she shook him off like a bear.

Garrett and another officer quickly intervened.

Madison, too, had somehow wrapped herself around Kathy's nonslapping hand and whined, "Mom, don't. Everyone's watching." Kathy was about to come at me again.

The other officer guided her away, and Garrett walked me to my car, his arm out trying to protect me from the microphones and telescopic lenses thrust in my face.

"Any comment on being slapped?"

I peeled out of the lot.

Around the corner. I sat in my car. Stunned. My hand pressed against my stinging cheek. I could still see the police station. The Wilkeses were surrounded by more people in white Joanna T-shirts. A woman was passing out candles. It was clearly the beginning of a prayer vigil.

I was talking to myself—"What the fuck, Lucas, where are you? What the fuck"—when a woman knocked on my car window. I rolled it down, just a crack.

"I'm Vanessa Lee. I'm a reporter from the Minneapolis *Star-Tribune*." She was short with shampoo-commercial hair and spoke incredibly fast. "I know you're going to get a lot of offers, but I really want to deliver three-dimensional coverage here, not get sidelined by the juiciness of the teacher-on-student aspect of this story. I want to delve a bit deeper into who Lucas is and would like to do a more extensive interview with you about him. It could be your chance to really share Lucas's side of things. Right now, it's assumed he's guilty. You could maybe turn that around, put some reasonable doubt in our readers' minds." She took a breath, then proudly stated, "We're the most read out-of-state newspaper in North Dakota, and number one in Minnesota. I write an opinion column and make it a point to take a contrarian point of view, to investigate behind the headlines."

I didn't say anything. I white-knuckled the steering wheel; my hands ached. I didn't know Lucas's side of things.

She twitched at my nonresponsiveness. "Here." She dropped her card in the open slit of my window. It fell into my lap. "If it's any consolation, if Lucas had been a woman and Joanna a sixteen-year-old boy, the media attention would be far worse."

"Well, at least there's that," I answered sarcastically. I made a point to toss her card into the backseat.

It was the first time I'd regretted not maintaining a friendship with anyone in Wayoata. I wanted to sit at someone's kitchen table, have them press a cup of tea into my hands and agree with me that this was just a misunderstanding. But my friends had been girls like me, ambitious and anxious to leave Wayoata behind. And it wasn't like I could call any of my friends in Chicago. Where would I even start? *Hey, you know that family I never really talk about? Yeah, well, my brother might be a murderer.* It would require too much backstory. Take too much explaining. I'd have to reveal too much. I was alone.

The makeup bag started calling out to me (For no good reason, when a craving set in and my makeup bag started talking to me, I always heard Seth Rogen's deep, gravelly voice), *Hey, hey, hey, I'm here for you, just dip in. Take a chill pill. Relax.* Its zipper mouth grinning up at me from my purse.

No. I better not. My left eye twitched with the struggle not to take a pill.

I guess I lied. I tend to do that when it comes to pills. Lie to myself. The past two years, while I'd been relatively sober, I hadn't won *every single battle* against my triggers. *There were just so many of them.* That smell of burning dust and dead skin when the furnace was turned on for the first time in my building put me right back in Wayoata. Back in that shitty house, in my upstairs bedroom, feeling all that powerlessness biting at my skin.

Listening to a mother and daughter chatter amiably while waiting for a prescription (the mother actually asking questions and listening to the answers like her daughter was a gift). Talking to my twin, the one person who knows me better than anyone else, and feeling like a liar. An entire day of listening to cranked Muzak and knowing I could do better than retail pharmacy, that I should go back to school for my Pharm.D. and work in biotech. Invent the most blissful pill on the planet and name it after myself.

When I needed to treat the sting of guilt that sometimes hit me like a bad flu.

It's not like I'm an unabashed user. I take breaks, sometimes for months. And I always feel bad about starting up again. But then I just take a pill, and I feel better.

Anyway I couldn't take a pill even if I wanted to. I had to go and pick up Lucas's things at the school later. So I went back to the apartment and waited for something to happen, for Lucas to appear, for good news, while the walls closed in on me.

It was just after 3 P.M. School didn't let out for another half an hour, but students were already milling about outside on the front steps of Westfield High. The same spot where the most popular kids hung out during my time there. Eleven years had passed since I was in this high school, the miniature version of this watchful, judgmental town.

Starting in ninth grade, our mother's town bicycle reputation seemed to cling to me like a bad household smell. A double standard that didn't apply to Lucas, of course, whereas I reeked of slut everywhere I went. I could feel people watching for signs that I was like her. As if my vagina were going to click on any minute like a Hoover vacuum. (For this reason, and a rabid fear of pregnancy, I'd never had sex on Wayoata soil. I waited until college, where I lost my virginity to a gentle English lit student with a Zoloft prescription.) Having these big breasts didn't help things. Rumors would come in waves, random and unprovoked and without a wisp of truth. Boys that I supposedly sucked and fucked in Dickson Park, the frozen hot dog that broke off inside me and caused an infection that led to me missing a week of school (it was really appendicitis), hand jobs for the football team for a case of light beer (the light beer was the part that really bothered me—like I would have done it for anything less than regular beer).

Adolescent self-consciousness still seeped into me as I walked by a pack of freshman girls wearing low-slung jeans and hairbands. Their T-shirts were tied tight in the back, exposing their narrow midriffs. These girls looked alarmingly young. One of them whispered something, and they all looked me over. Stared as I climbed each step, wearing matching mean-girl smirks and performing a synchronized slow tilt of their heads like they had practiced in a mirror.

A basketball practice was going on in the gym. The squeal of sneakers hitting the floor was sharp and made my nerves even more jagged. I made a point to pass the cafeteria. The lights were off, but I could still easily see inside. The lunch lady—I knew this because she still had her hairnet on—was sitting, bent over, changing from her black grease-spattered shoes into white sneakers. Clearly struggling with her own big-boned inflexibility, she looked sweaty. She caught me staring; we made eye contact before I could look away. Even from where I was, I could see a shadowy upper lip. She scrunched up her face, cracked her neck like a prison guard, pointed to the CLOSED sign.

The guidance counselor's office was in the same spot. The door was half open, but the room was empty. I spotted Mr. Lowe's motorcycle helmet on his desk, so he hadn't left yet.

I decided to wait a few minutes and sunk down into the middle of the same blue couch from when I went there. Its threadbare cushions now covered with a Mexican blanket. The coffee table was the same too, only now it was covered with even more initials loving other initials corralled in jagged hearts. I WANT TO BLOW MR. LOWE was still there, near the edge of the table but marred by the overlapping carved declaration that ANAL IS THE NEW ORAL!!!!

I could have written it. The part about Mr. Lowe. I'd had a blinding crush on him my sophomore year and spent several months malingering with anxiety attacks just so I could spend an hour with him. Not that we ever really talked much. Instead, after I gave him a rundown of my symptoms that I'd lifted from a pamphlet, he told me that music helped him "mentally flatline" and so that's what we did, we listened to music. Music he took upon himself to introduce me to (nineties alt-rock), and whenever his dark brown eyes made contact—mesmerizing eyes—he made me feel so fucking visible that I'd run home and find out everything I could about some obscure West Coast band.

He even had me listen to his own freshly cut CD and asked me what I thought of it. Of course I panted and swooned and said all the right things, and he gave me a copy. I listened to it night after night, lovesick, searching for hidden meanings in lyrics that could be about me, and fantasized about riding on the back of his bike, parking and wandering off into back lanes or construction sites or derelict buildings. (I was not the sort of schoolgirl who fantasized about having sex on plush beds with candlelight; I wonder what that said about me.)

I guess as counselors went, he wasn't really great, but at the time, under the influence of a schoolgirl crush, I knew he was just biding his time until he got his big break. I felt like we had this whole on-the-margins kinship; both me and Mr. Lowe belonged in big cities. Together of course.

I stopped coming to our "sessions" after my mother's accident. At the time, I felt that I was no longer worthy of his attention. I needed to feel punished.

"Mia? Hey." His voice set off a reaction; I was back rolling around in my bed listening to him sing. He closed the door. "How are you holding up?"

I answered with a stammered "I'm fine. Considering."

"I know. I know. God. What you must be going through . . ." Mr. Lowe gave me an agonized look like he was really struggling to come up with the right words to console someone whose brother could be a maniac. I shook my head to tell him he didn't need to say anything. He blew out a frustrated breath. "It's nice to see you, I mean, not like this. . . . It's just that I've thought about you over the years. Lucas told me you were doing really well in Chicago."

Mr. Lowe did look genuinely happy to see me. He hadn't changed much at all. Older. Probably fortyish. The black-rimmed glasses were new, but his dark brown hair was still thick with curls. He was wearing a blue button-down, giving him an overall sexy nerd appeal.

"It's nice to see you too. Are you still playing music?"

He gave an embarrassed chuckle. "I'm in the house band at Detours Bar . . . so if you count that, then yeah, I'm still playing."

"Well, that's good." It wasn't really. Detours was a dumpy bar that sold dollar-special beers and had a fog machine that set off asthma attacks.

"So here's, uh, Lucas's things, or at least what the police didn't take." He set the box down on the coffee table. A rolled poster of Shakespeare sticking out.

Beholding my brother's teaching career whittled away into something that could fit into a box was a miserable sight.

"He didn't do what they're accusing him of, Mr. Lowe." I had to say this, had to keep saying it to as many people as possible. Try to turn the tide wherever I could.

"Eric. Call me Eric. Lucas is so well-liked here, as a teacher and coach." A good dodge on giving an opinion regarding Lucas's guilt. He sat down across from me. Elbows on knees, his fingers loosely steepled.

I decided to cut to the chase. "Can you tell me anything that would help me understand how this is happening?"

He scratched at the back of his neck. "I'll tell you everything I told the police; they interviewed the entire staff. I did not personally witness anything untoward going on between your brother and Joanna or any other student. If anything, it was Lucas who was pestered. He had a bit of a following with the teenage girls. I mean, I've been the object of a few crushes over the years." I expected a look or a nod that counted me among the enamored, but there wasn't one. "But nothing like what Lucas had to put up with. It seems your brother's a pretty good-looking guy. He asked me several times how to handle it. How to let them down gently without damaging their self-esteem. He was very sensitive about it. I am as surprised as anyone by the accusations."

A second or two passed. I was hoping for something more, more conviction in his voice. A firm proclamation of my brother's innocence.

"You've got a hand mark on your cheek." He broke the brief, awkward silence.

"What?" I touched my cheek as if I could feel the outline of Kathy's hand.

"Ice. Let me get you some ice. I'll be right back." Eric was out of the room before I could stop him. I glanced at the pamphlet rack, half empty. Just a few crumpled looking scraps on HPV and sexting. I noticed a dog-eared poster hanging loose on the wall next to the rack. There was something about it. I stood and pushed back its corner. It was Garrett Burke doing his best UNCLE SAM WANTS YOU riff, but in blue shirtsleeves that hugged his bulging biceps and chest a little too tight. Deputy Gym-Rat was clearly trying too hard.

THE WAYOATA POLICE WANT YOU TO TAKE THE PLEDGE TO DRIVE SAFE. Written in marker at the bottom were the details for an April school assembly on safe driving.

Huh. I wondered how many pledges Garrett had helmed as WPD's hot poster boy. Bet all the girls showed up to take their abstinence pledge, don't-text-and-drive pledge, an anti-binge-drinking pledge, don't-hit-your-girlfriend pledge, a wear-a-helmet pledge. How bored was he, before Joanna's body turned up? Did he feel a tiny tinge of relief that there was a murder to solve? That something was actually happening.

Eric was back, ice pack in hand. "So what happened?" Maybe because I was standing, maybe because he was just being kind, he leaned in, tucked my hair behind my ear, and placed the ice on my cheek. Without meaning to, I startled at this simple act of gentleness. Then because he looked worried that he'd done the wrong thing, I thanked him for the ice and gave him an abbreviated version of events at the press conference in a way that made me sound less antagonistic than I had been.

"Kathy can be . . . I mean I shouldn't be saying this, but she's very, well—how to put it?—she had a strong personality even before losing Joanna." He made a face, like he needed to be coaxed to say more.

"What does that mean?" My mouth felt numb.

"It means, you probably don't want to cross paths with her on a good day."

"Yeah, Kathy has quite the arm. Does she do that a lot? Go around hitting people?" I wanted him to say something bad about her, but I also knew I was setting myself up to hear *No, just the sister of suspected murderers.*

"No, no, nothing like that. Kathy is just very aggressive. Even with Joanna, she was constantly hovering over her, clearing obstacles. Perceived obstacles, I should say. The dad, Ian Wilkes, was pretty easygoing. Hardly ever saw him." That didn't surprise me. Ian had just stood there when Kathy pulverized my cheek. He struck me as a weak wisp of a man, fine-boned and nervous behind his reflective specs. "But if it looked like Joanna wasn't going to get the lead in the musical, Kathy Wilkes marched in and strong-armed the drama teacher into giving it to her. I mean, the Wilkeses sort of run things in this town, don't they? I think if Kathy didn't own the only competitive dance studio in Wayoata, Joanna probably would've been subject to a lot more torment."

Somehow I knew that Kathy ran a studio, Shooting Stars. It was on the second floor in a strip mall. At night, with the lights on, you could see the girls in bodysuits with wads of hair gathered tight at the back of their heads and glimpse Kathy pacing up and down, adjusting arms, legs with a yardstick.

"So you counseled Joanna?" *Please tell me it was because some boy knocked her up,* I kept repeating in my mind.

"It was part of her probation."

"Probation?'

"Oh. Yeah, it's common knowledge that Joanna was caught with marijuana in her locker just before Christmas break. Swore she was just keeping it for her friend, but it's no secret her boyfriend was the school dealer."

"Boyfriend?" I interrupted.

"Dylan Yates. He's a bit of a wayward kid. Nineteen years old, should have graduated last June but was expelled for bringing a knife to school. He was trying to show off, play gangster." So Joanna had another side than the sweet, overachiever described in her obit; she was pregnant and dating a drug dealer. This was good. There was another suspect.

A burst of knocks at the door. "Sorry, jus' a sec." Eric opened it to a teary-eyed girl in a tank top and shorts with thin infected-looking scratches that laddered her legs and arms. She was showing off a new gash on her inner arm that was spurting some serious blood. Eric swung into action, had me grab wads of tissues to sop up the blood, and hustled the girl toward the nurse's station. He mouthed, "Sorry," over her head as I followed them tottering down the hall. I lagged behind when they reached the nurse's station and sneaked out. I didn't want to run into anyone else here.

I drove around looking for my brother like he was some kind of lost dog. I fought the urge to roll down the window and start calling out his name. It wasn't until I pulled up to the apartment block that I realized I'd forgotten his things back at the school. *Goddammit.* I did not want to have to go there again. The caretaker's daughter whipped into the lot in an old station wagon, jolted to a stop. Her head snapped forward. Then she started lurching back and forth, trying—badly—to park. She got out, slammed the creaky faux wood–paneled door with two plastic bags hooked on her wrists. The Harold's Grocers logo screamed out at me.

"You're not old enough to drive."

Bailey shrugged, tried for a no-biggie gesture, but her eyes darted around the lot. "I know how to, though. It's fine. I'm getting my beginner's soon." She fidgeted with the bags. Her homemade jeans shorts were cut too short; the pockets, each full of change, sagged past their tattered fringe like twin hobo satchels. Poor girl. I knew all too well what it was like to be the one who had to be the adult while the parent languished on the couch all day in a sour haze of booze.

"Need help?" One bag held three bottles of pop; it looked heavy and dangerously close to breaking.

"Nah. It's light." She did a kind of arm curl with the bags as if to prove how strong she was. This little show of bravado made me sad. I wanted to whisk her away to a teen Al-Anon meeting.

"Y'know, while I'm here, if you need a ride to the store or something, I can give you one." I was probably making an offer I couldn't fulfill, but still, I knew that it went a long way, that feeling when someone noticed the shit-storm you were weathering.

"Why?" She bobbed her head, clearly taken aback by the offer. "I can drive. Really."

"Well, what if you get caught? You might not be able to get your license." We walked into the building together.

"I don't do it often." She rolled her eyes, but a rueful smile flickered over her lips.

"Just be careful." In the foyer, Mr. Chin-puff, the ogler of girls just into their teens, was emptying his mailbox. Bailey cast him a cagey glance.

"Yeah, I will," she called over her shoulder as she scurried fast down the hall and into the property manager's suite.

Chin-puff followed me onto the elevator and pressed the button for the second floor. Who takes an elevator up one flight? He was wearing beige pleated Dockers and a blue T-shirt that said I.T. SPECIALIST in a SWAT-style yellow font across the back. I glanced at the magazine he had rolled up in his hand, expecting it to be some top-shelf porno type thing, but it was a guns and ammo catalogue.

He turned and faced me, sighing so theatrically my hair actually moved under the gust of his breath. "Hot out there."

"It is." I avoided making eye contact, but rather than getting the hint, he took it to mean he could look as hard and as long at me as he wanted. Normally I would have returned the stare-down (why should I be the only who's uncomfortable?), but something, the close confines of the elevator maybe, or the leather case hanging off his belt that I associated with penknives, told me that was a bad idea.

"Hey, you just move in?"

"Yeah, I did." This guy was either screwing with me or really out of touch with current events. I couldn't tell.

"Hunh." Finally the doors opened at their slow drawbridge pace. But before he got off, he pressed his thumb on the Door Open button. "My name's Dale Burton, 2D. You ever, uh, you know, need anything, just, uh, 'come and knock on my door.'" He started singing the *Three's Company* theme song. But there was no charm to it. He leaned forward in a near lunge, his eyes roaming my body. He didn't smile. When the doors shut, I heard an angry laugh.

At six o'clock I watched myself on the news while shooting back three bourbons, courtesy of my twin's bar. I sounded nervous and misguided, even neurotically loyal. Like those mothers of serial killers who still think their sons are innocent, despite all their sons' courtroom smirking when the crimes are described.

A picture of Lucas flashed across the screen. I wondered who chose it. He was obviously in the middle of coaching a hockey practice, his

Bulldogs Windbreaker zipped up to his chin, Bulldogs ball cap pulled low, the same ball cap that was on the coffee table right there in front of me. A scowl on his face as he looked out onto the ice.

A quick history: Lucas's hockey scholarship to Ferris State, his unfortunate knee injury. Cut to another picture with Zoey and Lucas, the one she'd showed me yesterday, the Saint Patrick's Day shot. Lucas suddenly looked much older than Zoey, laugh lines emphasized by the hard flash on the camera phone, eyes shot red, sweaty skin glistening with alcohol and horniness. It didn't help either (how did I miss that earlier?) that Lucas was glancing down Zoey's top. FORMER STUDENT was the caption.

The voice-over then reported that other girls in his classes had come forward to say Mr. Haas made sexual advances toward them. I choked on my bourbon. "What the fuck?" I yelled at the TV. It was like a grenade had been tossed into the room and there was nowhere to take cover. This was out of control. My twin, his life, his reputation detonated right in front of me.

The screen filled with a silhouette of a girl who wished not to be identified. In an altered robo-voice, she described how Mr. Haas would take her into the equipment room and ask if she had a boyfriend, told her how pretty she was, and then fondled her breasts for a while.

The girl was lying. The gym equipment room was an overfilled, stinky room. There was hardly enough room to stand, never mind get in a good groping. Not to mention it was always left open, and even if the door was closed, it had a window. It was probably the worst place in the school to molest someone. Why wouldn't he take her to the individual staff bathroom or his classroom and lock the door, or the book room off the library, where he had an actual shot of not being walked in on? The equipment room didn't make sense.

The story closed with a shot of the Wilkeses huddled close in a prayer circle—"A family grieves and prays for justice." A hotline number flashed across the screen. Lucas was considered dangerous.

I immediately called Garrett. He answered with an irritating hyperalert, "Hello, Mia."

"Those girls are lying. You know that, right? Come on, the equipment room? Westfield's equipment room is like a hoarder's spare bedroom." I should have done some thinking about what I was going to say before calling; this was a liquor-infused stream of thought. Focus. "Did you know there were other girls when you asked me to do the press conference?"

"You know I can't discuss that. How's your jaw, by the way?"

"Well, what can you discuss?" I stopped short of adding *asshole*. Stay calm. Breathe. I needed this apparently fake friendship too, so that I could glean my own info and steer him away from my brother. Not that I didn't think Garrett was clever, much more so than Pruden. I had to be careful around him. Unwisely, I tipped back the rest of the bourbon in my glass. "My jaw kills. Thanks for asking. Now, how do you know that that girl isn't just a high school drama queen out for her shot at some real attention? Like Josh Kolton? There's no way Lucas would take girls there and fondle their breasts. And, really, is Lucas a twelve-year-old boy? He's just gonna sit there and fondle breasts?"

"So you're saying he should have gone further?"

"I'm just saying it's bullshit! It makes no sense. Why would my brother kill Joanna and not these other girls, then? Why?" Garrett started to say something about how only Lucas would have the answers to that, so I kept talking. "He was never a violent person. I can't even process this. I can't. There's just no way Lucas did this! You could tell me that aliens abducted half of the earth's population and I would believe it before this. Did you know Lucas hated the sight of blood? He was a hemophobe." My voice sounded thick with too many hard edges, I slurred slightly on "hemophobe," and it sounded like "homophobe." I already regretted calling after three bourbons. Had I seriously just drunk-dialed the cops? "He-mo-phobe. It's a fear of blood," I tried again. More clearly this time. Not that Lucas full-out fainted at the sight of blood, but Garrett didn't know that.

"Have you been drinking?"

"Yeah, I've been drinking. I don't know what else to do right now but drink."

A long pause. He was probably deciding how to play this. Should he drop the friend act and go on the offense because I was drunkish? Or play it nice and cool, keep me thinking we had a friendly rapport because I was bound to trip up, reveal something worthwhile.

"Well, maybe, since you're under the influence, we shouldn't be talking about this right now."

"What *else* is there to talk about?"

"Oh, I don't know? Do you remember Mr. Arkin's paranoid prohibition of any video games other than *The Oregon Trail*? He was so convinced that all other games had hidden levels full of porn and violence that were just a secret code away, which of course we all knew, even *Mario Kart*! That man was so religious. . . ." So he was going to endear himself to me, maybe even hint at our computer club kiss. I could picture Pruden telling him, *I know the Haas women, and they like attention.*

"Garrett." I tried to cut him off, but he pretended not to hear me.

"I think you held the record for dead oxen. Am I right? You should've been charged for oxen neglect."

I smiled into the phone. "Garrett, please, stop."

He blew out a relenting sigh. "Fine. Mia, I can't say if these girls are lying or not at this point. Three of them have pressed charges, and we're investigating their allegations." He said this with so much kindness in his voice that I knew that the girls were being taken at their word. Why wouldn't they be, at this point? "But from what I saw, the equipment room is not in the same disarray as when you went there. In fact, it's not even the same equipment room. It's been moved and is now off the east gym."

"The equipment room has been moved," I repeated, like I couldn't believe what I'd just heard. Great. What did I really know? "And what about Joanna's boyfriend? Dylan Yates. Wannabe gangster? Is he not a suspect?"

"Dylan was with his dad when Joanna went missing. He was one of the first people we managed to rule out."

"Because parents never lie for their kids?"

"No, because his dad is a mechanic. Owns a shop on Eleventh Avenue, and other people, customers, also saw Dylan working there."

I let the hand holding the phone drop and covered my mouth to stifle a tormented sob.

"Are you still there? You OK?" I could hear Garrett from my lap. I was about to tap End. END. I wanted this to end—the accusations, not knowing where my brother was, being in Wayoata. Then the phone was at my mouth again.

"Was Joanna Wilkes pregnant?" It just slipped out. A drunken verbal turd that popped free of my mouth.

Garrett's voice dropped. "Where did you hear that? I need to know how you heard that."

Fuck. Again Mimi in my ear: *Tattletale, tattletale.*

This time I did hit End. Garrett's voice disappeared. I couldn't believe I'd just screwed up that bad. Oh shit, what had I done? An image of Lucas raging at me from behind bars. *Let me get this straight. You sucked back MY bourbon, from MY bar, in MY apartment, and then decided to call a cop and hint that I got my student pregnant? And you're wondering why I'm locked up? What were you thinking?*

I went downstairs and got Vanessa Lee's card. It was stuck to the floor mat in the backseat, where some gummy juice had been spilled by a previous renter. I agreed to give her an interview in the morning. There was another angle to this story—the Lucas-was-innocent angle—and Vanessa seemed willing to write it. I could undo some of this. He was still just a person of interest. People needed to be reminded of this. I had to dust off his golden-boy, hockey-hero image. (How much easier this would have been if Lucas had made it to the NHL; then he'd have had that pro-athlete Teflon glaze, and there'd need to be actual footage for people to be convinced he was a murderer. And even then . . .) This was something I could do, I could remind people my twin was not a killer.

After I hung up with Vanessa, I languished on my brother's sinking couch, booze-sour and bilious. Thought about taking an Ativan.

A knock at the door. I jumped up. I thought it was Garrett; was he parked outside the building watching me? Watching for Lucas to make an appearance. Then some part of me, the drunk part, thought it could be Lucas, hands in pockets, all casual. *Oh hey, saw you on the news and thought I better hightail it back here. What the hell is going on? I know the police said don't leave town, but I didn't think they really meant it.* But why would he knock on his own door?

It was Eric. Tanned, white T-shirt and blue jeans. Motorcycle helmet dangling from one hand, Lucas's stuff tucked under his other arm. "Hey, so you are staying here."

"So I am."

"I tried buzzing. Maybe I punched in the wrong code? Lucky for me, someone was on their way out, and I let myself in. I was going to leave this out here, but thought I should knock, in case you were here."

"Do you want to come in?" I opened the door wider to let him inside, made a bad joke about the shoddy security here at the Terrace. Went back to the couch and waved the bottle at him. "I'm drinking. Do you want a drink?"

"Yeah, I'll take a drink." Eric set the box down by the front closet. He looked around the apartment, and I could tell he felt weird being there. I wondered if he and Lucas ever just hung out. Just came by for an after-school beer. I got Eric a glass, poured a generous portion, topped off my own drink. "So how's your cheek?"

"It's fine. The ice helped. The bourbon too."

"Well, ice and bourbon are kind of a cure-all." He slugged back a mouthful and smiled. I felt warmer.

"Did you watch the news?"

"I did." He offered up a furrowed, sympathetic brow.

"Do you know these other girls? The ones who are saying Lucas touched them?"

"Not personally, no. I know who they might be, but none of them came to me first or anything."

"Who are they?"

"I can't say. . . ." He gave me a helpless shrug.

"OK, just nod once if they're histrionic, attention-seeking sluts who've done this sort of thing before?" Long past tipsy, I'd hit the drunk and unguarded stage.

He didn't nod. Instead he put his hand on my shoulder and half whispered, "Mia."

"Sorry, I didn't mean to . . . It's a terrible word, 'slut.' I've always hated it." I grabbed the bottle, freshened up our drinks (so much for the Ativan). Eric grabbed his and finished it off.

"I'm catching up." He winked and poured himself a refill. I liked that he was in the mood to drink. "Listen, why don't we not talk about this for a little while? Let's just talk about something else, anything else, for fifteen minutes."

"That seems to be the theme of the night. Getting me to talk about something else."

Eric's eyebrows wrinkled. "We don't have to. But I'd like to take your mind off . . . this awful thing you're going through, if you'll let me."

"OK, Eric." I hit the "C" really hard. I hadn't said his name out loud yet, and because it sounded strange in my mouth, I giggled a tad too girlishly. He gave me a look that said he wasn't sure if I was making fun of him.

"I'm just saying, as your previous counselor, it might be good to just—"

"Mentally flatline."

"You remember that?" He looked impressed. "But yeah, exactly. Good idea." He pulled out his phone, tapped the screen, and played music from it that I didn't recognize. It wasn't the aggressive Indie music I would've expected from Mr. Lowe, with menacing guitar hooks and distorted vocals, instead this was softer, more soulful. "Well then, tell me, how's life in Chicago?"

"Good. Tell me, why are you still here?" I noticed the bottle was empty, went to the liquor cart, and broke open a new bottle of Jim Beam. I never drank this much. In college my friends were always impressed by my self-control around alcohol. *That's it, just one drink?* I'd nod, with a tinge of self-righteousness—*I'm just such a lightweight.*

When really I was secretly coasting on the buzz off a fentanyl patch. Not to mention drinking made you too sloppy. Pills, on the other hand, when taken under a pharmacist's care, made you a better version of yourself. Tonight, I guessed, I'd get sloppy.

"Well, I did move away for a while. Not that long after you graduated. I decided I'd give myself two years in Los Angeles. I was there for one. My wife got pregnant, and she wanted to move back here to have the baby."

"You're married?"

"Not anymore. Divorced."

"So do you have a son? A daughter?"

"I have neither. She miscarried not long after we moved back. She blamed me, kind of. I mean, she didn't blame me for the miscarriage. She was just angry that I wasn't more upset by it. She knew I didn't want kids, not at that point. . . ." Eric let his words drift.

"So why didn't you go back to LA?"

"I don't know. I mean, I do know—it's just hard saying it out loud. At first I was trying to get back together with my ex, and then eventually I just used that as an excuse to stay. I'm comfortable here. I know what I am doing here. Out there, all the unknowns, it's kind of terrifying, and I was starting to feel too old."

"Well, hey, I don't exactly lead a life of glamor in Chicago. I'm a pharmacist. An overworked pharmacist." He gave me an appreciative smile that said he didn't believe me.

After another round of drinks, the conversation turned to my high school graduating class. (Eric had a surprisingly keen memory of past graduates. I wasn't sure whether to be impressed by him or depressed for him.) A where-are-they-now game with so few surprises it was sad. I read once that whatever your first-grade teacher writes about you on your report card will be true for the rest of your life. If you're quiet and withdrawn at six years old, it's how people will describe you at forty. I was glad Mimi wasn't the kind of mother to stockpile such childhood keepsakes.

We had slumped back into the couch. Mellow. Nearly an hour had passed. "You know, I thought about you for years," he said.

"I find that hard to believe."

"I did." His voice cracked with mock outrage. "You were so self-possessed, maybe. Older. Like you wouldn't be swept up in all the superfluous things adolescent girls tend to get swept up in. You had substance. I knew you'd be OK."

"I'm not sure any sophomore high school girl is self-possessed."

"You were."

"No, you're thinking of the wrong girl."

"I'm certain I'm not. You look really good, by the way. Did I tell you that already?" He started playing with my hair, twirling the ends around his fingers. I realized he was drunk. I said something lame about how good he looked too and how upset his girlfriend must be with so many women chasing after him. He smiled.

"Nope, no girlfriend. I'm between girlfriends. How about you? Anyone special back in Chicago?"

I'd hit that point of drunkenness when I was part of the scene unfolding, and yet far away. Blurry. "Not really." I hadn't slept with anyone since my boyfriend.

"I'm surprised by that." He moved in closer. The sagging couch cushion tipped me toward him. He grinned, tucked his thumb under my chin and kissed me. He smelled like citrus-scented soap and tasted like whiskey. I drew in closer, and his lips went to my neck, his hand reaching up the back of my head, gently gripping my hair. His other hand was on the move, tentative at first, waiting for me to deny things going any further, but I wanted this. Him. Mr. Lowe.

He kissed me again, and I was soaring on a geyser of unrequited love/lust. There was an adolescent urgency, on my part. I tugged at his jeans as he pulled off his T-shirt. He lifted my tank top and pulled my bra up and cupped my breasts. His mouth glided over my nipples as his fingers slipped under my underwear. And then my own jeans were off and he disappeared between my thighs. The room spun, and then his tongue was in my mouth again and I could taste myself.

I guided him inside of me. My one leg curled tight around him, the other anchored to the floor as he thrust. Gentle at first, then harder. It was only when the leather became slick with sweat and my head bumped hard into the armrest and all I could hear was my own heart pumping and Eric's wet breath in my ear, that I came. Seconds later, he shuddered.

A queasy, sick feeling came over me the moment it was done. What sort of person did this? Mimi. This was something Mimi would do. My brother was missing, and I was taking the opportunity to fuck my old guidance counselor. Lucas's co-worker. I pulled my bra and tank top down. My jeans were easy to find, as they were still dangling from my ankle. Eric was watching me. It was too dark to tell if he was panicked that I was turning on him, that I might claim he took advantage of me.

"You OK?" He slipped his jeans back up. Sitting upright again, shirtless. I liked that he didn't apologize. I nodded, though he must have noticed something was off in my eyes because then he asked, "Do you want me to go?"

I shook my head no.

He reached out, hooked his finger through my belt loop, and pulled me back to the couch. I let him. We fell asleep, blanketless, our bodies curled into one another.

6

DAY 4
SATURDAY

Hours later, I was meeting Vanessa Lee at a small coffee shop called the Daily Grind. Attempts had been made to evoke a sort of urban feel, with a chalkboard menu and subtle lighting, primary yellows and blues. There was a cluster of couches at the back. A nice place, but it was nearly empty. Being outcoffee'd, no doubt, by the new Starbucks.

I arrived fifteen minutes early because I wanted to be in control of where we would sit. This was when I'd expected we wouldn't be practically the only people there. Still, I picked out an island of a table near the bathroom, swished down mouthfuls of strong coffee, and mulled over last night. When I woke up, Eric was gone—just a note on the back of a gas receipt left next to Lucas's Bulldogs cap on the coffee table.

HAD TO GO. DIDN'T WANT TO WAKE YOU. HOPE I GET TO SEE YOU AGAIN.

—E

I wondered, if the situation were different, how I'd feel about sleeping with him. If I'd be swept up in schoolgirl giddiness right now, if I'd want to call a friend so I could moon over him and replay the night before in excruciating detail (or at least the details I could remember) and overanalyze the note he left. (Did he really want to see me again or was it a polite exit line?) Or would I feel a shade of disappointment because Eric in real life wasn't quite as good as he was in my teenage imagination? (There was no quivery ride on his bike! No guitar serenade!) As it was, right now, at the first tickle or murmur of excitement, my stomach clenched and turned to sludge, and I felt racked with guilt sharp as an ice pick.

I dipped my finger into a pill bottle in my purse and licked off the grainy bitterness as Vanessa entered, looking fresh-faced, dressed in a shimmery blouse and an A-line skirt. I felt suddenly aware of my baggy-eyed, sandy-pored hangover sheen that even makeup couldn't cover. Then reminded myself it was a print interview and it didn't even matter.

She tried for small talk as she ordered a coffee, but I was not in the frame of mind to offer more than one-word responses on the current heat wave. Thankfully, she gave up. All business, she slid her phone out into the middle of the table. "I am going to record this. Is that OK?

"That's fine, but first, I want to know why I should talk to you. When you said you wanted to take a 'contrarian' stance on this, what exactly does that mean for my brother?"

"I want to write an against-the-grain article. That means I want to explore other possibilities. That someone else murdered Joanna."

"Why?" A rush of optimism, heavily spiked with caution. I had to be sure I wasn't being duped here into giving an exclusive, that my words weren't going to get twisted.

"I'll be blunt. It will draw more attention than if I write the same articles as everyone else. A few years ago, someone from my graduating class, and I won't give any names, won a Pulitzer for an against-the-grain series that exposed shoddy police work in a small town much like Wayoata. I see that there's potential here to write something similar."

Good. It made sense to me if Vanessa was getting something out of this. I sat up, told her about my mother's accident. Her head injury. Pruden's ineptness. The black glove. I told it the way Lucas would have told it. "Someone set it up to look like an accident."

"A black glove—how very OJ." She nodded, but I think mention of the glove stretched my credibility. It was too pat. "But your mom, she's OK. She's still alive?"

"She's alive but suffered extensive brain damage. She lives in a care home." Vanessa's shoulders drooped. I fidgeted with a sugar packet.

"So you've already had issues with the Wayoata Police Department."

"Even if I hadn't, the Wayoata police have focused on my brother solely based on rumors that've been flying around."

"Well, that, and he did take off, and there's the text message exchange about a romantic weekend getaway." Vanessa tapped a heavy-looking engagement ring against her yellow stoneware mug, a tic likely to make sure people noticed it.

I flinched. "Did you read the text exchange?"

"Sorry, didn't mean to do a one-eighty on you. See? Always the contrarian. No, the police haven't released anything. I just heard about it. So you're right. Hearsay and rumor based on students' claims of having spotted Lucas and Joanna together when they shouldn't have been, as well as Lucas's sudden departure, are all the police seem to be operating on. The body was submerged for three weeks, which can make finding viable DNA difficult, and once the police did discover Joanna's body, sources tell me the crime scene wasn't properly secured, so any DNA they did find won't hold up." My stomach twisted. DNA. That magic bullet, aimed and whizzing toward me. I hoped her source was someone more credible than the kid who found Joanna. Vanessa pressed Record. "But tell me first about Lucas. What's he like?"

I said everything I could to elevate Lucas to saint status. "He cares for our mother; he's so gentle. He loves sports, loves teaching, loves kids, or well not *love* love—did I say how he cares for our poor mother? He would never, ever hurt anyone. He wasn't even that put-you-in-a-headlock-till-you-cry-uncle sort of brother. He really made it a point in his life to get along with everyone."

"So why do you think he ran?"

"What other choice did he have? He was being harassed by the police and threatened by people here who think he's guilty because of a few rumors. His truck was completely trashed. He left because he feared for his life. What else could he do?" I was surprised by the conviction in my voice, because I didn't really believe it. I couldn't see Lucas leaving because he felt threatened. He'd stay and set things straight in spite of a slanted investigation, in spite of everyone already thinking he did it. If anything, it would drive him on.

"Good. That's a good quote. Why do you think he hasn't contacted you, then?"

That was the crucial question, wasn't it? The question that wrecked me every time I looked at my phone—*Why hasn't he called me?* I couldn't say "no comment." That was what people said when they didn't want to lie. And here again the ugly, dark unthinkable came at me in a gust of panic that Lucas never left at all, but was inside some deep freeze next to hunted meat, in a gloomy paneled basement. I shook it off. "I'm sure he has his reasons. He probably doesn't want to get me into any trouble." I lost control of my voice; it rose at the end like I was just rolling out excuses to see what worked.

"That makes sense." Vanessa looked like she had to stop herself from adding, *I guess.* I could tell that she was contemplating pushing the issue further, but the details that made Lucas look guilty didn't help her article either, so she let it go. It didn't make sense. Not at all. Lucas should have called, and I had no good answer why he hadn't. "Do you think it's possible that your brother might have taken his own life, and that's why you haven't heard from him?"

"No! Never! He would never do that. He's innocent." I suddenly felt really tired and in danger of crying, so I gave her my best shiny-eyed smile, like the idea was so ludicrous it struck me as funny.

"Do you think someone else might have hurt your brother? As you said, he was being threatened." Vanessa tipped her chin into her chest and gave me a grave look that made me gnash my teeth.

"I . . ." My voice went dry and creaky. "I've had those thoughts, yes." I started nodding, yes, yes, yes. It really was the only thing that made sense as to why he hadn't contacted me. My chest started to burn. I could feel blood pulsing in my neck.

"Then again." Vanessa's chirpy voice snapped me back from the edge of panic. "I mean, the police would have probably found him by now. Vigilante murders are not usually covered up. The killer wants people to know justice has been done."

I looked at her. I felt like I was being tossed around inside a dryer. What was wrong with this woman? "I thought of that too." I took a deep cleansing breath. Shook my head. What was I thinking? Lucas was fine. He was alive, just inexplicably *unavailable*.

Plus, I'd know. Even if I haven't had a single mystic belief in my entire life before now, I realized at some point I started to subconsciously trust that if Lucas was dead I'd get some shivery, goose-bumped reaction that would let me know. A kind of twin-telepathy. I'd be doing something and an icy-cold sensation would crawl into me, and I'd drop whatever was in my hands (and here I envisioned holding a teacup and saucer even if I didn't drink tea, because it felt Victorian, when spiritualism was at the top of its game), my spine would go rigid to the point of shattering and I'd just know.

And that hadn't happened yet.

Or maybe it was the old Haas active-denial (who thought something so damaging would come in so handy).

When it was clear that I was not discomfited enough by the awkward silence Vanessa was forcing, to start filling it anything more on the Lucas-is-dead theory, she made a puckering noise with her mouth, and said with jarring pertness, "Onward. I'm assuming you've heard the name Dylan Yates?"

"Just recently, from the school guidance counselor." I could still smell Eric on my skin.

"Not from the police?" Vanessa was shaking her head, like it was the most ridiculous thing she'd heard.

"No. Well, eventually, but I asked the police about him. They told me he wasn't a suspect. He has an alibi."

"One provided by his father and his father's friends. Do you know that Dylan was arrested in February for breaking into the Wilkeses' home after Joanna broke up with him?" Her voice turned conspiratorial. "He was found in her closet. It looked like he'd been there for hours. He'd been relieving himself in an empty pop bottle. Joanna filed for a restraining order. A week later, he was found in their garage, in the back of Joanna's car, with a sleeping bag."

"I didn't know that. The police aren't telling me anything!" My arms dropped hard on the table. Now I was pissed. Suddenly wired from this emotional whiplash. My legs jittered under the table. *Yes. It's always the boyfriend. Everyone knows that.* (Here, I actively chose to ignore that technically the police were working from the angle that Lucas could have been her boyfriend too.)

"Well, you have to wonder why the police aren't leaning harder on Dylan Yates, given that he was stalking Joanna. I think it's because his father, Greg Yates, the one who gave the alibi, was an informant during a six-year stay in state prison for grand theft auto and drug trafficking. You asked me what my angle is, and this is it. I have an appointment with Dylan Yates this afternoon." She tapped her engagement ring, three times, quick, like an end-of-round boxing bell. "The police are under a lot of pressure to deliver, considering who the family is, and this can cause tunnel vision. They want to get someone behind bars as fast as possible."

We stood. Vanessa told me to call her anytime. She gave my arm a delicate squeeze in a show of solidarity, and I wanted to bear hug her back. My ally.

When I left, I felt much better. I felt a sense of vindication. Joanna had a drug-dealing ex-boyfriend with an ex-con dad. Maybe Lucas had been threatened. Maybe I was telling the truth and that was why he left, but it still didn't explain why he hadn't called me.

7

GREG'S GARAGE—HONEST 1ST RATE SERVICE (a claim that made you think the opposite) was sloppily painted over MARSH AND SON'S GARAGE. It was a dirty white building with two bays. One was open, one halfway shut, its roll-up door hanging crooked. The lot was full of rusted-out cars up on blocks, hoods left open, their parts picked out. There was a single gas pump that might or might not have been real—it looked so retro it could have been decoration. I parked. My head still had that fuzzy, hungover feeling. I was there because I wanted to see Dylan, as if I could pick up some kind of murderer vibe off him.

There was a group of four guys standing next to an old Hyundai with an oversized fin. They stared at me as I stepped out of my car and walked inside. I could see one of them nodding toward my PT, and the others laughed. I waited for several minutes, breathing in gulps of pine-scented air freshener, before a man in grease-stained coveralls broke away from the Hyundai group and came in after me. He wiped his hands on a filthy rag, stood behind the glass counter, and nodded at me.

"How can I help ya?" GREG was stitched into his coveralls. He was early forties, short and wiry, with damp-looking hair tucked behind his ears.

"I'd like an oil change."

"Oh, yeah? How about a lube job too?" He leaned forward, elbows on the counter, looked me up and down all slitty-eyed. One of the guys who'd been by the Hyundai was now standing in front of the door like a bouncer. I was getting nervous.

"No. Just the oil change."

"You want an oil change on a rental?"

How did he know? I looked out the window at the PT, at the license plate frame advertising the rental company. Shit. "Well, I just want to bring it back in tip-top shape." God, this was going south fast.

"I know who you are. You're the sister of that teacher, the murderer. What're you really doing here?" He stood upright, leaning now on his fists.

"I was hoping to talk to your son, Dylan." I said this in my best assertive-but-still-pleasant voice that women spend years honing.

"What do you want with my son?" Again that smile like everything was a dirty joke I wasn't in on.

"I just wanted to ask him about Joanna Wilkes. As you evidently know, my brother is being accused of something he didn't do. The media is following up on this too." I went with an assumed sales pitch, tried to sound like this was the acceptable truth or at least would be very soon. I nodded, as if demonstrating how to be agreeable. Greg's leer just got bigger. Men like this loved to watch women squirm. He probably gave his son advice like, *Women like to be controlled. It's in their nature—look at those goddamn erotica books they read. It's all about getting choked, so just choke a bitch when she needs to be reminded who's boss.* "In the meantime I'm trying to find out as much as I can about this, um, situation that the police have so royally botched."

"Botched? Huh. You think the police have done a botched job of this, Travis?"

Travis was now standing inside. He lit a cigarette, inhaled deeply, pretended to think about the question. "No way. For once I think the police have it right." He blew smoke toward the ceiling.

"Well, there you go. Travis here thinks the police are doing a fine job." Greg crossed his arms. "So no need to talk to Dylan. I don't really want no sister of a murderer talking to my son anyway. Too dangerous, I think, 'cuz things like that can be genetic, right, Travis? Pedophilia runs in families, don't it?"

"I think that's incest."

Greg laughed, a loud churlish growl. Stepped out from behind the counter. "That's right, Travis, that's right."

I turned to leave, but Greg stepped out in front of me. Light-streaky fast, like he'd just appeared. Every inch of his sinewy body seemed to be twitching. I felt a moment of pure panic. Something bad was going to happen to me. I should've called someone before going there. Let them know. I flashed first to Garrett, but he would've just tried to stop me. Eric. I should have left a message on Eric's phone. Greg could snap my neck right now, stuff me in one of those oil barrels, and have his parking lot posse roll me into some ditch off the highway, in the miles and miles of nowhere land that surrounded Wayoata.

Greg leaned in close to my face, his nostrils flared, his lips curled back into a gruesome smile, his teeth coated in sickly yellow saliva, like he had a chunk of chaw tucked somewhere in the back of his mouth. "Don't go anywhere near my son, you little bitch." His voice dropped to a gravelly pitch. "I'll only say that once." Then he winked. "Now, you go have yourself a first-rate day."

I scurried out of the garage. Travis followed me to my car, a few paces behind. The other two guys in the lot were clustered around my PT. I expected something from them, menacing catcalls, or outright threats, something like that, but they just stared silently, which was somehow more unnerving.

I fumbled with the keys; my hands were shaking too badly. Finally I started the PT and hit Reverse, jumping the curb as I sped out of the lot.

I pulled into a Perkins parking lot, and looked up the Yateses' address on my phone (this took three tries because my nerve-jangled fingers were too uncoordinated to win the quick-draw with auto-correct, that turned "Wayoata" into "Wayne." There were two Yateses listings in Wayoata. One number was disconnected; the other rang indefinitely. An odd, eerie sound nowadays. At least I had an address. My way of thinking was, I knew Greg Yates was at work, so if I wanted to talk to Dylan, right now was the time to do it. I knew too that Greg could be on his way home that very second to make sure I heeded his warning. This was a very stupid, dangerous thing to do, but I had to get to his son before he did, before I lost the chance, however slim, to wrest something from Dylan that could make the police discount his alibi. I couldn't count on Vanessa to do it. Her "angle" would change if something juicier came along, and she'd leave us twisting in the wind. It had to be me.

The Yates house was a flaking stuccoed bungalow, same boxy style as the one I grew up in. I pulled up to it, my head screaming, *TURN AROUND*. I was not feeling like a brave person. I froze like a lawn ornament when threatened. I'd frozen when Sticky Ricky thrust his hard-on against me. I'd frozen at my mother's hospital bedside, when Lucas asked me why I was acting so strange. I'd frozen two years ago, fresh out of rehab, when a tweaked-out man wobbled a gun at me and demanded Oxy. Moving into action only when I heard the click of the hammer. Lucas came down to Chicago that weekend to stay with me. We spent the afternoons in pubs, getting dozy drunk, playing rainy-day games like Uno and Scrabble. Lucas rebuffed a pretty bartender attired in a leather bustier so he could spend the night watching my comfort movies. If he were some budding murdering pervert, wouldn't he have gone home with her and engaged in some light erotic asphyxiation? She looked like she would have been into it.

I had to do this. Felt a flash of anger at Lucas for making me do this.

I couldn't decide if it was better to park a few houses down, so that if Greg did drive by, he wouldn't see my car next to his house, or park closer in case Greg showed up and I had to make a run for it. I decided to park close.

The driveway had three cars, each in a state of dismemberment. Heat shimmered off the metal in tiny waves. It was just past noon and already getting hot and humid under the unfettered prairie sun. My shirt was sticking to me.

I knocked on the front door, rang the bell. No answer. Went around to the back. An empty dog run next to an air conditioner that hummed loud. The yard was an overgrown mess littered with scrap metal and engine parts. I picked up a rusted screwdriver, flung loose into the grass, and slid it into my waistband. There was a fire pit in the center of the yard, surrounded by a scattering of spare tires, overturned lawn chairs, beer cans with hordes of wasps swarming above them. What jumped out was a rusted girl's bike with a pink flowery basket and handlebar streamers leaning against the back fence. The sight of it set my teeth on edge.

I knocked on the door again. Nothing. I was about to leave when I heard a low whimper coming from inside. I knocked again, called out, "Dylan?" Stayed still, listened. Scanned the side of the house to make sure Greg wasn't coming around the corner. Another mewl. I looked around the yard for something to boost myself up. I needed to see who was inside. I had a flash of a ticker-tape parade. Lucas and me atop a float, holding hands over our heads in a we-are-the-champions grip for setting free whoever was inside this house. For collaring Joanna's real killer.

The lawn chairs looked too threadbare to trust. I spotted a bucket with hardened cement in the bottom next to the shed. I dragged it over. When it hit the lumpy trail of sidewalk slabs by the front door, it made a loud gritty noise. I went rigid, ready to run if the back door started to open. My hand moved to the screwdriver, hovered on the handle. I took the crouching stance of an Old West quick-draw. Sweat trickled between my breasts. A vein in my temple started to thrum. Nothing moved, not even a shadowy flutter in the windows. I lifted the bucket in two hands, slow and quiet, and in a waddle, brought it up to the house. Tipped it over and looked into the window. It was the kitchen, overflowing with dishes and cardboard Hungry Man frozen dinner packages. A garbage bag sat out in the middle of the room.

Was there another girl inside? Joanna's replacement? Or maybe some feral woman kidnapped as a girl years ago and held captive by Greg and company. The one they'd decided was a "keeper." I tried to think of other missing posters in the police station, but there was only Joanna's face.

I got down, dragged the bucket over to the next room. A bedroom with a black-and-orange Harley-Davidson flag for curtains that only half covered the window. Unmade bed, a massive television, and some gaming console with wires stretched halfway across the dingy carpet. I guessed this was Dylan's room. Empty.

Again the whimpering, growing more high-pitched, a panting whine. I checked the yard again for Greg, certain now that that rag sticking out of the back pocket of his coveralls was probably doused with chloroform. I went to the third window at the back of the house. It was higher, and I had to reach to the bottom ledge and pull myself up. My feet barely touched the bucket. The bathroom. Truck-stop dirty. My sight line was between the toilet and the tub; the shower curtain was open. Someone was in the tub. I could see the top of a head. Brown hair. I wasn't high up enough to see over the lip of the tub. My arm muscles were giving out, and I had to dip back down to the bucket. I berated myself for not going to the gym more often. I pulled myself up again, higher. It moved. There were streaks of blood.

It took me a second to register what I was really seeing. A very large dog, on her side, giving birth on a nest of blankets in the tub. There was already one fleshy-looking puppy writhing under the dog's tongue.

"Looking for somebody?"

I startled, the bucket skittered, and I fell, my ass catching the edge of the bucket and then the ground so hard I bit the side of my tongue. The screwdriver jabbed into my hip. A grizzly, bearded man in a black T-shirt that stretched tight around his thick gut, smirked. Didn't offer a hand, which I was happy about. I hauled myself back up. Swallowed down the taste of blood.

"I'm looking for Dylan?"

"Yeah? Through the window?"

"I owe him some money, and I wanted to get it back to him before I spent it." I did some kind of girlish ditzy giggle. "I'm bad with money." I surprised myself at how quick I could think on my toes. It made sense, though, that Dylan the drug dealer would get people showing up at odd times, looking in windows.

"Dylan's only around during the week. Stays at his mom's on the weekends. You want me to hold on to it, give it to him on Monday? I won't spend it, I proooomise!" A Cheshire Cat grin.

"No, that's OK. He said I had to pay him today." I looked down, like I was really worried what was going to happen to me if I didn't get this money to Dylan. Maybe this guy would tell me something, like, *Oh yeah, you better worry because Dylan is violent and unpredictable. You know what happened to that Joanna girl? Well, you get the picture.*

"His mom lives in Sunstone Estates. Try there. But if you want a little something now, I might be able to hook you up." He invited me over for a beer and a toke as courteously as if for fine wine and cheese.

"Oh no, really I'm good for now." I motioned, like I'd had enough to eat.

"Suit yourself." He hocked into the grass.

"Thanks, though. Um, there's a dog in there, having puppies."

"Oh, yeah? Good. I'm taking one outta this litter. Don't worry, she's an old hand at it. It's her fourth."

Only when I was back in my car with the door locked did I feel like I could breathe again. The bearded neighbor offered me a limp wave like he was disappointed I wasn't staying. I turned the AC up high; it puffed a humid breeze at me as I headed toward Dylan's mom's.

8

Sunstone Estates was Wayoata's only trailer park. I'd expected worse, but there were enough well-maintained trailers to keep the whole place from sliding into total dump status.

I had trouble finding the Yateses' trailer. The lots weren't consistently numbered, and only some of the narrow gravel roads had names. It had the feeling that a bunch of people had showed up at the same time and just sort of parked. I was on my second loop when I stopped to ask a shirtless, shoeless ten-year-old-looking boy where I could find it. He just pointed in the direction my car was already aimed and mumbled something about pinwheels. Did not elaborate. When I pulled away, he threw a handful of rocks at my back window.

The trailer was tin-can small, but effort had been put into making it look nice. Too much effort. There was an overkill of lawn ornaments and, yes, a crazed number of pinwheels. A very large, nasty-looking dog barked from a dog run next to the trailer. The likely offspring of litter one or litter two. The door swung open. A woman told the dog to shut up. I guessed it was Dylan's mother. "Yeah?" She had on a pair of black tights and a bejeweled tank top; everything looked too tight. A cigarette dangled from the corner of her mouth. And so the stereotype lived on.

Three white Chihuahuas with reddish eyes were immediately at her ankles, yapping and baring teeth, trying to get past her, which made the other dog even more frantic, thrusting its muscular body against the gate of the run. She had to engage in some kind of spastic dance to get the Chihuahuas away from the door. Frustrated, she just waved me inside.

"Dylan, goddammit, your dog is scaring the shit out of my babies, and why the hell is Tia's diaper off?" Apparently Tia was in heat; she was dripping blood all over their beige carpet. She scooped up the bleeding dog, held her at arm's length. "So, what do you want?"

I realized I didn't have a plan at all. I had no idea what exactly I was going to say, so I gambled that Vanessa hadn't shown up yet. "I am the reporter who called? From the *StarTribune*?"

"You're early. Dylan . . . Dyyyyylaaaan!" she screeched again to the back of the trailer.

I wanted to ask her how early. How much time did I have before Vanessa showed up? The woman, suddenly composed and offering me a polite smile, introduced herself as Serena, then directed me into a dark living room. "Have a seat. I'll make us some iced tea."

I sat down on a padded folding chair angled toward the corduroy blue sofa. All set up for an interview. On the wall over the sofa was a poster of a holographic wolf, howling at the moon when I shifted to the right, snout closed when I shifted to the left.

A full minute later, Dylan emerged, looking sleepy or stoned. He pulled on a T-shirt as he entered the room and dropped onto the couch. Immediately I could see how Dylan would appeal to a sixteen-year-old girl. He had boy-band looks: the foppish hair, the feminine full mouth, same compact build as his father, all offset by a thick gold chain and a ball cap he grabbed off an end table and placed delicately on his head. The chain and ball cap looked like bad-boy, drug-dealer props. Even his arms were suspiciously hairless, and I wondered if he shaved them to look younger. At nineteen, he likely had only a year or two left before he was considered that washed-up creepy older guy. His pool of potential girlfriends would shift from cute high school girls en route to college to clingy single moms wanting an energetic male role model for their unruly kids. Then again, his interest in freshman high school girls might simply be pragmatic, as in, someone to move his drugs in the high school.

Close behind Dylan was a girl in pajama pants and a baggy T-shirt. She plopped down next to him and stretched her tree-trunk legs over his lap like they were going to hold him in place. So Dylan already had a new girlfriend. Another very young girlfriend. She had a bland baby face, and her eyes opened too wide like a doll's that flicked shut when you laid her down. Dylan licked his lips three times before speaking. I could see the girl practically swoon.

"Hey, so what d'ya want to know?" The smell of marijuana wafted into the living room. I pretended not to notice.

I introduced myself (as Vanessa Lee of course).

"You don't look like a reporter," the girl piped up. She was right. I didn't. I had a streak of dirt up my pant leg and backside from falling. I'd sweated off my makeup. It didn't help either that I was nursing a welt on my cheek from Kathy.

"It's print. And you are?" I dug around in my bag for a pen and paper, and found a pad with my pharmacy's logo in bright red at the top. I crossed my legs and rested the pad there, curling the top page over.

"I'm Skylar. But I prefer just Sky. Sky Cuthbert. You want me to spell it?"

"Shut up, Sky. She's not here to see you." Dylan shifted uncomfortably under her legs, but didn't push her off.

Dylan's mother fluttered back into the room, carrying a tray of drinks and a half-empty box of Abdallah candies. She had reglossed her lips, likely hoping I might at some point pull out a camera, and sat down on the arm of the sofa. "Have some iced tea." She grabbed her drink off the tray first; it was a different, more amber shade than the others.

"Thank you."

"He's getting paid for this, right?"

"I can talk to my boss about payment." Was boss right? Should I have said editor? I was drawing blanks. I took a glass of iced tea. There was far too much sugar in it. It stuck to my tongue.

"Well, he ain't saying nothing until he's paid." She folded her arms. I wished she'd go away. It was going to be more difficult posing as a journalist with another adult in the room. Though technically, I reminded myself, Dylan was an adult too.

"Mom, it's fine. I don't want any money," Dylan snapped at her.

"Well, isn't that great that you're doing this for free. How nice of you when you don't pay the bills and don't have a job."

Dylan ignored her, didn't even look at her, stretched out his arms. I caught sight of a homemade tattoo on the back of his hand, between his thumb and index finger. A wobbly JW. Did he tell Joanna the pain and probably skin infections were all for her? That she couldn't leave him after he'd branded himself with her initials?

Dylan's mom was about to say something else, but I cut her off. "I'm wanting to fill in some of the gaps about the weeks before Joanna went missing. There's been talk of other suspects."

"Oh, yeah? Well, I'm not one of them." He cocked his head, jutted out his chin. Again with the wannabe gangster posturing.

I looked at my pad of paper, like I was trying to reorient myself. "So how did you and Joanna meet?" I thought this was a safe place to start.

"I went back to Westfield for the fall semester. I was a couple credits short. It was important to me that I graduated." The conviction in his voice was a little overdone. He paused, waiting for praise.

I murmured a token "Good for you."

"So anyway, she had a spare at the same time I did. One day in the cafeteria, she left her binder behind, and I caught up with her, which was easy because she was on crutches." He smiled. Skylar pouted.

"How long were you together?"

"The first time was from September until just before Christmas break, so, like, almost four months." I noted to myself that this was around the time his high school drug mule was caught with weed in her locker. "Then we got back together end of January, but it was all on the down low."

"Down low?"

"Yeah, no one knew. Joanna wanted to keep it all secret so her mom wouldn't find out."

"Why did you break up?"

"Both times it was because of her mom. Total bitch. She wouldn't let Joanna date anyone. Like I said, her mom didn't approve. She just kept chipping away at her, saying shit like I was too old for her, that I dealt drugs, which I don't. That weed in Jo's locker didn't come from me." His mom rolled her eyes at him. He was a bad liar. "That I was using her for money. Just a bunch of shit. That whole family is fucked up."

"Dylan, language," his mother scolded him—I knew for my benefit because Dylan looked confused.

"No, seriously, I've been to Jo's house. Her bedroom, it was like a baby's room. Bright purple bed with that drapey thing on top, purple walls, white little-girl furniture. Purple was her favorite color at, like, seven, and she was never allowed to change it. There was all this ballerina stuff all over. She still had dolls and stuffed toys on her bed." His voice softened as he described her room, like he was wistful about squinting through the slats on her closet door, drinking in all that innocent girlishness. Skylar crossed her arms, her bottom lip sagged. A community-theater version of grumpy. I wondered if Dylan had been seeing both of them at the same time. Skylar finally winning out by sheer availability.

"And then Joanna took out a restraining order on you." Not a graceful segue, but Vanessa could get there anytime.

He sat up. "That was total bullshit. Her mom made her do that. I wasn't stalking her. No way. I don't need to stalk any girl. Jo invited me over, and when her mom came home, she had to hide me. I had to stay in that fucking closet for hours. After that, I didn't want anything to do with her." His mother rubbed his back, lit a smoke, took a drag, passed him the rest.

"But you were caught a second time. In her car?"

Something dark passed over Dylan's face. "What is this? Are you trying to make me look bad in your article? You said you just wanted some backstory."

"We're the ones who should have got a restraining order against them," Dylan's mom piped up. The ice in her drink jingled as she shifted in her seat. She hadn't put her "iced tea" down once. "That bitch, Kathy, she'd call screaming at my son to stay away from her daughter. Calling my son trash? Really? When her daughter's the one sleeping with a grown man, her teacher, I think it's pretty clear who the trash is. Was."

Skylar let out a trill of laughter. With a touch of incredulity, she said under her breath, "I was gonna have Mr. Haas next year for homeroom."

"Mom! Jesus Christ. She's dead," Dylan barked.

"I don't care, Dylan. It upsets me if anyone talks about my son that way." Dylan rolled his eyes while his mom nodded in my direction, making sure I noticed what a good, protective weekend mother she was.

I wanted to say that technically Dylan was considered a grown man by law. I could see why Kathy wouldn't have wanted him around her daughter.

I put my pen down. "I have a source, who of course I can't reveal, but this source has told me your alibi is being further investigated."

"What? Who said that?" Dylan shoved Skylar's legs off of his lap and leaned forward.

"Again, I can't reveal my source."

"Well, whatever. Your source is bad."

Skylar started biting her bottom lip. I looked at her. I could tell she wanted to say something. "Well, again, according to my source, there's proof that you weren't at your dad's shop." I flipped through the pages on my notepad.

Dylan's mom jumped up. "You know what, this interview is over. I don't like where this is going." She took my glass of iced tea away and stood there double-fisted. "You should leave."

Skylar started crying. "You could go to jail, even just for lying. It's perjury."

"Shut up, Sky, for Chrissake," Dylan snapped. "Just fucking shut up."

"I would have to say, there could be legal repercussions." I was trying to think, make quick calculations in my head. If Skylar was going to have my brother for homeroom next year, that meant she was just getting out of eighth grade. She was, at most, only fourteen years old. The age of consent in North Dakota was eighteen, and a class-C felony if the minor was under fifteen years old. So Dylan was five years older and could go to prison for statutory rape. I'd looked this up when I desperately wanted to think that maybe, if Lucas had an inappropriate fling with his student, she was old enough to consent. But Wikipedia had told me what I already knew—Joanna wasn't of age, and it didn't matter anyway because Lucas was her teacher.

"Tell them you were with me. You have the media right here, baby. Just tell them about our love story. There'll be sympathy for our situation." Skylar had that dreamy wisp in her voice. She was picturing magazine articles and interviews. I could tell she was the type of girl who relished in her proximity to a tragedy, coyly doling out hints that she was the current girlfriend of the dead girl's ex-boyfriend, wanting so much to come out with it.

"Oh my God, Skylar, don't you know how to shut your mouth?" Dylan dropped his head into his hands. "I'm not saying shit."

"Get out!" Serena kicked at the air in front of me. Iced tea splashed all over. Skylar was full-out weeping. Hands up, I retreated. Closing the trailer door behind me with a gentle click.

Outside, the sunlight hit me hard. The dog started up again with his killer barking. I was getting into my car when Dylan jogged up behind me. "This interview, the part about my alibi, I want it to be off the record or whatever. Just don't print it."

"OK. I won't."

"Oh." He looked surprised. "Good. It doesn't matter anyway,

whether I was with my dad or not. I mean, even if the cops do find out I was with Sky, I might go to jail for that, but not for Joanna. I still have an alibi. Sky's parents were home all night."

"All right, then." I noticed Skylar peeking out at us through the window.

"Thanks in there too for not mentioning the money. I mean, I'm still getting paid for this, right? This thing about the alibi doesn't change anything, does it? You still have a lot of other stuff to use."

"Yes, of course. The check will be in the mail."

9

I stopped in at a greasy spoon. One I used to eat at because they had the best waffles—I hadn't yet found something as good in Chicago. A couple, obviously just passing through, kept pointing their infant son toward me and chirping, "He's flirting with you, what a ladies' man. He's making eyes." Everyone else in the place glared.

I was starving. I hadn't eaten anything since the day before. A headache was blooming, and my hangover had moved from the nauseated-I-can't-eat-anything stage to the I-am-ravished-and-need-grease-and-salt stage.

I ordered a stack of waffles with extra whipped cream and strawberries, runny eggs, and a side of bacon, extra crispy, off a hostile waitress I pretended not to recognize. Laney Goudge was a popular girl from my class, who had literally fallen from grace in an abandoned grain silo while high on ecstasy. The town council had made a big stink about razing any deserted silo that could be used to hold those *friggin' rave parties.* Laney spent the second half of her senior year in a plastic neck brace avoiding the boys who tried to shoot pennies into the slot-sized opening under her chin. Nothing happened. The silo was still there; I'd driven by it on the way in.

The food came quickly. Laney half dropped the plate on the table, and the food slid all to one side. When she turned around, she did so stiffly.

I slathered on syrup, even dousing the eggs. I managed only a couple of bites before that sickly miserable feeling kicked in. Green around the gills, longing to call Lucas, just dial and get all the answers.

I took out my pad of paper and looked at the scratches I'd made at Dylan's trailer. Incoherent scribbles to make it look like I was writing something down. So Dylan had an alibi. He was hiding something, just not the murder of Joanna.

A list. The act of making a list would make me feel better. Places Lucas could be. In Chicago, there was that woman he was seeing who owned that restaurant—Alyssa, Alicia? Didn't one of his dormmates live in Des Moines? What was his name again? Because he'd hole up someplace, with someone who couldn't be easily connected to his life, right? Only if he was guilty, which he wasn't.

Instead, I wrote the name Dylan, followed by several check marks.

My phone chirped. The call was blocked. Vanessa had already left an angry voice mail—"Thanks a lot for burning my lead; I'm trying to help *you*"—so I didn't think she'd call again.

"Hello?" I sounded like I'd hiccupped, my mouth went so dry. *Please-be-Lucas, please-be-Lucas, be-Lucas.*

"This is Tom." I blinked, eyes stinging with near lethal disappointment. It took me a couple of beats to remember who Tom was.

"Right. Hi, Tom, this is Mia Haas. I'm Lucas Haas's sister." I half whispered because I didn't want to draw any more attention to myself, to who I was. "I'm calling because I found your name and number in my brother's apartment—"

"I know why you're calling." Tom's voice was a lispy drawl. I thought he would continue, but nothing, just dead air.

"OK . . . well, I'm hoping you could fill me in a little about how you know Lucas, if you've heard from him at all?"

"No, I haven't. I would like to, though. He owes me some money."

So Lucas was gambling again. "How much?"

"Well, that's changing every day, when you factor in the interest."

"How much?" I asked again.

"Thirty-six hundred dollars today. Tomorrow it'll be thirty-seven hundred."

"You're charging him a hundred dollars a day interest?" *Who borrows money from someone charging that kind of interest? Who charges that sort of interest and expects to get their money back?*

"That was the deal."

"Well, whatever your deal was, I'm sure he'll take care of this when he gets back into town. As you likely know, things are a little hectic for Lucas just now."

"Oh, I know all about that"—a hard chuckle—"and I'm not worried. Everyone knows I get paid no matter what. Lucas took out the family and friends plan." He ended the call with a cryptic "We'll be in touch."

I put my phone down, watched it go dark. Its glassy surface reflected the Tiffany-style light hanging from the ceiling; two bulbs out of three were burned out. Again I was desperate to call Lucas up and ream him out—*What the hell are you thinking, getting into debt like this, at a hundred dollars a day interest on a teacher's salary?* This somehow was the worst part, this constant reaching for my phone. A muscle memory move that could not catch up to the knowledge that he was unreachable. I gave in and called anyway. I pictured his phone ringing in some Ziploc bag marked EVIDENCE. It went to his voice mail, and there was his warm, happy voice, right there, pressed up against my ear.

"Now, that's breakfast." It was Garrett, standing over me. Lean and fit in his navy-blue uniform, he looked like he could be on his way to perform at a bachelorette party. "Mind if I join you for a second?" He dropped down, taking up the entire booth. He smelled like a hearty mix of aftershave and the outdoors. I pushed the plate away. "How are you feeling today?"

I hated when people referred to the night before like this. I'd rather the more honest approach: *Gawd, you were so wasted last night. How are you even moving right now?*

"Fine. Good."

"Good." He flashed a white smile. "I was worried."

"No need. Really."

"Well, I was. How's your mother anyway? I realize I didn't ask the other night, and I felt like a jerk." I pictured for a second, what it would've been like to bring Garrett home to meet Mimi. Would Lucas and I have come up with some game, like a jelly bean guessing contest, for how many times Mimi would find a way to brush against him, touch his solid chest?

"It is what it is." My voice drifted. I didn't want to talk about Mimi. Garrett gave me an understanding look with those baby-blue eyes that made something inside me snap like a tendon and then I did want to talk about Mimi. A rash, second-long flicker of wanting to confess, take the blame. Short-lived as a single heartbeat. He just had that thing about him, that made you feel you could tell him anything. He was in the right line of work.

"Well, I was just heading over to your place when I saw your car in the lot." Here I thought this was just a chance encounter. That was the thing about Wayoata. You could go looking for someone and find them within an hour.

"Why? Is it Lucas? Did you find my brother?" The hopeful edge to my voice made me feel foolish, even childish. If he had, he wouldn't be casually sitting across from me.

"No, sorry." Of course. "That's not why I'm here. You in a better frame of mind today to talk?"

Great. We were back to yesterday's drunk dial. I ignored his question. "Dylan Yates's alibi was bullshit. FYI."

"I just heard. If you ever want a job as a cop, I'll get you an application. A very nervous Serena Yates called me to tell me that she was certain an undercover cop posing as a reporter just left her trailer, so they wanted to get out in front of that. Dylan confessed he lied and informed us that he was really at his underage girlfriend's house."

"So? If he lied about working at his dad's shop, then he could easily be lying again."

"Listen, I get why you felt the need to talk to Dylan, but you have to understand that there are factors other than the alibi he gave us that ruled him out."

"Like what?"

Garrett nodded back at the conspicuous eavesdroppers in the booth behind him who had stopped talking the minute he sat down, he plucked up my pitcher of syrup, moved it to the end of the table, and leaned forward. His voice a low whisper. "Well, whether he was at his dad's shop or his girlfriend's place is secondary to the fact that he was logged into an online video game that overlapped with Joanna's disappearance, and his phone did not ping on the tower near Dickson."

"And my brother's phone did?"

"I can't discuss that with you, Mia. Sorry."

"Please just tell me. As a friend." The sugary sweetness of all that syrup and butter was coming at me in vile waves.

He eyed me, assessing if it was worth keeping up the facade of this "friendship." "No, OK? Lucas's phone didn't ping there either. But that said, it's also likely he left his phone behind for that very reason or else he was using a burner phone."

"God. Seriously? Damned either way, huh? Lucas can't win with you guys, can he?" I let out a tense breath.

"Mia." He said it consolingly, but his teeth were clenched.

"Maybe Dylan left his phone at home too? Maybe it's as simple as he forgot to log out."

Garrett was already shaking his head. "No. We just talked to Skylar Cuthbert's parents. They were able to confirm he was there. Their house was broken into last summer, and so they'd set up an intense alarm system—outdoor cameras, the whole shebang. Skylar snuck Dylan inside just after dinner, before the nightly lockdown. Dylan went in and didn't come back out until long after the Cuthberts left for work the next morning. I'll go over there later and look over their footage and so on, but I think it's on the up-and-up. So now Dylan really does have an airtight alibi. We know what we're doing, Mia," he added, a hair too defensively.

I nodded dumbly. Tried not to look defeated. It was not at all what I wanted to hear. "Does Wayoata have bookies?"

"Why, you need a loan?" He gave me a bemused look.

"No, I just got a call from someone named Tom, who said Lucas owes him money."

"Tom Geller?"

I shrugged. "He didn't tell me his last name."

"What did he say?"

I told him.

"It makes sense. Your brother frequented a lot of gambling Web sites, Mia. Call me right away if Tom Geller contacts you again. He's not a good guy."

"But what if Tom Geller has Lucas? Maybe that's where he is?"

"No. That's highly unlikely. Tom is only interested in money, so if he was detaining Lucas somewhere, there'd be some action on Lucas's ATM card by now. He'd clear out Lucas's account and let him go. But if it'll make you feel better, I'll check in with him. Anyway, last night on the phone—" Laney was back, friendlier now that Wayoata's finest was sitting with me. She brought Garrett a cup of coffee he didn't need to order and asked if he wanted his usual. "No thanks. Not today." Gave her a wink, and Laney's cheeks went girly pink. Clearly, Garrett was used to being a hot commodity around town. The bachelor all the women wanted to land. His face dropped when he turned back toward me. "You need to tell me how you found out Joanna was pregnant. Did Lucas tell you?" His voice was a near-inaudible whisper.

My skin went cold and clammy. "If Joanna Wilkes was pregnant, and you think Lucas was the father, couldn't you just test the embryo?" This was what I really wanted to know. Was a fetus floating in a test tube in an overworked lab somewhere, getting closer every day to the front of the line?

"Test samples were taken and sent." He cocked his head proudly. "But unlike TV, DNA testing is not so instantaneous. There's not a lab next to the station's lunchroom. We have to wait weeks to get the results. So I'm wondering, how is it only the police, the medical examiner, and Mia Haas know that Joanna Wilkes was pregnant? No one else knew. None of her friends or family came forward with this information. So how do you know?"

"Sorry, I don't remember saying anything like that. I hardly remember calling you." My shoulders had gone tight and were creeping up to my ears. "I mean, like you pointed out, I was pretty wasted last night."

"I didn't say you were wasted."

"Well, I was. I told you I'd been drinking."

He let his head fall forward in defeat. Leaned back into the chair, not noticing the beads of syrup stuck to his sleeve. "I was hoping you wouldn't play that card."

"I can't help you build a case against my brother, who is innocent. You have to understand that."

"You keep saying your brother is innocent. If you came by this information honestly, why wouldn't you use it as leverage to get us to stop looking at your brother?" I didn't have an answer for that. Garrett scowled. Shook his head like he was very disappointed in me. "You not telling me how you found out, that's obstruction of justice, Mia. That's an accessory to a crime after the fact. Do you know how much time you can get for that?" He looked at me. Waiting.

I dabbed a finger in the syrup on his sleeve and licked it off. Garrett stared at my lips. "So then arrest me."

Laney was back, trying to refill our mugs. We both covered our mugs at the same time, both paper in a game of rock, paper, scissors. A truce for now. Garrett stood up, tossed some cash on the table. Too much for his one coffee. "We'll talk again soon. Hopefully you'll come to your senses. And, by the way, you're lucky there's no law against impersonating reporters, but I wouldn't do that again." He gave me the same wink he'd given the waitress and left.

10

"Mia?" A hand waved at me from a poolside lounger. I'd decided to go back to Lucas's apartment; I needed to change. I needed a drink. Something stronger than a drink. "It's Mia, right?" A girl, wrapped in a towel, looking very small, walked toward me. She blocked the sun with her phone. Its screen glinted. It took a second to register, and when it did, my eyes popped. *Madison Wilkes.* "I just want to say sorry for my mom yesterday. She's upset—well, like obviously, my sister's dead." She shivered, her shoulder popped out of the towel, delicate and sharp looking. She wasn't as pretty as Joanna. Her face was a bit too long, not quite horse-faced but almost. She hid it well, behind a long mane of blond hair and carefully applied makeup. Her friends likely always voted her prettiest girl in the class.

"I understand. It's OK. Do you hang out here a lot?" I realized she was the white bikini girl I'd seen thc other day. Why was this girl here? Of all places to swim, why at the apartment building of the man who supposedly murdered her sister? The heat of the sun was behind me, and sweat beaded on my back. You'd never think a town that gets so dark and so cold could ever get this hot. Weatherwise, it was the most bipolar place on earth.

"The public pool is gross. Swimming helps me mourn." Her voice went up at the end, like a question. She tucked her hair behind an ear. Her fingernails were long and purple, a diamond-looking sticky in the middle of each. Women love their nail appliqués in Wayoata. Madison saw me noticing. Stole a quick disapproving glance at my own unpolished nails. "I got them done purple in honor of my sister. It's her favorite color."

I nodded. "Nice. Well, thank you for the apology. I appreciate it." Turned to walk away. Feeling strange and foggy like I'd just been spooked by something I couldn't be sure was real or not.

Her voice, small and sweet, called at me again. "I just want to tell you that I don't think Mr. Haas killed my sister."

I stopped, swiveled back around. "You don't?" My voice caught, went too high. I hadn't expected that.

"No, no way. First, he'd never be interested in her. Oh, that sounds bad. I don't mean it to. I just mean Joanna wasn't the kind of person who would get involved with a teacher." She was looking down now, at her nails.

"Who do you think hurt your sister, then?" I prodded. I shouldn't have been prodding a fourteen-year-old girl about her sister's murder—I felt like I was doing something wrong. Exploitive. Screw it, she might tell me something that could exonerate my twin.

"I don't know. Don't you think if I knew I would tell the police?" She eyed me, chin out. I felt like I was being accused of something. Her phone trilled. A text. I could see the restraint it took for her not to look to see who it was. (Same as when I abstain from another pill.)

"Of course you would. I was just wondering what makes you so certain that it wasn't my brother." I wanted something I could take back to Garrett.

"Well, people at school are saying the lunch lady did it. I could see it. She's a total bitch to everyone, but especially to the girls. She kicks out the girls way before she does the boys. It's, like, so she could look prettier to them or something by being the only woman there." She puckered her lips, her tongue pressed to the inside of her cheek so it looked like she was sucking on a jawbreaker.

"But what reason would she have to hurt your sister?" I was almost wincing, waiting for this girl to disintegrate because I was pressing her too hard. Nothing to see here, just another Haas acting inappropriately with an underage person. Some pesky kid, I couldn't see where he was, was playing with a remote-controlled car that kept circling near my feet and bumping into the chain-link fence, reversing, then bumping into it again where Madison stood. She looked agitated each time it hit the fence.

"I don't know. Who knows what goes on in the minds of people like that? It's like you want it to be your brother or something?" Madison kicked at the car, the fence shook.

"No. Not at all." I kept my voice soft and coaxing. I didn't want this girl to turn. "I appreciate what you're saying about my brother, about Mr. Haas. It really means a lot."

She nodded. Looked up at me with very large, watery blue eyes. "I think it could be Dylan Yates too. He was stalking my sister, y'know. And I wouldn't be surprised if Skylar Cuthbert helped him do it. My sister's dead, and they're running around like a happy couple." She shook her head with a wariness she was far too young for.

I nodded. Noticed that, besides Dylan, her two other suspects were women, or a girl and a woman. I thought about Joanna's hair. How cutting it off had a distinctive feminine violence to it, the whole wreckage of a woman's crowning glory or whatever. "I think it might be helpful if you talked to the police about some of your suspicions." I realized this was self-serving. The police would just explain to Madison about her list of suspects' alibis, but it would make Lucas look better if Joanna's sister doubted he was guilty.

"I tried to, but they were just interested in hearing if I ever saw Joanna with Mr. Haas, talking to Mr. Haas, texting Mr. Haas, meeting Mr. Haas. I was like, um, no." She glanced down at her phone.

I nodded. Tried my best to look reassuring. The toy car circled again. This time when it thumped the fence, Madison took off her flip-flop, slipped it on her hand, bent down, and whacked at the toy like it was a fly buzzing around. The fence billowed and the car teetered onto its side, wheels spinning in a frantic electric wheeze. I turned it back over, and it disappeared behind a garbage bin. "God, that's so annoying." Her phone trilled again; this time she looked. Her nails clacked against the screen. "I have to take this."

I was being dismissed by a fourteen-year-old.

As I made my way to the door, I nearly ran into Dale Burton. He was leaning against the building. A massive remote control at crotch level. A vein popped in the center of his forehead. Was he trying to get my attention or Madison's? He looked up me like he'd been waiting, smirked. "Keep your doors locked, sweetheart."

I scrunched up my face, brushed past him. *What the fuck is that supposed to mean?*

Back inside Lucas's apartment, I ran the kitchen tap for a full minute to try to get cold water, but all I got was slightly above room temperature water that smelled like chlorine. All the ice trays were empty. He never refilled them. I sat down at one of the kitchen stools. Something was off about the apartment. I'd felt it the minute I walked in but thought I was just being cagey. The Christmas Polaroid Lucas had on his fridge was gone. I checked under the fridge, in that slit of space between the fridge and the stove, in case it'd slipped out from under its magnet, but it was definitely gone.

I looked around, took the living room in. His ball cap, the one he was wearing in the photo that flashed on the news last night, was also missing. It'd been on the coffee table. The note Eric had left me was still there. Our two glasses from the night before looked completely undisturbed, but the half-finished bottle of bourbon was gone.

I dug around the couch cushions, thinking maybe I'd moved his ball cap and the Christmas photo when I was drunk. Did I put on his cap, cry into the Polaroid after Eric passed out and then completely blacked it out? Had I just thought he left his note next to it, while still in an early morning stupor? Maybe I'd tossed the bottle of bourbon out without thinking before I left to meet Vanessa?

Nothing in the couch cushions. I dropped to the ground, looked under the couch, felt my heart in my belly beating against the floor. The ball cap wasn't there. I stalked down the hallway to this bedroom. I couldn't tell what was missing from his closet, but there were bare wire hangers when there hadn't been any before. In the bathroom, Lucas's razor, hair gel, and cologne were also gone. Could Eric have taken them? Gone on a little impromptu shopping spree through my brother's apartment while I slept? But why would he take the Polaroid? Why would he want a picture of me at twelve years old, of Lucas and Mimi? He wouldn't. And I knew, *knew,* the electric razor was in the bathroom because I'd almost knocked it off the sink while I was getting ready and had moved it to the shelf over the toilet.

Ohmyfuckinggod.

So Lucas was in Wayoata. He'd been hiding in Wayoata this whole time. He had to know I was there. Where was he? Rage rattled through me. How could he do this? To himself? To me? I found myself pacing around in a small circle. What reason did he have to hide? *Because he's guilty* sliced through my mind. I pushed it away. Maybe he wasn't running at all because of this Joanna thing but from Tom Geller because he couldn't come up with the money. Could he really be that big of an idiot to choose lying low to avoid a loan shark over staying put and clearing his name of murder?

I sprinted back down the stairs. Outside, Dale and his car were gone. Was that what he'd meant by "keep your doors locked"? He'd seen public enemy number one enter then leave with an armful of his clothes. How did that even make sense? It was Lucas's apartment. Plus, it had hardly seemed that Dale was offering up a concerned warning. He was trying to be creepy. *Come and knock on my door—if not, I'll just let myself in.*

Madison was reclining in a lounger. Her towel gone, drinking from a small silver flask, staring at the pool. I considered asking her how long she'd been by that pool, and if she'd seen Lucas, or anyone who looked like Lucas, go in or out, but decided against it.

I got in my car and drove around. Visiting our old childhood haunts. An outdoor hockey rink where Lucas had practiced Saturday mornings, so early it was still dark. The air so icy it took your breath away. I passed the house of one of Mimi's old boyfriends, where she'd leave us sitting in a cold car waiting for her to come out and where we had shared our first cigarette swiped from her pack. Lucas had turned to me, woozy, lips blue, smoke coming out his nose. *We're gonna grow ourselves up,* he said, and I knew exactly what he meant. Behind the convenience store where we'd inhaled bags of candy, back to our old house. It was all stupid. I knew it. He wouldn't be in any of these places. But I couldn't think of anywhere else he would be. I couldn't see Lucas camping out in Dickson Park. He wasn't an outdoorsy kind of guy, and it'd be too easy to spot a fire, not to mention an all-around bad place to hide out if he had any intention of trying to clear his name.

It was dusk when I pulled into the Tall Pines Motel, an L-shaped drive-up motel that still bragged it had cable television and kitchenettes. The check-in clerk was a greasy-haired guy with impossibly thick eyebrows.

I stood in the office, trying to think of code names Lucas might use, but the desk clerk knew right away who I was. "You're the sister, aren't you? I saw you on the news." I nodded. "You need a room?"

"No, I was just—"

"I know what you're gonna ask. If your pedophile brother was staying here, I'd turn him in. So if you don't need a room, get out."

So that was that.

I couldn't help thinking now that Lucas really was about to do something rash. That suicide was a real concern. Maybe he just felt fucked every which way—financially, his professional and personal life in ruins. He was going to kill himself because everyone already believed he was guilty. There was no other reason he would still be in Wayoata. But then, why take hair gel, cologne, a razor, and a ball cap? Did he really want to leave behind a nice-looking corpse? Was he going to gel his hair in case his cap fell off when he was jumping off a bridge or in front of a train? It didn't make sense. Maybe he was back at the apartment. He'd just stopped in, grabbed a couple of things (would explain why later), seen I wasn't there, but was now back, waiting for me.

A black truck showed up in my rearview mirror. Right away I knew it was the same truck from two nights ago. My hands gripped the steering wheel tighter, my heart started to whirl. I checked my seat belt. The truck was much dirtier, like it'd been off-roading somewhere muddy. It had the same overkill cab roof lights. I tried to get its plate number, but it was covered up with what looked like strategic streaks of grime.

This time I wasn't going to putter along, road-chum to this shark. I pulled a sharp U-turn. The truck had to veer out past me, but it easily scaled the paved median and caught up with me. Who the fuck was this? I kept thinking it had to be this Tom guy; he was following me hoping that I would lead him to Lucas, but he wasn't being very discreet about it, and so that sort of defeated the purpose. Greg Yates? But this had started before he even knew who I was. I reached inside my bag for my phone to call Garrett, but the truck came up fast beside me and clipped my side-view mirror. It snapped off and dangled by a wire, thumping against my door.

Asshole.

I swerved to the right, hitting the gravel shoulder, jostling like a pinball. My phone went flying. It took three tries, the tires chafing the ridge of the pavement, the car lurching, before I managed to get back safely onto the road without tailspinning into the ditch.

The truck was now in front of me, so I zagged down a residential street. Whisked through a maze of suburban loops. Parked in someone's driveway. I waited. A kid on a bike wobbled past me, a reflective orange flag dangling limply off his back wheel, an LED light blinking between the handlebars. His helmeted head showed no signs of distress, no Mr. Big Wheels charging up behind him. I put my car into reverse; before I was halfway down the driveway, the truck was back, blocking me in. It revved its engine. Flashed its lights.

This was ridiculous. I ignored the blood pounding in my ears and swung open my door. I was not going to be intimidated. I wanted a name and license. This person had damaged my rental! Obviously so, and now there was no returning it and playing dumb about the dent and the rattle in the back, turning over the keys, and fleeing the rent-a-car lot. I was going to be stuck with paperwork and claims and deductible fees. Whatever else that needed to be done. Fuck. As if I needed to deal with this bullshit right now. I was about to confront the jerk when the owner of the driveway where we were holding the standoff came out their front door, yelling about what the hell was going on.

The truck skidded back and was gone.

The apartment was empty. I looked for a note. Picked through his things again. No note, nothing else was missing.

When our mother was in one of her interested-in-her-kids moods that usually came between boyfriends and during bouts of boredom, she'd turn into a pathological snoop. She'd play concerned parent and poke around our bedrooms, believing she was being careful not to leave any evidence of her intrusion, but there was always something she forgot. How meticulous could a drunk really be? I could usually tell when she had been in my room because of the wet rings from her glass on my dresser. After my first kiss, I wrote in my journal that I went really far with a boy (especially laughable now, because this boy was Skinny G). An exaggeration, but it was so momentous that it felt that way. That week Mimi took me to my pediatrician and put me on birth control. She didn't even tell me what the appointment was for until we were locked in the room with Dr. Bernard, a kind-faced man who looked like he always had a Werther's Original in his pocket to offer you. I'd been going to him since birth.

"Put this one on the pill, stat! I can't raise another one." Mimi laughed. An ugly sound in the tiny room among all those instruments of healing and the cartoon wall decals. I stared at Eeyore.

"We'd have to do a pelvic exam first." He eyed me in a way I didn't like. I had no idea what a pelvic exam was. I was likely the dinner topic at his house that night. I could see Dr. Bernard shaking his head, between bites of mashed potatoes and Shake 'n Bake, full of dismay. *Can you believe how early kids are starting these days?*

Mimi consented, all flirty. "Whatever you need to do, Doctor."

In the car on the way home, there was no talk about respecting my body or abstinence, just "Don't get pregnant." A simple instruction. Probably Mimi's most shining parental advice, until she added, "Least not till you get your own place."

So Lucas and I developed some time-tested hiding spots that, as far as we knew, our mother never discovered. I stored the weed I bought once and never smoked (my drug days were lying in wait for me at college) in the battery compartment of an old toy, not because I'd get in trouble for having weed but because Mimi would smoke it. Lucas taped his condoms to the bottom of dresser drawers. He kept love letters from Carolyn down an air return vent. We both hid money behind my bookshelf, taping it there inside an envelope, because Mimi was also terrible for "borrowing" money and not paying me back. If I asked for the money, she'd point out that I really owed her for the amount of electricity I'd used since being born. Initially, when Lucas and I got our own places, we laughed about how we still hid things. Old habits died hard. Maybe, out of habit, Lucas had put something in one of those spots.

I opened his bottom drawer, felt around. Nothing. I opened a vent, unscrewing the grate with a butter knife, but came up with a handful of dust. Checked the back of his kitchen cupboards, under the kitchen drawers, under the cutlery tray. I didn't even know what I was expecting to find, really. A reason, I guessed, why he wasn't there. Something meant just for me. He must have known I'd come.

Nothing. I cursed. Slammed my fist on the counter. I sat down again on the couch. Felt tempted to sail into oblivion on Valium. Lucas had been gone now for six days. Six days if he went missing the day he sent Zoey the breakup text. Some part of me was still hoping that he was going to simply show up with some story of a stalled truck on his way back from a deep-woods retreat or white-water rafting up north. Not that Lucas even had his truck, or would ever venture into anything rougher than a Holiday Inn.

"Where are you?" I howled at the flat screen. Gripped my hair. My eyes darted around the room.

I looked at the books on his bookshelf. Dog-eared paperbacks of high school required reading. Then I looked at the shelf itself. It was pushed back tight against the wall, but the top teetered forward ever so slightly. I pulled off the books. Dragged the shelf out, felt up the cardboard back of it. A manila envelope was taped to the back with duct tape. I carefully pulled the envelope free, peeled opened the glue seal, and stuck my hand inside. Feeling something feathery and soft, I flinched back like I'd touched something sickeningly dangerous, like a junkie's haphazardly discarded needle or a rabid animal that bites. Something infectious. I set it on the coffee table, gingerly, as if it could blow up at any second.

I sat down on the couch and stared at it. Nothing was written on the envelope, not *TOP SECRET—Mia's eyes only.*

A flurry of knocks on the door. The urgency made my heart drop. *He's back, he's here.* I got up, opened the door without thinking, expecting Lucas to slink inside, collar up, a fedora tipped low, all incognito. *I can explain.* I hid the envelope behind a toss cushion on the couch and answered the door.

It was the caretaker, Russ, looking pie-eyed and reeking strongly of body odor and stale everything: skin, smoke, beer, whiskey, motor oil. "Hi. Jus' want you to know you can park in your brother's spot."

"OK." What fucking time was it? After eleven at least. Didn't anyone use a phone in this town? Plus, I'd been parking in Lucas's spot since I got there.

He tottered forward like someone had pushed him. "It's closer than visitors."

I nodded. "OK. Great." My hand started to let the door go.

Russ's eyes jumped around. "Your brother, hear from him at all?"

"No. I . . . I have to go."

Russ said something incomprehensible, followed by garbled laughter. His face stretched out into some warped fun-house grin.

I started to close the door. His arm swung up with surprising speed, held the door open. "You alone?" This was like the start of a really bad horror movie, when the teenage girl answers yes or lies so badly she might as well have said yes.

"Dad!" It was Bailey, standing in the hallway, barefoot, her face red with fierce embarrassment. Russ turned, slurred something about it being past her bedtime, turned back to face me. Bailey grabbed him by the arm, her large hand easily encircling his wrist like a handcuff.

"Fuck off. We're just talking." He tried to buck off her grip, but couldn't. He was too drunk. I started to tell Russ to settle down, but Bailey shook her head at me. A stay-out-of-it glower. Every family member of a drunk has their own specific way of handling them, so I backed off. Gave her an I-know nod.

"Now." Bailey's other hand was on her hip now, her foot almost tapping like she could stand there with him all night if she had to. Russ belched in her direction, offered a smeary 'scuse me. "Sorry. He's never like this. It's his new meds. He's not supposed to drink on them."

"I'm not on meds," Russ grumbled and swayed. I could tell he was losing focus on whatever he'd had in mind when he pounded on my door.

"Come on." Bailey managed to lead her dad all the way toward the elevator while keeping her viselike grip. He staggered next to her like a toddler. She pushed the Down button with her foot.

I locked the door, both bolt and chain.

I kept my back against the door for a minute, as if my body weight added the extra security necessary to keep trespassers out, before moving back into the living room. To the couch.

I pulled the envelope out and dropped it on the coffee table. I went through a mental tug-of-war of whether it could've been planted, by the police, by someone else who was trying very hard to make Lucas look guilty. But the police don't miss *planted evidence*. And if someone had been trying to set him up, why would they do such an effective job of concealing it that the police missed it? No, you'd toss it in a partially opened drawer or something. Plus, who else would know the money hiding spot aside from Lucas?

I thought of all the forensic things that might be on it, saliva, fingerprints, maybe a shed eyelash or two. Things I already disturbed by reaching inside it. I told myself not to touch it again. Don't touch it. I stood up, took a step back, my hands planted on my cheeks. Did I really want to see what was inside it anyway? My twin was part of a major murder investigation and I just found a hidden envelope, there could be nothing good in there.

And here again I flexed my muscle for pathological denial. It's probably nothing. I blinked once, like I'd just brainwashed myself. Easy-peasy. Nothing to see here. Move along. I breezed down the hallway toward the bathroom and showered in my brother's shower. I soaped under my fingernails, where that thing inside the envelope touched my hand. Then toweled myself off with one of his gross bleach-stained towels. He needed new towels. Why couldn't he recognize that and go and buy some towels? Was that so fucking hard? Maybe if he spent less time at Casey's Bar and more time at Bed Bath & Beyond, he wouldn't be in this situation. I balled the towel up and threw it at the tiny garbage can, knocking it over, which just pissed me off more. I wanted to go home. To my own apartment, where my linen closet was stacked with new, fresh towels that weren't frayed at the edges in long knotted braids that snagged at my nipples. Where a woozy, sweaty caretaker didn't make late-night house calls. I wanted to sleep in my own bed. Go for a run and hear the wind tunneling between skyscrapers. I wanted to see crowds of people I didn't know. I wanted to know my brother was there, safe and sound, going about his life. Country mouse to my city. I grabbed the red makeup case, pulled all the bottles out, put them back in. Left the case on the bathroom sink and slammed the door shut.

Back in the living room, I made up a bed on the couch with Lucas's pillow and comforter. Eyed the envelope, the shape of its bulging innards. Who the fuck was I kidding? I grabbed it and dumped the contents onto the coffee table. A cell phone clunked out. A notebook, pages fluttering, dropped onto the table. I picked up the cell first and tried to turn it on, but it was dead. I flipped over the notebook, and something dropped over the edge of the coffee table. I think I knew what it was before I even looked. I'd already felt it. I leaned down, picked it up. A lock of hair, alarmingly similar in color to Joanna's, held together by a purple elastic. Similar. As if. Even I couldn't fool myself that much. It was Joanna's hair. I could almost smell the teenage fruity scent of hairspray emanating off it.

I jumped up. My vision went starry. I was light-headed, like all of my blood was draining. Printed neatly on the front of the notebook was "Joanna's Journal."

11

I started bouncing up and down like I was standing on hot coals, my hands spastically fanning the air. Something wild was clawing its way out of me, and I managed to grab a couch cushion just in time to cover my mouth. I let out a guttural, animal scream. The cushion button crashed into my teeth. "He fucking did it. He did it." I kept repeating it, a savage panting. More screaming and then I didn't have the strength to hold the cushion to my face anymore and I dropped it to the floor, fell to my knees, and pushed my face into it. The cushion smelled both musky and like sickly floral Febreze, and I was choking on it, and I wanted to choke. My mind skipped to the pills in the bathroom. Why not swallow them all? Maybe the Haases were meant to die off, go extinct before we wreaked too much havoc. Mimi was half gone; the budding Haas in Joanna was gone. Lucas had gone off the rails.

Thinking about it now, since he'd moved back to Wayoata, our conversations had become shorter, flimsier. "How are you?" was always answered with "good" and "busy." We didn't pick that hard at each other's surfaces. Maybe the things I thought I knew, the absolute certainties, were just stats from our childhood: Pepsi over Coke, pizza was better cold, always the ability to fly over immortality. It wasn't like Lucas knew that I could pop pills like Tic Tacs. But my belief that I *knew* him knew him was gone.

Once, Mimi, in one of her fits of whimsy, decided she would play fun mom. She covered the kitchen table with newspapers and served us spaghetti for dinner. The playful catch: we were supposed to eat it without utensils. We were fourteen, way too old for this kind of thing. I refused to eat it. She poured herself a giant glass of red wine and watched a shirtless Lucas plow through his plate, smearing the tomato sauce all over his face, dangling strands of spaghetti from his mouth, hamming it up while Mimi laughed.

All this time, I'd believed I got the brunt of Mimi's meanness. But maybe Lucas got something far worse. He had the role of pleaser while I was Mimi's "difficult" child. Maybe all his aim-to-please character was just a facade after so many years of tap-dancing on demand for his drunk mother. The humiliation of Mimi giving it to one of his friends was too much, and something dark, a seething rage that had been secretly building all those years from Mimi pushing him into playing man of the house in between her boyfriends, ruptured that night. It settled in, had free rein like an undiagnosed cancer, and all along under his affable grin, there was this dark and vicious thing blooming.

The hair. The hair Joanna had wanted to donate to kids with cancer. Why did he shear her, take home this sick memento? I thought of the numerous times we had pulled Mimi from the tub because she had passed out there. How Lucas had started doing it himself because he was stronger, Mimi's wet hair slapping him in the face. It stood to reason that with a mother like ours, Lucas would go Norman Bates-y.

I mean, I'd nearly killed her. We were not a nice family. The black glove. He kept it. What did he do with it? My mind skittered to some twisted masturbation thing. A glistening glove full of lube. Oh God.

And what about the blood? I guess it was an aversion he got over, then got a taste for. My mind shuttled back to the Sticky Ricky incident, how stealthily Lucas had moved, how he'd just walked right up and cracked his stick into Ricky's back. Two good wallops. Not saying a word, he watched Ricky writhing on the ground afterward like it was a curious thing, then stalked back to his room. But he was protecting me. I knew him to his bones. He didn't have a bad bone in his body—that was what people said about good people.

I'd been wrong. I sniveled into the pillow. Wrong.

The Lucas I knew would not have had the hair of a murdered teenager in his apartment. Like mother, like son. It must run in the genes, the sexual assault of minors.

He never stood a chance.

And now it was too late. It was all too late. The damage was done.

Finally, finally, finally, when I felt I could lift my head free of the snot-soaked cushion and breathe, I went into the bathroom and swallowed an Ativan and a muscle relaxant. Longingly cupped the other bottles, like they were pet hamsters, put them back. Made up my mind.

I gathered it all up, the journal (and here I flipped through the pages fast, unable to stomach the perky writing, the dated entries so hopeful in their plodding progression toward the free-fall days of summer break. Lucas's red check marks in the bottom corners like inverted scythes. Checking off the days until he could kill her), the hair, the phone, and stuck it in a black garbage bag and snuck down the stairwell into the parking lot and stuffed the bag under the driver's seat of the PT Cruiser. Got in and started driving. I made it to the intersection just before the police station. It was 3 A.M., and some part of me hoped it'd be closed, but the lights were aglow.

The traffic light flashed red. *Guilty, guilty, guilty.* It pulsed inside my head, a red ember that started to smoke in the middle of my brain. I smacked the steering wheel. *Go. Go. Just plop the bag down on the front desk and walk out.* I couldn't lift my foot off the brake. My body was going puddly from the relaxant.

Tomorrow.

I'd go tomorrow. I'd be able to think better tomorrow.

What's the rush, anyway? The police already think he did it.

Yes, I'll come back tomorrow. I did a squealing U-turn.

Back in the Terrace parking lot, in Lucas's parking spot, I pulled the cell phone out of the bag before going up. It'd be my only chance to see what was on it before I turned it in.

I tried my own charger for the cell phone, but it didn't comply. I guessed it was the secret cell he'd used to communicate with his teenage lover. Maybe there was something on it that could explain all of this away. A text from Joanna asking him to hold on to her journal, a text that went with the lock of her hair that clarified it was meant as a romantic gesture. Something was going on between them, but that didn't mean he killed her. I had to see what was on this phone. Before—and here I felt a hard twist in my chest, *Tattletale, tattletale*—I turned it in to Garrett.

12

DAY 5

SUNDAY

In the morning, after a ragged sleep, I waited until the stores opened and went shopping for a charger that would work. Before I left, I fished Scotch tape out of a drawer from the kitchen. Outside in the hall, after I locked the door, I pressed a small strip of the tape across the bottom of the frame and door so it was almost impossible to spot unless you were looking for it, another trick we'd used to tell if Mimi had snooped in our bedrooms. A strategically placed strip of Scotch tape can be as good as a wax seal when it came to catching interlopers. I noticed above my ribbon of tape there was already the sticky remains of floppy Scotch tape. A few pieces, actually. So Lucas had been worried someone was coming into his suite too?

I sensed I was being watched, whipped around, and noticed the peephole on the door across the hall from Lucas's was dark. I knocked on the door. "I'm Mia. I am staying in my brother's suite across the hall, and I'm just wondering if I could ask you a couple of questions?"

"Don't bother trying, dear, she won't answer. Doesn't come out of there at all." Lucas's right side neighbors were just exiting their suite with their matching Rollator walkers. They started on a slow shuffle toward the elevator. They looked they were on their way somewhere nice, both smartly dressed in their Sunday best. The hallway filled with a mix of perfume and aftershave.

"She's one of those, what're they called again, Doris?" The man turned and aimed an ear toward Doris.

"Oh Stan, don't tell me you forgot to put in your hearing aids?" She huffed back at him. Her lips wobbled with irritation. "Go back inside and put them in." Stan looked back at his apartment door, and then waved her away. Like he'd come too far to turn back. "Anyway, she's an ag-ora-phobe. That's what she is." Doris was practically shouting it, over-enunciating, so Stan could hear, and I was certain the "agoraphobe" could hear her as well.

"You the sister?" Stan's rheumy eyes scanned me.

"I am." He grunted something and Doris cut him off.

"Last winter when Stan had his stroke Lucas would come by and ask if I needed a ride to the hospital or if I needed groceries." She said this like she was reminding her husband of Lucas's kindness. Stan's face tightened, and I could tell he was thinking about how many times his wife was alone in a car with Lucas. I thought about asking if they had anything go missing from their suites, but didn't want to stir up any anxiety. Stan and Doris parked in front of the elevator and when Doris reached to press the Down button, her massive bejeweled purse started to slip from the seat of her walker. Stan reached over and caught it. He pushed the purse back into its place and they got onto the elevator.

Still standing in front of the "agoraphobe's" apartment, I heard the sound of something brushing up against the door. Maybe the sleeves of a sweater? As if this person had her back pressed against the door to keep it shut. I knocked again. Someone who peeped on life through holes and crannies and lifted curtains might know who'd been coming in and out of my brother's suite. Might even be able to vouch for Lucas's lame alibi of being home alone all night. This woman could have heard his door close and corroborate that he never left until the following morning. She probably played blind and deaf to the police, worried they would compel her out of her apartment down the road to testify, but she might tell me what she saw because I didn't have the power to force her out. A long shot, I knew that.

No answer. Forget it.

Dale Burton. He really had been warning me. Keep the door locked, and I did lock it. Of course. I should have thought about it before. I stomped down the stairwell, pissed as hell. Knocked on unit 11 "PROPERTY MANAGER," hard and incessantly, until I heard stirring behind the door. "Yeah, yeah, keep yer panties on," I heard Russ grumble behind the door. He wasn't wearing a shirt. His stomach bulged out; it didn't even look real but made of smooth latex. A movie fat suit.

"Yeah, what can I do fer ya?" There wasn't even a glimmer of recognition in his face that he had banged on my door last night. He hadn't been looking to get lucky in the way I'd thought. Lucas had a good bar. I was sure Russ had told himself a bottle here and there wouldn't be missed, and hey, while he was at it, might as well borrow a bottle of gel and cologne and an expensive cordless razor. Snagged the Polaroid too. *Never know,* he probably reasoned, *it might be worth something if this thing gets on* Dateline. And why not go for some red sneakers too, which cost almost two months' worth of rent in this place? But looking at Russ now, he seemed more a fluffy-haired, narrow-toed, cowboy-boot sort of man.

"I want you to stay out of my brother's apartment, or else I'll report you to the police."

"Not sure I follow?" His eyebrows furrowed. He cracked his neck.

I could smell his stale warm beer breath. An alarmed-looking Bailey lurked in the background, eating a Pop-Tart. I wondered if Russ had already been an alcoholic when he named his daughter after a liqueur. I spotted the bottle of bourbon on the kitchen counter, front and center in a cluster of other booze bottles next to the microwave.

"Oh, I think you do. I think when you're running low on your own booze, you go dipping into the tenants' cupboards searching for more. Don't do it again." I gestured toward the bourbon but Russ didn't even look.

Instead he just snorted like I'd said the most ridiculous thing he'd ever heard. "Now, you listen to me, girlie. I don't take kindly to being accused of something I didn't do. Think you'd understand that, going around saying your brother didn't kill that little girl. Unless you got me on hidden camera or somethin', then you better watch what you're saying. You don't want to be accused of slander with everything else you gotta worry about. Now, I'll be a gentleman and forget this conversation ever happened." He closed the door. Still, I heard him say to his daughter, "Can you believe that cunt?"

So Lucas wasn't back in Wayoata.

I avoided Walmart. There was no way I wouldn't run into someone I didn't want to see at Walmart. I decided to try Eddie's Electronics. The shop was full of old fax machines, giant fifty-pound printers, and tube televisions. I had turned to leave when Eddie came out of the bathroom, still tucking in his shirt as he introduced himself, toilet midflush. "What'cha looking for?"

"A charger for this phone." I held it up. Eddie ducked behind the counter, brought out a box with CHARGERS written on it in marker. I dug through the box, finally finding one. It cost me $1.50. On my way out, after he made his sale, Eddie cleared his throat and said he'd gone out with the search parties looking for that poor girl and hoped my brother would burn in hell. He added, "Such a pretty girl," as if ugly girls were more deserving of having their heads smashed in.

Back on Main Street, I drove right past her. She was a flicker on my peripheral vision that didn't come into mental focus until I stopped at the lights and wrenched the rearview mirror down to look back. I did a sharp U-turn on the red and pulled up next to her, grazing the curb.

"Mimi?" I hollered through the open passenger side window.

She was walking, fast, bent forward, as if against a strong wind. Still in her floral nightgown, but instead of the nursing home–issued flip-flops, she had on black rubber boots that in this heat must have been making her feet ooze sweat. She glanced up at me, but did not break from her power-walker's stride. I parked. Jogged up behind her. "Mimi, please stop." She still didn't acknowledge me. "Where do you think you're going?"

She jerked her head back, like someone had pulled hard on one of her braids, and aimed an aggravated gust of breath toward the sky. "Like you really want to know. I have to go."

"Mimi, I don't think you're supposed to be out."

She turned, again that smile. "No I'm not. I'm like the bad kitty who got loose when no one was looking." She curled her hands up into paws and rubbed her face, her tongue flicking out. Playing a cat grooming herself.

"I can take you back. Please. My car's right there."

"No!" She slung the word over her shoulder, and I knew there was no way I could get her into my car. I was too afraid to touch her, too afraid to rile her up.

I pulled out my phone and called the LightHouse. "My mother is out walking down Main Street right now. How is this happening?" The staff was always so quick to inform me when Mimi's antics resulted in a bill that needed to be paid, and yet conveniently left out that she could escape. How shoddy was this place?

The nurse assured me that there was a "crisis intervention" team out looking for Mimi this very second, that she'd never broken out before. She droned a list of their safety protocols that I couldn't possibly have cared less about at that moment.

"You need to come and get my mother. It's dangerous." I wasn't sure if I meant the world was a dangerous place for Mimi or Mimi was a danger to the world.

Mimi, now several feet in front of me, stopped suddenly, as if she'd hit a windowpane. She turned back, and in her wicked singsongy voice said, "You shouldn't have done that," and broke out into a surprisingly fast sprint down a side street. I went after her, gave the nurse her exact whereabouts so she could radio it over to the crisis team. Mimi didn't slow her pace, which didn't seem possible, given how much she smoked. She suddenly veered to the right, up someone's driveway, and into the backyard. A girl stared at us from her massive trampoline, never breaking from her steady, springy jumps.

Mimi hiked her nightgown up and scaled the fence with shocking ease. She was moving like a fucking werewolf. I struggled over the fence and found her again on the sidewalk, still trotting along at an even stride. Finally a white van pulled up alongside Mimi. Two burly medics got out. I thought there'd be a showdown, that Mimi would kick and spit and bite, but instead she greeted them like old friends. There was even a shoulder squeeze and a handshake. No way this was her first prison break.

I locked eyes with Mimi as the medic opened the van door for her, and again, that thing, the essence of who she was before the accident was back. The sharpness in her eyes. Where had she been going? Did she even know, or was it some illusory destination conjured by her broken brain?

I watched the white van wend its way down the side street and disappear. Got back into my rental, rested my head against the steering wheel, and sucked on a Klonopin like it was a dinner mint.

My mind shot back to ninth grade, when a pretty classmate asked me to stay for dinner two nights in a row. Maybe she sensed my reluctance to go home, that the whole normalcy of a sit-down, well-rounded supper with glasses of milk had enchanted me. In the Haas household, there were no mealtime rituals. The second night, just as bowls of mint chocolate chip ice cream were being served, my mother showed up with a suitcase full of my clothes, shouting, "You might as well move in," and drove off. I dragged the suitcase home, where Mimi was sitting on the couch, the room hazy with cigarette smoke. She patted the cushion next to her and gathered me into her. *You're my daughter—don't you forget it.*

How could I? You won't let me.

Back at the apartment, Eric was walking down the hallway toward me, away from Lucas's door. He had a tray of coffee with an oily looking brown-paper bag tucked between two paper cups. "I was just about to give up. I thought you were inside ignoring me."

I was already feeling the relaxed, slow-mo effects of the Klonopin, and so I could not think of anything witty to say in return.

"Is this not a good time?" Eric gave me his best guidance-counselor furrowed brow, and I wanted to curl into him and sleep. Just sleep. Sleep until this all turned into a dream. No, now wasn't a good time. I was never going to have a good time again; my brother was a murderer. It wasn't a good time because I needed to see what was on this phone. I needed this Klonopin out of me.

I shook my head. "No, no, sorry. I'm just tired."

"Well, aren't you glad I brought coffee, then?"

I glanced quick at the Scotch tape as I unlocked the door. Still intact. Was it Mimi coming into the suite? Was she headed here? She was certainly a strong contender for bourbon thief. But even if the nurse was lying and this wasn't the first and only time Mimi had gotten out, I doubted she had a copy of Lucas's keys, and then there was the practical matter that Mimi didn't even have pockets on her nightgown, so how would she courier around a razor, cologne, gel, clothing, and a bottle? No. It was definitely the slobby caretaker.

Inside, I made a mad dash for the bathroom, ran the water, and threw up the Klonopin. I brushed my teeth and drank the water from the tap. In the mirror, my eyes were glassy and the bruise on my cheek was darkening. I was glad I hadn't bothered to open the blinds before I left; the apartment lighting was so murky. I pulled my hair up and took several deep meditative breaths before going back out to Eric.

Eric, who at any other time would have been heart-shatteringly adorable because he'd unpacked the coffee and some strudel-looking pastry and set it all out on the coffee table like it was a nice place to drink coffee and eat cake. The coffee table, where his note still lay between our dirty glasses, where my brother's ball cap no longer lay. The coffee table that was next to the couch where I got laid, where my evil twin plotted how to get away with murder, the table that Joanna's red hair was strewn across just last night. I needed to get hold of my muddy, muddy thoughts. I deeply regretted the Klonopin.

Eric started to say something about not knowing what I took in my coffee and so he had cream and sugar and milk. I waved it away; it didn't matter. I'd drink it black.

"Tell me about Joanna?" I took the coffee he handed me and sunk into the couch. I needed to know what it was about her, about Joanna, that would have set my brother off, and yes, I knew this was an appalling thought. Laying blame with Joanna, but I was clearly still tripping out on denial.

He gave me a wary look. "Like what?"

"Just, tell me about her. I mean, my brother's being accused of killing her, and I don't know anything about her. You counseled her, right? I don't think confidentiality extends after death." I sounded a tad too callous. I tried again. "I just want to know what you think. Do you think my brother killed her?"

"God, Mia. You're putting me in a tough spot here." If he'd been in a dress shirt, I would have seen him tugging at it, hot under the collar. "I don't know. I really don't. When I first heard Joanna was missing, I wasn't even worried about it. I thought she just ran away. The girl had been heading toward a major rebellion for a while, and so I thought she just wanted to give her parents a scare.

"Kathy was in the middle of making plans to move to New York with Joanna next year, and Joanna didn't want to go. Her mom had her at the dance studio every afternoon after school and on weekends. She had a lot of trouble with the other girls there. They disliked her; she was always accused of getting special treatment because her mom owned it. Kathy made her a feature dancer in everything. There was probably a lot of jealousy there too because, from what I heard, Joanna was really talented." He took a careful sip of his coffee. Swallowed.

"She also had a falling out with her best friend over something dance related. Again the whole dealing drugs thing, the loser boyfriend.

She told me she was—" He suddenly stopped talking. It was like he'd just dropped off a cliff. *Pregnant.* I mentally finished his sentence.

"She told you she was what?" Now I was just being masochistic. It was clearly something I didn't want to know.

At this, he blew out a heavy breath. "Mia." He said my name in a way so bloated with sympathy that I flinched.

"What?"

"She told me she was seeing someone older that she didn't want to get in trouble. All this time, I thought she meant Dylan, but maybe she meant Lucas. I'm sorry. I feel like an asshole telling you this."

"OK, so if that's true, what I don't understand is how did Joanna have a relationship with my brother if her mother kept her under twenty-four-hour surveillance?"

"Kathy must be asking herself the same thing. But unless you keep your child in a locked room, you can't be with them every second. I think in a way, Kathy's possessiveness ironically made Joanna and Lucas very creative about coming up with ways to be together and not get caught. That's why the police are having such a hard time tracing the trajectory of their relationship."

"So you do think Lucas did it."

Eric drummed his fingers against his black jeans. Getting grilled like this was probably not what he had in mind when he dropped by.

"Nooo . . . not exactly. It doesn't matter what I think, anyway. Whatever happened, the truth will come out. I believe that." Eric wrapped his arm around my shoulders, pressed his lips to my temple. Easiest way to slip out of deep conversation? Tell someone everything happened for a reason. Any other day, this would have annoyed me, but today, now, it was all I wanted to hear. I wanted the easiest way out. "Do you want to get out of here? It's kind of gloomy."

I was hours away from turning my brother in. I glanced at the phone that I wanted to charge. That I wanted to put off charging. Did I really want to see what was on it? I don't know why I assumed it was Lucas's phone, it could be Joanna's; either way, the optimism I felt last night was gone. There could be nothing good on this phone. He hid it for a reason. And here something squirmed inside me, why wouldn't he take it with him? Why did he leave the evidence behind? But then how did I make sense of a man who helped little old ladies get their groceries, and fucked sixteen-year-old girls?

"Where would we go? I'm, like, the town pariah right now," I answered, my throat sticky. It *was* gloomy in there.

"I don't know—for a drive? You can wear my helmet, put the visor down, and no one will know who you are. That way you can be an undercover pariah." I appreciated how Eric was trying to cheer me up, even if it all felt askew. Like small talk at a funeral.

"How did you bring coffee here, anyway, on a bike?" I sucked air in, and made my voice go light and easy. Fake it 'til you make it (to the police station). Now there's a cliché I could get on board with right now.

"With great talent. Like a circus bear on a unicycle, balancing plates." He wiggled his eyebrows.

"Funny."

"No. I parked it here. Walked down the street, bought the coffee, and walked back. C'mon let's go." He tapped my thigh, stood, held out his hands. I put my hands in his, gave him a limp smile, and let him draw me up.

Outside in the parking lot I straddled the bike feeling tangled and strange. The air was muggy and the sun was hazy and hot. Nothing felt real for a second, as Eric kick-started the engine. This was what I needed. A day to get lost. Just one more day being someone whose brother was not a killer (officially anyway). A few more hours of denial. (With any luck, the caretaker would come moseying into Lucas's apartment and take the phone anyway, and then I wouldn't have to include it. I should probably have left the hair and journal out too, for Russ to pilfer.)

I curled tight into Eric. His skinny rock-star waist. My helmeted head resting against his back, smelling his Bounce-infused T-shirt as he took me up and down Main Street.

Eventually he parked at a bar called the Stagger Inn. "If you're worried about the locals, keep your head down until I find us a nice dark spot." It turned out I didn't need to worry. It was only noon, and the place was pretty dead. I followed him to the neon-lit bar, staying behind him when he ordered up a pitcher of beer.

We made our way to the pool tables, and played a couple of games. I was no good at pool, and Eric found this funny. He stood behind me and showed me how to properly hold the cue. When I made a side pocket, we clanged our mugs of beer together. I felt like I was in a pharmaceutical commercial, looking like I was having the time of my life as a cheerful voice-over listed all the dire side effects. Uncontrollable muscle movement, incontinence, heart failure, coma, sudden death.

When a couple of guys came in that I recognized from high school, I tugged on Eric's arm. We ducked back to our dim cavern of a table next to a House of the Dead pinball machine (its frantic, attract-mode music a perfect soundtrack to the tension crawling up and down my back) that made me think about Garrett. How he'd accept the envelope with Joanna's hair and journal with grim-faced sympathy, saying things like *You're doing the right thing Mia—the family can have peace now,* while his heart pounded with triumph. I didn't want to think about him.

I took another mouthful of flat beer.

Eric and I spent another hour talking literally about nothing. He was either the most incurious guy I'd ever met (which was nice right now) or else he really was working hard at trying to take my mind off of things. He regaled me with witty stories from his days in Los Angeles, bands he'd played in, and his most clueless students, and I felt warm bewilderment. *Here he is (again!)—Mr. Lowe. Full access. All mine.*

When Eric eventually went up to replenish our pitcher, I was starting to feel beer-blurry. Tired and drunk. Whatever Klonopin I still had in my system was giving the beer too much of a boost.

I dug through my purse for an upper. "What are you taking?" Eric had crept up and dropped down across from me. Beer splashed over the edge. I was going to lie, but then realized I didn't need to. I had the drunken confidence that Eric would understand. He was my counselor, after all, so I told him.

"And what does that do?"

"It keeps me awake."

"That's it?" He made a face that said he didn't believe me.

"No. It makes everything come into sharp focus. Like you can feel all of your nerve endings humming along in perfect harmony. Like you're a second away from unlocking all of the secrets to the universe." God, I sounded like a dealer at a high school party. I smiled.

"Hmm. Sounds cool. Can I have one?" His begging look gave me the feeling this wasn't his first pharma dalliance.

"Don't you need to work tomorrow?"

"Tomorrow's the first day of summer break. I'm officially released of all responsibility." He put his arms up like a marathoner crossing the finish line.

"Summer break already?" How the days had scrambled. Right now I could hardly think of how long I'd been in Wayoata. This time of year, I'd start doling out the passive-aggressive *Must be nice* remarks to my brother, and he'd wisecrack back, *It is, it really is.*

"C'mon, I'm feeling adventurous." Eric held his hand out.

"Mm. In that case." I tapped out a small white pill into his palm. He shook it around, like a fine wine swirl, and popped it into his mouth. "But remember, the first one's free. After that, it's gonna cost you. . . ." I eyed him up and down like a pimp.

"Ha. Cute. But this won't interfere with my bad heart, right?"

"Don't even joke." I gave him a light punch in the arm.

"How many did you take?"

"Three."

"Three?" He mocked loose-jaw shock. "You're not a beginner, then?"

I shook my head, feeling a burst of relief that I'd finally told someone. "I know what I'm doing."

"I hope so. You're the pharmacist."

We finished our beers and left. Back on his bike, we kicked up gravel down a back road that took us near the Harold's Grocers processing plants, then drove off to the outskirts of town. We motored alongside Dickson Park, a blur of shimmery green that went on for miles. I spotted a coyote skulking along the shoulder of the road, like it was hunting something down. When I blinked, it was gone. Eric sped up and we cut down the highway like a razor. I was, I guess, feeling self-destructive. Part of me wanted to let go of Eric's waist and skid across the highway, my head bouncing off asphalt, knocking out what I knew. I wanted the bike to wobble out from underneath us in a fiery, drunken, doped-up bike wreck so I'd never have to turn my brother in. Maybe I'd join Mimi at the LightHouse care home, our cracked-up brains sitting loose between our ears like bath loofahs. We'd be even-Steven and the plastic bag with a dead girl's English journal and lock of hair would get lost under the seat of an abandoned rented PT cruiser.

Eventually Eric turned off near the sandpits, where limestone made the water glow like nuclear waste. I held on tight as we jolted down a sandy hill and circled back out. Wind whipped across my face and into my ears, suffocating all thought. I felt a weight sweeping off my chest at each passing mile out of town, and then returning, all at once, when our ride was over and we passed the welcome sign. By the time Eric took me home, the sun was setting. And the sky was a swirl of candy-floss pink as if a plug had been pulled and day was being flushed.

It was my *Fear and Loathing in Wayoata* afternoon.

Back at the apartment, Eric stood by the door, leaning into the wall. He was drunker and more wired than me; his pupils were narrowed discs. "Is there anything more I can do for you right now?"

He said it as if he'd just handed me a menu of sexual favors. Or maybe it only felt that way, because this entire day felt like a last meal before the shit-storm came hailing down on me.

What more could he do for me? Give me an orgasm? Fuck me senseless so I'd forget about all of this for a little while longer?

I started to undo his belt. Yes, I wanted to be fucked senseless. We stumbled toward the couch. I'd felt queasy sick about doing this the first time, and yet I couldn't let myself think ahead to how I'd feel. Because maybe this would be the last nice thing I'd feel in a long time.

He moved me onto his lap. Unhooked my bra and pulled off my shirt. His mouth was on my nipples, as his hands kneaded my back, traveled up my neck and into my hair. He pulled me back suddenly by my hair—it stung in a good way—then pressed his mouth hard against my lips. We shared an almost violent kiss; his teeth caught my bottom lip. I tasted blood. He peeled off my jeans, picked me back up onto him, then he gripped my hips and moved me back and forth. His mouth pressed into my ear, and I listened to him moan my name. *Mia, you feel so good.* It was over quickly.

13

DAY 6

MONDAY

Eric and I slept in and said an awkward, hungover good-bye at the door.

From the window, I watched him leave. He crossed the parking lot toward his motorcycle, which glinted in the late-morning sun. Madison had already set herself up by the pool, and when she saw Eric, she yelled something. He stopped, moved his sunglasses to the top of his head. Walked over to the pool. A scowl on his face. He was probably wondering what the hell she was doing there. She looked like she was teasing him about something, then stood and went over to the fence. He said something, and her head dropped and she wiped her eye. Then Eric's hands moved across the fence to her bare shoulders and stayed, I thought, a second too long before he got on his bike and drove off.

I couldn't put it off any longer. I plugged in the phone and waited for its slow resurrection. I scrolled through the contacts first, thinking there'd just be one: Joanna or Lucas. It was a secret cell, after all. But there was a long list of contacts. I didn't recognize any of the names.

I wasn't listed, neither was Wyatt. There was no contact info for Madison or her brother Ben or Dylan Yates.

I'd been avoiding the camera icon. I took a breath, tapped the screen. There were at least a hundred pictures. I started sliding through them, the first few a blurry series of a hockey rink, then a couple of close-ups of a thick, bleeding steak, several teenage faces I didn't recognize. Then a leg. It took me a second to fully grasp what I was looking at or, more accurately, who I was looking at. Legs bare, spread-eagled. A towel underneath her pelvis. Under the towel, a boy's quilt decorated with fire engines. Panties half pulled to the side, a hand making a V gesture next to her crotch. I could tell from the angle that the hand did not belong to the person taking the picture. In the next picture, the fingers were inside her panties and another person was standing above the girl's head, his hand resting near his groin. In the next, the panties were gone. In the next, her shirt was pulled up. Next a beer bottle was pressed against her inner thigh. It was Joanna Wilkes, her face slack, clearly unconscious.

Then, jarringly, a can of SpaghettiOs. Then the can next to Joanna's crotch, then the can being poured out on her vagina. Then three more pictures of the runny mess disappearing into folds, that unnaturally bright red-orange sauce spreading down her pale white thighs. I bit the inside of my mouth. Horrified at this bizarre act of degradation. What was this? A sexual assault, some kind of sick Internet thing that people posted and passed around?

The one thing I knew for sure was that this wasn't Lucas's phone.

There were four saved text message exchanges. A few between "Me" and "Mom."

ME: What for dinner, starving!!
MOM: Come downstairs and you'll find out

One with "Me" and a girl he was badly sexting.

ME: Ur head is gonna slam into the headboard when I stuff all four of your holes

JESSICA: Where's the fourth hole?
ME: Oops. I mean three. HAHA. Send me a pic of UR boobs
JESSICA: Seriously, BOOBS?
ME: Fuck u then

Then another between "Me" and "Rooster."

ROOSTER: U suck!
ME: WHATEVER, U suck dick
ROOSTER: LOL. Ya ur mom's dick
ME: WHAAAT??? U wish homo

This pointless exchange went on for a while. I scrolled down. Looked at the last couple of one-sided texts sent to "Oz," two hours apart.

ME: Hey BIATCH u out of bed yet? Haas pissed you missed practice. U getting benched!
ME: BAHAHA. . . . Rooster called you a PASTA PUSSY
ME: Yo. U awake yet??? Gonna send u tasty pic.
ME: FUUUUUCK . . . Haas knowsssrghjk%

All communication dropped off. The date of the last text between Me and Oz was January 17. There was no other activity on the phone past that date.

I went back to the pictures. I didn't have Me's name, but I had his face, or least the face that showed up in most of the other pictures in the photo gallery. Rooster, Oz, and Me made sure their faces were not in any of the assault pics. Me looked how he sounded: shaved blockhead, thick neck, a menacing smile. A teen movie bully from central casting.

From my phone, I called the numbers listed under Rooster and Oz; both were disconnected. I called Me's home number. A woman answered in a clipped voice. A child whined at her. "Stop—Mommy's on the phone. . . . Hello?"

I was about to say, *I have your son's phone,* but then thought, *Why would I tip them off?* That I had this phone, these pictures.

"HELLO?"

I pressed End.

Haas knows. Lucas coached these boys and knew about the pictures. What did that mean? If he did, why wouldn't he have turned the phone over to the police or even to the school administration? Why was it in his apartment? Joanna could have told on these fuckers anytime for sexually assaulting her and catching it frame by frame for her full humiliation. Did they kill her because she threatened to do just that? Did it mean they'd killed Lucas to get the phone back, but he'd hidden it?

At this moment was he in a ditch off some back road or in a shallow grave in Dickson Park and just hadn't been found because no one was looking for his body? Maybe this was why airports and bus stations and border control had yet to intercept him. Something else was going on. He'd kept this phone for a reason. Maybe to protect her?

But there was the hair. The red, wavy hair. Why did he have Joanna's hair? Had he seen these pictures and flown off into a violent rage and somehow, what? Killed her for getting too drunk and making herself susceptible to assault? It didn't make sense. That wasn't Lucas.

I sent the texts and the photos of Joanna to my own phone. When I was done, my phone buzzed. It was Garrett asking me to come down to the police station. There was a hit on Lucas's ATM card.

Chief Pruden was waiting for me by the front vestibule. Someone had ordered in Chinese for lunch, and the whole station reeked; fried batter and sweet and sour sauce tickled the back of my throat. He grunted a hello and made no eye contact, his face blank. I tried to read him, see if I could detect what this ATM hit meant, if it was good or bad for Lucas. Pruden motioned me to follow him. I felt queasy. He led me to the same interview room I'd been in a couple of days ago. Empty white boxes were stacked at the end of the table, and a pile of fortune cookies was gathered in the middle.

"Wait here," he growled, his thumbnail picking at his bottom teeth.

Garrett was already in the room. "Glad you could get here so fast."

I sat down across from him, feeling inexplicably guilty about my night with Eric. Nights. Like Garrett could tell what I'd been up to by looking at me. Another Haas crossing some student/teacher line, even if it was retrograde. I don't know why I cared. "Of course. What's with Officer Friendly?"

"Pruden? He's just a little pissed about the article."

"Article?"

"Don't tell me you haven't read it yet. I guess us 'bored, overzealous small-town cops with too much time on their hands'—that's a direct quote, by the way—have all the time in the world to sit around reading the Minneapolis *StarTribune*."

I'd forgotten about the article. Shit. This was a bad time to irritate the police, now that there'd been an ATM hit, now that I'd discovered the phone, now that I really wanted us all to get along and work together.

"Oh? It was just supposed to be an article about Lucas, his character. Anything else must've been at her own, I guess, creative discretion."

"Hunh. Right. Well, it's not important anyway. How are you doing?"

I motioned to the room in a how-do-you-think-I'm-doing gesture. Garrett nodded, gave me a sympathetic half smile, half wince, like he knew all about how I was feeling. "Just wanted to make sure you were, y'know, holding up OK. You look . . . weighed down. You can talk to me—you know that, right?" He was about to say something else, but Pruden was back with an open laptop. He set it down and took a seat next to Garrett. The screen was on screen-saver mode, and a little WPD badge bounced around.

"Who does Lucas know in Springdale, Arkansas?" Pruden asked.

"Arkansas? No one."

"Before you answer, I want you to take a minute to think."

"I don't need to think. We don't know anyone in Arkansas. We've never even been to Arkansas." I ran my hand through my hair.

Pruden frowned at me. "Lucas withdrew everything from his account. All six hundred and eighty dollars of it. What do you think of that?"

I didn't know what to think. I felt queasy and angry and confused, and I just wanted to see the video. See if it was him. "I don't know." My voice sounded dry.

"The footage we have was caught in Springdale." Pruden scowled at me. "You sure Lucas doesn't have anyone down there that might want to help him out?"

"Yes."

"All right. But it's possible that Lucas could have a friend there that you don't know about? Someone he went to college with? Or even someone he met more recently?"

"I mean, it's possible, but I don't think so. Can I please see the video?" I looked at Garrett, who just sat there, giving me this empty expression.

"Hey, don't look at him. I'm the one asking questions right now," Pruden snapped.

"And I answered you. He doesn't know anyone in Arkansas!" I shouted, and immediately regretted it, because Pruden smirked. He liked that he'd got me to react like this. Was it because of the article, or because he thought he had me rattled and was a few questions away from getting me to blab about Lucas's escape plan?

Pruden grabbed the laptop, logged in, and pushed it toward me. "All you need to do is tell us if you recognize the person, or if anything is familiar about the person on this tape." He got up, walked around the table, stood behind me, and pressed Play. I took in a deep breath and held it.

The footage was dark and grainy; the time said it was just after 1 A.M. Whoever it was had on an oversized hood that concealed most of his face, except for a couple of glimpses of his chin.

"I can't tell. It's not Lucas. I don't know who this is."

Pruden kept reaching over me and replaying the footage—"Have another look"—like it was some kind of numbers game and I'd magically see through the hood after x number of views. "Is it anyone you recognize? A friend of Lucas's? A friend of a friend?" I could feel and smell Pruden's salty breath on the top of my head.

"I have no idea who this is." I felt a mix of relief that it wasn't my brother and panic because the chin was mostly hairless. That could be due to meticulous grooming or because whoever this was, he was still in high school. *A hockey player.*

Pruden made a frustrated sound at the back of his throat.

I pulled the phone out of my pocket and slid it across the table, past the laptop. "I found this in Lucas's apartment today." They both stared at it.

"Whose phone?" Pruden asked. He went around to the other side of the table, hovered over the phone like it might try to get away. Garrett's back went very straight.

"One of the hockey players on the Westfield Bulldogs. There are pictures on it of Joanna Wilkes being assaulted. Have a look. It will certainly make you rethink your dogged investigation into my brother."

Pruden left and returned with gloves for himself only, which seemed to annoy Garrett.

"Where did you find this?" Garrett asked. "We thoroughly searched Lucas's apartment."

"It was behind the bookshelf." Garrett made a face, turned his attention back to the phone.

They both sat across from me, huddled over the phone. Pruden did the scrolling, making disgusted noises in the back of this throat. Garrett chewed at his thumbnail. Finally Pruden stood, left with the phone. He didn't explain.

Garrett pulled his chair in again, leaned across the table. His face somber. "Mia, why do you think Lucas had this phone?"

"He likely confiscated it. Who is he? What's his name?" I could see Lucas coming into the locker room, standing behind Rooster and

"Me," and seeing what they were looking at as they tapped through their catalogue of pics to send to Oz. Me noticed who was behind him, tried to send out a warning to Oz before Lucas wrenched the phone from him (causing the streak of gibberish at the end of "Haas knows"). Me fell to the ground whimpering as Lucas smacked him around.

"It won't take much to find out who Rooster and Oz are. I know who the other kid is, but I can't tell you. We need to follow this up first. Plus they're minors. Listen, why do you think Lucas wouldn't have turned the phone in earlier, when Joanna was missing and almost the entire town was looking for her? Why would he hold on to this?"

"He was probably being sensitive to her humiliation? Not to mention, he didn't trust anyone here after being harassed by you guys and thought it would just be buried as you tried to build a case against him and only him." I couldn't think of a single good reason why Lucas wouldn't have turned this phone over to the police, but there had to be one.

"You have to admit that it's strange to hang on to it when it could have helped his case and, for all he knew, helped find Joanna. If this happened in January, then he's had nearly five months to turn it over."

I shrugged; my hands went up a little too wildly and dropped back heavily into my lap. I tried very hard not to get angry, not to lose my temper. Scream, *Fix this*. "We need to find him so we can ask him. Right? I want to find my brother. I feel sick. I mean the text ended with 'Haas knows.' Don't you think that's a little ominous? And now some guy has my brother's ATM card? Lucas could be badly hurt or dead, and you guys are trawling Greyhound stations when maybe there should be search parties in Dickson Park looking for him. He went missing the same day Joanna was found. It has to be connected and not in the way you guys think it is."

An image of Lucas being struck in the back of the head with a shovel by Rooster in full hockey gear shuddered through me. I could hear it, the sound of his skull splitting. I dropped my head into my hands. My hands smelled like plum sauce from the table. I looked up again. "Do you know that even Joanna Wilkes's sister believes Lucas is innocent?"

"You've been talking to Madison Wilkes?"

"She's been at the apartment block, using the pool. She waved me down and told me exactly that. 'Mr. Haas and Joanna were *never* together. *He did not kill my sister.*' " OK, so Madison didn't say this exactly but I needed to make my point.

"I don't think Madison knows what she believes or thinks these days. She's fourteen years old and just lost her sister." Garrett gave me a look that made me feel unreasonable. "We'll talk to the players and go from there. Mia, this is definitely a new piece to the puzzle that we need to explore. If something has happened to Lucas, if he's been harmed in any way, we'll find out. I agree with you that this could change things, but I also don't want to get your hopes up that it means Lucas is no longer a person of interest. Maybe this can be chalked up to bad luck for this poor girl. A coincidence. I don't know. But I promise you, I'll do everything I can to find Lucas. I'll call you as soon as we have more information. Here." Garrett slid a fortune cookie across the table at me, his lips twitching up with encouragement. "Maybe there'll be some good news in it."

I pocketed the cookie and left.

Still in the parking lot, I called Wyatt and popped an Adderall. I needed that impenetrable tunnel vision to find Lucas, without the interference of a lingering hangover and go-to-pieces heartache. As assistant coach, he had to have known about Joanna Wilkes's assault by three of his players. Why wouldn't he have said anything to me or the police?

Someone picked up before it even rang on my end. A long silence full of heavy, wet breathing. "Hello?" No response. I asked to speak with Dad. In the background I could hear the catty shredded voices of a reality show blaring and a boy crying "Owie" over and over. I pictured Carolyn draped on the couch, trying to shut it all out. Whoever answered hung up.

I decided to try Wyatt at his work instead. Eden Green was its own low white-stuccoed building, with green shutters and a large plastic green dewdrop with a smiley face next to the entrance. Across the street was Rita's Glazed Buns, a name that had always amused us as kids.

The secretary was on the phone, looking bored as she recited the virtues of lawn aeration.

She covered the receiver. "Can I help you?"

"I'm looking for Wyatt?" But then I saw him crossing the hall behind her, in a green golf shirt and cargo shorts with a brown paper bag in one hand, tossing an apple up into the air with the other. He looked up, then quickly away, as if he hadn't seen me. As I followed him into what was obviously the lunch room, the receptionist called after me, "Miss?"

"Oh hey, Mia, it is you, thought I was seeing things. How are you?" He made a point to look up at the clock on the wall, brow furrowed like a bad impersonation of a worried, time-is-money businessman. The smell of spicy baloney emanated from his paper bag.

"Who's this kid?" I had my phone out already, flashing the Opie-looking blockhead in front of Wyatt's face.

Wyatt glanced at my phone. "Um, why?"

"Just tell me. I know you know."

"He's one of my players. Well, he will be again this fall."

"What's his name?"

Wyatt took a bite of his apple, followed by slow, measured chewing. "Cody Jackson, goalie. A really good goalie. Nice kid. Why?" I suddenly remembered Wyatt acting in a school play. He'd been as stiff and obvious as he was now.

"He assaults girls."

Wyatt swallowed, sat down at a table covered with Eden Green flyers; his leg jittered under the table. "Now, why would you go and say something like that?"

"He took pictures; the police already know. Lucas knew and took his phone away. I know he would have talked to you about this."

"He didn't. It's Joanna Wilkes, isn't it? The girl you're saying Cody assaulted?"

I didn't answer him.

"That's the only thing that makes sense to me. Midseason Lucas just up and kicked Cody Jackson and two other players off the team—good, vital players. He wouldn't say why, just that they weren't working hard enough, which wasn't true. Of course that didn't go over too well with the parents or the school administration, but the players said they agreed with Lucas, and that was that. Lucas was so tight-lipped about the whole thing. After each game we lost, I kept asking him to put those boys back on the team, but Lucas just said the same thing over and over—they didn't deserve to be part of the team. I knew he had to have something on them. One player moved out of state to play on another team, and Westfield dropped to the bottom three last season."

"He must have told you something."

"He didn't, really he didn't. I don't know why he wouldn't have told me or said anything to the admin. I mean, other than he was banging his student. He took serious flack for kicking those boys off the team."

"What are the names of the other players?" Wyatt shook his head, no.

"I don't want to get involved in this. I'll be coaching two of those players next year."

"So hockey is more important to you than Lucas? Than finding out who really murdered Joanna Wilkes?"

"If the police want to come here and ask me questions, I'll talk to them."

"But not to me?"

Wyatt shrugged.

"Why?"

"Unlike Lucas, I want to take the *proper* channels with something like this. You're just telling me these boys assaulted Joanna. I'd like some proof first."

I could have pulled my phone out and showed the disgusting images to Wyatt, but I had a feeling it wouldn't make any difference. I already had one of their names, and that was enough. "You know what, Wyatt? You're a shitty friend."

"Oh, and like you're such a great sister. Where've you been? You never came back to help him out with your mother."

I had nothing to say to that. It was true. "I'm here now. That's what matters. And I'm not leaving until I find my brother. You know what? I think you're enjoying this a little, Lucas's downfall. How long have you been his sidekick for? Huh, Wyatt? Finally, after all these years, you get to be the head coach, the main guy. Maybe even now your wife can stop fantasizing it's my brother when the lights go out."

"Get out."

A search on a reverse phone lookup, and I was sitting outside Cody Jackson's house. A faux chateau made of plastic on a treeless street. It was Wayoata's newest housing development, a gap-toothed cluster of McMansions built circa 1996. It was the kind of property Lucas had always pointed out that I could afford here. I'd harbored fantasies on the way over that Garrett and Pruden would already be there, leading this Cody kid out in cuffs. Something blunt and bloodied dangling in a plastic Ziploc from one of their hands. Case closed.

No such luck. Nothing was happening when I got there. How long would it take them to pull this kid in for questioning?

Again, I didn't have a plan. I was just there. I needed to be doing something, I needed to feel like I was looking for him. I popped another Adderall, then two more. If I'd ever needed cognitive enhancement, it was now. I needed to put it all together, the phone, the hair, the journal, the players. With nothing to do, my mind galloped along at a frenetic speed. I punched a series of searches into my phone like it was a Magic 8 Ball I was violently shaking for answers. I tried Lucas's page again as if it'd be reactivated and there'd be a selfie of him in some truck stop bathroom with *Just dyed my hair, how's it look? Heading to Mexico. YOLO.* Cody Jackson had a Facebook page. It was exactly what you'd expect—Cody drinking, videos of Cody setting off reworks, Cody playing football and hockey. At the top of his friend's list was the Joanna Wilkes's memorial page. I tapped on it.

There was a proclamation of always remembering, and x's and o's, and we miss you's. The digital hereafter was just as insincere sounding as in life. I wondered how many of these people Joanna had really been friends with; it had sounded like she didn't have many friends at all. There was video of an earlier prayer vigil, this time in the funeral home's parking lot. Clearly it was just after Joanna's service going by how creased and rumpled and sad everyone looked. There were 602 Likes. I pressed Play.

It was obviously taken with a cell phone camera. The image was jumpy and nauseating, and it looked like it was taken by someone standing a fair distance away. I did catch a glimpse of Kathy, ruddy and tear-streaked, clasping a small white container. The group held hands and prayed. A man's voice, off camera, announced that it was time to release the butterflies, calling it a flight for hope. Anyone holding a box opened it, and a sparse cloud of monarch butterflies floated upward, ascending like messengers.

I saw something that seemed off. A face looking down when everyone else was looking up. It was quick, and I couldn't be sure. I had to watch it three more times. At first I thought he was just stepping on a cigarette butt, pivoting his foot back and forth to be sure it was out, but it didn't fall to the ground like a cigarette. On my fourth viewing, I was certain it wasn't a cigarette.

One of Ben Wilkes's butterflies didn't fly up like it was supposed to, so he stepped on it. Ben, the butterfly killer. He ground it into the cement with his foot, then made a heart shape with his hands and aimed it at the sky. How fucked up was that?

14

Just after 5 P.M., the front door of the house opened. Cody Jackson came out with a skinny, sleepy-eyed girl in tow and peeled out of the driveway. I started driving behind him. Slow, and far back enough that I wasn't noticeable, as unnoticeable as you can be in a red PT Cruiser with a broken side mirror. Cody dropped the girl off at her house, his fish lips all over her before she finally got out, then continued on to a fast food restaurant (get rid of the girl, then get some food; what a cheap dick). He went inside.

I was on full Adderall speed now. The police weren't fast enough. I knew better. I was faster. I was speedy-fast-speeding. I could do this better than Pruden anyway. I should shake this kid down. *Bang, bang,* just like that. The song "Shake That Thing" rushed through my head at chipmunk speed. Fuck, I needed an Ativan to counterbalance. A pill to offset a pill to offset a pill. "Shake That Thing" was replaced by "There Was an Old Woman Who Swallowed a Fly."

Find Lucas. Find Lucas. Find Lucas.

I followed Cody Jackson inside.

He was a big kid, six foot two and over 220 pounds, at least. He'd really fill out a hockey net. Seriously, how had that tiny girl lived through an afternoon nap with him? He ordered a heaping tray of burritos and cheesy fries. Once he was sitting down, I went over.

"Cody Jackson, right?" I attempted a schoolgirl voice, but my words crashed into one another. Reminded myself to slow down. At least it gave the effect that I was nervous to talk to him, which he seemed to like.

"Uh, yeah?" A bit of burrito tumbled out of his mouth when he spoke.

I sat down across from him. "Goalie?"

He grinned, nodded, wiped his mouth with a napkin. "Yeah, that's me. What's your name?"

"Mia."

"All right." He forked some fries and twirled them around in the Day-Glo cheese sauce. "Whassup?"

"I just noticed you sitting here," I purred, leaning in and letting my breasts rest on the table, "and I had to know, is that Cody Jackson, the Westfield goalie?" Cody nodded, gave me a chubby-cheeked wink. I wanted to punch him.

"That's me in the flesh." He pushed his yellow straw up and down into the plastic lid. A squeaky simulated fucking.

"Good. Wow, I couldn't help myself. . . . I just had to know, am I really in the same restaurant as Cody Jackson, the Westfield goalie and photographer?" At this he scrunched his face. I got my phone ready with one of the least graphic pictures of Joanna and flashed it in front of his face. "And the disgusting pig who assaulted Joanna Wilkes and took pictures of it?"

"What?" He flinched back, hard, almost as if he'd been Tasered.

"I found the phone my brother took from you."

"Wait, you're Mr. Haas's sister?" He squinted, searched my face.

"That's right, asshole. Tell me where my brother is, or I'm going straight to the police."

"I have no idea where Mr. Haas is. Why would I?" He pushed his tray away.

"Tell me what happened after you sent the text 'Haas knows' to

Oz, because you know what? It looks really bad for you. It looks like you and your friends killed Joanna as payback for getting you all kicked off the team. Then suddenly my brother is gone. Did you kill him too?"

"What are you talking about? Mr. Haas killed Joanna."

"No, he didn't."

"I don't need to tell you shit."

"Fine, OK." I started to stand up, continued in a loud voice, "The police will get it out of you anyway. I mean, it's pretty clear that Joanna told my brother what you did to her, and you got really angry and killed her. You tried to set my brother up—"

"Stop saying that. Stop saying I killed Joanna." Cody cast nervous glances around the restaurant, and his face went a dark crimson purple, like he was choking. I sunk back down into the booth, watched his bottom lip droop out even farther. He was crying, making soundless airy noises, like a tire deflating. Flecks of ground beef and orange cheese glazed his tongue. He started repeating "Oh my God" over and over. Three tables away, a kid poked his head over the plastic seat and stared, a tiny cardboard sombrero that came with the kids' meal askew on his head.

"I knew I shouldn't have gone along with it. I can't believe this is happening. I just took the pictures." His head pitched forward; he covered his face.

"Gone along with what?"

He looked up at me, all doe-eyed and snively. "Last year a girl—something like that happened. She got really hammered, and some pics went around with her making out with three dudes at a party. It was bad for her. She had to be homeschooled for the rest of the year. Someone wanted us to do something like that to Joanna. They paid us. But, like, we're not rapists."

"So you what? Lured her somewhere?"

"No. Not lured."

"Tell me what happened."

"And I'll get my phone back?"

"Yes."

"Jesse Campbell asked Joanna to his house party. She said yes, because all the chicks say yes to Jesse, and we knew she was off with that douche, Dylan. So he poured her really strong drinks, she got hammered fast. I seriously think that was, like, the first time she'd had alcohol. Which is funny because she was selling weed outta her locker. Anyway, Jesse took her into his little brother's room. Joanna kind of just flopped down on the bed, totally wasted. She just sort of passed out. I think Jesse might have added something more to her drink, I don't know, but she was out. Then that's when we did what we were paid to do."

"Who paid you?"

"I don't know. None of us know. Whoever wanted it done sent an e-mail to Jesse. The money was taped under a bench in that park by Wilson Elementary."

"How much were you paid?" Lucas and I had both attended Wilson Elementary; it practically shared the backfield with the high school. It was where the lunch lady worked as a night janitor. Had she done this?

"We each got five hundred bucks, in total. Two fifty before, two fifty after. But we didn't get the second payment because the next day was Saturday and we had practice. We slept in. Jesse didn't even get up at all for it and missed the whole practice. So we were gonna e-mail the pics after practice but then Haas found us looking at them in the dressing room, asked if they were the only pics, and took my phone. Couple days later, he kicked us off the team, said if he ever saw or heard anything about the pictures again, he would turn my phone in to the cops and we'd be charged with child porn. He said he was making us a deal. So obviously we didn't have any pics to e-mail back, and we didn't get our second payment."

"Did my brother know you were paid?"

"No. No one knows."

"It doesn't exactly look like you're hurting for money, so why would you agree to do it?"

"I'm saving for college." He jutted his chin out, like saying this made him sound good. This kid had a car, brand-name clothes, money for a tray full of burritos; surely there were other corners to cut before he resorted to rapist for hire.

"So why you guys?"

"I dunno," he mumbled. "Like I said, Jesse gets girls." There could be more to this, but I didn't think so. Most of the time horrible things happened due to stupid, weak reasoning like this.

"How were you contacted?"

"E-mail. Jesse got the e-mail. I probably wouldn't even have been in on it, but I was there when he got it, and he offered, and I just couldn't turn down the money." Cody felt the need to reiterate.

"Oh, so you're a victim of circumstance."

He shrugged. "I'm telling you, we didn't have anything to do with Joanna's murder. Mr. Haas did it. I know he's your brother, and you don't want to hear it, but that's what everyone's saying. I mean, he really overreacted, kicking us off the team. Like I said, we didn't, you know, touch her in any way."

"But you poured SpaghettiOs on her vagina and took pictures of it."

A slight tremor of something on his sticky lips, the start of a smile? Or was he going to cry again? He had one of those faces, the kind that looked on the brink of some kind of strong emotional outburst. "Whoever it was wanted that part in it."

"Why?"

"I don't know? We didn't ask. It was harmless. I mean it wasn't like she was actually raped or anything. The whole thing was weird. I thought it was Dylan, to be honest. He wanted her to go out with another guy and have a bad experience and run back to him."

Which she had done. I stood up. I needed to tell Garrett this.

"Wait, can I have my phone back?"

"Oh, right." I fake-rummaged through my bag, pulled out my middle finger. "Oops, I already gave it to the police."

As I pushed through the greasy glass door, Cody yelled, "Bitch."

Garrett's house was a well-kept Craftsman with a cruiser parked in front of the jutting garage. I rang the doorbell twice, heard a dog bark inside, and was about to leave when he answered in a towel. Rivulets of water still rolled down his broad, sculpted chest. A chocolate lab poked its fleshy nose out at me. Garrett hissed, "Down," and the dog lowered itself to the floor.

"I tried calling," I explained. I had, three times. Each call turned over to voice mail. I'd tried the station, and the receptionist said he'd gone home. Relying on that NoDak need to be helpful, I just asked her where Garrett lived and she told me. I glanced at his towel, made a concentrated effort not to gawk at his action-hero chest, but it was too distracting. A chest like that was a discussion piece. Something to be appreciated. I cleared my throat. "Do you want me to come back?"

"No, that's fine. Come on in." He led me into his living room, quickly gathered up papers off the coffee table, and stuffed them into a file, then dropped the file on a side table. "I'm not usually so messy, but the case . . ." His voice dropped off, and he took a sharp breath in through his teeth. "Anyway, I'll be a second. Have a seat." He motioned toward the couch, then disappeared down the hall.

Garrett's house was bigger than it looked from the outside. Vaulted ceilings and a stone fireplace gave it a cottagey feel. The living room was messy. There were newspapers and files all over the place in piles of various heights, a week's worth of clothes draped over the back of a plaid recliner, and another week's over the kitchen chairs.

Garrett returned freshly shaven, in a gray T-shirt and jeans, still barefoot. Extra clean-cut. "Want a Coke? I'd offer you a beer, but y'know, I wouldn't want you to black out."

"No thanks." He sat down in a chair across from me.

"So what's up?"

"I just talked to Cody Jackson."

"You didn't." He groaned, leaned back into the chair, looked up to the ceiling. "Goddamn it, Mia. I told you not to do that. I thought you were here because you finally wanted to tell me how you knew about Joanna's pregnancy."

"He told me that they were paid for it."

"Well, that's great! Now that's he talked to you, he's gonna start thinking up something to make himself look better. He now has time to talk to his friends, and they'll cover each other's asses. We talked to Cody's mom, and she's bringing Cody in tomorrow morning. I told you that we would handle this. Fuck." A vein throbbed in the middle of his forehead. "You think you're helping your brother, but you're making things worse."

"I'll be a witness if they try to change their story." My eyes were starting to throb. The Adderall swimming around in my blood was starting to feel like a school of piranhas, and I was trying not to go all hot and fidgety. I did feel chastened. Having come down a few notches from the Adderall high, I realized I'd done a very stupid thing, and maybe Cody would try to cover his ass, but the kid seemed so dim I wasn't too worried he'd do a good job of it.

"Right, because you'd be considered unbiased? It doesn't work that way. Tell me what exactly he said."

"They were each paid two hundred fifty dollars to put Joanna in a humiliating position. Cody thought it was Dylan." I explained about the e-mail. "It requested the SpaghettiOs."

"That's a lot of money for someone like Dylan, especially paid out to three people. The SpaghettiOs—I mean, I don't even know what to say about that other than it's completely fucked up. But I guess that was the point."

"Dylan deals drugs. He'd have the money, and he was obsessed with Joanna. I know he stalked her. When she first broke it off with him, he shamed her into coming back to him, then when she dumped him again, he tried stalking. When stalking didn't work, he killed her."

"First, Dylan isn't much of drug dealer. I doubt he'd have that kind of money, but let's say he had something to do with this. It still doesn't change the fact that he has an alibi for the night of Joanna's murder. These pictures of Joanna might not have anything to do with her murder."

"Maybe his dad helped him out. Maybe Greg Yates killed Joanna for his son."

"Mia." Garrett sighed.

"Or what if Dylan and Greg Yates hired someone to kill Joanna because she dumped Dylan? Or maybe over some drug deal gone bad? And when they saw it looked like Lucas was being considered as a suspect, they just killed him. Made him disappear, so it looks like he's on the run."

"I think that's a highly convoluted and unlikely theory. I can check their phone records, e-mails, see if anything aligns with these hockey players. We can question Dylan about these pictures. We will look into it, and by 'we,' I mean the WPD. Either way, Mia, this doesn't undo the evidence against Lucas. I think you know that."

I sat there, quiet. The lab came and put his head in my lap. I stroked his velvety ear, not minding the streaks of drool left on my pants.

"Now can you tell me how you found out Joanna was pregnant? I need to know."

I was about to tell him the lie I came up with: Eric told me. That Joanna had confided in the school counselor and I didn't want to jeopardize Eric's job (*we've become close the last few days, y'know*) and so on, but Garrett's phone rang.

He dug it out of his pants, swore under his breath. "Just a sec. OK?" He stood and walked out of the room.

I could leave, right now. Avoid lying. I could overhear Garrett talking in a low drone somewhere down the hall.

I eyed the file Garrett had left on the end table. I moved to the end of the couch and lifted the file's tab. It fell open to the photograph of Joanna Wilkes lying on a metal slab in the morgue. Her face a puffy, swollen mess. Waterlogged. Broken blood vessels spidered all over her face, and her neck was a pulpy purple-black. Her hair, what was left of it, looked like it had been hacked at with a hunting knife. Its long-short patchiness reminded me of a cherished Barbie doll that Lucas had once cut the hair off of when we were kids. It came out of nowhere, this memory. He'd propped the half-sheared doll in the middle of my bed and waited in my closet until I found her. Watched me as I wailed. Snickering.

Garrett came back into the room and snatched the folder from me. "You can't look at that."

"I'm sorry. It was just there. I shouldn't have looked." My voice went weedy, my legs soft and boneless. I had to tell myself to breathe. I really shouldn't have looked. "Why the hair? Why do you think whoever did this cut off her hair?"

"I think, to be honest, it was a trophy. Something to remember the murder by, or else it was something to remember Joanna herself. Her red hair, I guess, was sort of her trademark. It was what people noticed first about her."

"I should go." I whispered this; my voice wasn't working. I bumped into the coffee table on the way to the door.

"Wait, Mia, you need to tell me about how you knew Joanna was pregnant. Think about it. We'll find out anyway if Lucas was the father. Why get yourself in trouble over this? And who knows, maybe in conjunction with the phone we'll be able to eliminate Lucas as a suspect completely." It was a good try, but Garrett sounded way too artificial, too Splenda-coated, to trust. Plus finding something in my brother's day planner was in no way going to get him scratched off their one-person suspect list.

"Eric. Eric told me." I left his house before he could question me further.

Up until then, I'd been trying not to think of Joanna as a real person. I'd only been focused on Lucas, and Joanna was the meat hook I was trying to unsnag my brother from. But now, thinking what her last months were like, and the fetus that had been beating along inside her, I felt overwhelming sadness.

That poor, poor girl.

My head was starting to hurt. I was hungry for something. More pills or maybe just food. When had I last eaten? I needed something to take back to Lucas's if I was going to stay put at the apartment for a while. I obviously couldn't go to the more convenient Harold's so instead braved Target, where at any given time, half the town was shopping.

I wheeled an ambulance-red cart with a wayward front wheel around, loading it with the kind of food I'd eat when I shut myself in and was going through withdrawal or a painful craving. When I'd spend all day bingeing on Netflix and sugar. I grabbed chips and white powdered donuts, Gatorade and bananas, four premade sandwiches that would expire the next day, dark M&M's, and Swedish Berries. At the last minute, I added a salad kit I knew I wouldn't eat, just to see a pop of natural green among all that hypercolored food dye and white bread. I lingered for a minute by the cold medicine, peeking into the pharmacy. Professional curiosity, I guess. I had to check in at work. I would. I just wasn't up to it yet. I listened in as a young, clearly inexperienced technician instructed a woman to take her iron pills on an empty stomach with a full glass of water. When the technician was finished, I coasted up behind the woman. "Iron pills can feel like a bag of nails in your gut. Better to take them on a full stomach, with orange juice. The vitamin C helps absorb the iron. Grab a laxative too."

The woman swung around, gave me an appreciative smile. If she recognized me, she pretended not to. "Thanks. It's my darn Aunt Flo—it's just so heavy." I could never understand why women felt the need to use a euphemism for a period. "I'll keep that in mind."

"You betcha." You betcha? Where the fuck did that come from?

I pulled into a checkout, but the cashier, a woman with severe zebra highlights, pulled out the CHECKOUT CLOSED sign as I was about to load my groceries on the conveyor belt. She looked at me and snapped her gum, daring me to do something about it. I backed out and went through the self-serve.

Outside in the parking lot, a man was leaning up against the PT. Mid-fifties, bald, dressed like he'd just come from a bowling alley. He gave me a big toothy smile. "I saw you inside the store, recognized you from the TV." This man stretched the word out in a goading way, *Teee Veee*. I didn't like this. "I figured this must be your car, and I was right." He snickered, his arms snapping up in mock-surrender style, and moved away from the PT Cruiser. It took a second to get what he meant, but then I saw all the glass. The back window of my car had been smashed in. Glass was everywhere, all over the backseat. I felt a surge of panic. Joanna's lock of hair, her journal. Enough to put my brother away for a very long time. It took a dizzying amount of self-control not to fling myself into the car and check that the garbage bag was still under the seat.

"Tom Geller." The man reached out his hand. A medical bracelet glinted. I didn't take his hand. He made a *meh* sound. "Guess you're not so well liked here." Again, that smirk.

"Stop following me."

"I don't know what you're talking about. This is a happy coincidence." He leaned against the side of the Cruiser again, put his hands in his pockets and started to jingle some loose change.

"I'm warning you to stay the fuck away from me."

"Whoa, whoa, settle down. This is a just a friendly reminder that your brother's debt is now at four grand. Might not seem like a lot to someone like you, but it's best to deal with these things before they get out of control."

"Four grand?"

"That's right."

"And what does four grand get me?" My mind started working. Maybe Garrett was wrong, maybe Tom figured the police were monitoring Lucas's account, so he was waiting until I was desperate and scared enough to pay him off. No questions asked. No police.

"It gets your brother debt-free."

"That's it?"

He tilted his head. "What do you mean that's it? Being debt-free is a beautiful thing, doncha know?" Then offered me up a greasy smile.

"Will it get me my brother back?"

Geller made sucking sound with his lips, like he was thinking about it. "That I can't say. Up to him isn't it?"

I stared him down. Tried to think of a way to ask if he was holding my brother for ransom, without outright asking because it seemed like we were talking in some kind of criminal-speak where you didn't use incriminating words. I couldn't come up with an innocuous simile for ransom. "That's not good enough for me. If I give you the four grand you're asking me for, I want my brother back. Isn't that how ransoming works?

"What now?" He hooted, loud. His eyes went watery like I'd just said something hilarious. "If I had your brother, you really think I'd be asking for a measly four grand? Tell me how that makes any sense?"

I didn't say anything. Worried I'd just driven up the price or else he was telling the truth and this whole conversation was useless. "How do I know Lucas even owes you money?" I tried, hoping he'd set up a phone call with Lucas or offer another kind of proof that he was alive and well and then I'd pay him anything he wanted.

Geller stared me down, his tongue running over his front teeth. "You called me remember?" He let that hang there for a second. "Let me make this real simple fer ya, when this sort of situation arises in my business, the loan always goes to next of kin, and I'm not someone you want to owe money to." He shifted, his foot crunching on glass. Another blast of dread that the journal and hair were gone, that Geller had them and his next move was going to be classic extortion. Worse, he really didn't have them and there was someone else out there running straight to the police station with them.

"Fine, fine." I started digging through my purse, the plastic grocery bags swinging violently on my wrists. I pulled out forty bucks and tried to hand it to him. Geller tipped forward on his toes, peered at the money and balked. "It's all I have on me." I threw the money at him and it landed in a wet parking lot pothole. My voice had gone shrill. I didn't even sound like myself. A woman pushing a squeaky cart shot me a dirty look. This was how it must feel right before you snapped. Blind frustration. I was being reckless. Really, this guy could have pulled a gun or a knife or just attacked me. He'd already tried to run me off the road! I'd let the publicness of the parking lot make me feel safer than I really was, because I seriously doubted anyone would come to my aid if this guy tried anything.

Tom just stared at me, two beats long, like he was trying to decide something. "Well, I'll be seeing you soon. Take care of that window."

He bent down, pocketed the cash, and whistled as he walked toward his silver car. Not a black monster truck, but a silver sedan.

I flung open the driver's door, bent down, my knees crunching into a spray of glass on the pavement. Heart-in-my-throat frantic, I dug around under the seat, glass scraping against my palms until I felt the plastic bag.

It was still there. Thank God, it was still there.

Back at the apartment, Madison Wilkes was at the pool again (I had to think she left at some point?), joined now by two of her friends. It was half past eight in the evening and getting too dark to swim. They had arranged themselves in a tableau of sexy poses on the loungers. Knees bent, leaning back on elbows, passing a bottle of raspberry-flavored vodka between them. Bailey was there too, wearing mannish khaki shorts and an oversized green T-shirt. Her hair pulled into a tight ponytail at the back of her head. From where I was, she looked like she could be the hapless forest ranger, not at all clued in that she was the butt of the joke.

Madison was pointing. "There, get it out—it's fucking gross." A pair of tighty-whitey underwear was floating in the middle of the pool. Bailey was standing next to the deep end, wielding a net, trying to scoop it out. Snagging it, she brought it up, dropped it poolside like it was a big ugly catfish. The girls squealed. Madison stood up, hand on hip. "Well, you can't leave it there. Throw it out." Bailey picked it up with one finger and thumb and held it away from her as she ran to the garbage can that was chained to the fence.

One of the other girls let out a shriek. "That's so gross. She touched it with her hands." The other one fake sneezed the word "dyke."

I felt a burst of protectiveness and had a brief urge to call out Bailey's name, whisk her away from the catty taunts. Even serve up a dire warning on bullying, but I was too full of self-defeated heaviness, a chin-in-my-chest grief that had, for now, punctured all of my rage. I felt like a runny abscess on legs. I'd probably do more harm than good. No fourteen-year-old girl wins over the popular crowd by getting bailed out by an adult. Never mind one who was the sister of the suspected murderer of the queen bee's sister. My thoughts were going soggy too.

As I passed, Madison had gone stone quiet, her X-ray eyes on me. I had an overtired paranoid thought that she could tell what was in the bag based on the way it was shaped. I gripped it and hustled by.

Again, I checked the Scotch tape on my door before entering—still intact.

I needed darkness, my head felt like it was creaking, like I could actually hear fine little fissures spreading along the inside of my skull. I went into Lucas's room, pulled his blinds, and lay down. I took Advil for my headache, half an Ativan, half an Ambien (it was a triple-A sort of night), and a shot of rye and slept. A hard, sweaty kind of sleep. I woke up six hours later, in the middle of a dream of Lucas standing before me, arms out, with something in his hands. Tangled seaweed. No, hair, dangling between his fingers like crimped tendrils. "Here, take it," he kept repeating. "Take it."

15

DAY 7

TUESDAY

It was almost 2 A.M. Someone was knocking on my door. This time, I looked through the peephole before opening it. It was Bailey. I opened the door just a crack, and the plastic bag crinkled under my hand where I'd left it hanging when I came in earlier, blurry-eyed with migraine, post-pill-binge aura.

"Yes?" I looked behind her for dear old Dad, but it was just her.

"I want to apologize about my dad the night before."

"Don't worry about it. It's OK, and you're not the one who should be apologizing anyway."

But Bailey wasn't listening. Her eyes were traveling all over the place; she looked panicked. She cut me off. "Can you help us? Please?"

Was she asking if I could help her and her father? Still in the midst of a heavy brain fog, I wasn't sure, but then I saw who she meant. Slumped against the wall, on the ground next to the door, was Madison. Her coltish legs were splayed out at an odd angle. Her head had pitched forward, and her blond hair fell over her face like she was a puppet put away. I stepped out of the apartment just as Bailey lifted Madison up, like it was nothing, and brought her inside. She dropped her onto the couch. "She took something—I don't know what. You're, like, a doctor, right? Can you help her?"

"No, I'm not a doctor! I'm a pharmacist. I'm calling an ambulance." I went for my phone on the coffee table. Bailey grabbed my arm, her face full of the desperate anguish only a teenager could muster. "You can't. Her mom will kill her. *Please, please doooon't.* I mean, just look at her first. *Please!*"

Already I was thinking it wouldn't look good that when a drunken teenage girl found herself in trouble in the middle of the night, she would knock on Lucas's door. I knelt down and rubbed Madison's sternum with my fist to try to wake her up. Her breathing was even, but she was unresponsive. Close up, she reeked like cough-syrupy alcopops and hairspray. Her eyelids looked weighed down by a thick crust of metallic eye shadow: smoky eyes.

I asked Bailey again if she had any idea what Madison could have taken, but Bailey had backed up close to the door, looking terrified. Her hands tucked behind her, pressed into the wall. I dug through Madison's pockets and found a white, half-crushed pill, definitely Vicodin. "How much did she take?" I held the pill out at Bailey.

"I don't know. I didn't see her take anything."

I ran to the bathroom, rummaged through my red makeup case. I kept naloxone with my pill stash, which I guess was an admission of sorts that my pharmacy degree didn't exempt me from losing control or mixing up my pill pairings. It made little sense, though, because I lived alone, and if I was overdosing, it was unlikely I'd be able to self-administer it. Still, it was like an expired EpiPen; probably useless but it just made me feel better having it on hand. Back in the living room, I administered two shots in each of Madison's delicate nostrils.

This roused her. Her stomach started making heaving noises. "She needs to throw up." Bailey and I carried Madison to the bathroom, where she threw up a watery, yellow mess. "Get some water." I had Madison drink three glasses of water before I arranged her on the couch on her side and put a pillow behind her so she couldn't roll onto her back.

I spotted the plastic bag hanging from the door. *Fuck*. I got up and ran over to it. "Just a sec," I mumbled to Bailey, and stuffed it in one of Lucas's dresser drawers.

"Can I sleep on the floor next to Mads?" Bailey panted, oddly cheery. Like this could still turn into a pillow-fight, Oreo-gorgefest variety of slumber party.

"That's a good idea." There was no way I was going to be here alone with Madison Wilkes overnight. "Where were you both, anyway?" Bailey was still in the same shirt/khaki combo, while Madison looked like she was dressed for her first number on a stripper pole.

"A party," she answered. I tried to press her further, but she was skittish about giving out details. "Can I turn on the TV? I can't sleep without it."

"Keep it on low." I handed her the remote. She turned it to the Home Shopping Network, drew the sheet up that I gave her, and closed her eyes to a pantsuited woman purring over a five-piece quilted luggage set.

I monitored Madison for another hour, sitting in the beat-up recliner across from her. When I was sure she was stable and in a deep sleep—she'd be sleeping it off for hours—I decided it was safe to go back to bed.

I half woke again, no idea of the time, sensing movement next to me. A light gust of air brushed against my neck, mascara-stiff eyelashes prickled against my skin, the weight of an arm wrapped tight around my stomach. I felt a dreamy calmness that I wasn't alone. My eyes flicked open, wide. I was being spooned.

I rolled away, looked behind me. "Madison?" Her eyes were open, her face lit up by the strange light from the sole parking lot lamppost coming in between the slates of the blind. In the semidarkness of Lucas's bedroom, she looked nothing like she had before. Now she looked like a feverish child. Her makeup had rubbed off, and pressed against the pillow (my pillow!), her cheeks looked fuller. Almost moonfaced. She looked like her sister. I wanted to run from the room.

I looked at the drawer where I'd put the plastic bag, my vision full of squiggles. It didn't look like it'd been opened. I fought an urge to check.

"Can you tickle my neck?" She twirled the end of her hair into her mouth and sucked.

I sat up. "What are you doing in here?"

"I'm sorry, I just miss her so much. So much. We used to do this. I'd come into her room if I had a bad dream and we'd take turns tickling each other's necks." Her voice was weepy. "Did you and Mr. Haas do things like that when you were young?"

"I'm sorry if you had a nightmare, but I think it's better if you go back to the couch, Madison." I pressed my back farther into the headboard.

"No, please, don't. I'm afraid." She reached up and gripped my wrist and started sobbing, loud, bed-quaking sobs. "I thought you'd understand."

"OK. Fine. You can stay here, just for a little while. All right? Just until you feel better, then back to the couch. Or why don't I call your parents? They're probably very worried about you."

"No, don't bother. They don't give a shit about me. I could disappear, and they wouldn't even care. I hate being at home. My mom is always angry and crying. My dad's gone, like, totally silent. I'm sick of Officer Burke being there all the time. He sits in my sister's room for, like, hours, like, on the edge of her bed, just looking around, for what, I don't know. It upsets my brother that he's in her bedroom. No one even notices I'm never there." She buried her face in the pillow. I could see Garrett, crossing over from dedicated to obsessed, desperate to spot something in Joanna's bedroom as if it could all come down to a *Where's Waldo?* moment. I wanted to say something consoling, tell Madison that the downward spiral of her family would eventually end. Even get better. But I didn't believe it. There were things that people did not recover from.

"I'm sure that's not true. I'm sure they'd be very worried. What you did was very dangerous. Those pills are not something you should be messing around with. Why did you take them?"

"I don't know. Maybe part of me just wanted to die, like Joanna.

It's not like anyone would notice. It's just Joanna, Joanna, everywhere I go. You know what people say to me? Your sister is an angel now. She was a drug dealer, and now it's like that never happened. Maybe I want that too. To be perfect."

"Don't say that. You can't mean that. You're actually quite lucky. Your friend Bailey really saved you tonight. You might not be here if it wasn't for her."

"She's not my friend." Her head snapped up off the pillow.

"You're not friends?"

Madison dropped down again, flipped onto her back. "Ugh, no. Bailey is, like, obsessed with me. I think she's a lesbian. She made us friendship bracelets that are so lame." She lazily stretched her arm out, but I couldn't really see it. It was lost anyway among a stack of other bracelets that extended partway up her arms and made a jingling sound as she dropped her arm again. "She's, like, I made these so we will always remember this year, and I'm, like, whatever. She even dyed her hair to match mine. I hate it."

"Well, imitation is a form of flattery right? Anyway, I think you should get back to the couch now."

"What was Mr. Haas like in high school?" She was trying to stay longer, I knew that. But I couldn't resist plugging my brother's virtues.

"Popular, athletic, and very kind."

"What were you like in high school?"

"Hmm . . . I don't know what to tell you. Mostly I just studied because I wanted to get out of here."

"I looked up your graduating class on the wall at school. You're much prettier now." Of course this was what mattered, not the journey out of Wayoata, college, or a career in the big city.

"Thank you. Are you ready to go back to the couch yet?"

"Are you and Mr. Lowe getting it on?"

"What? No. Where did you hear something like that?"

"It's OK. I think it's a good thing. It might make him stop trying to counsel me." She said it in a way that hinted to something lascivious that made me squeamish. My skin twitched.

"OK, Madison, I really think it's time for you to go back to the couch." I was about to climb over her if I had to and turn on the light.

She ignored me. "Sometimes, when I'm trying to make myself feel better, I think maybe it was all for the better, Joanna dying."

"Why would you say something like that?"

"She was terrified of disappointing our mother, and now she never will. No one else knows this, but I saw a pregnancy test in the bathroom garbage at the dance studio. I knew it was hers. She tried to hide it by wrapping it all up in toilet paper and two maxi-pad wrappers but I saw it." There was something so unseemly about this girl going through her sister's garbage with the thoroughness of a crime scene investigator. I had to bite my tongue to stop myself from saying so because I needed her to tell me what she knew. "It was positive. I asked her if she was gonna start, like, vitamins or whatever or get an abortion, but she just screamed at me like a maniac. She was crazy pissed at me. She shook me so hard my teeth rattled."

My body clenched. "Do you know who the father was?"

"I don't know. I wasn't gonna ask after that. Dylan, probably. I thought she was still a virgin, but then there were rumors that she was having sex with a bunch of different guys."

I was suddenly grateful to her, that she hadn't gone around telling people Joanna was pregnant. It would have made things even worse for Lucas.

"It would have totally destroyed my mother if she found out her prima ballerina was with child."

Odd wording, that—"with child"—and I could feel Madison was trying to endear herself to me. Make herself sound sweetly precocious.

"My mom was a teenage mom too. She wanted to dance professionally. It ruined her life."

"I'm sure it didn't." Technically, if I remembered correctly, Kathy was just out of her teens when she got hastily married. It was something the town paid attention to, felt good about. All that money, and their daughter gets into that kind of trouble as well.

"No. It did. It would have ruined Joanna's too."

I didn't know how to respond. If it made her feel better to think that, then I didn't want to take that away.

"Every family has its secrets right? That's what they say. I hope Jo, wherever she is now, knows I kept hers. Oops. Well, I guess except for telling you. But you won't tell anyone, will you? Promise?"

"Promise."

She started hugging my arm, gave a little-girl sigh. "I just feel so close to you. No one else could ever understand what we're going through. Tickle my neck?"

I forced her up and back to the couch. I tucked her in tight, and when she asked for a kiss, I pressed my lips to her forehead and said, "Sleep tight."

When I woke up again, Madison and Bailey were gone. So were five of my Ambien that I carelessly left out on my brother's nightstand.

16

I checked the drawer, opened the plastic bag. The hair and journal were still there. The flap of the envelope was still tucked inside so it didn't look like it'd been messed with. Even so, I wished I had licked the glue seal and then I'd know for sure. I dug around Lucas's kitchen for anything with caffeine, and the best thing I came up with was an energy bar. No pills today! I said this to myself with the springy bark of a boot camp instructor all up in your face. No pills. None. Today I was going on the straight and narrow. I was going to find my brother.

I carefully extricated the journal from the plastic bag, to avoid seeing or touching the hair, and dropped it onto the coffee table. The English writing journal was always such a joke because the teacher got to skip out on the last fifteen or twenty minutes of class, intoning, "Think, explore," just before taking off for a cigarette.

I started flipping through the pages. Reading random parts. It was all hand printed. *These kids can't read cursive writing. It's like some ancient hieroglyphic to them,* Lucas had told me, incredulous.

At first it had the sanitized treatment of a school journal with the requisite exploratory responses to novels.

> Lord of the Flies *is, in some ways, a lot like dance tryouts. The savage girl in all pink taffeta, her flexed toes pointed like spears, her tight scalp-pinching bun rests on her head like a plush throne ready to receive the crown she is vying for (a solo!), her glittery makeup, red, red lips like warrior paint. Ready to do battle.*

I skipped to the next entry.

> *. . . Lennie Small reminds me of my brother: big and oafish and totally capable of killing something from overpetting it. (Who would ever let Lennie run a rabbit farm?! That would be an all-around bad business decision.) OK, just kidding (humor is my only defense against such a depressing book!). But I do worry about my brother sometimes. He's, well, delayed in some ways, and that makes him a little vulnerable to manipulative people. He likes to do what's asked of him, without thinking much about what he's being asked to do. Does that make sense?*
>
> *ANYWAY . . . On the bright side (of a very dark book), my own personal economic "depression" has ended—I just got my first job! So excited. I can work during my spares! My boss is already hinting toward a promotion. Paycheck = I-N-D-E-P-E-N-D-E-N-C-E.*
>
> *p.s. Full disclosure: You said the only rule to apply to our journal writing was to be honest writers. So here goes . . . I didn't finish the book. Not yet anyway. I bailed when I overheard someone talking about a dead puppy. I wasn't sure what was worse, you knowing I didn't read it and getting a bad mark or thinking I did and had such a lame response. I will try (against all odds!) to finish before our essays are due.*

Several entries, four months' worth, extolled the virtues of her BF, Dylan. He was the only one who really understood her, who let her be her. All was big bubbly letters and hearts. Then it was over with Dylan.

> *. . . I am trapped behind glass, waving a white flag. I see you go on like it was nothing, and my heart breaks. You said it was forever, but forever for you is four months. You let her get to you, I know it. All feeling gone, an empty heart.*

The sanitized feel had loosened up. Turned increasingly candid. Like a reality star who claims to forget the cameras are even there, Joanna seemed to be doing the same thing, ignoring the fact that her journal wasn't private. Three quarters of it was about her mom.

> *My mom wants me to be part of her grand delusion that I am going to be famous. Anytime I try to tell her that I'm not good enough, it's like she can just blink that truth away. Just like that, three rapid blinks, and the delusion is back, intact, and I'm forced back on board. I have to show her. Somehow.*
>
> *I tried going out with a friend after dance class. Just a friend, but oh no, my mother had to join us for hot chocolate. She talks about all the other girls in the class, and I get so embarrassed.*
>
> *My mom took me shopping (she never just gives me a credit card and lets me go like she does for Madison—no, she wants to come with me). She actually makes me feel bad if I say I'd rather go with friends, then she'll make some excuse that she can't give me any money. I'll point out that I would get a job if I could, if she didn't make me practice all the time. (She doesn't know about my job so I have to keep asking her for money, so she doesn't suspect anything. It sucks having money I really can't spend.*

But makes saving a cinch.) We'll fight, and somehow I end up with her at the mall buying things I don't want to be seen in. I cried in the change room, as I took off a white blouse she insisted that I get. I didn't want it. It was way too young for me. But she bought it anyway, and she thinks I'm wearing it right now, because that's what she wanted me to wear today. She actually put an outfit out on my bed today! I'm sixteen years old! Who does that? I'm so glad she hasn't caught on that I change at school.

Maybe I'm too hard on my mom. I won first place last week in Minneapolis!! The judges' comments were amazing, and I felt incredible. I didn't even like the dance she choreographed, but I guess she was right. Sometimes she is right. I forget that.

UGH! I can't even believe I wrote that last week. Things are terrible again. She wants to send me to rehab! Who goes to rehab for weed? (Sorry—I know we aren't supposed to include any "illegal doings" in here that you would have to report, but the drugs found in my locker are pretty common knowledge at this point.) I told her I don't need rehab, I just need more spending money. She doesn't listen. She just blames Dylan, but he didn't have anything to do with it. You know what? It was fun. I liked being a drug dealer. I liked being seen as less than perfect. I even got along better with the girls at the studio. There, I said it. (Don't report me.)

My mom has sicced my brother on me like a guard dog. He watches me. He drives by the school parking lot all the time to make sure my car is still in the lot. I think he likes it. Watching me. I hate her.

Ben, the butterfly squasher. He was a big boy. Took after his mother, more so than his twiggy father. The only entry on Madison read:

In a way I wish I could be more like her. She does what she wants. Yesterday I didn't get home from the studio until eleven at night to reheated steamed vegetables and a salmon patty, while Madison got to have her friends over (all her loyal followers) and bake frosted cupcakes, her lips and fingers all pink from gorging on all that icing. She thinks our mother favors me. Even when she's trying to be spiteful toward me all I want to do is trade places with her. She came into my bedroom and ate a cupcake in front of me (which doesn't sound terrible, but she knows I'm on another one of Kathy's "special diets"), relishing each and every nibble. All I want to do is trade places with her. "You're so gifted," Madison will say to me, but in a way that's kinda mean. She's so lucky she can't dance.

The tone of the journal shifted after her assault in January. Entries were left half finished, it looked like she just dropped off. Like she couldn't be bothered to continue or didn't have the energy. She quoted sad lyrics from songs and filled the margins with drawings of girls with really large, watery eyes. When Joanna and Dylan reunited, things lightened up again, but Joanna sounded wiser. She never retreated into the puppy and rainbow thing of their early romance.

By February, the entries grew increasingly personal toward Lucas.

You wanted to know when I last felt safe. I'll tell you. . . .

I think I felt safest when I spent my summers at my grandparents' lake house. Carefree days by the dock with cucumber sandwiches and tall glasses of lemonade. The smell of my grandfather's cigar smoke that everyone hated but I kinda liked. This was before Kathy totally hijacked my life. Then it was summers in the studio, all day long. Before the whirlwind dance conferences in LA and NYC, and those midnight flights back to Wayoata so I didn't miss school. When the days were all loose and easy.

My favorite room in the lake house was the attic, under

a circular skylight. At night, if it was a full moon, it would look like this giant orb glowing on the floorboards. I'd lie in the middle of it and stare up at the starry sky through this massive *peephole. It had this fairy-tale feeling, like I could slip through it, upward into the stars, into an alternate universe, and return with special powers that'd make me great at everything I tried. Or else I could almost convince myself I was moving. I was in a spaceship traveling away, up, up, and away. Whatever. Kid stuff. Still, it was like nothing could touch me when I was inside the orb.*

I will never feel safe like that again.

Other entries were like listening in on a frustratingly one-sided phone conversation on the bus.

You know that thing I mentioned yesterday? Well, never mind. It doesn't matter anymore. I've been thinking about what you said, and it's true—it's better not to worry so much. Great advice. (You're so much more helpful than Eric, who just asks a bunch of questions, then never says anything other than trying to get me to listen to lame music when I want advice. LOL)

What thing? What advice? What should Joanna stop worrying about? And not that I thought Eric's music therapy was exclusive to me, but I couldn't help feeling a little crestfallen. It seemed almost pitiful that it was something he still routinely pulled. Was he really trying to connect with kids through music (music their parents listened to?), or was he just trying to get out of doing any actual work? Or worse, was he straining to still come across as the youthful, cool teacher? (I did notice yesterday he was wearing a leather wristband!) And here my brain started to fizz like an Alka-Seltzer—was the music thing what he did with girls he took a special interest in? Girls he thought were especially "self-possessed" and could handle a more "mature" relationship with him. Wasn't it weird that he'd slept with me? I was his ex-student! But then Zoey was Lucas's ex-student. I couldn't have it both ways. I read the next line.

> *I thought about you before I fell asleep last night, and I felt safe. I felt like you were right, that it might all be OK. I just need to wait it out.*

Wait what out? Her mother? High school? So she and Lucas could run off together?

There were also several references to various injuries:

> *I know, I know, I'm on crutches again. :(THANKS for helping me this morning with my books. . . .*
>
> *. . . SORRY for the sloppy writing. At least I have an excuse—my wrist is sprained (again!). . . .*
>
> *. . . THANKS for letting me sit in your classroom over gym class. Bummed though that I have this stomach infection. . . .*

She brought up an "accident" that involved her BFF Abby. That was how she wrote it, in quotations, meaning it might not really be an accident:

> *. . . Sometimes I just want to get Abby and Mrs. Peters alone, explain everything, but Abby just looks at me like she's scared of me. Then sometimes I get angry—like how could Abby really think I was involved? That I would just stand by and let my mother do that to her? She knows me better than that, or least I thought so. I guess my mom really is making sure we are heading toward some Grey Gardens existence. (See! I told you I didn't fall asleep during the movie, which for obvious reasons, I hated!☺)*
>
> *If you weren't there for me . . . Well, like you say, "what if" are the two most dangerous words when put together.*

Why would her friend be scared of her? What did Kathy do? When did Lucas start peddling self-help clichés?

> *OMG. Now I know why Eric doesn't say anything. You'll never believe what happened yesterday. I came home for lunch. I wasn't feeling well, and who's there sitting across from my S'mother???? Eric!!! There was money on the table!! I can only assume that my mom was paying him to find out what I've told him. So this whole time I've been confiding in Eric, he's been telling my mom everything. It makes sense now, how my mom found out Dylan & I were back on. That's disgusting—there should be a law against it! Thank God I didn't tell Eric everything!!! Can you imagine?*

So Eric was auctioning off Joanna's secrets to Kathy. That was not the guy I hung out with. What kind of lowlife could do that? How did I sleep with such a lowlife and not even know it? Were my teenage girl goggles that rose-colored?

It was so two-faced. To Joanna. To me. He acted like Joanna was any other student.

I felt fooled by him. Was his side job selling teens' secrets to their parents? Those deep, dark things that kids managed to hold back from social media. Was he playing me too? Waiting for me to drop some gold nugget he could sell to the press? But it wasn't like he was soliciting me for information. He didn't even seem to care if I talked at all, which I took as him being *sensitive*. How was I going to solve anything if I couldn't even figure out who was an asshole and who wasn't?

I went over the day we spent together. Nothing stuck out. It was nice. A *nice* day! That's how I would describe it.

I thought of his hand on Madison's shoulder. Lingering there. What was that? Who was he? And what kind of mother would even think to buy off the guidance counselor?

You're the only one I can trust. I trust you completely. p.s. Sorry again about being late. It's really Mrs. Thompson's fault—I'm working for her again. She's never on time, and if I wasn't making such good money working for her, I'd quit. (I didn't know you two dated!)

Mrs. Thompson. Carolyn! I leaned back into the couch. Joanna was working for Carolyn? She'd acted like she didn't even know Joanna. Was this why Wyatt had seemed so squirrelly? Distancing himself from Lucas. They were involved somehow. The entry was dated the month before she went missing.

Joanna's last entry:

I can't wait for our St. Roche trip. Finally!!! My mom would kill me if she ever found out. Xo

The "Xo" was etched in so deep, the paper bubbled around it like a burn blister. So Lucas really was sleeping with her. All of this was happening because he couldn't keep it in his pants. I felt a stunning blast of anger, of plunging disappointment, *you idiot* turned into a minute-long mantra. How could he? How could he cross the line (and how many teenage girls did he cross it with)? *Xo*. St. Roche didn't sound like a trip for paternity testing or an abortion. It didn't sound like Lucas was pressuring her into going. The exclamation points made it sound like a happy outing. They'd planned on going to St. Roche. Then what? Plans fell through, so he lured her out to Dickson Park and killed her?

I poured myself a drink to quell the itchiness to take something stronger and went through the journal again, cover to cover, three more times. I read for anything that might have hinted at something abusive going on between Lucas and Joanna. For that abused-wife whimper in Joanna's writing, something that made her sound afraid of Lucas. But the only person Joanna sounded afraid of was her mother. Even the emotional slump that came after the assault was not addled with fear in the same way as when Joanna wrote about her mother (not that I didn't think the hockey players couldn't have done this, or that whoever was sick enough to pay them wasn't capable of murder), but on nearly every page, Joanna referenced her mother with some level of anxiety. Dylan said Kathy wouldn't let Joanna grow up. Kathy paid off Eric. Kathy caused an "accident" to befall Joanna's BFF. She was a mother hen who'd rather suffocate her chick than let her out of the nest. And what was with all of Joanna's injuries? *My mom would kill me if she ever found out. Xo.* Maybe this wasn't some teenage hyperbole but literal.

I felt a rush of guilt for thinking Lucas was a closeted psychopath. I was sorry for the Norman Bates comparison. I knew my brother. I did. He was my twin, and we could see right into each other with one look. Every time I played it out in my mind, it just didn't work. It couldn't work. It couldn't be him.

I downed the rest of my drink. Why did I keep doing this? Why did I keep placing his traits and childhood memories on a weighing scale? It was beyond logic; my brother was innocent. End of story. It couldn't be him because it wasn't him. He was guilty of sleeping with her, of poor judgment, of having a barely eighteen sexual predilection (even if Zoey was twenty-one she looked younger) but he did not kill Joanna Wilkes. Belief was a choice. I was choosing to believe he was innocent.

I flipped through the journal again.

Eric.

Carolyn and Wyatt.

Kathy.

I had one answer at least. No wonder Lucas had hidden this.

17

I wanted to bust down Carolyn's door. Her car was in the driveway, but no one was answering my machine-gun doorbell ringing. Curtains were drawn, and so far, no small faces had peeked out, but I could hear them. I called, and the phone trilled inside the house until it hit voice mail. I was about to leave when I heard a yelp and a splash. The backyard.

I swung open the gate. It was lighter than it looked, and it smacked into the fence. The backyard was a long sprawl. Two girls in a sandbox startled and started crying. There were about nine kids, spread among two play structures and a kiddie pool.

A teenage girl came jogging over. "Hello? Can I help you?" She was dressed in a bikini top and jean shorts. She looked around the yard, skittishly pulled out her phone, and tried to smile while also frantically texting.

"Where's Carolyn?"

"Mommy's not heeeeere," one of Carolyn's melatonin-starved kids screeched, his white-blond hair sticking up with what looked like hardened yogurt. I looked back at the teenage girl, who was still texting.

"Where the hell is Carolyn?"

"Bad word, bad word," some kids chanted.

"She just stepped out." The girl finally looked up from her phone, startled. "Oh. I know you." I took a step forward. She flinched, her hands formed into a shield. "I never wanted to say anything." She moved toward the gate. "Carolyn said that we could help the police arrest Mr. Haas. Please don't hit me."

"I am not going to *hit* you. Why would I hit you?" My head snapped back. A two-second daze in which things quickly stitched together in my head, and then I got it. "What did Carolyn tell you to do?"

"I'm sorry, sorry, so soooorry." The girl started walking backward out of the yard, then scampered barefoot down the driveway, like I was revving a chainsaw over my head. The other Haas twin knocking round town, looking to find another teenage girl to kill!

"You can't just fucking leave," I yelled at her, but a passing plane muted my voice.

"Bad word, bad word."

"Carolyn should be back any second. I'm sorry." She called over her shoulder before disappearing down a walkway. So this was what Joanna must've been doing, babysitting Carolyn's day-care kids, so Carolyn could go off and do what? My neck went stiff with tension. I rolled my shoulders. Looked up. Jet stream bisected the blue sky, like a cat's eye glaring down on me. But it didn't make any sense that no one else knew Joanna worked here. Parents would have seen her here at drops-offs and pickups. And even if Joanna made herself scarce during those times, the kids themselves would surely have mentioned her name at home? Especially with her missing poster plastered all over town.

Maybe she just babysat Carolyn's kids?

I turned back toward the tiny tot chaos. Noticed in the far corner of the yard there was a shabby-looking hoop-style greenhouse. Something pulled at me. I waded through the sea of kids. "We're not allowed over there," a potbellied four-year-old girl screamed at me. The door was padlocked in three places. I cupped my eyes and tried to look inside, but the plastic wrap was milky white and heavily coated with dust. I couldn't see anything definitive. I had a sudden movie-reel vision of Wyatt driving Joanna home after she'd been babysitting his kids. His sweaty hand moved from the shift stick to her thigh—why should Lucas have all the fun? He pulled into Dickson Park for some privacy. Carolyn was waiting back at home, knowing, hoping that her husband did something to Joanna so she could exact her twisted bitterness on Lucas. *Guess your little teenage piece of ass isn't so special. She handed it out to Wyatt.* (It was like an anvil dropped on me: Carolyn could have paid the hockey players to humiliate Joanna. She would have known the boys through hosting season windups and team parties. But it didn't turn out how she planned—she didn't get the pictures.)

Maybe Wyatt hit Joanna when she rebuffed his advances, and she died. He would call Carolyn. She'd come up and help him discard the body. At some point, Carolyn decided to cut Joanna's hair. Maybe she planned to use it to taunt Lucas, to strategically place slender hanks of her hair in unexpected places (his desk at school, his truck, his apartment) to drive him mad. To show him she owned his ass. But then something better occurred to her. Why not send Lucas to jail for Joanna's murder? Save themselves, and there in jail Lucas could never have another woman and would come to appreciate her visits. She changed her mind again; she rolled toward Wyatt's white pimply back in the middle of the night and dozily announced, *Let's just kill Lucas too.* And here he was, becoming fertilizer in this greenhouse.

I dropped down onto my knees and worked at ripping the plastic up from the frame.

"Jayden hit meeeee."

I stopped, stomped back across the yard, and broke up a fight over a yellow plastic shovel, its handle now broken. Kept the shovel. At the greenhouse, I used the pointed end of the snapped shovel to stab into the greenhouse's sheath and pull it up. I rolled in under the opening, between its metal ribs. Rows of potted marijuana plants. A grow-op hidden in plain sight. I walked up and down the aisles, looking for a bloody shovel, rubber gloves, red Nikes. And then I remembered something (funny considering what I was breathing in), the offer for a toke of some "original green Kush" by the kid who found Joanna's body. Original green. Original sin. Eden. Eden Green. Carolyn. Wyatt and Carolyn were Joanna's supplier, not Dylan. So Carolyn was hiring high school girls to help at her day care, then seeing if she could convince them to take up the more lucrative business of dealing weed? Except Joanna. She would have gone straight to selling pot because she didn't want her mom to know she had a job (a job she went back to even after the pot was found in her locker). *It's really Mrs. Thompson's fault—I'm working for her again. She's never on time, and if I wasn't making such good money working for her, I'd quit.*

This was what they were hiding? It was all so fucked up.

A boy started whining frantically for juice, setting off a mini-riot. I tried to use the sugary sweet voice adults use when talking to preschoolers as I told the boy I'd find him some juice, but he eyed me suspiciously.

An hour later, when Carolyn finally pulled into the driveway, I was coated in sticky residue, topped with a coating of sand. I heard the car and saw she was being dropped off by a bald man in shirtsleeves. She leaned over, quick, and kissed him on the lips. He smacked her tiny ass as she got out. Then she saw me.

"What are you doing here? Where's Kira?" She trotted into the backyard, did a quick head count.

"She left about an hour ago. So this is your thing, huh? Get teenage girls to run your day care so you can run off and do whoever you're doing?"

"Oh God, Mia." She cut me off. Flipped her hair over her shoulders. "It was an emergency; I wasn't gone long at all."

"I'm sure the parents of all these kids would love to know their Precious Treasures are being watched over by only a sixteen-year-old without an adult on-site, while the person they're paying to care for their children is getting her rocks off somewhere else." Carolyn sniffed, looked the other way, like she couldn't hear me. "Not to mention the grow-op you got going on over there." I spoke up, using my best self-righteous voice.

"It's hardly a grow-op." She rolled her eyes and scoffed. "Just some flowers for my garden, and yes, maybe I have a single plant, but it's for personal use."

"Don't bother, Carolyn. I looked inside. So how do you go about deciding which teen babysits and which one deals your weed? Do you give them an aptitude test or something?"

"Leave, Mia. Get off my property." She said this through clenched teeth, as she crept toward the sandbox and made cooing sounds at the sand castles.

"I know Joanna Wilkes worked here, and I know she was selling your weed."

She stopped and backed away from the sandbox, but two of the kids had wrapped themselves around her legs like barnacles. "She came to me. Kathy Wilkes wouldn't give her anything. Can you imagine? All that money, and they wouldn't give her a dime. Joanna said she was saving for something."

"Saving for what?"

"I don't know. It's none of my business." She shook her kids off. "Probably to run off with your brother before he decided to kill her."

"Fuck off, Carolyn, you know Lucas didn't kill her." *Baaad word.*

"No, I don't!"

"Then why are you making a teenage girl lie about Lucas molesting her?"

"I don't know what you're talking about." Carolyn's eyes went big and innocent. I wanted to shake her.

"Yeah you do. The girl that was just here, Kira, she told me everything. She said she's going to recant." Not exactly true, but I needed leverage. "You know what I think? You heard the rumors that Joanna and Lucas were involved, and you were worried she told him that you were her supplier. You wanted to make sure he was arrested."

"Lucas killed that *poor* girl." She said *poor* like a weepy Chicken Little. Even tossed her head back and looked up. "A girl that I came to know and care about. I was just so sick of seeing him around town, flaunting his twenty-year-old slut while Joanna was still missing. He still thinks he's the town darling and that he can just do whatever he wants. Someone needed to wipe that smug grin off his face. Someone needed to push the police to try harder."

"So that's it? The old college obsessiveness. It never went away, did it? Your stalker tendencies. You just couldn't stand to see him with anyone else, even now?"

"I am not going to ask you again. Leave."

One of her kids started chanting, "Watch-me-Mommy, watch-me-Mommy," as he sat on top of the slide.

Carolyn closed her eyes for a second too long, flared her nostrils. "I am watching, OK? Just go down the slide."

"For all I know, Carolyn, you killed Joanna. Maybe a drug deal gone bad? How big is your operation? A landscaping company is a pretty good front."

"I would never hurt that girl. How dare you? I am a mother." Carolyn pounded her chest with her fist.

"See how far that gets you with the police."

Suddenly Carolyn sunk down onto a child-sized bench and looked up at me with big eyes. Her yoga pants puckered out and exposed a lacy G-string. "You know what, Mia, I'm just trying to make ends meet here."

"Oh, OK. That's fine, then. That totally justifies using teenage girls to sell drugs to minors and having them watch over your charges while you pick up ass on the side. Then, yeah, carry on."

"*God, Mia,* it's not like I'm peddling meth. It's weed. Please don't say anything. Wyatt doesn't know about any of this. There's no operation. He wouldn't. Our marriage has never been great. I won't lie to you, I had feelings for Lucas for a long time, and I think Wyatt knew that. I didn't come forward about Joanna working here because we need this money. I couldn't risk losing the day care. Wyatt is so fucking bad at running the business."

I felt a sudden, brief, supernova burst of satisfaction. "I'm telling the police, Carolyn." I turned to go. She got up and the bench turned over with a loud thud. The children in the yard went still as garden gnomes.

"Well, I guess you were both bound to turn out fucked up, with your mom running all over town," she taunted. I ignored her, but she followed me down the driveway anyway. "If you go to the police, you'll regret it."

I swung back around. "Are you threatening me?"

"How did you even know Joanna was selling my product," Carolyn said this quaintly, like she was referring to homemade scented candles or baby blankets, "when no one else knows? Not even the police—and yet you know?" Her voice sharpened. "Did Lucas tell you? Because if he did, then I guess he really was doing her."

"This isn't some game, Carolyn. This is my brother's life that you're fucking with." She was right, though; she could say whatever she wanted. It wasn't like I could bring out Joanna's journal as proof.

"I'm just saying, who's going to believe you? Because you know what? This is what really happened here: you found out my employee was one of Lucas's teenage victims because he told you about her. You came here to get her to recant. You attacked her. I have nine impressionable young minds in the backyard to back me up on this."

"Fine, Carolyn. Bring your posse of preschoolers down to the police station, then. They shouldn't be here anyway when the police start busting up your greenhouse."

"I could get rid of everything before they ever got here, and Kira will quickly realize that no one wants to be known as the girl who lied about being molested. Trust me, once I'm done talking to Kira, she won't recant a word."

An urge to unleash on Carolyn, body-slam her into the driveway, invaded me, but then I saw two toddlers weave out of the yard, through the open gate. I gestured at them with my thumb. "I can't believe anyone lets you watch their kids." Carolyn rushed over, corralled them back behind the gate and closed it, then stood up straight like nothing happened.

"You need to leave. I'm working," she said, without a sliver of irony in her voice. I made a *psshht* noise with my lips.

"By the way"—I walked up the driveway toward her—"after Kira took off, I recorded the whole last hour on my phone, not a single child care worker in sight. Isn't that child abandonment?" Not a bad idea—I wished I'd thought of it before. "Get those girls to recant, or else I'm going to the police with my video and calling every one of your Precious Treasures' parents to tell them that their children are being watched by a sixteen-year-old while you're out screwing some guy."

Carolyn bared her teeth in her signature mean-girl smile. "You're so delusional. He did it. He killed her. Joanna was so moony over him."

"You don't know what you're talking about."

"I heard them talking on the phone."

"You have twenty-four hours." Eyes burning, I retreated down the driveway.

I drove over to Abby Peters's home, perched on the edge of my seat, feeling like a cross between a bumbling gumshoe and Liam Neeson. I had a list of names that I was going to see, that was my plan. When I called (the phone number was an easy find, thanks to a teenage disregard of safety on Instagram), Abby's mother was more than happy to talk to me about Kathy—"Oh, yah, you come on by. That woman is a real bitch, doncha know." (OK so some of us do have accents, and I was relieved I was hearing it again because that meant mine hadn't returned.)

She seemed not to even care I was the sister of an alleged murderer. This made better sense once I got there and realized she was the much older sister of one of my friends in high school. "It's Jenny! Cheryl's sister?"

"That's right. How is Cheryl?" There was only one degree of separation in Wayoata. I remembered Cheryl Fitz; she'd defected from our insular group mid-sophomore year in a frenzied campaign for popularity. It had ended badly. She couldn't live down a threesome with two guys at a house party, and was thereafter called Cheryl Fitz-All. We welcomed her back with open arms.

Jenny went on to tell me all about Cheryl, how she was married and living in Boston now. Just had her first baby. A girl. Findlay. Good for Cheryl.

"I'm surprised you're here. I mean, God, if I was going through what you're going through, I think I'd just curl up into a ball and die."

"It's a difficult time."

"So do you think he did it?" Jenny's eyes were practically bulging out of her head. I could tell she was already retelling the gossip to her friends. *Guess who dropped by? Lucas Haas's sister. Yah, can you believe it? I just had to ask.*

I realized then no one had outright asked me that yet.

"No. Of course not." She waited for me to say more. I didn't.

Jenny looked disappointed, like I'd really let her down. "Oh. Well, come on in. Just slipping a hot dish into the oven." It's always a hot dish or *hoddish* here, never a casserole. The kitchen had obviously just been updated; its ultramodern look did not fit in with the rest of the house. She invited me to sit down at an expansive kitchen island. She wiped up a puddle of water left by a half-empty bag of melting Tater Tots—those made the crunchy top layer of most Wayoatan *hoddishes*—and tossed out a can of mushroom soup. Jenny shined the granite countertop and showed the rest of the kitchen off like a trophy, opening cupboards as she talked, sliding out drawers. It was a hushed demo, since everything was soft-close. "My husband never knows when I'm mad at him now." She giggled.

I accepted an offer for lemonade, which was premixed and in the fridge.

A girl, who I assumed was Abby, was sitting in the living room in front of a mounted TV, oblivious to my arrival as she watched a home movie of her preteen self practically twerking in a sparkly unitard on a bright stage.

"Abby, turn that off. Come on in here." Jenny put her hand up and whispered to me, "No sixteen-year-old should be reliving her glory days." Abby came sulking into the kitchen. She was of cheerleader stock. Tawny and tiny with honey-colored hair halfway down her back. I noticed a slight hobble as she sat down on a stool next to me.

"That looks like a pretty bad sprain."

"Sprain?" Abby snorted. "Kathy Wilkes broke my ankle in two spots five months ago. I had to miss school for two different surgeries, and I might need a third one."

They told me in turns what had happened. Abby and Joanna were rehearsing with Kathy at the studio late one night. They were two weeks away from a competition in New York. Kathy had choreographed both their solos, and as usual, Joanna's was supposed to be better. It was more sophisticated. Shooting Stars was Wayoata's only dance studio, and Kathy did win competitions, they reminded me, so everyone just sort of put up with it. But this time, it was obvious that Abby's solo was way better. Joanna wasn't trying very hard, and if Jo's solo wasn't great, then no one else was allowed to be great.

Kathy started saying that Abby kept landing a jump with her foot turned inward, but Abby didn't see it. "After, like, the fiftieth jump—Kathy is such a hard-ass—she came over and bent down, lifted up my left foot to show me how to land, and *snap*. It happened so fast, it was like I saw the top of her head and then heard the bone crack. I screamed. Kathy denied she even touched me. She said I landed wrong. Joanna said she didn't see anything but she was right there. She saw what happened. I know it."

I pictured Kathy's washerwoman arms on this tiny-boned girl.

"All Kathy could say was 'Uh-oh, SpaghettiOs.' " Abby shook her head.

"Uh-oh, SpaghettiOs?" I repeated it, slow. Blinked rapidly, feeling like I'd just been spritzed in the face with ice water. My skin puckered up; my muscles tightened at each syllable. *Uh-oh, SpaghettiOs.*

"Yeah, it's her catchphrase for everything."

"Kathy's catchphrase?" My voice creaked. My stomach went into spasm.

"Yeah. She says it all the time."

"Like how often?" I asked, anxious.

Abby made a face at me, then drew out her words, as if I didn't speak English. "Like all the time." She shrugged. *Oh my God.* I'd been trying to think up all sorts of sexual significances for the SpaghettiOs, but I couldn't. Aside from the obvious vagina and tiny rings of pasta comparison. But it wasn't a vagina reference. Kathy was behind it. She plotted her own daughter's sexual assault and ended it with a literal uh-oh, SpaghettiOs. Did Joanna know? Did she wake up with the SpaghettiOs in her lap, or did the boys clean her up after the shots were taken? It was Kathy. *Holy shit.*

"Hello? You still with us?" Jenny waved at me.

"Sorry, yes. So Kathy denied everything?"

"We're suing." Jenny smacked the granite island. "In a way, it's too bad. Abby was sure she could have brought Joanna around as an eyewitness eventually, but, well." Tears welled up in Jenny's eyes. "I guess that's not going to happen. I have to remind myself things could be worse. I still have my daughter."

"So Joanna was afraid of her mother?" I ignored Jenny. I'd become immediately uncomfortable around people who cry on cue, in all the right places. Looked only at Abby.

"Yeah, totally. Kathy controlled everything about Jo's life. Joanna had a bunch of injuries over the last couple of years, sprained wrists, twisted ankles; she was always at Dr. Bernard's. At first I thought it was from Kathy pushing her so hard. Joanna knew how competitive her mom was, which was why I was so pissed that Jo wouldn't have stood up for me. I mean, sometimes you won't stand up for yourself, but you will for someone else, right?"

I made a hmm sound, because I didn't have anything to add.

"But then something happened."

"What?"

"I saw Joanna do something that made me think she might've been doing it to herself."

"Doing what to herself?"

"Injuring herself. It was weird. One day, this was, like, before my injury, we were in the studio and Kathy had gone to get Joanna something to eat. That was the other thing about Kathy, she was always watching what Joanna ate. It was only smoothies with chia seeds, or fish and steamed vegetables. Kathy called it clean eating but obviously she didn't follow her own diet and she didn't want Joanna to get fat like her. Anyway, Joanna said she was going to go outside and get some air. I told her I'd come with, but I had to use the bathroom first. Next thing I knew, Joanna is lying at the bottom of the stairwell holding her knee. It had this bloody gash. She said she tripped but there was something not right about it."

"What do you mean?"

"Well, it's not like there was anything to make her trip down the stairs and it's not like Joanna was eighty years old and her hip gave out. Basically there was no reason she fell. She just did. I think she liked it, being injured or, well, the benefits. She got to sit out of dance for a while. She had time to herself. She got to see Dylan. I mean, even her relationship with Dylan had to be top secret because Kathy would never let Jo have a boyfriend, and that was even before some weed was found in her locker. After that, her brother was practically, like, her babysitter."

"How so?"

"He followed her around, checked in to make sure she was at school. If we went for a coffee or whatever, he'd show up. It was so creepy."

"Doesn't he have a job?"

"Oh no," Jenny interjected with a guffaw. "Maybe some part-time work at the grocery store, but Ben has a borderline IQ. Kathy made sure he graduated with everyone else. No one in this town is going to piss off one of the biggest employers, right? This whole thing between us and Kathy is a real David and Goliath story."

I gave Jenny an I-know-what-you-mean nod.

"Do you know Jo didn't even come and see me after my first operation? I had to get a pin put in my ankle," Abby continued. "We'd been dancing together since kindergarten, and it was like she didn't even know who I was after the assault—that's what we call it around here. Assault. Her little sister, Madison, did. She brought flowers. She's a sweet kid. People have the wrong idea about her."

"They do?"

"Kinda, yeah. It's nothing, really. She just runs a little wild. But Madison was totally on my side. You know what she said? Joanna might've even told her mother to do this to me. That Jo only acted all noncompetitive when she was number one, but when my solo turned out to be better than hers, she couldn't handle it."

"We asked if Madison would write out an affidavit, but she said she was too afraid to," Jenny added.

"Well, no kidding!" Abby lifted her leg a couple of inches off the floor. "In a way, Madison's lucky she can't dance. It means she's free of Kathy. If Miss Kathy thought you had any talent, then she was a bitch. That was the shitty thing. If she was all sugary nice to you, then you knew you sucked."

"Do you think Joanna would have told her mom to hurt you like this?" I didn't think so, not the Joanna I'd caught a glimpse of in her journal. But then there was that caveat that if the journal was her flirty communiqué with Lucas, then Joanna would be hiding certain sides of herself.

"One time I saw Jo's feet—they were like raw ground beef, and her toes were all crooked and blistery. She had to practice that much. I think it was all Kathy."

"Do you think Kathy could have hurt Joanna as well?"

Both Abby and Jenny recoiled slightly. It was too much of a stretch for them, I guess, that Kathy could go from breaking legs to murder.

"Oh, I don't think so. Not her little superstar. I mean, that's why she broke my daughter's leg, so Joanna could win. It was all about Joanna, so why would she—" Jenny started. She licked her lips; she finally had her slab of gossip: . . . *And guess what she wanted to know? If Kathy did it. Can you believe it? And we're right in the middle of it all.*

"I guess I never thought about it," Abby interrupted. "Everyone just said Mr. Haas did it. 'Cept for Josh Kolton, who keeps saying the lunch lady did it, but he's a total stoner. But maybe. I wouldn't put it past Kathy. I mean, look at what she did to my ankle; that takes a certain kind of person, right? And Joanna didn't want to move to New York; that was Kathy's plan. That they were going to live together. And there's something else. Something Joanna told me that made her mom sound totally psycho." Abby paused, let the word "psycho" linger. It took sheer willpower not to shake it out of her. "When Jo was, like, twelve, Kathy was doing her hair for a jazz recital, and there were too many tangles for Kathy, and so she just cut it all off.

Like, grabbed a pair of sewing scissors and just chopped it into this awful chin-length bob, all uneven and jagged."

I could almost feel the silky texture of Joanna's hair between my fingertips. Kathy killed her daughter because her little superstar didn't want to be her superstar anymore. Or because she was pregnant! If Madison saw the pregnancy test in the garbage, then Kathy could have as well. No wonder Joanna's funeral was held less than forty-eight hours after her body was found. It meant that she had to have been cremated just hours after the autopsy. Kathy wanted zero opportunity for her daughter's body to be exhumed, in case something turned up that incriminated her. Maybe she paid the players to humiliate Joanna too, to literally chasten her, and when that didn't work and Joanna ended up pregnant, she just snapped and then she needed someone to take the fall.

Suddenly, I could see it. It wouldn't be hard. Kathy dropping in on the drunk caretaker. Maybe she brings a bottle and some concerned chatter about her younger daughter spending so much time there. He passes out; she slips the key off the ring. Lets herself in. Plants Joanna's journal, her hair. This would have to be after she knew Lucas wasn't coming back. How could she know that, unless she'd done something to him? But why frame Lucas? Because he was sleeping with Joanna? Maybe that was all the reason she needed. Of course, there was that niggling fact that the journal and hair were in one of Lucas's old hiding spots. It would have made better sense for Kathy to put it somewhere more obvious so the police could find it, but maybe she thought it would seem less authentic that way.

"And you know what? I never bought the whole Mr. Haas and Joanna secret relationship thing. So many girls threw themselves at him and would have gladly given him whatever he wanted, but he always shot them down. So why Joanna of all people? I mean, Haas turned down way hotter girls than her. He could've taken me out to the woods anytime he felt like it."

"ABBY!" Jenny sputtered on her lemonade. "How could you say such a thing? Did he touch you?"

The conversation was over.

18

Wayoata's skate park was a run-down little embedded bowl not far from a grazing pasture. There was no parking lot, so I parked on the side of the road. I tapped out two Xanax. I know I resolved not to take any pills today but I needed a little something to get past these crawly, fire-ant pinches on my skin. Tomorrow I'll stop (and yes I knew that was the addicts' classic sales pitch to themselves but tomorrow really *did* work better for me). I washed the pills down with warm bottled water and walked in. The air was heavy with cow dung. Serious weed smokers hung out at either Dickson Park or the skate park, at least in my day. I was trying the skate park first. Three lonely-looking skaters circled around each other as two girls watched, sharing a wine cooler, their legs dangling over the lip of the bowl.

They looked up when I approached. One of the girls waved. Friendly.

"Is Josh Kolton here?" I asked. It was a long shot that he'd be here, but then again, it was summer in Wayoata and there wasn't a whole lot to do. The girl squinted her eyes, tried to follow the trio of boys gliding back and forth, and then just pointed at the center of the bowl, which didn't help at all.

The girl sitting next to her cried out, "Joshie . . . you're in trouble!"

"Joshie" rolled up to the lip of the bowl and kicked his skateboard into his hands. He was a shaggy-haired kid with a knitted cap, despite the heat, that stood up high on his head like it was made of meringue.

"Yeah?" He walked toward me, as I moved away from the girls.

I introduced myself as Mr. Haas's sister. I noticed Josh held his skateboard a little bit more tightly and angled in such a way that it would shield him in case murdering Westfield students ran in our family. "Sorry to bother you, but I've heard around that you witnessed someone, not my brother, with Joanna the day she went missing." I didn't specify "lunch lady." I wanted to hear it directly from Josh.

"Yep. No one believes me, but I swear I saw the lunch lady. I even got suspended over making inappropriate comments about school staff. Three sweet days off."

I asked him exactly where he was standing, how far he'd been from Joanna. The girls were making impatient noises.

"I was sitting at one of the picnic tables, and I saw Joanna first. I yelled, 'Hey, JoJo,' at her. She turned around and waved at me. I thought she was going to come over, but she just kept hiking into the woods."

"So you saw Joanna for sure?" The picnic tables were a good distance from the trail.

"Yeah, she waved at me."

"Then what happened?"

"I was looking for my lighter to spark one up and then not even a minute later, the lunch lady came up behind her on the trail. It was, like, weird because I've never seen the lunch lady in Dickson Park before. She wasn't with anyone."

"What did she look like? What was she wearing?"

"I can't remember what she was wearing, but it was her. I know it was. Then Joanna went missing. It's like that fat bitch ate her or something." He said this last part really loud, hand cupped around his mouth, laughed this loose-jawed *haw, haw,* but when his mouth closed again, it was tight and serious. "I saw the lunch lady. I told the police, but they thought I was just stoned."

"I believe you."

"You do?" His dull eyes sharpened.

I nodded. "I do. I believe you saw a woman, maybe not the lunch lady per se, but someone who looked like her." From far away, the lunch lady was the right height, the right build to be Kathy. The hair color was wrong. Kathy had blondish hair, and the lunch lady had dark hair. Still, if it was late afternoon and the lighting poor, then it would be easy to mistake hair color.

As I started back toward my car, I saw the black truck idling behind it. I slipped behind a straggly bush, pulled out my phone, and dialed Garrett. It went to voice mail. Tried again. Voice mail. I couldn't even see the license plate number because the truck was right up against my bumper. I left a panicky message. "Garrett, it's Mia, someone's been following me. I don't know for sure, but I think it's Tom Geller. He's tried to run me off the road a couple of times already. I'll send you a picture of the truck."

I held my phone between the branches and zoomed in but was still too far away. I wanted the plate number or his face. The only way I could think to get a clear shot was to run at the truck, paparazzi style, take a picture, and run back to the skate park before he could mow me down.

I held my phone out in front of me and started to jog toward the truck. My heart was in my ears, beating frantically, like the wings of a trapped insect. Inside the cab, all I could see was a man in sunglasses and a baseball cap pulled down low hunched over the steering wheel. I aimed my phone at him, his truck. The truck shot backward, then pivoted into the middle of the road leaving snaky black tracks. Filling the air with burned rubber. I moved to follow him, a stupid rather than ballsy move, and kept trying to get shots of the plate, but whatever I managed to snap was likely blurry. He just kept backing up.

The truck stopped a couple of hundred yards away. The front grille glinted in the low sun. I zoomed in as much as I could and pointed my phone at the plate, my finger was about to press the camera button when the engine revved. The truck gunned forward, fast, straight toward me.

I took a few clumsy steps backward and bumped into the back of the PT. Half tripped. The Xanax was suddenly working too well, as if it had just gone off in my bloodsteam like fireworks.

Dulled anxiety clotted my adrenaline and slowed my reaction time. The truck picked up speed, and its kettle-whistle noise momentarily stunned me. I felt cornered. My second-long hesitation was broken by shouts to run from the kids at the skate park.

I scrambled along the driver's side of the PT Cruiser and dove headfirst in front of the car. The first layer of skin on my bare forearms grated off into the concrete. I felt a rush of wind as the truck sped by, then swerved onto the shoulder, kicking up a cloud of dust that made me choke and half blinded me. I rolled toward the passenger side, tried to squish myself under the car, and waited, my back pressed into the hot metal. Unable to catch my breath. Certain the truck was going to come back and take another shot at squashing me into the road. Or even smash into the PT, which would then roll and flatten my head. Still, I stayed there. Listened for an engine. Teeth chattering. Bones rippling. My arms burned, blood oozed into the sleeves of road dust. There was a high-pitched hum in my ears, a soundtrack to my repeating thoughts. I was almost killed for four thousand dollars.

I'd started to inch back out from under the car when I noticed something stuck to its undercarriage. A box with a small green flashing dot. It was held there by a magnet. I pulled it off. It had PROPERTY OF WPD stamped across it. Fucking Garrett. He must've put it on the day I got here. How else could he know there was a box of Kleenex in my rental unless he was lurking around my car? While I sat in the interview room staring at Joanna's missing poster, he was in the station's parking lot, planting a GPS. He'd been tracking me the whole time. He knew I almost went to the police station at 3 A.M. the other night. That was why he was acting like he could read me, asking if I was weighed down by something. It was probably why he hadn't arrested me for withholding information about Joanna's pregnancy, in case I did lead them to Lucas.

"Holy shit! I totally thought that guy was gonna hit you." I jolted, my head bumped into the car. It was Josh Kolton, skating up to my car. I put the GPS back.

"Did you see the license plate?" I got up, slow.

Josh shook his head. "No way, man. He was going too fast. Are you OK? You're bleeding— Whoa that's crazy road rash. Do you want me to call somebody?"

"I'm OK, thanks."

"I seriously thought you were gonna be like, splat." He slapped one hand into the other. "You sure you don't want me to call like an ambulance?"

"No. Like you said, it's just road rash. You didn't get even a number or letter off the plate?"

"Nah. I was, like, way over there." He squinted to the skate park as if it were some distant hill. Josh skated up and down my car three times, and then he just kept going. Shaking his shaggy head.

I flipped though the pictures on my phone. Blurry. It didn't help either that the screen was cracked. But I thought I could make out an "A" and "7." At least I had Josh Kolton and his stone-head, wine cooler–swilling pals at the skate park for witnesses. Witnesses no one took seriously.

Garrett called back. "Nice timing," I barked.

"What's going on?"

"I was almost killed is what's going on." And then all the panic and fear welled up inside of me and I let out a blubbery, angry sob.

"Where are you?" I wanted to answer, *Really? Oh, I think you know exactly where I am.* But I'd already decided that pretending to be oblivious to the fact that they were tracking me could come in handy.

"The skate park."

"I'll be right there."

In minutes, Garrett pulled up. Lights flashing. One look at my arms and he grabbed his first aid kit from the trunk and led me to the passenger side of his cop car. "Let's treat this first. Now hold your arms out." I did. He crouched down on one knee in front of me and dabbed alcohol on me; my eyes watered. He gently dug out pieces of gravel lodged under my skin with tweezers. He held on to me, firm, murmuring, "Almost there, almost." I felt his breath on the inside of my arm. "You have a high pain tolerance, huh?"

"Guess so," I murmured back. He looked at me, first at my mouth, then into my eyes. Something in my stomach twirled before a stab of worry hit, that he was going to narc-out and ask me if I consumed any drugs or alcohol this fine evening.

"So, tell me what went down here." He went back to work on my arms and I told him everything. "And the back window? The guy in the truck did that too?"

I explained what had happened. How Tom Geller broke the window and draped himself over the shattered PT in the Target parking lot like a car calendar girl. How he picked my two twenty-dollar bills out of a puddle.

Garrett took a break from tweezing my arms and went through the pictures on my phone, flicking on the dome light, flicking it off again, tapping the screen to enlarge the images, then shrinking them back down. He handed my phone back. "Can you e-mail those to me? The guy who does our IT stuff should be able to do something with them. Was it a Ford? It looks like a Ford in the pictures."

"I don't know. It was just a big fucking truck."

Garrett nodded. "OK, I'll write that down." He gave me a half smile. "Big fucking truck." I tilted my head forward, giving him a don't-patronize-me look. He went back to picking at my arms.

"Listen, I have some good news for you. The girls who said Lucas molested them have recanted their statements. They called in quick succession, blurted out a recantation, and hung up. Odd. You didn't have anything to do with that, now did you?"

"How could I? Well, there you go. Lucas is innocent!" So Carolyn had come through. She must have wanted her weed business more than she wanted my brother to suffer. *Thank God high school weed is so lucrative*. "Are you finally going to start looking at other suspects, then?"

"Hold still. It doesn't work that way exactly. I mean, it leaves open the question whether the girls are lying now or if they were lying before but it definitely helps Lucas, that they recanted."

"They're not lying. I mean, they were lying before. They're telling the truth now. Lucas didn't molest them. I was literally almost killed. It has to be related. It has to be! Maybe it wasn't Tom Geller, but someone else. I never actually saw his face. I'm getting close to finding out the truth, and whoever was in that truck is threatened and wants to take me out."

"You really need to hold still. I checked and Tom Geller does own a black truck. A Ford. He's obviously escalating and trying to scare you into paying off Lucas's debt. You're the next best thing, because once Lucas is in jail, he won't be able to pay him."

I pulled my arms away, the tweezers caught in my skin. I cursed.

"Sorry, I meant to say *if* Lucas is guilty. *If*."

"No you didn't."

"What are you doing out here, anyway?" He pulled back like he was trying to get a big-picture look at my face. His eyes narrowed to analytical slits.

"I wanted to talk to Josh Kolton. I wanted to hear what he had to say."

"Ah, the lunch lady again." Garrett rolled his eyes, and started to wrap up my arms with gauze. "I told you she has an alibi."

"Do you know that Kathy Wilkes's catchphrase is 'Uh-oh, SpaghettiOs'?"

"No." He looked surprised. "I was not aware of that. I've never heard her say that." He snapped the first aid kit closed.

"Well, it is. Around the dance studio, anyway, she says it all the time. Garrett, I think Kathy set up the assault on her own daughter."

He made a face, and stood up. "I can't see any mother inflicting that kind of sexual humiliation on her own daughter. Why would she do that?"

"I think to manipulate her. I think Joanna was starting to rebel and was rethinking what she wanted to do in life, that she didn't want to dance anymore. Kathy wanted to scare her, show her that the world's a frightening place out from under her talons."

Garrett shook his head. "It would take a whole lot of convincing for me to think Kathy Wilkes would ever do that. A lot. And if that was Kathy's catchphrase as you say, wouldn't Joanna know it was her mother? Wouldn't that make her want to leave Kathy even more?"

"Maybe it was a threat. To keep her in line."

Garrett shifted. "Mia. It wasn't Kathy. Those boys did what they did; they're to blame. This whole thing about being paid, about money being taped under a bench, sounds like total bullshit. There's no proof. It's just a way to try to avoid responsibility. Two of those boys have younger sisters, and like most Wayoata girls, they could have passed through Kathy's studio, and that could be what planted the sick fetish. Maybe one of them came home saying uh-oh, SpaghettiOs, or whatever. Who knows? But this was the boys' twisted idea of a good time."

"Cody said they got an e-mail asking them to do it."

Garrett sighed; he was starting to look really annoyed. "I know what Cody is saying. If that e-mail ever existed, which I highly doubt, we won't know because Jesse Campbell is on his third laptop since Joanna's assault."

"Could you check Kathy's computer?"

"I'm not doing that, Mia."

"So you're not even going to consider it, are you?"

He just looked at me. "No."

I felt myself verging on an outburst. I wanted so badly to tell him what was in Joanna's journal, all that frustration. All those feelings of being smothered. I wanted to tell him that I thought Kathy Wilkes murdered her own daughter, maybe even murdered and framed my brother because there were already so many irresponsible rumors flying around that would make it easy for the police to follow, because he had the phone and knew what she did to her own daughter. I couldn't. Not yet. Not until Garrett could be persuaded to look at Kathy as a suspect. I thought of that reporter, Vanessa Lee. Her hankering for something controversial.

I sucked in a deep breath. "You're there a lot, aren't you, at the Wilkeses'?"

"I have been. That family has been through something so horrific, so I try to be there. It makes them feel better to see how hard we're working at finding Jo's killer. They really are a nice family, Mia." He glanced at me sideways. I could tell he didn't want to get me started on a Lucas-is-innocent diatribe.

So I asked about the ATM withdrawal.

"We're still gathering footage from surrounding businesses. Speaking of which, I should go. Get some statements from the kids at the skate park before they light up again and their brains scramble. I want you to promise me you'll go home and get some rest. I'll deal with Geller."

"I will," I lied.

Half an hour later, while I was walking the aisles of Home Depot, ticking off a shopping list for tools to commit a break and enter, Garrett called. "Tom Geller's truck doesn't match your description or the truck in the pictures. His truck doesn't have that front grille. This doesn't mean he couldn't have hired someone else to harass you, but at this point we can't arrest him. I'll keep looking into it. In the meantime, try to stay off the road."

19

I used to break the law all the time. But what I used to do, swiping a pill here and there from the hospital dispensary, was all sleight of hand to avoid cameras and co-workers. Skimming off of my friends' careless parents in college was easy enough to deny. No one ever counted their pills. If they did notice a shortage, there was always bad memory to blame: *Did I double dose last week?* Or even better, someone else to blame, some twitchy nephew who'd stayed too long in the bathroom. I doubted that parents ever suspected the quiet, science-loving dark-haired girl their daughter had brought home for the weekend.

But this.

This was something entirely different.

I pulled into my old pediatrician's office, parked in the back lane.

Joanna and I (and Lucas) had shared a doctor. Dr. Bernard was the quintessential friendly country doctor, attentive, good bedside manner, and easily distracted. I'd swiped my first prescription pad off him when I was in college. I'd faked a head cold that first visit back for Thanksgiving. I wasn't officially an adult until November 30, and around these parts you stack with your pediatrician right up until you turned eighteen (at which point you just dusted your childhood off and crossed the waiting room to the adult side of the clinic). My face turned beet red every time he renewed my birth control prescription after a stiff and awkward yearly pap test, where I'd stare at the Winnie-the-Pooh wall decals and yell at Mimi in my head. Dr. Bernard handed me a lollipop afterward with an apologetic smile. There was no way he'd upgraded to digital files, and he'd likely put up a big fuss about never doing so. He'd say charming things to his patients like *It's not broke—why fix it?* or *I've been doing this for forty years without e-mail.* At least this was what I was counting on.

I was also counting on the idea that the Wayoata medical examiner had gotten only a copy of her medical file, not the original, or else that the clinic kept back a copy and gave the police the original. There was a better chance I wouldn't find anything at all and I'd just get arrested and there'd be no one left to find Lucas. I'd be written off for being as crazy as Mimi.

I got out of the car. Nervous as hell. Felt like a thousand cameras were aimed right at me, like I'd been hit with a bout of criminal stage fright.

At least I'd remembered to drop the GPS off at the apartment. I stuck it to the side of the winter plug-in. (In college I'd have to explain to those from more temperate states that I was not referring to a Glade plug-in but that cars in North Dakota *really* needed to be plugged in overnight if you planned on going anywhere because it kept the engine from freezing over. The block-heater itself was a Grand Forks invention—how could it not be?) I then spent fifteen minutes in the parking lot rewatching lock-picking videos on YouTube. A technique called lock bumping looked easiest; you slid a key into the lock, and then hit the back of the key with the handle of a screwdriver and somehow (I forwarded through the boring mechanical explanation), you could turn the key and unlock the door. Armed now with a screwdriver, I stood at the back entrance of Dr. Bernard's clinic and went through my key ring. Only my own apartment key slid partially into the lock. I took a deep breath, felt like I was tipping over the edge of a cliff. Looked behind me again. Brought my arm up and hammered my key with the screwdriver. Way too hard because my key broke off. One end of it clattered into the dark back lane.

Fucking hell. Now what?

I eyed a window.

Good thing I had also bought a flashlight, heavy-duty metal, for backup. I pulled the car up closer to the building, climbed onto the hood, and knocked the flashlight against an exam room window, expecting it to shatter into nice icy chips. But it just made a loud *thunk*. Not like the movies, or maybe I was weaker than I thought. It took three tries, my face turned the other way, my legs skittering on the hood like it was ice. (And here I got a vision of myself falling and knocking myself out, waking to a future as the star of a stupid criminal video. *Why, why did I not think to wear a balaclava?*)

I doubled-handed the flashlight like a baseball bat before I managed to smash the glass. I reached inside, unlocked the window, and slid it open. Setting off a high-pitched sound. An alarm. How stupid that I hadn't expected that! Five minutes—I had to do this in five minutes.

I climbed inside headfirst. My arms and legs tangled in the dusty aluminum blinds.

I stepped out of the exam room. It was so dark. The screech of the alarm was narrowing every single blood vessel in my body. I was going blue. I had to be. Felt turned around. Blinded by panic. Couldn't figure out where to go.

Right or left? Left. Gawd, get it together. Don't get caught standing here like a deer in headlights.

Files.

Get the file. Get out.

Go, go, go.

I raced down the hall.

Next to the receptionist's desk. A wall-length bank of files.

I flung open the heavy drawer marked "W" so hard the cabinet shuddered. Found it. Wilkes, J. Sandwiched between Ben and Madison's much thinner files. I tucked it under my arm and was about to make a mad dash back out the window when I took a stunned second to glance into the waiting room. The long cartoon ruler where Lucas and I had once measured our respective heights was still there. My mother had always added a couple of inches for Lucas to make him feel better. He didn't really shoot up until he turned sixteen.

On the way out, I grabbed a prescription pad and a handful of lollipops.

I pulled in next to a Dumpster at McDonald's and watched a single police car race by, blue-red light ablaze. I didn't want to be seen driving away from the clinic. The dome light and the yellow glow of the golden arches provided enough light for a quick peek at Joanna's file. Her medical history was typical, occasional sore throat, the chicken pox, a broken arm when she was seven. Until two years ago. Then things started to change. Multiple complaints of stomachaches concluded to be irritable bowel syndrome, numerous sprained ankles and wrists. A pulled hamstring, a fractured radius. In the months before her death, the injuries grew closer together. In the last six months, she had sprained her wrist twice and her right ankle three times.

Apart from the fracture, arguably most of these injuries could have been faked, but I was sure Kathy would have caught on pretty quick if her daughter was malingering. It takes a lot of dedication to keep up the act of being hurt, limping with the same leg, or staying consistent that she could not open a jar of peanut butter or whatever and needed help. That would have been annoying for Joanna, hating her mother as she did, to need her for little things. No, Kathy brought her daughter to the clinic each time. She believed her because she was the one who had hurt her. She didn't even bother to cover it up by avoiding the clinic. Kathy needed Joanna to mend properly if they were going to go to New York and Joanna was going to dance.

Finally, after fifteen minutes, it looked like the coast was clear.

I said this out loud, laughed some strange hyena-like sound. Delirium had set in. I needed sleep. Real sleep.

Back at the apartment, I was about to pull into the lot when I spotted the black monster truck waiting in a parking spot not far from Lucas's. I circled past, pulled fast into someone's driveway. Sunk down in the driver's seat, bit into my lip. Scared he had seen me, but the truck stayed dark.

I watched it in my rearview mirror, popped two Provigil, a narcolepsy med, to stay awake and alert. Chased it down with a watermelon-flavored lollipop. I was going to outwait this bastard, without a doubt. I was going to follow him home, then call Garrett. Two hours later, the truck turned on. Cab lights burned into the dark like pinholes.

I trailed behind at a safe distance. Five minutes outside Wayoata, I knew where we were headed.

The truck pulled into a sprawling brick house with a four-car garage. A sign at the end of the circular driveway said PRIVATE PROPERTY, followed up with WELCOME TO THE WILKES HOME.

Four abandoned-looking media vans were parked neatly on the side of the road.

I drove in behind the truck, parked next to three Jet Skis up on jacks. Turned my car off. The driver's door swung open, and Big Ben slid down out of the driver's seat. I stuffed Joanna's file under the floor mat. Got out, hollered under the full influence of fearless rage, "Why the hell are you following me?" My hands went jittery. Side effects of Provigil were nausea, tingling, aggressiveness, and uneven heartbeats, and suddenly I was feeling them all at once.

"Private property. You're trespassing," Ben yelled back, blinking wildly as if surprised at the volume he produced. His arms hung by his sides like a gorilla's.

A porch light turned on. Kathy at the door. "Ben? Is that you?" The wind had picked up, gone fierce, and her voice was muted by the swaying branches in the trees lining the driveway.

"Over here, Mom." He backed away from me. Nodding, as if to say, *Now you're gonna get it.*

Kathy stepped farther out. She was in a pink fuzzy robe that caught in the wind like a cape. "Who's with you?"

"That lady." His voice went babyish. Simple. That lady? As if he didn't know who I was. As if he hadn't been shadowing me since I got here.

Kathy marched down the steps, barefoot. "What the hell are you doing harassing my son on my property?" she roared, retying her robe. Tight. Double knotted. "Call the cops, Ben. Now." Ben took out his phone. His chubby face went ghoulish in his phone's light.

"Yes, call the cops. Your son almost killed me today. He's been following me for days, and I want to know why."

"You want to know why? She wants to know why?" Her mouth widened into a shocked grin, addressing some audience in the dark front lawn. "Why the hell do you think? We want to find out where your pathetic excuse for a human being brother is and bring him to justice."

"I'm here to find out the same thing. Where's my brother?"

" 'Scuse me?" Kathy came closer, her head snapped side to side on her neck.

"I know what you've done." My hair whipped across my face.

"Yeah, what've I done?" Hands on hips. Her mouth curled up into this bemused grin. Briefly, she looked past me, at Ben. A flicker of something ran across her face.

"Justice is just a little bit closer to home, don't you think, Kathy?"

"What the hell is that supposed to mean?"

"You know what it means. It's just a matter of time before the police put it all together."

"What are you talking about? You know what, I don't even give a shit. You're psycho. Your whole fucking family is crazy. Everyone in Wayoata knows that much. I bet you're just like her, your mother. A slut in the big city. You're all sexual deviants. Stay away from my family. I hope your brother burns in hell."

I blinked back the angry tears that were heating up my eyes. My stomach tightened with fury. "Tell me, did you enjoy abusing your daughter? I bet you did."

"What did you just say to me?" Kathy said this with eerie calmness. A beat passed. Then she came at me, her shoulder hitting me hard in my stomach and knocking the wind out of me. I slipped on the dewy grass, my legs suddenly gone. Kathy was on top of me, pinning me down at my shoulders. Her robe had come undone, exposing a plunging lace-trimmed nightie underneath. A shadowy glimpse of a butterfly tattoo, deformed by weight gain, its tie-dyed pattern looking too green, like it was moldy. Her hair had loosened and blown upward, porch light casting it into some Medusa-like corona.

She punched me in the jaw, hard—a white light exploded behind my eyes. My teeth jingled like loose change. I got my left arm free and managed to block her next blow. I twisted loose from under her, did an army crawl away; pain shot through my arms, then Kathy grabbed for my legs. I kicked, hit her somewhere, because she let go and I managed to stand up, but Big Ben was right there and he pushed me back toward his mother. Kathy grabbed me from behind, her arm came up around my throat into a choke hold, and she started to squeeze. Ben stood there watching, expressionless, like this was all perfectly normal for him. All I could hear and feel was her hot wet breath in my ear, repeating, "You fucking bitch, bitch, bitch."

I couldn't breathe. My legs kicked out wildly in all directions. The veins in my neck were blood-thick and throbbing. The black night rippled like I was underwater. The porch light scattered and sparked. I was going to pass out. Flashing blue-red lights, for the second time tonight. Kathy released me. I dropped to the ground, gasping for air. Clawed at the grass.

Garrett was out of the car, shouting, "What's happening? What's going on?"

Kathy said something I didn't catch over my own jagged coughing. Garrett lifted me up by the armpits. "You OK? Do I need to call for an ambulance?" I dipped my head forward so I could take in deep breaths.

"Oh God, she's fine. Trust me." I could hear her now. Kathy was behind me, claiming I just showed up in the middle of the night, knocked on their door, and attacked her. It was all in self-defense.

"She attacked me!" I sputtered. In the corner of my eye, I could see a cluster of bobbing lights. Cameras. Good. "How much did you get? Did you get all of that?" I called out in a hoarse voice in the direction of the cameras. No response.

Kathy's husband, Ian, had come running out of the house and was by her side, looking eyeless behind his glasses that reflected the lights from the cruiser. His arm was around her, and Kathy started to sob. She stooped down so she could bury her head against her husband's chest. All soft now. Grieving wife and mother. Gone was the woman who had just python gripped my neck and called me a bitch. This was all for the cameras.

Rage flashed through me, and my fists balled up like a child's. "She just tried to kill me. Her son tried to kill me. They're the ones. They killed their own daughter. They have Lucas."

"Get her out of here now," Ian growled. A big voice for a small man.

Garrett flashed a penlight in my face. "What are you doing here?"

"He's the one who's been following me. It's Ben Wilkes who almost ran me over today. Look, his truck is right there. It's the same truck as in the pictures. They've been following me."

"What're you on? Your pupils are the size of dimes."

"Nothing. Jesus."

Garrett glanced at the reporters, back at me.

"You don't believe me, do you? My brother is likely here, buried in their basement while you hold their fucking hand. They set him up to look guilty, so they could get away with it." I started to raise my voice again so the reporters could hear me.

"Don't do that." He grabbed my wrist, firm. I winced. He directed me toward his cruiser.

"What the fuck, Garrett? Let me go!"

"You'll just make this worse for yourself if you don't settle down."

"Get your hands off me. What are you doing?"

He ignored me. Ordered the reporters—there were four now—to

stand back. Stand back? Why wasn't he telling them to leave? "You're arresting me?"

"Just get in." He opened the back of the cruiser and pushed me inside. His hand on my head. It closed with a dull thud. I tried the door. Locked. The reporters swarmed.

I smacked the windows with my palms, a frantic drumroll. "She attacked me! Kathy attacked me." The cameramen (one was a woman) took turns aiming their cameras at me. White lights beamed into the backseat as they baited me like a zoo animal. "Could you repeat that? What happened?"

I tried to explain through the glass, but the reporters kept talking over one another and were having a hard time hearing me. No one was following what I was saying. They lost interest after a few minutes when their jumbled questions started about Lucas and I refused to answer. Moving like a singular body, they scurried toward Garrett and the Wilkeses talking on the front lawn. It was getting light; the sky had turned purple-pink, the color of an old bruise. Something moved in front of the Wilkeses' home. Madison. Red hood up over her head, swinging gently back and forth on a porch swing. Unnoticed.

Garrett squeezed Kathy's shoulder. He kept nodding. Ben said something, his palms out in an I-don't-know pose. Kathy burrowed her head again into her husband.

Garrett glanced back at the reporters, more than once. His stance was a tad too wide. Hands on hips. He was mugging for the cameras. He'd just arrested an alleged murderer's twin sister, who attacked the grieving mother. He was going to make every news show there was tomorrow. This here was his big break. This would overshadow Pruden. Put Garrett right at the helm, so at the next press conference, he would be the one standing at the podium taking questions about the other violent Haas twin. I leaned my head back. Tired and wired. The worst combination ever. The Provigil rolling through me like a leashed stampede. A green pine air freshener made the air in the car stuffy and thick. I had to fight off claustrophobia.

Finally, Garrett was back. He dropped down into the driver's seat.

I'd managed to pull it somewhat together. With a calm I was surprised I could muster, I stated flatly, "She killed her daughter. She killed Lucas. Or she had her son do it. I don't know. She said she hopes Lucas burns in hell. Why would she say that, like he's already dead, if she didn't know he was dead?"

He adjusted the rearview mirror to look at me, then readjusted and started backing out.

"What about my car?"

"I'll get an officer to bring it over to the station."

"Let me out of here!" I tried the handle again.

"Mia, you need to calm down."

"Calm down? What the fuck! That woman just tried to kill me. Her son has been trying to run me over for the past week. That whole family is obviously very violent."

"Their daughter was brutally murdered!" His rising voice was all edges. His rearview eyes were looking at me like I was the abuser here. "They were searching for her for over three weeks, they didn't eat or sleep, and then you show up and make these terrible accusations. Don't you think they've been through enough? Did you really need to come to Kathy's home in the middle of the night to accuse her of killing her daughter? What's wrong with you?"

"You need to talk to Abby Peters."

"The Peterses? I know all about them. They've sued about three other people over the last year. They sue so often it's practically become a saying around here, that I am going to 'Peters' you. Hell, why didn't you call me before you came out here? I could have talked to you about all of this." He chuckled, but it sounded mean and spiteful.

"I know you want to write me off as crazy. It makes your job easier. But Kathy was abusing her daughter. She was always hurt."

"No, Mia, Kathy wasn't. I don't know what Abby Peters told you, but I can imagine. Joanna suffered some dance injuries, minor sprains. Nothing serious, nothing to indicate abuse. And you know what? If someone really did pay to have those pictures of Joanna taken, my first suspects would be the Peterses, not that I really think that."

"But Joanna hated her mother, she was afraid of her—" At the last second, I caught myself. I was about to mention the journal, cite Joanna's comparison between malleable Ben and Lennie Small.

Garrett shook his head and stared ahead.

"Did you even look into Tom Geller? Or did you know it was Ben this whole time?" He had to have known it was Ben's truck from the pictures I took. How could he not? He was at the Wilkeses' all the time.

"No. Of course not. He just told me he'd been following you, but said he wasn't trying to scare you. He thought you could lead him to Lucas. I think that Ben might not have realized how aggressive he was being. He's . . . I don't know, I think he could be on some spectrum."

"Riiiight. Well, you saw my arms. I just, what? Threw myself into the pavement? He was trying to run me over."

"I spoke to Ben, and you don't need to worry about him again." Garrett said this with an annoying amount of confidence in his own authority.

"So my brother is an official suspect based on your measly 'eyewitness' accounts, whereas Ben just tried to turn me into roadkill and he gets off with a stern warning? I have an eyewitness too, you know, if that's all it takes. Why aren't you arresting Ben?"

"Yeah, I know. Josh Kolton." He shook his head in a way that suggested I might as well have said the tooth fairy. "Ben was antagonistic, Mia. I'm not saying he wasn't. That was wrong. But like I said, he's a little off, and he thought you'd take him to Lucas."

"Too bad, then, that you didn't tell him sooner that you had it all covered and he didn't need to tail me. I found the GPS, Garrett," I added, just to wipe that smug confidence off his face. "Do you have a warrant for that?"

Garrett craned his head toward me. Spoke through the side of his mouth. "Yeah, I do have a warrant. We're just trying to locate your brother."

"Well, you should put one on Kathy's car, then. They know where he is."

"OK. Let's just say your crazed theory is true. Why would she involve Lucas? Why would the Wilkeses go to all this trouble to set up your brother? Why not just say she ran away?"

"Because maybe my brother was sleeping with Joanna, I don't know? And they wanted to make him pay for that? They thought he was the father of her baby? Maybe Joanna wanted to have the baby and continue seeing Lucas. I know she didn't want to dance anymore, and maybe that's all it took for—" My words were crashing into one another. Desperate. This was desperate. The emotional equivalent of gnawing off a limb to set myself free. I had to concede Lucas could have been sleeping with her to make this work.

Garrett cut me off. "*For what?* You think Kathy murdered her own daughter because she didn't want to be a ballerina? You think this was some kind of dance-mom honor killing? Come on, you must know how ridiculous that sounds. It's like reality is a multiple-choice questionnaire for you." We stopped hard at a four-way intersection, car jerking; the traffic lights dangling from the wires were all blinking red. He went through the lights, pulled over to the side of the road, and parked. Put his hazards on, though the roads were deserted. Their timed ticking filled the car. He drew an audible calming breath and turned around to face me. "I am glad to hear, though, that you're finally admitting to yourself that there was a relationship between Lucas and Joanna."

"That's so condescending, Garrett," I snapped. An angry, sticky sound erupted in the back of my throat. Shook my head. He eyed me, still looking wary of my wide-eyed intensity.

"I am just saying, that it's a step in the right direction." I knew what was coming next. "But I know that Eric Lowe did not tell you Joanna was pregnant."

"Well, Eric Lowe isn't exactly good at keeping secrets—"

"Don't bother lying! I know the school guidance counselor didn't tell you because he didn't know. If he'd known, he would have told Kathy. They were meeting regularly to discuss Joanna. When I told

Kathy her daughter was pregnant, I could see it in her face. She had no idea. So how did you know she was pregnant?"

I couldn't blame Madison either because I'd be pelted with a *when, where, how* line of questioning and any remaining credibility would vaporize. "I just figured it out. I saw something scratched out in Lucas's planner, OK? That's how I knew. I'll admit, maybe Lucas was sleeping with Joanna and it was his baby, but don't you see that that gives the Wilkeses a reason to go after him? Kathy killed her daughter because she was ruined and then went after him."

"Let's stop talking about the Wilkeses for a second, OK? Let's talk about you. What you know. You knew Joanna was pregnant. We scoured Lucas's apartment, and yet you found something in his planner we missed, and you're the one who found the cell phone. You're the one hiding something, Mia."

"It's not my fault that I'm a better cop than you and Pruden." I wrapped my arms around myself like a sullen teenager.

"You're so full of information, and yet how? There's only one answer to that: Lucas told you. He's just waiting somewhere, isn't he? For his sister to clear his name. He told you where that phone was hidden."

"No."

"You talked to him the day he took off. Where is he?"

"That call was a fucking pocket dial. Do you really think I was lying to you this whole time? I told you I don't know where he is. I wish I did. You have no idea how much I want to talk to my brother right now. And what about you?"

"What about me?"

"This whole time I've been thinking you've wanted to make a quick arrest and pin this on Lucas because you are that bored small-town cop trying too hard to prove himself, but I know you're the safety liaison at Westfield. You probably saw Joanna all the time." I knew I was starting to churn out accusations with the discrepancy of a lawn sprinkler but I couldn't stop myself.

"*What the fuck are you saying?*" Garrett's voice thundered back at me. An angry, bone-splintering bellow. I flashed to something.

Skinny G in computer club. An obnoxious group of eighth-grade boys sneaking in and unplugging his computer midgame. Garrett lost it. His face blazed red. He slid off his plastic chair and flung it at their ringleader, narrowly missing his head. It clattered hard against the wall. Garrett went for another chair. The bully, clearly panicked, backed out of the room. I'd thought Garrett would feel good about his retreat, but instead he sunk down and started hitting his head against the wall. A dull thud, over and over, until I got Mr. Arkin, who had to call his parents. I felt suddenly scared. In the deserted early morning I was alone with someone who could do whatever he wanted and get away with it.

I softened my voice cautiously. "I'm just saying, what if you'd been the one seen with her, talking to her when you shouldn't have been, maybe if she'd stolen a kiss off of you when you didn't expect it and someone saw? You could be in Lucas's position this very second."

"That would *never* happen. Where the hell are you hearing this shit?" Garrett hammered the steering wheel once, sounding off a weak honk. Followed by a breathy silence. "I would never plan a trip to St. Roche with a high school student. But Lucas did. Even you can't write that off as misconstrued perception. You're grasping at straws, Mia. You need to accept what this is and start telling me what you know and how you know it. You need to tell me where Lucas is."

"And I'm telling you, you need to look at the Wilkeses." Another thought hit me. If Kathy had bought off the guidance counselor, why not Garrett too?

Garrett made a blowing noise. "You're a piece of work." He shook his head once, like it was my loss that I couldn't tell him what he wanted to hear, and pulled away from the curb.

We didn't talk for the rest of the short ride to the station. Once there, Garrett fingerprinted me and took my picture. I spent the next four hours lying on a thin cot, bug-eyed and mind-fizzled, staring at the tiniest watermark on the ceiling.

20

DAY 8

WEDNESDAY

When I was released, Pruden stood nearby, cross-armed, and stared at me with slitted eyes as I signed some paperwork (the official reason I was put in jail was public intoxication) and collected my car keys. I wanted to yell, *Really? I'm the one you're worried about slipping through your butterfingers?* Instead, I grabbed my keys and made a beeline out of there.

The PT was parked outside the station. In all of this, I'd forgotten I had Joanna's file. I flipped up the car mat; it was still there. Of course it was; otherwise, I probably wouldn't have spent the night in just the drunk tank. My bag was still zipped closed and parked on the floor. I didn't know if it was a lack of a search warrant thing or because the WPD still had plans to surveil me and wanted to make me think I was in the clear.

Back at the apartment, I plucked Garrett's GPS off the outlet and tossed it in the Dumpster. Inside, I sat on Lucas's couch, bloodshot and grass-stained. My eyes felt raw, my jaw ached, I had an annoying ringing in my right ear. My arms felt and looked like they'd been through a blender.

Sounds from the pool crept through the window—children laughing, splashing. Someone was playing some headache-inducing club music. I took a Percocet. This time it really was for pain.

I scrolled through my call log and found Vanessa Lee's number.

She answered after half a ring. "Hello?" Her voice breathy, excited.

"Hi, Vanessa, it's Mia Haas. I'm wondering if we could we set up another interview? I have a lot to tell you, the Wilkeses—"

"Mia, what happened last night? Can you comment? I've tried calling you several times this morning."

"Comment?" I was feeling that slight mental doziness that Percocet gave me.

"You're all over the news today. Haven't you watched?"

"No, I haven't had a chance. I've been in jail." I started in about how I was unjustly kept in a cell overnight, how my rights were probably infringed upon, but was interrupted by a muffled noise, like she'd covered the phone with her hand. "Are you recording this?"

"Oh. Yeah. Is that OK? It's so I can be as accurate as possible when I write my articles."

"Fine. Whatever."

"So, can you comment about why you were at the Wilkeses' home last night?"

"That's what I want to meet about. Kathy Wilkes killed her daughter. I think she might have killed my brother."

A pause. "Oh? What are you basing your theories on?"

"I saw Joanna's medical file. She was hurt all the time. I think her mother was abusing her. The police aren't looking into this. You have to print all of this."

"How did you see Joanna's medical file?"

"I went and got it." Not a smart admission, considering she was recording the call, but I was past caring. "I have it here, and I can show it to you. You could see for yourself the frequency of Joanna's injuries. Something else was going on in that house."

"OK. Let's meet. How about same place, in an hour? And you can show me that file."

Vanessa's voice had shifted to gentle and cheery, like a kindergarten teacher, and I knew she wasn't going to write another article about the WPD's incompetency or Lucas's possible innocence. She wasn't going to look at this file and publish a reproachful piece on the Wilkes.

I was her story now.

I sat there, mouth breathing into the line, trying to think but not thinking. The Percocet numbed my mind like a head cold.

"Hello?"

I pressed End.

I Googled myself, and a list of articles came up from newspapers across the Midwest. All with headings that closely paraphrased the first hit: SISTER OF SUSPECTED MURDERER ASSAULTS GRIEVING MOTHER.

There was a shot of me, a close-up. My arms were out at my side, midflail, so it looked as if I was posing in a messiah position. It was clearly taken when I was yelling at the cameras. My face was splotchy; grass was in my hair. And I did look crazy. I did. For a full minute, I wondered if I was. If the pills had made my brain go runny and soft. That maybe I couldn't trust any of my own memories. That for me, reality was a multiple-choice questionnaire. That maybe I had pushed Mimi way harder than I believed, that I had intent to kill. That I wanted to crack her head open like an egg. What if I had her by the hair and I hit her against the counter, over and over, and just blacked it out because I couldn't handle the truth? What if everything good I thought about my brother was invented? A see-no-evil head case like a wife completely oblivious to her husband's child porn studio in the basement?

And then there was Eric. My most recent example of poor judgment of character. And any instincts I did have (if that sick, queasy feeling after I slept with him the first time could be labeled as intuition and not pure guilt) I quelled for a good time on his motorbike. What was wrong with me?

Even those things I thought were missing from the apartment—were they really missing, or did I move them and forget all about it? Had my brain gone that mushy? Sievelike. A few steps short of dementia? Was there a room next to Mimi's with my name on it?

I dumped my phone on the coffee table. Slumped back.

God, I missed my brother. I missed him so, so, so much. This was agony. I felt like I was gasping for breath. Everything ached. My heart was wheezing in my chest, shuddering against my spine. I was scared, something beyond scared. I felt black. As if I were fading away, like a chalk picture on the sidewalk in the rain. He had made me feel anchored to something. To our upbringing, to our shitty childhood. We confirmed each other's origin story. He was there. He *knew.* We were each other's personal Rolodex for *Mommy's fault* excuses. *With a mother like ours, no wonder . . .* we'd say to one another if we fucked up, as we patted each other on the back and tried again to be better people. No one else would know me like him, from beginning to end.

I felt gutted.

Kathy had done it. Kathy and her son, Ben, killed Joanna, killed Lucas, and nearly killed me. Kathy had snapped last night. I could still feel her arm around my throat. She wouldn't have stopped squeezing if Garrett hadn't shown up. I would have died on their front lawn, and Big Ben would have tossed my limp body over his shoulder and dumped me next to Lucas, in our twin burial sites.

It had to be both Ben and Kathy. A mother-son killing duo.

I needed to find Lucas. I needed to know what happened to him. I needed a funeral and closure and to know exactly where he was, even if it was in a graveyard. And justice. I needed justice most of all. Then I thought about Zoey. Zoey and Ben. Their ages matched up. They must have been in school together. I texted her, asked to meet. She responded almost instantaneously.

OFF IN AN HOUR. MEET IN BAR.

I quickly jumped in the shower, brushed my teeth, tried to do something with my hair. I padded on a layer of makeup to conceal the bruises on my cheek and neck. All courtesy of Kathy. I re-dressed my arms and made sure to wear a long-sleeved blouse to keep them covered, cuffs left unbuttoned and loose.

I noticed Lucas's hair gel and razor had been returned, but not the cologne. I blew out a gust of relief. See? I'm not crazy! They were sitting in a corner, between the toilet and the wall. So this was the caretaker's apology? He still came into the suite without permission. Asshole. I needed to call the rental agency.

On my way out, I saw Dale Burton standing at Russ's door. "More stuff is missing from my place, Russ, and I want it back," he said. I thought of how Dale carried around a guns-and-ammo catalogue, and didn't want to think about what the booze-addled caretaker was now packing.

Russ stepped out, his voice all wet squeaks. "I don't know whatcha talking about."

"Bullshit. You do know, and if I don't get my shit back, then you need to pay me for it. Those were expensive hunting knives." Dale poked him in the chest, hard enough that Russ stumbled back into his apartment. "You have two choices."

Dale glanced over, saw me, gave me a told-you-so nod, and I nodded back appreciatively (confirmation of my sanity by an outside source was *the* gold standard after all). Turned back to Russ and kept talking in a lowered voice. Good for Dale, leaning on Russ. If I could, I would've joined him.

21

I sat down at the bar and ordered a coffee, black, from an unfriendly bartender who had a newspaper open next to a bottle of Windex. I could see my face in the paper, a close-up from the press conference. Stray watermarks made me look deformed. I watched the bartender pour my coffee; I couldn't trust that he wouldn't do something to it, like add a helping of Windex. He set it down on the bar, hard, so it splashed over the side.

I waited for Zoey who kept circling around a table of three guys in khakis and golf shirts nursing their beers, asking if they wanted anything more or just the check. One dewy-lipped guy, who I had pegged as a church pastor, delicately said no thanks to both. Finally Zoey flopped down on the stool next to me. "Fuck it, gave the table away. If they're gonna milk a single beer for that long, I doubt the tip was gonna be much anyhow." She leaned across the bar and had an almost flirty exchange with the angry bartender that ended with a joke I was pretty sure was at my expense.

I caught a whiff of coconut body butter, and I thought this was always how these girls smelled. Like a tropical holiday, all sun and fruit and soft beachy sand. He served her a large, sugar-rimmed glass of strawberry margarita.

"So? You here to attack me, too? I can't believe you went after Kathy Wilkes. How are you even showing your face in public right now?" She took a long sip. With her other hand, she stroked her hair like it was a pet ferret. Had she always done this? Or had she developed this subconscious tic only after it became widely believed that my brother had chopped Joanna's hair. Like she had to keep checking that her hair was still there. Proof of Lucas's love because he hadn't harmed a *hair* on her head. "He wanted to boot you outta here"—she nodded toward the bartender—"but I said no, she's here to see me."

"I wanted to meet with you because I wanted to apologize about what I said before. Lucas didn't get anyone pregnant. I was wrong." A lie, but I wanted Zoey back on my side. "And . . . and I think Lucas might be dead." My voice went teary.

Zoey swiveled toward me, fast enough she almost threw herself off the stool. "What? The police found him?" Her bottom lip trembled.

"No. The police don't share my belief."

She clamped her hand against her chest—her breasts did not move—and let out a loud, brief shriek. "God, you scared me." But her eyes had welled up with thick, heavy tears. It was the first time that I believed Zoey might have actual feelings for my brother, deeper than infatuation. I felt a puff of warmth toward her.

"As you know, obviously, I don't believe my brother was responsible for Joanna's death, and I've come to believe he isn't on the run at all. I think something has happened to him. The police of course are not looking at it that way, and so I guess I'm trying to put things together on my own."

"Like what?"

"Tell me about Ben Wilkes."

"Big Ben? Oh, wow. I mean, I don't know him all that well. Why? What d'you want to know?"

"You went to school with him, right?"

"Yeah. He's quiet. Shy. I was a cheerleader when he played on the football team."

"Was he ever violent toward anyone?" A profile. I could build one based on my TV wisdom alone. It seemed easy enough. I mean, everyone knew what to look for. Overbearing or promiscuous mothers, abusive or neglectful fathers . . . a profile that also sounded like Lucas.

"Oh, God no. Big Ben's like a teddy bear. Just a real sweetheart. I mean, he's a little touched, but that only makes him more gentle, I think. At one point, it became clear he couldn't follow the plays all that well, and given his size, he could have just razed anyone on the field, but he didn't seem to like tackling people. So he was spending most of his time on the bench, and I guess someone suggested he be the Bulldog mascot, and he just loved it. He'd put that furry dog head on and go out there and play the big goof. He was so good, he was seriously stealing the cheerleaders' thunder. But then his parents didn't like it. Thought he was being made fun of and made sure he was put back on the team."

"Hmm. Did he do better then? With tackling?"

"Yeah, actually he did. A lot better. Why?"

So Kathy could groom her son to be violent. I explained to Zoey why I was asking about Ben. Her pert nose scrunched up.

"So you think Kathy Wilkes murdered her own daughter because Joanna didn't want to move to New York with her, then had Ben help her frame and possibly murder Lucas as well?"

"I do."

Zoey stared straight ahead, jabbed her straw around the margarita. I couldn't tell if she was giving what I said serious thought, or was signaling the bartender to get rid of me. "Oh my God, you should talk to Carl." She spun around on her stool, looking around the lounge. "He comes in here every afternoon."

"Carl?"

"Yeah, he worked at Harold's processing plant. He's always going on about the Wilkeses." She called the bartender over. "Carl been in yet?"

Bartender shook his head. "Not yet."

Zoey turned back to me. "Talk to Carl—he'll be here soon. Like clockwork, every day he comes in for a couple of beers."

"What'll Carl tell me?"

"Jus' that he thinks the Wilkeses are evil. He lost three fingers last year working in their plant. He goes on about it all the time, hoping us girls here will take pity on him and give him a blow job or whatever he's got going on in his head. He's, like, forty and schizoid—as if anyone's going there. Anyway, he knows all this shit about the Wilkeses. He's always in before three." It was quarter to two now. "I just can't believe that my baby might be dead." Zoey licked the rim of her glass, and the sugar granules dissolved fast in her lip gloss. She grabbed the drink napkin under her glass and blew her nose.

The baby part jarred me, and it took a second to realize she meant Lucas. "So you believe me?" I asked, careful not to sound too incredulous about it.

"Well, it makes sense, doesn't it? Why would he have just dumped me like that?" *And we're back* to why Zoey was dumped, but I didn't care, so long as she believed me. Then she made this little startled noise, her eyes popped and her jaw fell loose, "*Ohmygod,* what if the Wilkeses threatened me too? I always felt like he was trying to protect me. Maybe he was protecting me from them. Like I said, I was supposed to go over after my shift that night and then I got that text, and that was that. I lied, by the way. I did keep the text he sent me. I just couldn't delete it. As awful as it was, I kept it."

"Can I see it?"

Zoey tapped and scrolled, then handed me her phone.

> I DONT WANT TO BE WITH U ANYMORE. SORRY. I AM IN LOVE WITH SOMEONE ELSE.

"He didn't write this." I couldn't see him dumping someone so harshly. He always made smooth exits, so whoever he was dumping believed they'd reached the decision together. If he did write it, it was to get the job done quick and effectively, like taking a chainsaw to an umbilical cord. And what was with all the capital letters, like he was shouting at her? In the box of school things that Eric dropped off, my brother had another classroom poster with a pensive-looking lizard asking, "What do people who type 'Y' and 'U' instead of 'why' and 'you' do with all their extra time?" Would Lucas use "U" instead of "you"? He was still an English teacher. So maybe he was protecting Zoey in some way? Or else Kathy or Ben used his phone to text Zoey and keep her away so that she wouldn't walk in on them. But doing what? It's not like they did anything to Lucas in his apartment. There was no blood, no sign of a struggle. How would they even have known that Zoey was coming over?

"I knew it. I knew I hadn't been dumped." Tone-deaf, Zoey sounded too pleased with herself, as if Lucas was better dead than having dumped her. She gave a triumphant nod.

"He didn't text that. Or else someone made him do it."

"We have to find him." She grabbed my hand. I squeezed hers back. Gratefulness that I finally had an ally shuddered behind my breastbone; I almost wept. Instead I took in a steadying mouthful of air so that I wouldn't.

"OK. OK, let's go back to before he went missing. Did Lucas talk about anything that seemed strange or off to you?"

"Not that I can think of. He certainly never mentioned having sex with one of his students."

"Anything at all, however small."

"Not really. I mean, sometimes we didn't do a whole lot of talking." A wistful giggle.

I rolled my eyes. Grilled her a little, got specific. "Anything about coaching? His hockey players? Cell phones? Gambling? Owing money? Ben or Kathy Wilkes?"

"No, nothing that was weird or out of the ordinary. Well, just before everything went down, he was talking about you a lot."

"Me?"

"Yeah, he said he worried about you. Things like that. Alone, in the big city. He said you thought you didn't deserve someone special."

"He said that?" I felt the sharp cut of betrayal as I pictured Lucas with his head in her lap, casually psychoanalyzing me as she stroked his hair. Why hadn't he ever brought this up to me?

She offered up a sympathetic pout and nodded.

I made my face go steely so I wouldn't show I was stinging. Put it aside. "Anything else?"

Zoey looked up, as if really trying to peer inside her own head. "Well, he also kept bringing up wanting to know who his father was."

"What did he say about it?" That surprised me. He hadn't brought that up for years. The last thing I remembered him saying about it was that if our father was worth finding, he'd have found us.

"Just that he wanted to know. It bothered him. It was a gap in his history, y'know?"

"Yes, I know." We shared the same anonymous father, and therefore the same gap-toothed history.

"He was working on it."

"Working on what?"

"Finding him. He said he was getting close."

"Getting close, how?" What the hell did that mean? Getting close? If he knew who our father was, why didn't he tell me any of this?

Zoey shrugged. "I don't know. He didn't get into details. It was kind of depressing to talk about anyway." The bartender refilled my coffee with the remaining dregs of the carafe, though I motioned for him not to. "Funny. Lucas hated coffee."

"Yeah, I know." Something tugged at me. "Or, well, he did. Supposedly he likes coffee now. He gets his students to bring him one if they're late."

"Uh, no, I don't think so. He can't stand the stuff. I always tease him about it. He doesn't even have a coffeemaker at his place."

So Bailey lied about that, a stupid lie, the kind teenagers tell that have no other purpose than to get attention in the moment they're telling it.

Zoey elbowed me. "There's Carl." She bounced over to Carl, put her elbows on the table. It looked like she was sweet-talking him into meeting me. Just like she sweet-talked the bartender into letting me stay. This girl had skills. She waved me over. We both sat down.

Carl had a wild look to him. It was the combination of a lazy eye, a full-out old West mustache worn in earnest, and a permanent look of sexual frustration, a sort of half wince. "I want to shake your hand." He extended a palm, with a thumb and three stumps. His index finger was intact, so I mostly held that as he pumped my arm up and down. "Wish I coulda' punched that woman in the face myself. Though, y'know, under different circumstances—not right after her daughter died, that's for sure." He eyed me like I was a psychopath, then lingered on my breasts.

Zoey snapped her fingers twice. "Over here, Carl. She wants to know what happened between you and the Wilkeses." I was glad Zoey had stayed. No need for small talk, just straight to the point.

"Here's how my saga all started. Lost my fingers on the job last spring. All three were sliced while I was feeding plastic film into the equipment that seals food into packaging. Everyone wants their food to come in nice little packages." He sneered, like this was completely unreasonable. "Thing was, the guard was broken. I'd brought it up the week before to the foreman, and he said it'd be fixed. It wasn't." He wiggled his stumps. "So, after getting offered a shitty workers' comp package, I decided to sue. Well, that Ian Wilkes wasn't having any of that." He took a gulp of his beer, the foam washing up on the shore of his 'stache. Then slammed the mug down on the table. "They fucking burned my house down." His voice went up, loud. I startled. Zoey cast me a told-you-so look, pretended someone had called her into the kitchen, and left. Carl watched her go with a creepy intensity.

"So the Wilkeses burned your house down?"

"Yup. Without a doubt."

"And what happened?"

Carl leaned in close. "Nothing at all. Firefighters said it was caused by a short in a heater I was using, but I know it was them. I didn't have no house insurance, so I had to take the damn compensation package. I couldn't afford to hire a lawyer and wait years for a payout." He paused for dramatic effect, and I knew I was supposed to say something sympathetic.

"Oh, that's terrible."

"Now I'm living at the Tall Pines Motel." He waved his hand around like a foam finger at a ball game.

"Have they followed you at all? Tried to intimidate you?" These details were what I needed to really flesh out my profile of Ben and Kathy and apparently even Ian Wilkes. There was always a trail of near victims before actual victims.

He started nodding, whispered, "How do you know?" A kind of paranoid look swept over his face. "They're watching me. Kathy and Ian Wilkes. Watching to make sure I don't make trouble."

"Ben's been following me too. Running me off the road in his black truck." I leaned in closer. I was really getting somewhere.

"Well, I don't know nothing 'bout no truck. I do know they've been tapping my phone and peeping in my window. Those bank fees I get on my statements, that's them stealing from me, and they get a doctor to take my blood when I'm asleep. I don't know why—do you know why they take my blood?"

I got it then. Carl really was schizoid. This was how I sounded to Garrett, to Vanessa Lee. It wasn't long before he started getting into government conspiracies, why supermarket meat didn't rot (carbon-monoxide-laced packaging!), and what the fluoride in water really did to the human body. Eventually I was able to get away, but not before Carl asked me to pay for his drinks. "It's only fair, considering how much confidential information I've given you."

I sat outside in Casey's parking lot. Someone had tossed a half-finished Big Gulp through the broken window into my backseat, and the whole car had a not entirely unpleasant scent of grapes baking in the sun.

I didn't go back to the apartment but drove to Eric's instead. During the night of too much bourbon, he had revealed where he lived with what I'd thought was a charming amount of embarrassment (a boxy condo complex not far from Westfield). I'd ignored the two texts he sent me, both asking how I was doing in a slightly different way. Before Kathy nearly wrung the life out of me, I might have been able to muster up some sympathy for Eric. Yes, it was a loathsome, jerky thing to sell off a student's confidentiality (again a tremor of relief I'd never seen him again after pushing Mimi—what would he have done with that info?), but the Wilkeses had a lot of money, and maybe Kathy had made an offer too sweet for someone on a teacher's salary to resist.

A glance in the rearview mirror. I had a ghostly, hollowed-out look. My neck had a collar of bright-red splotches that looked like I had tried to hang myself but then changed my mind. Eric opened the door, looking sleepy and smelling like a hangover. His hair was tufty. It was just after 4 P.M., and he was still in boxer shorts. He started to apologize for his appearance; he'd played at Detours until close last night—then he noticed what I looked like.

"What happened to you?" More asleep than awake, he reached out to touch my neck, his eyes hooded like he was going to kiss me better, but I brushed him off.

"Kathy, again. That's what happened to me. We need to talk." Good. He'd slept in and hadn't read the news yet, and being hungover, he was probably not at his sharpest. He invited me in, slipped on some track pants and a faded T-shirt, and poured me a strong coffee. Eric's place was exactly as I'd thought it would be, decorated like the Hard Rock Cafe. Band posters and two neon signs. A mounted guitar rack with three gleaming guitars.

He sat across from me on a barstool at a tall rustic table. Afternoon sunlight was streaming in through a window and hitting his face, hard. He looked tired, even starting to show signs of the next ten years. He had the creasy, blanched look that precedes haggard. I wondered if he did the occasional bump of cocaine to get him through those late nights (he'd been pretty eager for an upper!) or for the sweet rush of closing his eyes and trading in the crowd of depressed dart-tossing drunks for a packed stadium. I got that cheated feeling. Like I'd gone to bed with a ten and woken up to a five.

"I know that you were selling your sessions with Joanna to Kathy."

"What? I don't know what you're talking—" He had just the right amount of outrage in his voice. I might've believed him.

"Just don't, OK? I don't need to hear you deny it."

"There's nothing to deny, Mia." His lips twisted into an angry smile. He cocked his head, furrowed his brow in what was probably his best mirror-face, a face that made the ladies at Detours a sure thing. That had made me a sure thing. I'd have bet his stockpile of Los Angeles anecdotes and interesting music trivia were just finite party favors, and once they ran dry, Eric had to move on to other conquests before his hollowness was exposed. His hand traveled across the table and rested on mine. "I offered Kathy some extra counseling, if that's what you mean?"

"OK, whatever you want to call it." I moved my hand away. Eric made a face, like he was sucking on something sour.

"I'm calling it what it was."

"Except you were telling Kathy everything Joanna confided for a fee."

Eric sighed. "I'm a good person, Mia. I was only trying to help a concerned mother.

Why, oh why, had Eric not called himself a good person earlier? I never would have slept with him. The worst people I'd ever met started their sentences with *I'm a good person, y'know.*

"I'm not interested in getting you in trouble. That's not why I'm here. I want to know about Kathy."

Eric sniffed. His eyes narrowed like he was trying to think up a lie but was too hungover to think creatively. Resignation glided over his face. "What about Kathy? I told you that she was overbearing. What else is there to say?"

"Was Joanna afraid of her?"

"Afraid of her? No. I don't think so. I mean, if she was genuinely afraid of her mother, she probably wouldn't have acted out so much." He took a sip of coffee.

"Didn't you wonder why Joanna had all those injuries? Didn't you question it?"

"Injuries? No, why would I? She had some dance injuries. It happens."

"How did Kathy approach you? What exactly was she after?"

This made Eric start to fidget. "She just dropped by and told me she was worried about her daughter. That's it. She didn't want Joanna to repeat her mistakes. I didn't think she had nefarious intentions, if that's what you're asking. Yes, maybe she was one of those dance moms living vicariously through her daughter, but that doesn't mean she didn't want the best for her."

"By the best for her, you mean exactly what Kathy wanted her to be."

Eric rubbed his face. Held his hands on his cheeks, pulling down all his features, his eyes red-rimmed and distorted. I got the feeling that just the sound of my voice was annoying the hell out of him. Too bad. He looked at me from under those bowed eyelids, before he let go of his face and dropped his hands onto the table. His lips twitched. He sighed. "*Fuuuuck*. Fine! Whatever, Mia, OK? I don't know why you're so intent on trying to make me feel bad. But you know what? Joanna was a spoiled brat. OK? She had everything. Everything. I would have killed for the opportunities she squandered." Eric was practically shouting, his voice dripping with bitterness. He kept shaking his head, like I'd driven him past some point of no return.

"So you sold her out, because—why? You hated that she was still so young and had so much talent and an easy means out of here. While you're still—"

"Yes, I know I'm a failed musician. I don't need you to tell me that," he snapped. "I didn't hate her. That's ridiculous. She was just . . . like they all are. These kids. They're generic little copies of the kids I had last year and the year before, and the year before. They like the same music, shop at the same stores, and take the same selfies."

In my defense, both times I'd been around Eric, I hadn't been sober. Not that I was totally sober now. But even with a Percocet running thin in my veins, I could now see that when Eric wasn't set to music and soft lighting, he was an angry, resentful man.

"Did Joanna tell you she was pregnant?"

Something dark passed over his face. "No."

"What? It looks like you want to say something. Tell me."

He hesitated. Stood up, stretched his back, and grabbed a bottle of whiskey from a cupboard, then poured a shot into his coffee. Took a sip. Grimaced. "Hey, do you have any more of those pills?"

"I do."

"Could I . . . this hangover. I'm just feeling like shit here."

"I told you, only the first pill was free. You need to start talking to me, and I'll give something that'll fix you right up. So, again, tell me, did Joanna say she was pregnant?"

Eric sat back down. "Well, this one time— Let me think. I don't know how it came up, but she started talking about how adoption was one of the most selfless things someone could do for someone else. It led me to saying something about my ex-wife's fertility issues, and so on, and she wanted to know if my ex-wife—who's now remarried, by the way—would still want a baby and how amazing it would be for her if someone just gave her one. And so and so on." Eric started to make a yakky hand gesture then caught himself. "Anyway, I didn't think much about it, because that's what these kids do. They feign this grand capacity for selflessness and kindness without ever having to follow through. At their core, they're just attention-seeking statements. There's nothing to them."

"When did she talk about adoption?" Like all good Wayoatan girls, Joanna didn't think abortion was an option.

"I don't know? I don't remember exactly. Earlier in the year. Maybe January?" Could this have been Joanna's second pregnancy? Or had she been planning on getting pregnant since January? Was that her ultimate ticket out of dancing? Just like Mom. But then Joanna would have to keep it to make that work, wouldn't she?

"Did she talk to your ex-wife?"

"What? No. I doubt it. I don't talk to my ex anymore, but I'm sure she would have been in touch if a student had contacted her about adopting her baby. That's sort of a conflict of interest." *And taking cash from Joanna's mother wasn't?*

"Did you tell Kathy that Joanna was talking about adoption?"

"No. Why would I? I thought it was nothing." Eric shrugged a little too forcefully. It made me think he wasn't being totally honest. Or did Joanna really get in touch with his ex, and Eric couldn't stand the thought of his ex going on with some neat, tidy family?

Especially if it was his.

My throat tightened. During my sessions with Eric, the door had always been closed. No other staff members ever popped in. Not that I could remember. There was opportunity. I mean, there was even a couch! Was it so outlandish that Joanna could have been sleeping with Eric too? Maybe she was the school faculty Lolita. Maybe she knew how much it would piss off her mom to be sleeping with multiple men. And what a great cover for Eric to do recon on Joanna when he was the one sleeping with her. Then when he found out Joanna was with Lucas too, he fed Kathy stories, and that was why Lucas was dead right now and not Eric.

"Mia?"

I shook myself out of this line of thinking. I mean, I'd just slept with this guy! Twice! And now I thought he was the one who'd started it all? Clearly, my judgment was too skittish and couldn't be trusted. Besides, wild finger-pointing would not help my cause. And whatever Eric might have done was beside the point; it still boiled down to Kathy and Ben.

"You said Joanna mentioned she was seeing an older man. Did you tell Kathy that?"

"Well, like I said, I thought she meant Dylan, so yeah, I told Kathy."

"Did Kathy ever suspect Joanna was involved with Lucas, before Joanna went missing?"

"If she did, she didn't hear that from me." Eric said this so forcefully, I almost believed him. "What is this all about, anyway?"

I took a deep breath. "I think Kathy murdered her daughter and could have possibly murdered Lucas."

Eric just looked at me. Took another gulp of his coffee. "Huh."

"Huh? That's it?" I noted that Eric didn't once ask me how I knew what I did. I wasn't sure if that could be chalked up to a foggy hangover or something else.

"Well, you're allowed to think whatever you want to think."

My thoughts shuffled. "The other day at the Terrace, what did you say to Madison Wilkes?"

"Madison?"

"She was at the pool, at my brother's building. I saw you talking to her."

He blinked. "Nothing. She just looked like she needed someone to talk to."

"So what? You saw another financial opportunity?"

He scowled at me. "Well, I guess I deserve that. But no, I really just wanted to see how she was doing. Let her know I was here to help if she wanted to talk."

"Yeah, she probably *really* needs your help." I said this more sarcastically than I meant to. Eric flexed his jaw, let out a shallow snort.

"Listen, Mia, I'm sorry for your situation, I really am, but I am not a bad guy, and I really don't need this right now." He picked up his coffee mug, saw it was empty, set it down hard. He rotated it once, twice. I noticed his hands were shaking.

"Eric," I started, and was about to say, *I thought you were different* or *Whatever you need to tell yourself,* but it seemed too utterly pointless, and then there was suddenly nothing left to say.

Somehow Eric took this to mean something else entirely. He reached out again and made a play for my hands. Tried to look sexy-sheepish but instead looked old and washed-out. This guy really did think he had a magic penis—like some fairy godmother, he could just wave it at you, and you'd feel better. My stomach turned. I snatched my hands back. He gave me a chilly smirk.

"Can I least get that pill from the other night, then?"

I tapped out two Advil tablets and left.

I sat in my car. I didn't know what to do next. Crazy Carl was a dead end. Eric was a dead end. I was at a dead end. Maybe I needed to look at things differently. If Lucas was actively looking to find out who our father was, then I knew who I had to go see.

Mona and Mimi were proudly Wayoata's original "cougars." I still knew Mona's phone number by heart; her long-suffering husband answered. I was surprised she'd stayed married. I'd met him once, just for a minute when he dropped by to pick her up (she'd passed out on the couch). His name was Andrew, and he looked nothing like the jerk she complained about. He woke her so gently, I remembered feeling just the briefest grinding yearning for a dad while Mimi flitted around the room like she was worried about Mona, all the while casting flirtatious glances at him.

Now Andrew told me in a cheerful, what-are-you-gonna-do? voice that she was likely playing the slots over at the casino. "Again," followed by a stoic sigh. The casino was a half-hour drive away, off the highway. Pretty much in the middle of nowhere. The parking lot was gravel, and from the outside, it looked like some roadhouse in an eighties movie. This here, in better days, had been Mona and Mimi's stomping ground. They fancied themselves *Sex and the City* type gals, without the city.

Entering, I was hit with the strong smells of chlorine from a whirring glass cleaner behind the bar and the musky perfume favored by middle-aged women. I scanned the backs of people sitting in front of the slot machines. I tried to remember the last time I saw Mona. Something had happened between her and Mimi sometime before the accident, and they'd stopped talking. This wasn't unusual, they had frequent falling-outs, mostly spurred on by Mona's sober stretches, and then suddenly they were back together like nothing had happened and girls' night was back on.

After Mimi's "accident," Mona showed up once a week with a tinfoil-encased hot dish and made feeble attempts to tidy up the house a bit for us. She'd always corner me at some point during these visits, tell me how sad she was. Poor, poor Mimi. She'd talk about her like she was a good ol' gal, a best friend that'd been taken away from her. She prodded me to cry with her, she wanted a big sobfest—*A girl your age without a mother, it's just tragic.* She'd aim her shoulder in close. *I'm here. I'm right here.* If I was alone when she showed up, I'd pretend no one was home. I was not interested in a surrogate mother.

Finally I spotted her by her hair. It was the same bottle-red-bordering-on-orange that she'd always dyed it. Hair that never moved because it was sprayed so stiff with hairspray that it looked coated with shellac. A teal-colored silk scarf draped over her shoulders. Her lips were moving, cursing the machine. I sat down next to her, plunked a quarter in.

Surprisingly, Mona had aged remarkably well. I had pictured her marshmallowy puckered or sunken and drink-battered, but she looked good. Definitely had had some work done. Her eyes were more cattish than I remembered.

"Mona?" She hardly looked up. The blinking lights and chirpy music had full hypnotic hold over her.

"Uh-huh?" Her veiny hand dumped in another fistful of quarters.

"It's Mia Haas, Mimi's daughter." I pushed Spin and lost my quarter.

Mona whipped around to face me so fast it looked like it hurt. "Mia? *My God!*" She cried out. Her twiggy arms outstretched, a dry kiss pressed against my cheek, a second that landed on the corner of my mouth. I suddenly remembered that Mona used to get large blistering cold sores and my lips burned. She kept both her hands over mine. "Let me look at you, it's been ages," she purred. That's what both Mimi and Mona did: they purred or they drawled in husky voices. "I thought you would have come and seen me sooner. It's all such terrible business, what they're saying about Lucas."

"I honestly didn't think to. I wish I had." It was true. I remembered now how warm Mona was toward me before the accident. Before everything related to Mimi felt so tainted, so singed at the edges. She was the giver of those bad, tipsy haircuts, though she'd tried hard to replicate whatever picture I brought her. She'd pay me compliments about my eyes. Once when I had a bad cold, she brought me a package of M&M's and a *People* magazine (while my mother shot me a dirty look that said I was milking her friend for attention).

I knew she had two sons. Both were older than me, and I knew only vague things about them. One still lived in Wayoata; the other lived on the East Coast and worked in computers. I think Mimi had envied her for that, two sons. Some women should never have daughters.

Mona cashed out, and we made our way to a high table. She was a short woman, though this was easy to forget because she still wore stiletto heels when most women her age had long been sporting Dr. Scholl's. She had some trouble hauling herself up onto the stool. Finally she set down her purse on its side. Its opening faced me, and I could see sprinkles of tobacco stuck to the blue lining. I was always sure to buy a purse that zipped closed, for fear that I'd accidentally drop it and all the orange bottles would come spilling out.

"So, have you gone to see your mother?"

"Once."

"Mmm. Well, that's nice." She said this in a way that made me feel going to visit my mother only once since I got there was not that nice at all. "Well, I go to see her from time to time. She has no idea who I am, of course. Thinks I'm one of the nurses, but it's funny, because sometimes I'll tell her a story about some wild thing we did, and I'll get a glimpse of the old mischievous Mimi." Mona sniffed and let out a huffy sigh. "We had a good run. We did."

"I had that feeling too."

"Well, I guess you never know. Maybe some of the old Mimi is still in there."

"That's true," I murmured. Quick to move off that topic, I asked, "Did Lucas ever come to see you—asking about our father?"

Mona ran her tongue over her teeth. Her eyes sharpened. "He did. About three months ago." She nodded, drummed her *clickity-clack* nails once, twice. "Your brother seemed very stressed by it. I asked him why he was bringing this all up now, but he didn't really say.

Anyway, I'll tell you what I told him. I don't know who your father is. That was the one thing I could never get out of Mimi, not for lack of trying. Of course she'd toss little mysterious tidbits about him; he was quite a bit older than her, he was European, married, and very wealthy, but you know how Mimi liked to embellish." These were all things I already knew. I was disappointed, not for me, but for Lucas. "I know he gave Mimi child support whenever she started grumbling or threatened to tell his wife. In turn, she never went for more, because he said if she did, he would sue for full custody and win because he could afford the best. Now, whether any of this is true, your guess is as good as mine. Mimi always had a penchant for drama."

This was something new. It was the first time I'd ever heard of child support. To think some man out there had knowledge of us and had discussed us like some fluctuating stock was a punch in the gut.

"What did Lucas say when you told him all of this?"

"Well, he was most interested in the money. How much money did Mimi get, how often, how she was paid."

These were good questions, I guessed. If the man who fathered us could just toss Mimi some cash here and there, that meant he lived in Wayoata. Mimi always insisted that he'd moved away. That he didn't even know we existed. But he must have. Lucas would not have taken this news well.

"Of course I didn't have any answers for him." Mona shook her head apologetically.

"Did he say anything to you about getting close to finding out who he was?"

"Why, no! Did he find out? I would *love* to know." Mona leaned in. Licked her lips.

Smudges in my memory took shape, things that I'd never really thought about. Those wet conversations Mimi had in her bedroom, door locked. An empty bottle of wine on her nightstand by the time she hung up. Or in the bathtub, emitting little, ragged sobs through the door, a wineglass smashed against the toilet. Finding fine shards of glass for weeks after. I'd ask, *Who were you talking to?* And she'd just shake her head like she had no idea what I was talking about.

Once, once—how could I have forgotten this?—I picked up the extension. A man's voice, low timbre, saying things to her like *Calm down, don't disrespect me,* then cajoling, *Yes, fine, I know, I know.* Mimi not sounding like Mimi, because she was so pared down. The voice had been unfamiliar, which had made me think he was someone new, because we were still at an age when Mimi would have us call her boyfriends and ask things like when they were coming over or if they would like to do something with us sometime soon. Yet he didn't sound like someone new, because Mimi wasn't using her steamy voice.

"That night . . ." Mimi's intended destination that night had been something Lucas had fixated on right after the "accident." I knew better; I knew it didn't matter. She still would have had the brain injury. But Lucas always treated it as a missing piece.

"I know what you're going to ask me because Lucas asked too. Just like I told him when it happened, I don't know where Mimi was going that night. Honest to God." She held up her hand like a pledging member of 4-H. "Maybe she had no idea herself. She was always so up and down with everything. Unpredictable. She drove men away with her intensity and lured more in just the same. It's almost too bad that this artistic thing she's doing now didn't come earlier in her lifetime. I bought one of her pieces at a LightHouse fund-raising event and had it framed. It hangs right in my living room. She's quite the artist. The way she was, would make a great biopic wouldn't it? This town was just too small for her."

"She always said that, but she never left." So apparently it wasn't too small for her. Or maybe it was the deep-voiced man who kept her here, especially if he was married. She would have got off on traipsing us around in front of him. She'd cast him some vengeful looks at the supermarket over our heads, and we'd be oblivious that our father was right there. I really didn't like how Mona was romanticizing my mother, either. She wasn't deserving of it. "What happened to her, my mother? What made her so, I don't know, the way she was?" For a second, I thought Mona would play dumb, say something patronizing like Mimi tried at least to be a good mother.

"Well, you know Mimi didn't like to talk about the past." It was true. Five minutes could pass, and Mimi considered it the Past, and the Past was deniable and therefore immune to criticism. Bringing it up made one unforgiving and spiteful.

"I know she didn't get along with her own mother. Maybe that set the tone. The way Mimi talked about her, she was very cold and distant. She put herself first, even when it came to sharing Mimi's father. I think sometimes that kind of selfishness can run in the blood." Mona caught herself. "Of course that means you and Lucas have a lot to be proud of, becoming such considerate adults all on your own."

I had nothing to say in return. My head felt like it was filling with radio static.

Mona reached over, gripped my wrist. "You know, I always felt bad for you. I know Mimi was especially hard on you. Some women, they just don't know how to get along with their daughters. They can flirt with their sons, but they just don't know what to do with their daughters. I guess Mimi was more like her mother than she cared to admit, but she did love you in her own way."

"Hard on me" was an understatement. It didn't matter. Nothing would change how I felt about her.

We said our good-byes, and Mona wrapped me up in another tight hug, and I found myself clinging back. A feeling of intense tenderness swept over me. Even a dash of homesickness for this town. I suddenly didn't want to let her go.

When I stepped outside, the daylight burned into my eyes. The car was suffocatingly hot. I rolled down the windows, fought a wave of nausea. My thoughts were scattering, I needed a handful of Adderall to corral them in, Valium to calm down, an Ambien to blink out and disappear. Craving started to broil my skin. I drove to where Mimi had had her accident. She'd veered off Main Street and smacked into an old oak tree. Several trees lined this section of the street. She wasn't heading home, because our house was in the opposite direction. But who knew, maybe she got turned around in her drunken stupor or was in the middle of trying to do a U-turn. I parked, walked the sidewalk. Tried to see if I could pick out the tree. I could not. I'd have bet Lucas could.

The sky had turned a dirty yellow. Back in the car, I was driving aimlessly again. I found myself outside Kathy's dance studio, so I parked my PT in the lot across the street. I sat watching—for what exactly, I didn't really know. I guess, for Kathy to come out with a rolled-up carpet, Lucas's arm falling out at the last second as she loaded it into a minivan. The Wilkeses had a multitude of places where they could hide a body: at their food processing plant, in some unused vat, or in a freezer in pieces. I had a flash of him, lifeless, his eyes dark puddles.

I caved and took just a nibble of a Valium to keep my nerves steady, two Adderall to stay awake.

I was there, watching, because it felt like I was doing something.

From there, I drove past the Wilkeses' house twice. OK, three times. Just turned around at the end of the road, passed it again. Their sprawling ranch house was practically all windows. It was too bad I couldn't just park and watch them at home, comfortable in their natural habitat where they might make revealing mistakes that could lead me to Lucas, but there were double the number of media vans. Reporters likely hoping to catch another front-lawn confrontation between me and Kathy. After the second drive-by, reporters did notice me and tried to flag me down, their baiting questions rolling in through the missing back window. "Are you planning to attack Kathy Wilkes again? Is your brother a murderer? How many other students did he molest?" I sunk down and careered past them.

Now I was back at the studio watching Kathy go red-faced again as she yelled at little girls in pink bodysuits.

Ben drove into the lot, then out. Odd. I followed him. It was a short drive to a convenience store, where he walked out with a handful of Slim Jims. Then he sat there in his truck, gnawing on them in the store lot. Nothing was happening.

Maybe I was following the wrong Wilkes. What did Ian do with his evenings when Kathy was at the studio? I drove outside Wayoata to the processing plant, but a heavy-looking metal gate was drawn across the entrance.

I was literally driving around in circles. I decided to go back to Lucas's. I had the key in the lock, and plans to collapse on the couch with an Ambien-Percocet milk shake, when behind me the door to apartment 45 opened. Just a crack. "Hello?" A voice, high and gentle, little-girl-like.

"Yes?" I turned around, tried to peek into the sliver opening.

"My cat, somehow, somehow, he got out. Can you help me?"

"I . . . I can try." My voice shot up, not sure what exactly she wanted me to do.

"He's black with a white triangle on his chest. Can you look for me? I just don't understand how he got out, I just don't . . . We went to bed together and then I woke up, and he was gone." She sobbed, breathless. Oh, I knew how it had happened. Russ had gone rummaging for booze.

"His name is Edgar. Here." She dropped a foil bag of treats. Another cat let out a demonic growl.

"Shake them. He should come out."

I picked up the package of treats. Started down the hall, shaking them. "Edgar, Edgar, come."

I went down the stairwell, calling the cat, caught sight of a tail and nearly fell down the stairs. "Edgar, come. Come." I shook the bag of treats, with hard, desperate flicks of my wrist. I needed to catch Edgar. I could at least do that, catch a cat. I was hopeless otherwise.

I lost sight of the tail, but descended all the way into the basement anyway. Obnoxious, head-splitting rave music pulsed at full volume at the end of the hallway, where there were two suites. No crevices for a cat to hide in. I took a quick look, then went the other way toward the storage area. A bunch of closet-sized storage spaces with plywood doors, half with padlocks. No cat. The pipes ticked down here. I quickly scanned the hall. There was a mechanical room, but the door was locked.

There was another exit up a short set of stairs that led to the side of the building. I wasn't sure if the key I had worked on this door, so I propped it open with a case of empties someone had left, it seemed, for this very purpose. I looked around in the sparse bushes not far from the parking lot.

Back up on the main floor, I went outside again. Called out for Edgar, shook the bag. My voice echoed back at me in the parking lot. I looked by the garbage bin, hauled myself up to look inside. This was ridiculous. Then back inside and into the laundry room. A washing machine was spinning loudly, and foamy soap escaped through its lid.

I wondered if apartment 45 was really agoraphobic. How did that work with groceries and laundry? A flash of black fur. Edgar was behind the dryer.

"Here." I doled out a treat.

Slowly I drew him out, picked him up. He bit my hand. I dropped him, got him again. "I gotcha," I said out loud, more than once as I walked the cat back upstairs. "I got him, I have Edgar!" I said this through the door, absurdly triumphant sounding. My eyes tearing and dripping onto the top of Edgar's slick black head.

The door cracked open. "Shhh. No one can know. Cats aren't allowed." Edgar jumped from my arms and disappeared inside.

I was about to say, *I think the caretaker already knows,* and explain why, but the door snapped shut. "Put a chair under your doorknob." I pressed my forehead against the door. "You're welcome."

At some point, in a near coma with the golden assistance of a dangerous amount of downers, I felt someone take both of my hands and unroll the fists I'd made in my sleep. I could hear the squirting sound of a tube. A cool touch. Someone's hot breathing on the inside of my arm.

Small slippery circles were thumbed in my palm, then a greasy rubdown worked over each of my knuckles. Someone's fingers slithered in between my own, slow and methodical.

Unrushed. Not at all worried I'd come to. Like they'd watched me swallow a handful of pills.

I tried like hell to wake up, to snatch my hands away, but couldn't. I just kept sliding back down into sleep like a trapped frog inside a bucket. I couldn't judder a single finger. I couldn't lift an eyelid. I'd lost control of my body (that was the point of all those downers). I was in full sleep paralysis. Even my heart rate stayed at a slow, steady *thump, thump, thump* while inside somewhere, I was screaming in terror.

22

DAY 9

THURSDAY

When I finally woke up, the sun was coming in through the vertical blinds, casting its prison-bar shadows across the blanket. My hair was damp with sweat. I would have written last night off as a hallucinogenic episode or, at best, a really deep dream if I hadn't pressed the back of my hand to my nose and caught a sharp whiff of vanilla. I staggered up and grabbed my phone.

"Can you please check if Miranda Haas is in her room?"

"Of course she is."

"I need you to check; this is her daughter, Mia Haas."

The nurse brought the phone with her. I could hear her climbing the stairs. She breathed heavy into the phone. It couldn't have been Russ who'd lotioned up my hands, because I seriously doubted he would have stopped at my hands. Maybe if it'd been my breasts that were kneaded and smelled like vanilla, or worse, I would think it was Russ. Or if there were more bottles of booze missing. No. It had to be Mimi. It had that mother's loving touch. Maybe it had been Mimi the whole time; she was the one taking Lucas's things. Maybe she knew where he was.

"Did she get out again last night?" I walked around the apartment, checking the closets, behind the recliner, under the bed, sure my mother was about to pop out.

"No. We've taken better precautionary measures since she ran off. We've put a lock on her door at night. I realize that might sound extreme—"

"No, that's fine. Good."

"I am unlocking her room now." I heard a jangle of keys, the nurse cursing lightly under her breath. "Wrong key, hold on." Then the sound of Mimi shouting in the background *What'd ya want* at the nurse. "She's right here, Miss Haas."

"I heard. But there's a window in her room, right? Could she get out that way?"

"Well, of course there's a window. It would be against the building's fire code not to have one but Mimi's room is on the second story," and here the nurse paused, so I'd clue in that I should know this about my mother's living arrangements, "but she couldn't drop out from the window without injury. There's just no way she could have gotten out, Miss Haas."

No, but maybe someone else was letting her out. Could it be Kathy? Maybe she was whispering vicious things into my mother's ear while pressing Lucas's apartment key into her hand. Setting Mimi up to do her dirty work and get rid of me. And what? Instead Mimi slathered my hands with lotion? My mind went swirly, and I started to sweat again. There was always the chance I was still hallucinating, that I hadn't smelled what I thought I had. I pressed my nose to my knuckles again and nearly started retching. No. Someone lotioned my hands, while I slept. Back in the bathroom, I washed my hands, scrubbed until they were raw and I couldn't smell the faintest trace of vanilla.

I slumped down on the couch again, still coated with pixie pill dust from the night before. I felt violated. I felt crazy. I felt like the apartment, the TV, the bookshelves, the cowhide rug, a yellow Post-it note stuck to the bottom of the recliner, another day without knowing what had happened to my brother, were all a watery surface, and if I could just reach out and touch the air with my finger, everything would ripple.

A yellow Post-it? I reached down, teeth grinding, and pulled it off the recliner. It was full of inky numbers in Lucas's handwriting. An address.

I headed south toward a tiny touristy town on a marshy lake surrounded by oversized cottages referred to as summer properties and lake houses by those in Wayoata who could afford one. The town felt like a movie set, full of old-style storefronts with striped awnings. I followed Google's directions past a Dairy Queen with a horde of people surrounding it, past a farmers' market with a jazzy band playing up on a platform, past a patio full of midday drinkers. Lake life.

I almost missed it twice. The lake house was set so far back off the road, and its front lot was heavily treed. I knew it was the lake house from Joanna Wilkes's journal. I knew that before I even left the apartment. The Post-it must have been in the envelope I ripped from the back of Lucas's bookshelf, and somehow it fell loose and stuck to the chair. Was this where they met, Joanna and Lucas, for their secret sexual rendezvous? Did Lucas put a sweaty hand on the girl's knee as they drove out here after last period, saying things like *No one would ever understand us,* as one corner of his mouth twitched?

It looked like it had been closed down for a few seasons. The windows were boarded up, and an overall look of neglect hung over it. I turned the car off, listened to it tick as I tried the front door. Locked of course. But there was a tear in the screen. I reached inside, tried the entry door, but it was also locked. I walked around to the back, stepping up onto a tiered deck with stairs that led down to the dock and a boathouse. An animal was skittering around in the dead leaves under my feet. Tried the back door, also locked.

Down the steps, to a dilapidated boathouse. Water grass was spiking out at the shore here and around the dock. The lake itself shimmered with oil rainbows. I tried the door to the boathouse—locked. I used my car keys to tear a hole in the screen, a sort of miniature gnawing hacksaw. I slipped my hand through the scratchy opening and turned the little tab on the knob.

There was no boat here. I stepped carefully around the edges of the open water. There were missing boards, and the remaining dock was rotted. I was afraid the whole thing might give out. An old life jacket hung from a nail, a canoe was tilted and leaning on its side. A rusty jerry can sat under a workbench. Everything was covered in webs with raisin-like insects speckled throughout.

I don't know why I did it, but I crouched down and felt behind one of the oars. An image of a golden key flashed in my mind, and there it was, a key. Somehow I'd known it would be there. This startled me. My hands shook, and I dropped the key on a worn-out board near the water.

A sort of déjà vu had been lingering around the back of my neck since I got there. The first whisper of it was when I walked up the front steps. Like a callused finger tapping on the nape of my neck, which only became stronger as I went down to the dock, it was clawing at me now. I knew déjà vu could be a symptom of heightened dopamine caused by certain stimulative medications, and so maybe this wasn't a sensation I should pay much attention to, but how had I known exactly where to find the spare key? How had I even known there was a spare key?

Down on one knee, I snatched the key back up but not before peering into the water, thinking maybe if the Wilkeses had killed Lucas, he could be there, weighed down by something, his face bloated with terror, mouth opened. Drowning on his last screams. His now sodden features all running away from each other.

A cold panic swept through me. For a hideous moment, I saw my own face and mistook it for Lucas's. I jolted back; jagged wood dug into my palms. Dread took my breath away. I felt like I was being swallowed up. The sound of blood sputtered in my ears. I squeezed my eyes shut, listened to a boat whizzing by in the distance. Took careful, calming breaths though my nose. My teeth hooked on to my bottom lip.

Get it together. Fall apart later. But now get it together.

Outside as I turned to go back up to the lake house, I saw something out on the water. A formation of rocks sticking out of the lake, like the spiny back of some sea creature. Something about it jarred me. Again the déjà vu, but stronger, almost a memory, but not quite. It darted around my head like a hummingbird on methamphetamine, never staying still long enough that I could get anything more than an echo of its presence.

Back up the steps. The key slid into the back door, and I stepped inside a large mudroom, with a drift of dead leaves. The place smelled musty and oddly like rotten apples. I went to my right first, and before I went into the kitchen, I knew that it was where the kitchen would be. I'd been here. We were here. I didn't know what that meant exactly, but somehow I knew the whole floor plan of the house. I could clearly picture the furniture that was hiding under the dusty sheets.

I turned down a long hallway that led to five bedrooms and a bathroom, ending with what I knew was once called the *big bedroom.* I followed a set of stairs to the attic. Here was the circular skylight that Joanna wrote about in her journal. Now the feeling was almost visceral. Lucas and I had been here, running around this strange, angular room. Hiding inside an old steamer trunk, shadowboxing with that mannequin torso, and sitting there too in the orb of light shining in through the roof.

I heard the crunch of gravel. Someone was driving up. I looked through one of the wavy glass windows. Ben's warhead of a truck was parked tight behind my toy car. He dropped out of the driver's seat and started to head up the driveway. I shot back from the window, knocked into the mannequin torso, nearly tipping it over. Instinctively, I grabbed it. Leaned it against the wall and ran across the attic, then stumbled halfway down the stairs. A loud bang. The storm door. I froze midstep. What should I do? Should I make a run for the front door and hope that I could head him off and make it to my boxed-in car? Then what? No, I'd have to get to a neighbor's house, a neighbor who was home and willing to help me (assaulter of grieving mothers) over Ben Wilkes. I could feel my throat closing again, under Kathy's arm pressure.

I crept back up the stairs into the attic. I tried pulling up one of windows, my road rash splitting open from the strain, but it was painted shut, or nailed shut, or else it was never meant to open. *Fuck, fuck.*

I had my phone. I could call Garrett. But what would he do? I was trespassing again, and clearly his "stern" warnings had had no effect on Ben, who was still following me. And I couldn't be sure how deep Garrett was in with the Wilkeses. And even if, *if,* he did flick on his siren and buzz over there, it'd take too long. I'd be dead by the time he got there. Ben would roll me up in a tarp and drop me into the lake.

I looked around for something I could use—a weapon—but everything was boxed up.

I descended the steps again, quiet and light. Listened. I knew the layout of this house. I could use that to somehow go around him. A rustling, like someone was taking the sheets off the furniture. He was in the living room, and I needed to pass the living room to get to the front door. I ducked into the first bedroom right of the stairs, full of little-girl furniture. White wrought-iron bed frame, the bed stripped of sheets. White furniture and a white hope chest. I stepped into a half-empty closet and waited. The stinging smell of mothballs made my eyes water.

I pushed myself farther back into the closet. It hit me then: I'd been here before. Just like this. In this closet, inside this room. This was my bedroom. Somewhere buried in my memory, I knew that I'd claimed this as my room. I hid inside this closet, but it was Lucas coming to find me.

A slow, sort of loping sound drew closer. I inched off something from a hanger, a dress, and tried to hide under it. A floorboard creaked in the hallway. A hinge squeaked; he was checking the closet in the room next to mine. My room. *My room?* What the hell was going on?

I stood up. Could I make it if I bolted right now? The hinge squeaked again. No. He was in the hallway again. I crouched back down, expecting at any moment a shadow to snuff out the sliver of light coming into the cracked closet door. Expecting Ben to fling open the closet doors and drag me out by my legs.

I pulled out my car key, slid it between my index and middle finger. I'd plunge it into his eyes, at least carve a couple of good scratches on his pampered cheeks. He entered the room. I stopped breathing. Leaned forward, peeked through the crack. He dropped down onto his stomach and looked under the bed. A push-up and he was standing again. The way he was moving, slow and unworried, going room to room . . . he knew he had me.

He started toward the closet, and I curled into myself. Snapped into the fetal position like I was a human lawn chair. Key ready. His hand was on the knob, the hinges started to move—*ohmygodohmygodohmygod*—and then a thump in the attic. The mannequin had fallen over. It had to be the mannequin. Ben let go of the closet door and stalked down the hallway toward the stairs.

I bolted. Flung open the closet and ran toward the front door. I was on the front lawn and could hear Ben running up behind me. I dove into the PT. Hit the door locks. Ben ambled around my car like Cujo. I started the car and slammed it backward into his truck, then forward, back, then forward. I probably would have shattered my back window if I'd still had one. His front bumper popped off.

I lurched the PT forward again, went too far, and skittered into what was once a flower bed. My front wheel was hooked on brick edging. The wheels turned, and I panicked. My hands shaking, I shifted into neutral instead of reverse. Exhaust filled the backseat and then Ben stuck his arm in through the missing back window.

"Fuck off, leave me alone, get away," I screamed.

In reverse again, the car lurched, and Ben staggered back and half rolled off the driveway.

I wrenched the steering wheel all the way to the right, and scraping the front of his truck, I was able to cut across the front lawn. The ground dropped out, and I dipped into a shallow ditch that I doubted the car could climb out of, but somehow it did. I was back on the road. I glanced in the rearview at Ben, flailing his arms at me.

It wasn't until I passed the Dairy Queen that I could breathe again. My body started going from braced and rigid to all loose and rubbery. Spaghetti-limbed. My hands kept sliding off the steering wheel, and my foot felt like deadweight on the gas pedal. Lead foot. All I could smell was car exhaust and mothballs. I kept looking over my shoulder, thinking I'd see Ben's truck hurtling up behind me, but he wasn't there. What was he going to do to me? Duct tape me to a chair in the living room? The living room where I'd been before. Wait for Kathy, who'd circle around me, smacking her yardstick in her hand as she decided exactly how to dispose of me? Would I get a long, nefarious speech? Would they tell me what they did to Lucas before that last crack to my skull? The murderer's soliloquy with all the answers? No. Kathy would be all business, she'd hack me up in the same detached way she'd carve a turkey. The thought of Ben's icy cold eyes and Kathy's hot breath in my ear closed in on me again, and my heart started to power up in my chest. I veered out of my lane; someone honked and shot me the finger out their window. *Breathe.*

Why did I remember being there as a little girl? Sleeping in that same room with a canopy bed, hiding in that same closet where Ben had me cornered.

I sucked in my bottom lip. Something clicked. I knew what was so familiar about the lake. The painting in Lucas's living room. Mimi's painting. That was it, the view from the dock.

So what? Mimi dated a Wilkes or, really, a Russo? Kathy's maiden name was Russo. One of them took us out there? I couldn't think of any other reason that I would remember that place. I knew Kathy was at least ten years older than me. She had two brothers, but both were younger than her and significantly younger than Mimi. Then again, when had that ever stopped her? It all seemed too date-y, though, for one of them to bring her and her kids to the family lake house. Mimi was definitely too old to be brought home to meet Mom.

Kathy's husband was older than she was. Or at least he looked older. His hair was mostly thinned out and gray, but I doubted he was old enough for Mimi to have preyed on. Or maybe he was older than he looked. It would explain Kathy bringing up my slutty mother, who'd been "inactive" for several years, during our tussle on her front lawn if Mimi had initiated her husband into sex at some point. It made sense when Carolyn did it, because she was grappling for ways to insult me, but why would Kathy bring up Mimi?

There was something else, something I was starting to know, but I couldn't quite let it settle. Not yet. Not before I talked to Mimi.

Mimi was napping when I got there. All the residents had a daily afternoon nap like it was kindergarten. I pushed her door open, and there she was, on her back, her hair splayed out on her pillow like a gray-and-yellow corona around her face. Like this, her resting face was still beautiful. I remembered that when I was little, I would watch my mother sleep. Coming up close to her, studying her features when they were still, because she never was. Sometimes I wasn't sure I really knew what she even looked like. I stared at her until I couldn't bear to anymore.

I looked around her room, taking in her jars of cracking paint and cups of pencils. I searched for vanilla-scented lotion but couldn't find any. I leaned over my sleeping mother and checked the window. There was nothing to use to climb, no ledge to scale or hefty drain spout she could use to slide in and out. The nurse was right, it was a straight drop down.

I flipped through one of Mimi's sketch pads. More flowers, more gnarled trees, more grassy fields and watery sunsets. And then there were several sketches of Lucas. Lucas in a suit, Lucas walking in an open field, Lucas sitting on a chair, legs crossed. Hanging on the wall were the perfected watercolor versions of the drawings in Mimi's sketchbook. Haunting and beautiful, they surrounded her bed like a colorful explosion.

I sat down in a rocking chair next to the bed. I found myself doing it again, examining Mimi's face. Looking for myself in her tangle of crow's-feet, the delicate curve of her nose and smoker's lips that always looked like an invisible finger was holding up one side, as if she was smirking even while she slept. There was nothing. The first time I ever heard that every woman eventually turned into her mother, I was nine, and I spent the week wallowing in my bedroom. Then I did everything I could to be as unlike her as possible.

But with the chalky bitter-pill taste in my mouth, the fact that I had put my own mother there, and managed to have sex in the few days I'd been there, I had to say I was all-around unsuccessful.

Mimi's eyes switched open like a doll's. I said hello; she blinked.

"What are you doing here?" she asked, groggy voiced.

"I wanted to visit you." I didn't know if she'd remember I had turned her in the other day and if she'd still be angry with me. I'd moved the rocking chair out of her reach just in case.

"Oh." She pulled the threadbare afghan off her, sat up. "Well, hello." Her head drooped forward like a sleepy toddler. She rubbed her eyes with crinkly fists.

"I like your paintings." I already felt tired at the effort it was going to take having a full conversation with her. "They're all very pretty."

"My work sells out at the art shows."

"My work" was very adult sounding.

"I've heard. That's wonderful." I gave her my warmest smile, and she nodded. "I would like to buy one, if you have any for sale right now?"

She looked at me sideways, deciding something. A tight smile passed over her lips. "Well, that one's for sale." She seemed to point randomly at a coated wall.

"Oh, which one?" Her finger wavered around the room. "This one?"

"Cold! You're cold."

Ah, the hot and cold game, OK. I touched the painting next to it, and Mimi screamed "cold" again, then lit a cigarette. "Shut the door. We're not supposed to smoke inside." She stood up on her bed and slid open the window, then flopped down on her belly and pulled out an old water bottle with an inch or two of brown-yellow water at the bottom. The orange filtered butts circled like a school of bloated goldfish. "Keep going, keep going." She clapped.

So I did. Touched one after the other, finger just grazing the canvasses because I was afraid I'd scratch the paint. Eventually my finger pressed into one of Lucas. "I really like this one." I knew I couldn't be too obvious in wanting to know anything or she'd clam up. Dangle the information just out of reach like she always did.

"Cold, so cold." Mimi was starting to look a little pissed off.

"It's a very good picture of Lucas, though. Looks a lot like him in real life."

"That's not Lucas!" She let out a snort of laughter.

"No? I think it looks a lot like him." I stood, took a closer look, wanting this to be over. The face seemed to tilt ever so slightly, into someone else. The eyes were wrong. That's what it was. The shape, color, were more like my eyes. "Who is it, then?" My throat had gone dry.

"You know who it is, silly billy." Mimi leapt up from her bed, she was tugging at the front of her pink nightie like she had to pee.

And then I did. Just like that, it was Mr. Hideaway. Flashes of Mimi telling us to stay in our rooms, her guest would be there any second. Earlier she'd pulled out the hide-a-bed from the living room couch. Put fresh sheets on, plumped the pillows. She'd traded out the bottle of hard liquor she'd been drinking for a bottle of red wine, the ashtray emptied and wiped clean. She only ever wiped the ashtray clean for Mr. Hideaway. We called him that because he slept on the hide-a-bed (something about a sore back and Mimi's bed being too soft) and we had to hide away from him, and well, I guess, because Mr. Pullout just didn't sound right. Eventually one of us would need to use the bathroom or get a drink of water, and Mimi would call to us, and we'd go over and talk to Mr. Hideaway. Who now in my mind looked so much like Lucas, but that couldn't be right because Mimi had said I was the one who got our father's looks.

"It's Mr. Hideaway." I said it out loud. Mimi laughed some crazed chortle.

"Daddy, Daddy, Daddy." Mimi's voice reverberated off the walls. All the drawings and paintings seemed to curl at their edges, peel away from their sheer weight.

"Please, Mimi, tell me his name."

"Guess."

"I don't want to guess. I want you tell me."

She crossed her arms, shook her head no. "At least go through the alphabet."

"Alphabet, what are you talking about?"

"Say the alphabet, and I'll nod at the letters that spell his name."

"OK fine. ABCDE . . ." A blast of frustration pulsed through me. Of course she was making me do this. I started rushing. FGHIJ came out as a single rushed syllable. She was dangling the answer to who our father was, like she always did, and I couldn't trust that once I said the right letter she'd tell me. She'll probably say NO to all the letters I list, that'll be her fun. I skipped right to the letters I wanted. "W"? "R"?

"No, no, no. You're not playing it right." She lit another cigarette. "Start from the beginning again."

I stood there for a second, eyes stinging. Even before the injury, Mimi had always been the child, never the parent. She was sitting in the middle of the bed again, ears perked like a terrier's. I could sense a shift in her mood. I always could read her, anticipate the next emotion that would take over before she even felt it herself, while she knew nothing at all about me.

I didn't think I had it in me to ride this out with her, whatever was coming. "Fine. A, B, C . . ." When I got to "O," Mimi interrupted.

"I'm hungry. I have an idea. Let's go to a restaurant." She stood up and started opening the drawers on her dresser.

"No, Mimi." I pressed my hand over the next drawer she tried to open. "Tell me Mr. Hideaway's real name."

She started tugging harder on the drawer, arm muscles forming peaks under baggy skin. "Stop it. You're mean."

"Not until you tell me who my father is." My hand stayed firm on the drawer. My armpits were getting damp, my cheeks burned.

Mimi kept pulling, grunted. "I'll never tell you now. Move." She tried dropping to her knees and got the drawer to slide out an inch. Her hand slipped in quickly, just as I shoved it back in, accidentally catching her fingers. Mimi howled.

"Sorry, sorry, sorry, I didn't mean to do that." I just kept hurting her.

She leaned into me, and for a second I thought she was going to kiss me, but instead her teeth went for my shoulder. I held her at bay by her forehead until she scrambled up and ran down the hall calling for a nurse and then for Lucas.

23

In the car, still outside the yellow house, I dug through my bag, only to come up with an empty pill bottle. There was always something extra hiding at the bottom of my bag. I dumped it out, thought I saw a little white pill roll between the seats. I clawed around but couldn't find it, and then I wasn't even sure there was a pill at all. Suddenly it didn't matter because all the frustration and sadness and confusion descended upon me at once. The floodgates opened, and I released a primitive-sounding cry. Something savage, an angry war howl. Fucking Mimi.

Mr. Hideaway was our father. Mr. Hideaway was a Wilkes, or really a Russo, or someone who was good enough friends with the Wilkes/Russo clan to have taken us to their lake house when we were children. Lucas had read Joanna's journal, recognized the lake house, and what? Thought he'd seduce a potential relative? I knew he wouldn't have killed Joanna, but now I knew it even more. Joanna, who could very well be his, our, niece or cousin. Was half sister possible? If Lucas really was sleeping with her, if that had happened, could he have in some enormous fit of revulsion struck out at her? Or had it always been about getting to know her? There had never been an affair, just Lucas probing to see if he could find anything out about the identity of our father.

The test at GenTech. Maybe it wasn't a paternity test after all, but to see if Lucas was related to whoever he suspected was our father. How did that work? Was he using Joanna's hair as a sample? It would explain why Lucas came to have it. But there was so much. Why not just spit on a Q-tip?

I called GenTech. A woman with a cartoonish, high-pitched voice answered, said that all client information was private and there was no way I could access this information. Never, ever. She said it exactly like that—"never, ever"—like I was making some kind of audacious fairy-tale wish.

I had a picture at least of our father. Or Mimi's rendition of him. I had peeled one from the wall before fleeing her room. I found a pen and made his hair dark with black ink.

I pulled into the first bar I saw. It was in the "artsy" section of town, which meant it was between an antique store and Becca's Scrapbooking Emporium. Inside, the lounge was nice and shadowy, lit mostly by a single forest-green halogen lamp. It was on the main floor of the HI-Way Hotel (Wayoata's only official *hotel*), which advertised on its sign NEW ROOMS and the best sentence fragment ever, STATE OF THE ART. What exactly was state-of-the-art here, the HI-Way Hotel felt was self-evident enough to never specify.

I ordered a stacked cheeseburger from a bartender who eyed my bruises, sipped a beer while I waited, then carried my beer and burger to the remotest booth in the place. I took my phone out and started to tap research on its tiny, cracked screen.

Even the *Wayoata Sun* archives had been digitized (how adorable!). Once, when I was in middle school, we had to shadow someone in a career that interested us. At the time, I wanted to be journalist.

It was the most boring day of my life. I followed around a gigantic woman named Maureen who had overlapping teeth and traveled via scooter; her ass hanging off the edges like an awning. She was working a story about a bin full of dead hogs left out to rot that could be seen from the highway coming into Wayoata. To be clear, the story wasn't about the horrors of factory farming or even the dangers of improper carcass disposal, no, it was because these dead hogs were accidentally on display at the start of the fall corn festival. It was not good for tourism (which was a joke in and of itself). At the end of the day, with a dimpled frown, she turned on me. "I can tell you don't care an iota for Wayoata, but let me tell you, these things are important. Taking pride in where you come from is important. It means you take pride in yourself."

A one-time fee of twenty-five dollars would get me an account and access to the *Sun*'s archives. For some irrational reason, I pictured Maureen on the other end, taking payment. Nodding her jowly head as if to say, *Told you so.*

I looked up everything I could on the Wilkeses, the Russos, and Harold Lambert, founder of Harold's Grocers. It took me less than fifteen minutes to find a photograph of my father. It was a shot of a Harold's Grocers grand opening in Fargo. Now that I knew what to look for, he was easy to spot. He stood out against the gingery redheads that were the Lamberts, even in black-and-white. He had a smarmy, car salesman look about him.

Peter Russo. Peter Russo was Mr. Hideaway. I looked his name up in notices. Peter Russo had married Alice Lambert, daughter of Harold Lambert, on July 15, 1964. Which would make Joanna and Madison my nieces and Kathy my half sister. Which would make us one big happy, murderous family.

Alice had Joanna's corkscrew hair. Here's how it must have gone down: Peter married rich, then he met Mimi, probably at one of the four grand openings in Omaha. She likely got pregnant on purpose. I couldn't see her missing an opportunity for regular payments from someone who could make child support—never anticipating that it just might not be worth it—and she followed her golden ticket back to Wayoata. Or maybe she thought he'd get divorced and marry her. Maybe it really had been love. For Mimi it would only have been love if Peter didn't want her back. She never wanted the men who wanted her back, who actually liked her children.

A section of the social pages announced that Peter and Alice Russo had moved to Fayetteville, Arkansas, "where the climate will be kinder to my husband's lungs," Alice was quoted as saying. That was ten years ago. A few months after Mimi's accident. I called a few P. Russos in Fayetteville. On my fifth call, a woman answered with a thin, reedy voice. I hoped the background escalating argument between two drunken pool players in the lounge wouldn't be picked up.

"Is Peter Russo available?"

"What's this about please?"

"I am calling about his granddaughter Joanna Wilkes."

"You reporters." She hissed, clicked her tongue, and hung the phone up.

At least I had an address.

Lucas's ATM card had last been used in Arkansas. Nightmare images ground in my head. I could picture him driving there through the night, hands white-knuckling the steering wheel. He was finally, after all these years, going to see his father. Give him a piece of his mind. Red taillights flashing across his angry face, his lips a pencil-thin line. Not noticing Ben Wilkes's splotchy face bobbing up in the backseat.

Fayetteville was almost a thirteen-hour drive from Wayoata. I had three uppers left at the apartment. It would have to last me. Before getting on the highway, I stopped again at Home Depot and bought duct tape and a roll of clear plastic; and couldn't decide if I was getting dirty looks because I was a Haas purchasing half a murder kit or because I looked so strung out. Probably both. In the parking lot, I covered up the back window on the PT with the tape and plastic. I wished, wished, wished I had taken out the extra insurance. I drove through the night hunched over the steering wheel, feverish, my eyes bugged out, seeing things on the side of the road that weren't there.

I stopped only for bathroom breaks and a box of gummy cereal bars.

When I got there, I tried to freshen up a little bit at a Denny's. I really should have planned it better. Packed an alternative outfit to my now-crumby blouse and creased jeans.

I practiced smiling, and then smiling and saying "fuck you" at the same time.

24

DAY 10

FRIDAY

The house looked almost like a girl's private school, with its gray brick facade, stony turret, and huge oak doors finished off with a lion's head knocker. I rang the bell. A woman, midfifties, clearly the housekeeper, in a rubbery apron with a dish towel dangling over her wrist, answered the door.

I asked for Peter Russo.

"Alice isn't home just now. Is she expecting you?"

"It's Peter I'm looking for." I doubted she'd misheard me. Maybe Alice kept her husband on a short leash after his very reproductive affair. Or maybe affairs, plural. Maybe I had several half siblings. "I talked to Alice last night. She knew I was coming."

"She's not here right now. Could you come back in an hour?"

"I wish I could, but I'm just passing through town and it'd be such a shame not to see him, with everything that's happened. I wanted to pass on my condolences." It was a gross way to get inside. I did know that.

The housekeeper looked positively torn up about what to do, and so I took it as an opportunity to push myself inside. I chattered away, about how nice it would be to see Peter again, that I knew he wasn't well, how pretty Fayetteville was, and then she was leading me past a living room overdecorated with antique-looking couches and pillars topped with urnlike vases, and up a wide, curved staircase.

She knocked on the door as she opened it. "Mr. Russo? You sleeping?" I followed her into a master bedroom about the size of my apartment in Chicago. It smelled like reheated gravy and vegetable soup, mixed with the smell of sickness. The bedroom had a king-sized poster bed with a shimmery bedspread and a mountain of pillows perfectly arranged against the headboard. The bed annoyed me.

Peter Russo was sitting up in a wingback chair, looking out the window. An oxygen mask elasticized over the back of his head, still thick with gray hair. His eyes widened when he saw me, fear or shock. So there he was, dear old Dad, the abandoner in the flesh.

I'd been going over things in the car, how I'd introduce myself. *Hi, I'm your daughter* was what I'd planned, but now that I was there, so close to this waxy man who was my father, nothing seemed to come out of my mouth. I stood staring at him, like a baby. Knees shaking. I morphed back into that little girl from before I'd decided not to give a shit, when I still really, really wanted a dad. A dad who liked to give us rides on his back and called me his little princess and jokingly forbade me from dating until I was thirty. A dad who would teach me how to drive. A dad who somehow satisfied Mimi so she wasn't so fucking unhappy.

"Someone's here to see you, Peter." The housekeeper's voice had that ghoulish cheeriness that nurses put on when conversing with the dying. She turned back toward me. "What'd you say your name was?"

"Mia," I whispered my name, without meaning to. I hated that I sounded so awed.

Peter lifted the mask off his face—a bloody line slashed his cheeks where the elastic had been—and shooed the housekeeper out of the room with a crooked finger. He croaked out a hello and nodded at the other wingback chair angled toward him, where I imagined he and Alice must have had their most heated discussions about Peter's other children. Or maybe we were never discussed.

"Sit."

I couldn't move. "Sit," he said again. He was wearing a robe, silky red, his legs crossed at the knees; a Crocs sandal dangled from his left foot. Long, stick-thin legs, sparsely haired, nodded back and forth. He took a mouthful of water from a plastic covered mug, like an adult sippy cup. His hands shook. I noticed he had absurdly long eyelashes, just like my own.

"COPD, stage 3. Don't ever smoke—you don't smoke, do you?" He had an accent. I was usually terrible at discerning accents, but this was definitely Italian.

"No." I'd recently been popping several pills a day, though. My liver probably looked like a puffer fish.

"Good, good for you. Gotta be on this twenty hours a day, my leash." He motioned to an oxygen tank by his foot. There was an awkward silence.

"You knew my mother, Mimi Haas." I thought I should start there, ease into it. Like a gentle reminder that tells men to get their prostate checked.

"You're my daughter. I know." He said this with an annoyed resignation, took a few deep breaths from his oxygen mask, and I wanted to slap it off his face.

"My brother—" I started. He snapped the mask off again.

"Killed my granddaughter." He finished my sentence.

"No, he didn't."

He shook his head back and forth, a little too wildly, like he didn't want to look at something and I was forcing him to. "The police are looking for him."

"Have you talked to the police? Did you tell them that you—that we're related?"

He shook his head again. "No. What good would that do? To tell the world my illegitimate son seduced and murdered my granddaughter? Would it change the investigation? This revelation of incest? No. My daughter would never forgive me. I'll be gone soon, and she'd have to live with it. It would follow her everywhere. Ruin the Harold's brand, and how does that honor Joanna's memory? My poor Joanna." He said this, breathless, then when he had enough air, he added with wheezy indignation, "You two had both moved away," like it was Lucas's fault for returning to Wayoata, like he'd brought the plague back with him.

So Kathy didn't know, unless Lucas had also tried talking to her. I hadn't thought of that.

"There was no affair. Lucas was only talking to Joanna to find out more about you. He contacted you. I know he did."

"My other granddaughter, Madison. She saw them together at school, in his car. *Touching*. She told me herself." I doubted this was true. He was looking to justify keeping secret children.

"Did Lucas come here to see you?"

Peter shook his head no. "He called me, I know he did. A few times, but Alice, my wife, didn't"—his lungs whistled, a deep rattle churned in his chest—"didn't tell me. Once I picked up and listened." He nodded in the direction of an antique-looking phone with a gold-trimmed rotary dial on a nightstand. "He was angry. He thought we should pay for your mother's care, that we should make back payments of child support to both of you. He threatened to sue me. He sounded like Mimi. Lucas, I believe, took it out on Joanna to get to me. He had access to her—"

"Why didn't you talk to him, call him back?"

"It would have upset my wife."

"So it's your wife's fault, then, that you couldn't be bothered to acknowledge your own children's existence? Those are some really great family values."

"I'm not well," he said, his mask full of white condensation. For a second I wanted to laugh. Lucas was obsessed with *Star Wars,* and now I had some asshole sitting here with a mask on his face saying, *I am your father.*

"What's your excuse for the other thirty years of our existence?"

He lifted up his mask again. "As much as you might not want to hear this, it was Mimi's choice. She said it would be worse for you to know and see me around town with my other children. Mimi wanted all or nothing. That was how she was, most of the time. It wasn't even a long affair, just over eighteen months. That was it. When she got to drinking, she changed her mind from time to time. She'd show up on my doorstep at all hours of the night, demanding money, demanding that I take you both."

"She was a functioning alcoholic. She needed professional help." I couldn't believe I was standing up for Mimi, but at least she'd tried to take care of us. The functioning part might've been too kind but she did have a job, she bought groceries, she kept us alive (weren't these the benchmarks for functioning?) At least she'd acknowledged us.

"Don't you remember the time she just dumped you off at our house? It was about one o'clock in the morning. Late fall. Neither of you even had jackets on. I took you both out to the lake house with me before my own kids woke up. She didn't come back for you for a week. It got to be too much. Whenever she took up with some other fellow, it would seem like we could just all get along, but it never lasted."

"I remember you as Mr. Hideaway. You'd sleep on our living room pullout couch."

"She'd lure me back, here and there." He wrung his hands, as if he were the victim of some Venus flytrap vagina that kept snapping shut on him whenever he got too close. I started thinking about Mimi's accident. "You lived on Southland Drive?" I said it like a question, but I already knew. Everyone knew that big house where Harold Lambert's daughter lived. It suddenly mattered to me where Mimi was going that night.

His eyes flitted back and forth. He held the mask over his mouth and nose. Deep breaths. Took it off again. "Oh, I think you know the answer to that."

"Mimi went to see you the night of her accident, didn't she?" Peter didn't say anything, but I was able to hold the silence. I just sat there. Waiting. Thinking, *What if.* Thinking, *Maybe, just maybe . . .*

Peter's eyes wagged back and forth as I stared at him. I could hear his watch ticking. The housekeeper started a vacuum. Finally he broke.

"What if she did? I couldn't control when she decided to drop by. She'd show up at all hours of the night, drunk as usual. It was upsetting for my wife. When our kids still lived at home, she'd wake everyone up, and my wife would have to try to keep the kids upstairs so they didn't know what was happening. Later it would be the grandchildren if we had any staying over. Your mother, when she was in a certain hateful mood, was always trying to cause an upheaval."

"That must have been so hard for you." I was being sarcastic, but he nodded as if I were really sympathizing. "What was she doing at your house the night of her accident?"

"The usual."

"What's the usual?"

He eyeballed me, contemplated. "As I said, disturbing the peace. That was always Mimi's point. It happened less as the years went on, but when it did, it was almost more shocking because we'd convinced ourselves the last time was the *last time.*"

"You left your black glove in her car." I went with the assumptive close. Why not make him think I already knew most of what had happened? Something happened.

He closed his eyes, drew a few sharp breaths. "Yeah, well, that was a difficult night."

"For you or my mother who now lives in a care home?"

His shook his head again, like I just wasn't getting it. "What happened was her own bloody fault." He whined under his wheeze. "Like I said, Alice would usually shut herself up somewhere in the house, wait for it to be over. That night, Mimi was especially aggressive. She kept ringing the doorbell, even after I opened the door, to try to draw Alice out. She was calling out her name. I don't know if she was hankering for a catfight or what, but she was going on about how Alice was living in *her* house, living *her* life. How she deserved better, deserved more money from me. Alice was plain sick and tired of it. She came down and confronted Mimi on the front steps. She told her to go home to her children and get sober. Earlier that day there had been one of those rare winter rains, and then the temperature just dropped. The stairs were slick with ice. I'd planned to salt them after dinner, but I guess I just didn't get to it. Now, Alice didn't touch her in any way, I want to be clear on that, but your mother, as drunk as she was, didn't need much more than for someone to blow on her to get her to fall over."

It was true that sometimes Mimi could fall over like a bag of bricks. Just bang—like a narcoleptic, but it was from the booze. She'd get all sorts of bruises. When she told her concerned co-workers at the bank, *Oh, I just smacked into the doorframe is all,* they'd think some guy was knocking her around, but it really was just the doorframe, or the kitchen cupboard or whatever.

"Mimi tried to take a swing at me and lost her footing, slipped backward, and hit her head. I couldn't rouse her. She was out. I would have called an ambulance, but I knew how it looked."

I pictured my mother with a serious dent in her skull, blood gushing out of her ears like a tap had been turned on inside her head, running all over Peter's front steps. A mess to be cleaned up. But not my mess. My mother had never lost consciousness when I pushed her into the countertop. It hadn't been my fault. I didn't cause her injury. Something uncorked inside of me, and a whole range of high-pressured, raw emotion geysered. Relief, guilt for feeling relief, anger for having spent the last ten years believing I'd caused it, anger at myself for such enthusiastic self-hatred, for the pills. For the nights and days I'd spent alone with the curtains drawn, all itchy and hopped-up on an upper or drained-out on a downer, feeling nothing as the sun motored across the sky. Wanting, badly, to feel punished because I got away with it. A sadness for my mother that everywhere she had turned that night, someone was turning away from her.

"We didn't want the police there. Alice was worried they might arrest her, because no one would believe she didn't push her husband's mistress. There'd be press, and our kids would find out about my indiscretion, about their half siblings. Alice, my kids, my grandchildren still didn't deserve to pay for my mistakes. She went down on her own. She was trying to *hit me*; all I did was put her somewhere else. It was an accident, plain and simple. Mimi did it to herself. I figured she'd wake up in a few hours. She was used to tumbles like that. I knew someone would find her, get her help."

This guy was such an asshole. "So you just abandoned her?"

"I didn't put her on some deserted back road."

"But how do you know that she couldn't have made a full recovery if only she'd gotten help sooner?" It was a slightly hypocritical accusation, because maybe we had both contributed to her head injury. It wasn't like I'd called the police to stop her from driving off. The difference was Peter had put her limp body in the car. He had to have known the severity, whereas all I saw was a smear of blood on Mimi's temple.

"I don't. I have had to live with that."

"You've had to live with that?" I'd been living with it for the last ten years. "You? Not her two kids who are paying for her care? Then what? You just left Wayoata? In case Mimi woke up and remembered that she'd been at your house?"

"Nothing like that. It was just time for a new beginning. My kids were adults. They had their own lives, and I was getting sicker. I breathe easier here."

"I bet you do," I snapped. "You didn't think we might need help after our mother was turned into a near vegetable?"

Peter shrugged. "You were old enough to take care of yourselves. What could I have done?"

"We were seventeen!"

"Well, maybe I should have done things differently. Don't you think I've regretted that decision every day since? Because I have. And now, look, I guess I've had my comeuppance." He fidgeted with the oxygen tank's hose.

I didn't know what decision he was referring to: not calling an ambulance, ditching her car, ever meeting Mimi in the first place, regretting not acknowledging us.

"Your comeuppance?"

"Joanna, my sweet, sweet Joanna."

His dead granddaughter was his punishment. Her murder had happened to him. It was pretty obvious why Mimi and Peter didn't work. The universe rotated around each of them. How was it possible that Lucas and I were conceived by two of the most narcissistic people living in Wayoata? Seriously, what were the odds of that?

Peter started coughing and wheezing; his eyes went shiny. He slipped the oxygen mask over his mouth and nose, breathed in deep. I waited a full minute, but Peter wasn't going to take the mask off again. He'd wimped out and was now busying himself with the curtains behind him. I had a violent urge to bend the oxygen hose in half, enjoy a few brief moments of depriving this man of air, as he had deprived us. Of tormenting him, the way his absence and, finally, rejection had tormented my brother. There were a hundred different things I could have said, but I knew the odds were they'd be so inflected with rage that whatever I said would come out as an incoherent string of obscenities, and I didn't want to be mad at myself later for being so inarticulate. He wasn't worth the time or effort or the future replay.

Before I left, I asked the housekeeper if I could use the bathroom. I perused the medicine cabinet. Guilty conscience abated, I knew this was the moment I should ditch the pills, give them up completely, just toss them out the car window as I drove back to Wayoata, let them spray like a mini Pfizer hailstorm against the car windshield behind me. But this was not a good time to go through withdrawal. I managed to swipe a near-full bottle of Percocet, which was a score because I'd just run out.

I found a cheap motel three hours out of Fayetteville. It smelled like sweat, loamy sex, and stale cigarette smoke. The bedspread was an irritating polyester quilt, with a brown and orange geometric pattern. The fixtures, the doorknobs, the remote control were all coated with a stickiness.

I didn't really believe what Peter had told me. Or at least he had glossed over certain details. I think Alice very well could have snapped (the way I'd snapped earlier), and in her desperation to make Mimi leave, she pushed her down their tall, opulent front steps. Let gravity have its way with her. I knew from experience how easily she would have gone down.

I thought about calling Garrett. This would change everything, wouldn't it? Really bring things back to Kathy, her motives to pin Joanna's death on my brother. She could have known. I could see Lucas in their kitchen, hand over Kathy's, gently revealing the true nature of his relationship with Joanna. *I'm her uncle, see? Your half brother. I could never have been sleeping with her. Now let's figure out where she is.* Ben coming up behind him with a frying pan. Kathy refusing to divide up the Harold's Grocers fortune to include two more illegitimate siblings. Ian Wilkes's glare-filled glasses as he watched, holding Kathy's hand, while Big Ben beat my brother to death. And here the hypothetical goriness gripped like a seizure. Blood running down the walls from my brother's split head. His eyes popping out with surprise from the first hit, and then getting dimmer with each dent put in his skull. His blond hair, streaked bloodred (and here Kathy glimpses that with red hair, Lucas does look a little like her dead daughter and she instructs Ben to hit harder.) My twin's last words would be a dumbfounded gasp of *oh no* or *ouch*. Something so simple and human. Kathy praising Ben with a *good job, son,* as my brother twitched away the last seconds of his life.

My body clenched. The room started to swim. I had to shut my mind down. Force these sad, violent images to fade to black. *Skim,* I told myself, *skim like a Jesus lizard rather than sink into an abyss of grief and terror of life without my twin. Do not drown in this sadness. Not yet. Not until*—and here I ground my teeth—*not until I get some kind of vengeance. Not until the Wilkeses pay.*

I drifted again, to all those nighttime talks with Lucas about who our father could be. Shared fantasies of having some Daddy Warbucks out there (a pro athlete for Lucas; me, I liked all the men in aftershave ads who I pictured boarding private jets right after they smacked their cheeks up with stinging cologne), and here he was. Rich. And it was gut-wrenchingly sad that Lucas and I hadn't discovered him together, that we couldn't right now pick Peter Russo apart and vent all our disappointment.

The only thing that sat askew inside my gut was why Lucas had never told the police about it (or I should say the only other thing because it was pretty fucking inexplicable why he hadn't called me to tell me he'd found out who our father was). Why not say, *Whoa, that girl was my niece. Of course I wasn't sleeping with her.* Toss the chunk of Joanna's hair at them and say, *Test that.*

I could think of only two reasons why he wouldn't have: One, he was sleeping with Joanna and it wasn't until later he figured out that she was his niece. Two, if Lucas went missing the same day Joanna's body was discovered, then maybe he thought she just ran away from the humiliating pictures, from her control-freak unstable mother. He didn't help the police in any way because he believed Joanna was alive and well. Better off than she had been in Wayoata. Lucas knew what it was like to live with an unstable mother. He would have been in Joanna's corner all the way, especially if he knew she was our niece.

Or maybe there was a third reason—a much simpler, more straightforward answer. He'd planned to tell all in the interview, but something had happened.

Again I thought about calling Garrett, but I had the feeling I would just slur through the conversation and my credibility would be further shot. I had taken a Percocet (which, by the way, belonged to Alice, not my father. It gave me some pleasure to think that teetotaler Alice, the woman who pushed my drunken mom down icy steps, was a hypocrite). Just to sleep. To process.

25

DAY 11

SATURDAY

The water tower appeared on the horizon first. It was like some force field existed around Wayoata, and I kept getting boomeranged back there, into this alternate universe where its residents thought my twin brother was a killer on the loose. And then the Terrace came into view. It jutted out from the other low-slung town architecture like the creepy spire on a haunted house.

It was a gloomy, dark evening. Windy and hot. It was just after 6 P.M., and the sky looked like it'd been threatening rain all day, but the storm just stayed up there, taunting, ruining everyone's summer plans.

An ambulance was parked in front of the Terrace. The sight of the red lights flashing against the drab brick made my insides wilt. A gurney was being wheeled out the door.

As I hustled up, I caught a glimpse of Russ, his neck in a brace. His eyes were open, and as the paramedics pushed him past me, I could smell the reek of stale beer. We made eye contact, and a look of wild panic consumed his face. His lips were moving, saying some gibberish, I think about a leak.

"Don't try to talk," one of the paramedics ordered, and Russ's eyes fluttered closed.

Bailey was sitting on the front steps, her head buried in her hands.

"What happened?" I asked her.

"My dad." Her voice bubbled. She slapped at a mosquito on her sandaled foot, wiped her hand on the concrete step. She seemed hesitant to talk.

"Did something happen between him and Dale Burton?"

"Dale?" She looked up at me. She rubbed the tears and sweat off her face with her shirt, leaving a streak of cover-up behind on her collar.

"I saw them arguing the other day."

"Oh, that? That's nothing. Dale's just mad because he's getting evicted for not paying his rent." That didn't sound right, because Dale had been the one asking for money, but that must have been what Russ told his daughter when clued-in tenants showed up at his door demanding their stuff back. "No. My dad fell. He was drunk, and he fell down the stairs."

The ambulance was pulling away. "Do you want a ride to the hospital?"

She shook her head. "I hate the hospital. It's where my mom died." She pinched the loose end of her wiry bracelet and spun it around her wrist.

I sat down next to her. "Oh, I don't think your dad is in danger of dying, Bailey. You know what? My mom fell down some steps too, and she's alive and well." I didn't know why I was saying this. I had no idea how extensive Russ's injuries were.

"Yeah, but isn't your mom, like, brain-dead or something?" She looked up, blinked.

"No, she isn't. Who told you that?"

"Mr. Haas talked about it. Wasn't she in a car accident?"

"Well, I mean my mother does have a brain injury, but she leads a very good life. She's a successful artist." Why did I think it was comforting to tell her about my brain-damaged mother in this moment?

Bailey made some stuck-in-the-throat sound. "Could I come hang out with you for a little while?"

I went through a dozen ways I could say no. I was in no shape to console anyone. "Don't you have any family that can come and be with you?"

"My aunt's coming. She'll be here soon." Her voice was quiet; her eyes were fading out. I could tell she was under the influence of that water-submerged feeling that was shock.

Bailey followed me up into Lucas's suite and plopped down in the middle of his couch, mumbling something about being hungry. There wasn't much in the way of food in the apartment; the salad kit I had bought was liquefying. I pushed my finger into one of the white powdery donuts. It was still moist feeling, so I offered her some and a bag of chips. "That's all I've got. I haven't done much grocery shopping."

Bailey crinkled her nose but still wrapped her lips around a donut and cracked open the chips. "Do you want to order pizza?" Her voice had veered into something like bubbly. Almost cheerful. It was jarring, but I knew better than to think she should be acting differently in a moment like this. Children of alcoholics have no role model for normalcy.

So I obliged and ordered a pizza (with the extra toppings Bailey suddenly *needed* while I was placing the order with a squeaky-voiced kid). Her aunt would be there soon. While we waited for the pizza, Bailey peppered me with questions about living in Chicago. What did my apartment look like, what kind of restaurants did I go to, how many times had I gone to a Blackhawks' game? I indulged her, giving the "big city" the full mythical treatment. That was what a teen like Bailey wanted to hear, that there was an actual geographical place where it really did get better.

When the pizza arrived, I set Bailey up with some pop and a napkin and went to shower. When I got out, the TV was on. Bailey was laughing, loud and hard, as if she didn't have a care in the world. I shivered. Dried myself off and dressed in my last somewhat-clean outfit.

Finally, when it became apparent nearly two hours later that Bailey's aunt was not coming anytime soon, I told her I needed to go out. Again I offered to take her to the hospital; again she declined.

I was back at Shooting Stars dance studio or, really, in the parking lot across the street. A class was just ending. Girls scattered through the parking lot like pink confetti, disappearing into their idling chariots. Kathy left a few minutes later. Madison lagged behind her, awkwardly carrying a storage bin and looking really unhappy about it. *Kathy is my half sister,* I thought, and something twisted hard in my chest. I couldn't decide if I should follow her home. Knock on their front door again and tell her what I knew. I could tell the reporters to follow me. It'd be like a reverse Publishers Clearing House novelty-check moment. Peter Russo owed us something. Some slice of the Harold's fortune that was estimated at $1.2 billion according to Wikipedia (I'd checked).

That was what Lucas was after. He owed Tom Geller money, and it must have seemed like the sky had opened up and handed him this whopping reprieve when he figured it all out. But then it wouldn't have been only about the money with Lucas. It wasn't for me either. If Lucas had threatened to sue Peter, it was because that was the most tangible way to sling all of his anger and resentment at him. To pry us out into the open, to be acknowledged after a lifetime of being ignored, of being treated like twin bastards. It would force Peter to accept us.

But of course, money was always nice too.

And after Kathy killed her daughter, she thought, who better to pin it on than her half brother who might come after some of her rightful inheritance?

So then, what? She was coming for me next? It was soapy and outlandish and oh so media-friendly, and once this did hit the media, then the Wayoata PD would be forced to investigate Kathy as Joanna's and Lucas's murderer. The haze of suspicion hanging over Lucas would finally clear. He would want that, alive or dead. *Dead.* The word echoed through me; my bones jostled like I was a game of Jenga on the verge of collapse. I slapped my cheeks. *Not yet.*

I could test Joanna's hair against my own.

I sat in my car for a while longer, not wanting to go back to the apartment. Not wanting to run into Bailey. Not wanting to move at all. It'd been eight hours since I last took something to help keep me awake, and my body was turning to stone. I fell asleep. When I woke up, a light was on in the studio again, the blinds firmly drawn. It was one in the morning.

I got out of the PT, stiff-limbed, and crossed the street. The parking lot was empty. I tried the front door, locked. I went around to the back of the studio. There the door was unlocked. I slipped inside. A pulsing pop song was cranked up. Heavy padded thumps of feet were hitting the floor. The music paused. I heard the labored breathing of someone working out, then the music started up again. If I hadn't watched Kathy leave, I would have thought it was her. Maybe she'd come back.

I climbed a narrow staircase up to the studio. The door was propped open with a small plastic garbage bin. I pressed myself against the wall. A strong sweaty smell emanated from inside the room, overpowering even the fruit juice smell from the bin. I shifted, hugged the doorjamb, and peeked in. And then I saw who it was. I watched him watching himself hold his leg out in the wall of mirrors. Like a hippo in a tutu. Ben. He was wearing a witchy Halloween wig tied up into a bun. Red lipstick burned bright on his face, pink eye shadow circled his eyes making him look like a lab animal. Forehead beaded with sweat. He was in full drag. I could see it, clear as anything, the lunch lady. The lunch lady who'd followed Joanna into Dickson Park.

Sitting on the floor, atop a pile of denim, was a pair of red sneakers. My mouth went dry. They were so much like Lucas's that I was about to swing open the door and grab them, but thought better of it. I took my phone out, quiet. Waited for Ben to come back into my line of vision. I'd send it to Garrett. Finally, finally, the proof I needed. Ben spun back into view. My finger, poised triggerlike, hit the screen on my phone. The camera flashed. Dammit.

Ben saw me and screamed. A loud high-pitched siren of a shriek. He charged me. His shoulder crashed into my right breast, and I was thrown back into the wall. The garbage can went skittering down the steps. The studio door snapped closed as Ben busted through the back door.

I got up slowly, winded, my breast cramping hard with every movement. I called Garrett as I limped down the steps. Thankfully, he answered. I told him where I was and that he should come now. "You found Ben?" was all he said before I pressed End. When I reached the back alley, Ben was squealing out.

I stood there a minute, the darkness whirling around me. Short of breath, certain I would never breast-feed from my right breast, I took a mindless step forward and stumbled. I turned and went back up into the studio and picked up Lucas's shoes. No longer in pristine shape, but scuffed and double knotted. I hugged them tight against me, until my sternum ached. I wanted to swallow down a blister pack of anything that would make this marrow-deep anguish disappear. In the studio mirrors I looked dazed, and washed out, and insignificant. Scared and helpless. I needed to stay angry, I had to stay angry. I had to keep ahead of the snapping jaws of grief because once it got me, I knew that'd be it. I needed to stand up. Steel myself.

Garrett stepped into the studio and flicked the throbbing music off. Full of vindication, I was on him. "Ben has Lucas's sneakers. I was right. I was fucking right this whole time, and now he's gone." I was breathing too fast, my words were coming out wispy and rushed. "He knows where my brother is. I tried to get a picture. Evidence. He did something to him. He's going to get away."

"No. Mia, just calm down for a second, OK?" Garrett put his hand on my shoulder. "We won't let him get away. I need those." He gingerly took the sneakers from me and motioned for me to follow him back outside to his cruiser, where he placed them in an evidence bag. "We've been looking for Ben since this afternoon. Never thought he'd be here. The Arkansas ATM withdrawals, those were Ben. A camera on a convenience store caught Ben buying Slim Jims less than a block away a few minutes after the withdrawal. Which way did he go?"

"So he did do it, didn't he? He killed Lucas?" My heart was rising and breaking all at the same time. Garrett's cruiser was still idling. Insects made loops in the headlight beams.

"We'll know more once we bring him in. Just focus for a second and answer me, which direction was he headed?"

"South." I pointed in the direction Ben had turned out of the lane.

Garrett did a quick-draw of his radio and rattled off this info. When he was done, he gave me a solemn look. "We'll find Ben. Don't worry about that. Go home. I'll be in touch."

I wanted to say, *Like you found my brother,* but didn't.

I went to the station, even though Garrett said not to. Waited. Drank several cups of sludge-like coffee that left a silty taste on my tongue and tried to quiet the dread grinding inside me. I wanted to know where my brother's body was, because that's what it came down to now. Where Lucas's body was.

The police found Ben four hours later in Dickson Park, not far from Joanna's makeshift memorial. A dejected ballerina leaping around in the woods. A preliminary search of Ben's truck turned up nothing significant, no muddied shovels or bloodied baseball bats. Garrett texted me this, thinking I was at Lucas's place.

A cruiser pulled into the police station. Pruden and Garrett got out. Pruden opened up the back door and protected Ben's head with his hand as he pulled him up and led him inside the station. There were already a couple of reporters ready to go, who until that point had looked like confused geese who'd migrated too early.

"What are you doing here? I told you to wait at home," Garrett said when he saw me standing in the middle of the station's waiting area.

But I wasn't listening to Garrett or Pruden, or Pruden's reprimand of the receptionist working the night shift that she shouldn't have let me wait. Ben's hands were cuffed. Big Ben. My nephew, the man-child who most likely had murdered my brother. His own sister.

Makeup was still padded thick on his face. Mascara had muddied his eyes, bandit-like. The scoop neck of the ballerina bodysuit exposed a very freckled chest.

"Tell me where my brother is." I had practiced this, in my head. This calmness, and it surprised me that I could manage it. But Ben didn't look at me, only down at his scathed bare feet tapping out some rhythm only he could hear. "Please Ben, where's Lucas?"

He sniffed.

"I know you loved your sister, just like I love Lucas, so you can understand how I need closure. If you can give me that—" My voice caught. I didn't want this to be a weepy plea; I always felt weepiness got you less than your desired goal. I wanted to trick him into thinking I would forgive him, all I needed to know was my brother's whereabouts. "Ben, there's something you should know. Lucas was your uncle." I flinched at "was" and "uncle." "We're related. I'm your aunt. Your grandpa Peter had an affair with our mother." I was using that voice that I imagined good mothers used when explaining the bird and the bees.

His eyes shot up, his nose scrunched up, like he smelled something bad. He blinked. His eyes stayed open. "Huh?"

There was something in this, so simple and childlike, and I knew it was Kathy who'd told him to do it, to kill his own sister, my brother; more than anything, I knew it was Kathy. And the calmness I had scattered. "You killed the wrong fucking person! Lucas was just trying to locate our birth father, but I think you know that, don't you? I think Joanna told you that just before you bashed her head in and strangled her. Now where is my brother?"

Ben started taking fast shallow breaths, like a terrorized rabbit, and for a second, I went still, and I could feel the stillness come off Pruden and Garrett too. It was like a full confession was stuck on the tip of his tongue and any second it would lift off, easy, like dandelion fluff. Up and out, tumbling over those rapid breaths. It was brimming up, he made a sound in his throat, like he couldn't find the right word to start with, but then he was looking up, at his reflection in the flat-screen TV, off now, all the distressing stats gone.

But he wasn't looking at himself but at Kathy, who was waddling, quick, toward the station, an enormous purse flapping against her thigh. "Please, don't let her see me like this. She'll hate me." He whined into his chest, his face contorted into something ugly and alarming.

Kathy's hard voice cut through the air. "*Jessssus Chrrrrist,* Ben." It was a snarl of disgust, but not shock. She shook her head, like she was declining this version of her son. Garrett started to lead Ben away toward the interview room. "Ben, don't say a word. Nothing," she called after him. Her eyes flitted over me, then back at her son. "Mama's here, Ben. There's nothing to worry about."

"Mama, I'm sorry. Sorry," Ben called back before the door closed.

I braced myself for another blowout with Kathy, fistfuls of hair and scratched cheeks, but another officer was right there, leading her down the hall away from me. She didn't look at me, and all I managed to get out was, "Who's the fucked-up family now, huh?" But it didn't really have the teeth I wanted it to, because we were all related. Related fuckups.

I waited in Garrett's office during Ben's initial interrogation. Hoping that that moment when it had seemed like Ben was going to tell all would happen again. Hoping that he wouldn't heed Kathy's demand not to talk, but I knew when Garrett showed up at the door over an hour later that this hadn't happened.

"Nothing." He shook his head and sat down across from me.

I sunk forward. A high-pitched sound burrowed into my ear, like a tuning fork had been forced into the back of my skull. Every tendon that had been holding me up in the chair felt sliced by disappointment and frustration.

"He isn't talking. Not yet. He won't say anything about the ATM transactions or how he came to have Lucas's sneakers. He just keeps repeating that Lucas hurt his sister. But I have every confidence we'll eventually get him talking."

"So you think Lucas is dead?" I don't know why I even asked this. It was like asking a doctor if you had a sunburn when your skin was blistering red and peeling from the bone.

"I think we don't know anything for certain, not yet. But listen,

I owe you an apology. You were right about the Wilkeses' involvement, but we did what we could with the knowledge that we had."

It was a nonapology, but I couldn't even muster up a "Too little, too late." The letdown that he hadn't gotten something out of Ben was vise-gripping my stomach. Garrett quickly moved forward. "Was that true, what you said earlier, about you and Lucas being Kathy Wilkes's half siblings?"

"Yeah, it is." I told him everything then. Almost everything. I left out the part about the journal and the swatch of hair because it still sounded weirdly incriminating, but I told him that Lucas had been seen having intense discussions with Joanna, not because he was sleeping with her, but because he was trying to figure out who our father was. And he was right. "I think Ben killed them both on his mother's orders. Joanna was pulling away from her. She was pregnant, and Kathy couldn't handle it—maybe she thought Joanna really was having an affair with her uncle? I don't know. Kathy tried to rein her back in by paying the hockey players to sexually humiliate her own daughter. When that didn't work, Kathy killed her and saw an opportunity to pin it all on Lucas."

Garrett leaned back in his office chair; it squeaked. He rested his hands on top of his head. "Holy shit. OK, well let's test your DNA against a Wilkes tomorrow. That'd be the first step in building this theory of yours, because as of now, we don't have any evidence Ben or Kathy killed Joanna."

In the last several hours while I was waiting, I'd decided that even more than finding Lucas's body, I wanted him to be absolved of killing Joanna. I wanted it to be known that Kathy ordered her son to kill his sister. I wanted it to be known that Lucas's murder wasn't some vigilante reaping but cold-blooded. I wanted Lucas to be restored to his golden-boy status. I wanted everyone in Wayoata to feel terrible that they'd ever doubted it.

Garrett reached over and squeezed my hand. He looked stricken. His eyes, shiny and bloodshot, fixed on mine. His voice went heavy. "I am sorry, Mia. Really sorry I didn't do better by you in this investigation."

"Just promise me that when you go back in there, you won't come out until you get some answers."

Garrett nodded. "I'm going to use everything you told me before this lawyer Kathy called gets here. I'll keep you updated. I can text you every hour if that's what you want, but you need to get some rest. There's nothing you can do here."

I left the station, my eyes gluey and dry. Stepped into the bright, stunning morning that made the grief barbing around inside my body so intensely piercing that for a second I thought I might not make it to my car. I could just fall and die there, on the spot.

Lucas was gone. I was twinless.

26

DAY 12

SUNDAY

I entered Lucas's apartment, weak-kneed and in desperate need of something. I needed that ashy feel of a bitter pill between my molars, the taste of something dissolving on my tongue and the anticipation of looming oblivion. I popped three of Alice's Percocets, and while I waited for them to do their magic, I poured myself a king-sized portion of vodka.

The sunlight (I couldn't escape it) coming in between the blinds' slats slashed light across the coffee table. Across Bailey's forgotten plate littered with jagged grinning pizza crusts. Balled-up napkins dotted with tomato sauce. Her half-finished can of Coke, backwash coated and grease printed. I flicked open the box of pizza; there was one slice left. That girl had an appetite. The cheese had congealed into a white fleshy skin.

The smell of it was making me sick. I wanted to clear it all away, but I couldn't move. I reclined on the couch, my spine creaking out of its curled seated posture, and rolled onto my side. The Coca-Cola's squiggly "C" hooking into the "L" like a tongue, like a fishhook. My head was going fuzzy.

Eyes closed, I kept seeing Lucas. An agonizing fusion of nightmare and memory. Lucas submerged in water, his hair a floating wreath around his head, screaming so hard it looked as if the water was boiling in his open mouth. Lucas at seven years old, treading water, his scrawny arms in water wings that buoyed up beside his ears. Lucas in a burial plot, lighting a match over and over that kept going out. Lucas and me riding our jingly bikes. Lucas and me in Mimi's LeSabre, smoking cigarettes.

Finally the booze and the pills arrived, arm in arm like shiny partygoers. I slept. Sweet sleep.

But not for long.

The sound of knocking, a persistent knuckled drumroll, pierced the heartbeat sound pumping in my ears. Then I heard her. "Mia? Mia, are you in there? Helloooo? You there?"

Knock, knock.

Fucking Bailey. I couldn't lose her.

I had no plans to open the door. None. *Go away.*

"Mia?" The knocking was getting more insistent, harder.

Go away. I wanted to scream it, but then she'd know I was home and keep knocking.

Finally silence. I hoped she'd gone away, and I started to drop off again. But then the jangle of keys. I sat upright. The door was opening, the light from the hall spilling into my dim cocoon.

"What the hell, Bailey? You can't just come in here. You have no right to do that." I stood, stumbled off the couch, still in a heavy stupor.

"You're home." She looked startled, standing half inside the apartment.

"I was sleeping."

"Oh." No apology. She wasn't leaving.

"It's not a good time."

"It's just . . . I lost my bracelet. Is it here? I think it's here."

"I'll look for it later."

"I can look," she blurted. Then, baby-voiced, "It's just really important to me, and with everything going on with my dad . . ." She trailed off, because she assumed it was enough of an excuse to break in. She took another step inside.

"Fine, I'll take a look."

"No, really. I can."

I ignored her; she needed to be ignored. The bracelet was next to the couch. I picked it up and was about to toss it at her, fling it hard and tell her to leave, but the way it felt in my palm—the silky texture and the color of the threading. Something was wrong with it. I'd felt this before. This silky texture.

I rolled it between my finger and thumb, back and forth, and some of the threading came loose, and I knew what it was. Hair. Ginger-shaded hair braided up with the embroidery thread. It was the hair coming loose, going fuzzy around the thread. Now that I saw it, I knew.

I turned around, but Bailey was right on me. I bumped into her. Her face looked suddenly older, nostrils flared, her lower lip bent into a hard, stippled shell. Something was in her hand, and for a two-second beat, I thought she was trying to return Lucas's electric razor.

And then something bit into me, a sizzling pulsation. It went on forever. All of my muscles went hard and then slack. I had no control over my body and fell to the ground. I twitched all over, and my heart firebombed against my chest. My vision turned sparkly and sun-red, and I turned inside out.

I faded in and out. Felt myself being moved.

I was on a dance floor. The one I passed out on when I'd just turned twenty-one and had had too little to eat and too many of whatever I was taking. There I was, flat on my back. No one had stopped dancing. No one tried to wake me up, or even pulled me off to the side. They had just made a little circle around me and kept dancing, and when I woke up, I stayed there for a little while, under those laser lights spinning like spokes, watching everyone lurching and gyrating, all legs and wrists and chins. Fixated by the bizarre angle.

My eyes fluttered open, not to that dance floor but a food-stained linoleum. My hands were zip-tied tight; another zip tie had been looped through to leash me to the handle of an oven door. My arms felt drained of blood. Duct tape was pinching my mouth. The apartment was like Lucas's but smaller, a bachelor suite, and I was in the alcove kitchen. On the fridge was the Christmas picture of Lucas, Mimi, and me. Someone had carved X's into my eyes.

I looked out into the dim main room. There wasn't much furniture, just a pullout couch, two lawn chairs, and two substantial speakers throbbing out bass like thunder coursing up the walls, along the floor. I noticed the tinfoil window, and knew I was in the basement of the Terrace.

Something on the bed moved. Mr. Hideaway flashed in my mind. I tried to stand up and partially managed to get into some kind of half crouch and then I saw him. Lucas. He was turned the other way, facing the silvery window. He was wearing only boxer shorts and a bright blue tie that was tossed over his shoulder. Under the tie was something like a dog's pinch collar, with a metal chain, leashing him to the metal frame of the pullout. Even from the back, I could see his hair had been freshly gelled into some tousled style. The smell of cologne was overwhelming, badly masking rank body odor and the smell of urine. A bedpan was on the floor nearby.

Lucas, Lucas, Lucas. Luucaaas. I screamed his name behind the tape.

I couldn't tell if he was alive or not. His back was bed-marked red—it wouldn't be red if he was dead—and then I saw him move. I did. I tried to break away from the stove.

Lucas.

The oven door opened, and I slipped, my bare feet skittered against the linoleum. I tried to pull the stove out with me, toggling it side to side. Lucas rolled over and faced me. His mouth was duct-taped too, but drawn in marker on the duct tape was a set of oversized, ruby-red lips. Very worn, ruby-red lips. Attempts had been made to shave him, because his cheeks were a patchy combination of curly beard and bare skin. His hands were zip-tied behind his back; his feet too. His wrists and ankles were a pulpy mess.

He shook his head no. His eyes were bloodshot and terror-stricken.

A door opened somewhere in the apartment. From where I figured the bathroom would be.

"Oh, fucking great, Bailey, she's awake. I was hoping she'd just have a stroke or something with her stockpile of pills," Madison growled, and marched into the middle of the room, hand on hip. She was wearing a sleeveless black blouse like a micro-dress, her tiny waist cinched with a thin plastic belt. A heavy-looking, bauble necklace hung loose around her neck.

She was not wearing shorts and I caught glimpses of her silky underwear. She finished off her outfit with very spiky red heels that she skittered around on. She looked like a little girl who had raided her mother's closet (or some other tenant at the Terrace).

"I really don't know what you were thinking. You shouldn't have brought her here. You fucked everything up. Everything was fine. I just wanted time alone with my *boyfriend.*" She bared her teeth. "If you would just answer your fucking phone. Why did I even bother buying you a phone if you don't answer it when I call? What a waste of money. I would've told you, you had bigger things to worry about than your shitty bracelet. This is all on you. Not me. You!"

Bailey was in the room now too, sitting in one of the lawn chairs. Her head drooping, her hair now curtained around her face. Her hair, which had been dark but was now blond. Dark, just like the lunch lady's. She was the lunch lady, this pear-shaped girl who needed to be looked at carefully to see that she was fourteen and not pushing forty. It wasn't Ben in drag or Kathy. "Well, how do you want me to do it?"

"*Well, how do you want me to do it?*" Madison mimicked her. "I don't fucking care, just do it. And this music, Bailey—we really need something else. Seriously. I am getting, like, an aneurysm from it." She jumped onto the bed; the mattress heaved. She curled herself up against Lucas. In a flirty voice, she said, "This is all your fault too, y'know?" She flicked his tie like it was a little whip. "You've got too many women in your life, babe."

The sight of this girl climbing on my brother like he was an amusement park ride was sickening. My feet kicked at the floor as I tried to break myself out of the zip ties, but the oven just creaked open, closed, like some jabbering mouth.

I pressed my knees onto the door, put all of my weight on it, and it started to sink. A vision of breaking off the door and then swinging it around like some medieval knight's shield flickered clear in my mind. Then Madison was standing there, her high heels kicked off, bouncing back and forth like a boxer, and in a quick, jerky movement, she darted over me and turned the oven on high. I kicked at her, both legs thrashing. She let out a little giggle as she avoided me and said, "Feel the heat, bitch," and then skipped away and flopped back down again next to Lucas. The bedsprings squeaked harder. Madison kissed Lucas's neck, glanced up at me, half smirked, then leaned down and kissed him again. Where the tie encircled his neck I could see tiny bite marks, and down his chest, his skin had been rabidly sucked on, leaving a trail of fat hickeys.

Lucas shuddered squeamishly, turned his face away from her and tried to buck her off.

"Stop looking at us!" Madison hissed. "Oh, I get it. You want to watch. Sick. My aunt likes to watch me fuck my uncle. Lukey here told me all about it, Auntie Mia. It's definitely a bit of a mood killer, but you know what? It's not like Lukey here doesn't like doing his nieces. Isn't that right? Keep it in the family." She thrust herself closer to Lucas, licked at his ear. "Bailey, why are you just sitting there? Kill this bitch already."

Bailey got up, all slope-shouldered, and went around the corner.

I started again to pull at the stove, dragging it out from the wall. The veins near my wrists felt like they were popping. Madison rolled her eyes. Stood up again, lit some of the stubby candles on the floor that surrounded the bed, pulled at the sheets that had been bunched and tangled around Lucas's feet, gave up and left them there. Turned the music up. Got back into bed with Lucas, her head now on his stomach, dipping up and down on the ebb and flow of his breathing. Her finger circled his nipple.

On the wall over the pullout couch, written in loopy, clumsy cursive, was the word "destiny," like those sticky wall appliqués that were just as terrible as LIVE, LAUGH, LOVE coffee mugs. Hovering over it like it was a marriage bed. A teenage girl's sex crime was to want Lucas to love her back, for them to play house this way. To domesticate him, to make him her prince, the boy band member she could have all to herself. Some of his clothes were folded into tidy piles on the kitchen counter. Each had a distinct style theme. Lucas casual, Lucas formal, sporty Lucas. A human Ken doll they dressed up and undressed and made over. The Christmas picture was what? To make him feel more at home?

Bailey was back, with a serrated hunting knife. I started screaming, the sound raging through my throat. I tried to drag the stove farther out, but it was caught on a broken tile.

"Where should I stab her?" Bailey blinked, turned around to Madison.

Lucas thrashed around. "Settle down, babe." Madison put a hand on his shoulder, then yelled back at Bailey, "I don't fucking care."

Bailey raised the knife, and I tried to avoid it, practically tried to crawl inside the oven, the elements red-hot and licking at my face and arms.

"Well, don't do it here! God, Bailey, what the fuck?" Madison's arms were folded tight. "This is getting exhausting already." She grabbed her bag, pulled out her own stun gun, and zapped Lucas against his chest. He let out a deep growl, and his body arched up and went stiff, then sagged back into the mattress. "I said settle the fuck down. Goddammit, Bailey. Deal with this." Madison flicked her hand.

Bailey nodded, sighed. With the knife, she cut the zip tie that had hitched my bound hands to the oven door. I lunged at her, but Bailey was ready and struck me in the head with her hulky knee. Something crunched in my jaw.

"Get up." She hauled me up. This girl was strong, like carpenter strong, like handled-a-drunk-dad-for-years strong. She was stronger than me. She pushed me toward the door, the knife piercing the back of my neck. I hoped someone would be out in the hall, poking around their storage space. There was no one.

Ahead of Bailey, I saw my opportunity. I made a run for it, ripped off the duct tape, screamed for help. I made it to the main stairwell door, but it was chained shut. I shook the door, hard. Hoped someone would hear it rattle and wouldn't write it off as the pipes.

"Stupid bitch." Bailey had me by the shoulder again, but I twisted around, fast, and hammered her with fastened fists. Like I was dropping a mallet, as hard as I could, somewhere in the face. She stuck her knife out and up, and it speared into my wrist down to my bone, but also cut the zip tie. My hands popped apart. I shoved past her and ran down the hallway. I stumbled up four steps to the other door, the one that led out to the side of the building. It was locked, not with a chain but a dead bolt. My hands, slick with blood, shook as I clumsily twisted the thumb turn, took a step out. It was dark. There were two lonely cars on this side of the parking lot, and an abandoned shopping cart. The lot was practically empty. I screamed for help anyway, and then I felt it, the knife sliding into me from behind, just over my hip.

Bailey's arm wrapped tight around my neck in a choke hold. She half dragged me back inside, down the hall, to the mechanical room. A trail of blood ran thick along the carpet. Inside the mechanical room, with her free hand, the hand with the knife, she flicked on the greenish fluorescent light and pushed me hard to the ground. My shirt was hot with blood.

I crab-crawled back on the concrete floor, away from her, tried to press myself between a giant old boiler and a hot-water tank. Bailey walked toward me, slow, not at all worried.

"Bailey stop, just stop. You don't have to do this."

"Shut up!" She sniffed, tugged some hair out of her face.

"I just don't understand why you're doing this. I thought we were friends."

This gave her pause. She tapped the knife against her thigh. "Bullshit. You couldn't stand me. People think I don't notice, but I do. I was being friendly, and you were trying to get rid of me."

"What are you talking about? I was upset about my brother. That's all. Otherwise I would have been more talkative. We're friends,

Bailey. You don't need to do this. You just need to let me go, and we can still be friends." The room was going wavy, the mold growing behind the water heater was catching in my throat, a pipe was dripping somewhere.

Bailey shook her head. "Madison would never let me do that, and I know you'd tell."

"No, no, I wouldn't tell anyone. You don't need Madison. You really don't." My hip was burning. "I had a crush too at Westfield, on the guidance counselor."

"Mr. Lowe? Ew, he's so old."

"I did, though, and you know what? It passed. I just forgot about him. You need to go and tell Madison that, OK? That she'll get over it, she'll hardly even remember Mr. Haas. To just let him go. And if you have feelings for Madison, you need to know that one day—"

"Oh my God, just shut up already."

"Bailey—"

"I said *shut up*! She's my best friend. She really is." She jutted her chin out, in a dare-you-to-contradict-me expression.

"I know she is. But she isn't being a good friend to you right now. She's getting you into trouble. What will happen to your dad's job here when the agency finds out his daughter kidnapped her teacher and kept him in an empty basement apartment?"

Bailey, shaking her head, let out an airy snort. "It doesn't matter. I don't need to worry about him anymore or this shithole place. I'm going to live with Madison."

"You sure about that, Bailey? She's not very nice to you. How do you know she didn't just use you to get to Lucas?"

"I know because we were friends before that."

"Before when? Lucas has been living in this building for a while now."

"Whatever. Maybe she did use me in the beginning. I don't care because I used her too. Then we became real friends, and people are a lot nicer to me at school now that I'm BFF with Mads. Now I'm popular. I can get people things."

"By stealing from tenants?" So it had been Bailey coming into

Lucas's suite, not Russ. Not Mimi. One of these little bitches lathered me up in my sleep, probably Madison with her long purple nails, who equated a manicure with honoring the dead. She likely told Lucas afterward, as if it were a twisted day at the spa with her future "auntie sister-in-law," or maybe she framed it as a friendly, caring gesture, like she'd given me a makeover that would win over all the boys, hoping my brother would stop looking so queasy when she sucked on his chest. "Listen, Bailey, I know what it's like. I wasn't very popular in high school either, but then I left Wayoata and saw that there's a whole world out there and none of this high school nonsense matters."

"Oh, OK. Guess I'll just let you go, then. I'm sure you'll just let me come and live with you in Chi-ca-go." She overenunciated "Chicago," let the syllables ricochet around the room like a spray of bullets. "Do you think I'm retarded like your mom?"

"Bailey, think about it. Do you really want to live in the room next to a girl who killed her own sister? Who's letting her brother take the blame for it?"

"Madison didn't kill Joanna. We did it together." She held her arm out. The bracelet was back and tied so tight it carved a little valley in her chubby wrist. "See this? I took some of her hair that day and made these. One for me, one for Madison. We're, like, binded forever now. We did it together. And Ben'll be fine. He really will." Then she added airily, giving me a little-darling smile, "He likes the simple things in life. All it took was a pair of sneakers to get him to drive as far as he could to use Mr. Haas's bank card." And here I pictured the hot pulses of the Taser, the drag of a hunting knife, the glint of Madison's teeth as she clamped down on his skin, making Lucas spill out his PIN number. "Of course the idiot goes to where his grandparents live to do it. I don't care. Ben'll probably even enjoy prison, surrounded by all those dudes. Far away from Mommy, who won't let him be a guuurrrl." Another *haw-haw* laugh. "Don't worry, we'll smuggle in some lipstick for him."

"But why? Why did you and Madison kill Joanna?" I needed to keep her talking. The pain in my side was getting worse, sharper, like acidic bile was gathering inside the wound. My mouth was going cold and numb, and I didn't know how long I could keep this conversation going. Behind my back, my hands were scrambling for something. I picked up a short, rusty nail. Fucking great, so I could kill her by tetanus poisoning eight days from now.

"We didn't mean to kill her! Madison just wanted to give her a bad haircut because she was so stuck up. She was always, like, flicking her hair, acting like it was so precious." Bailey mimicked the act with her own thin, greasy hair. "We told her Abby wanted to meet her, and then I was just supposed to knock her out, and she'd, like, pass out, and Madison'd, like, hack it off. Joanna was supposed to wake up in Dickson Park all half bald. She'd prolly have amnesia, and have no idea what happened. I had to hit her hard enough for the amnesia." Something, maybe a wisp of regret, passed over her face. Obviously she'd had this amusing slapstick head bop in mind, like cartoon birds were going to turn up and encircle Joanna's head as Madison cut her hair off.

"But she was strangled. So it wasn't an accident."

She rolled her eyes, angry that I'd pointed out this minor indiscretion. "She woke up halfway through. She was mad and started yelling at Madison. Calling her all these shitty names, saying she was gonna tell on her, so Madison had to shut her up. It's so stupid how everyone thinks Joanna is all great now that she's dead. You know what? Joanna deserved it. She was not friendly. Not friendly at all. She thought she was gonna be this huge star in New York and made sure everyone was so impressed by her. Then she starts going after Madison's man? Like, seriously? Joanna knew Mr. Haas was off-limits." Mr. Haas—she retained this formality, this respect. Had they called him Mr. Haas the entire time? "Even after Madison tried, tried, like, really hard to give her a chance, to humble her before, y'know? Joanna still walked around like she was the shit."

Humble her. Madison had set the hockey players on her own sister. "Uh-oh, SpaghettiOs?" It just came out, like a question.

Bailey nearly doubled over with laughter, the knife wagging back and forth against her leg. I hoped she might drop it, that I might even be able to kick it out of her hand. "Hilarious," she heaved. Cheeks pink.

"So what does Madison think? That she and Lucas are gonna go off and get married? Have kids, live happily ever after? Because you have to know that's not going to happen."

"Maybe, maybe not. But they'll always have apartment 1B, won't they? And at the end of the day, Madison won. She got the guy. Not Joanna. For once, not Joanna, who had everything. Anyway I've gotta go." Bailey came down on me, and I kicked and clawed, lost the nail, but her knife just kept coming, slicing up my hands as I grabbed at the blade, at my arms, into my legs as I tried to draw into the fetal position, and then again into my stomach, and I went still. I couldn't move; I felt pinned to the ground. My lungs were twisting. Bailey stood over me, a black silhouette. Slowly, she drew the knife out and watched me, her head cocked as I emitted these strange, jagged rasps. I was either getting some air back or taking my final breaths.

She tapped her foot against my leg, and I didn't move. *Just play dead,* I thought. Then I realized that I couldn't tell if I was playing dead or actually dying. Finally, she turned and left. Switched the light off.

I needed to get up or I was going to bleed out in this mossy room. I was going to die in here. The girls would make it look like I just gave up and went back to Chicago. No one would even look for me for weeks. And Lucas would be chained up like a dog, dry-humped for who knew how many days, until he starved to death. Until Madison grew sated and bored? *No. No way. I am not letting two fourteen-year-old psycho bitches kill us. No.* My eyes slowly adjusted to the dark; all the little red lights on the various tanks were like runway beacons. I got up onto my knees, and realized that I should be in more pain than I was, then thought of the handful of Percocet I took how many hours ago. It was still in my system. (Thank God for a pill addiction.)

I tried to stand and slipped in my own blood; my arm shot from under me and landed on something under the hot-water tank. I dragged it out. A giant wrench, at least the length of my arm. I used it to stand up, like a cane. Its curved end wobbled. I could hardly pick it up, and so I saved my strength and dragged it behind me as I lurched forward, serial-killer style. It scraped against the concrete floor, but I knew they wouldn't be able to hear me over the music. As I opened the door, the hallway light crashed into my eyes and wooziness hit me. I nearly toppled over in the doorway. I spit out a gob of blood.

A few more steps to 1B. I knocked on the door hard, with the wrench handle. A shadow passed over the peephole, and I could hear Madison say, "It's her, Bailey. Good fucking job."

Somehow, I lifted the wrench, held it up like a baseball bat. My pulse accelerated, and I could feel my blood jetting out even faster. My body started to sway, my vision rippled. Bailey swung open the door, and I smashed the wrench into her face. She staggered back; blood sprayed from her nose like a fine mist as she fell back into the small closet next to the door.

Madison, who was behind Bailey, started backing up. She bumped into the bed. Then onto the bed. Scrambled over Lucas, to the far side of his legs. I brought the wrench up, walked the length of the bed toward her.

"No, please don't. I'm just so mixed up, Mia. I don't know what I'm doing. I need help. My mom . . . she just loved Joanna so much more than me. They were going to leave me behind. Remember the things we talked about when I slept over? It was a cry for help. Taking those pills, a cry for help. I need help."

I could see her hand inching toward her bag still on the bed, the stun gun. I brought the wrench down on her arm, and it cracked like a bird's wing. Her purse went skittering across the room. She screamed and writhed around at the foot of the bed, the clot of sheets fell off and onto a trio of candles. The sheets went up in flames, as if doused in gasoline, and I thought of the stink of cologne. They'd been dousing Lucas, the sheets, the bed, in cologne.

I staggered toward Lucas; any second, that mattress was going to catch. My hands were on the dog collar, unhooking the metal buckle, when I felt two arms wrap around my abdomen, squeeze. White-hot searing pain as I was wrung out like a dishcloth, blood drained. Half lifted up, my feet scrambling.

Bailey screamed, her voice thick and nasal, "Got her, Mads."

"Hurry up," Madison whined.

I struggled to find my footing as I was dragged backward and then thrown forward to the ground, my chin cutting against the tile. Bailey was on my back now, grunting. She grabbed me by the hair and started smashing my face into the floor. One, two, three dull smacks, like trying to break open a cantaloupe. My nose flattened back up into my skull. I couldn't breathe, more blood, so much blood. I was being dunked into a puddle of it.

"Fucking kill her, Bailey!" Madison's shrill voice cut through the air, like she was cheering on the quarterback at a football game.

I saw the stun gun under the bed. I twisted my body and swung my arm up wildly toward her face. I felt my stomach rip and let out a howl. My elbow connected with her already gushing nose. She fell back, taking some of my hair with her.

I started to crawl toward the stun gun, my fingers just grasping it as Bailey snatched at my neck. I flipped onto my back, pressed it against her neck, and pulled the trigger. She toppled down onto me. I felt all the air go out of my lungs. God, this girl was heavy. It took several attempts to roll her off.

I struggled to get to my feet. My muscles were seizing, something was clicking loose. I stumbled forward onto the bed, finished unhooking my brother. Stood, then sunk onto the floor. My body was giving out. Lucas rolled off the bed and started shuffling toward me, his feet still bound. He nodded toward the door. *Let's go.* He tried to reach out behind his back and grab my hands in an attempt to drag me, trailer-hitch like. The mattress was on fire now too. The whole room was hot, so hot.

Madison jumped out of the flames and onto Lucas's back, letting out some primordial growl. "You fucker. Where do you think you're going?"

Lucas twisted forward, his neck corded; he snapped his head back into hers. Hard and fast, and Madison flung backward, hair whirling like a doll.

And then the room, the spinning, smoky room started to shrink down into a pinhole. I heard Lucas talking, the sound of his voice through the duct tape, but could not make out what he was saying. I felt a hand on my ankle.

A faraway sound of voices. Someone was saying my name over and over. Madison wailed little-girl hiccups of panic. "Help, help. He raped me."

Then nothing.

27

DAY 16
THURSDAY

I woke up to a crackling jumble of senses: a bed, gauze, that antiseptic smell, and whatever was being fed through my IV. Lucas was there, sitting next to my bed, watching a muted baseball game on a TV someone had rolled in.

We were safe.

I tried to say something, but my voice was garbled, my throat sticky.

He heard me anyway. Stood, let the remote fall off his knee, and hobbled over. "Hey, sis." He held up a mug of water and aimed the straw at my mouth. The ice water prickled down like shards of glass. My nose was packed with gauze, and I immediately started coughing. My abdomen felt like it was tearing.

"Hey, hey, take slow sips. Whoa, slow down, you bruiser. You've been out for three days. Don't try to move." I smiled at "bruiser."

"You OK?" My voice was a nasally slur, but Lucas understood.

"Yeah. I'm fine. Don't even worry about me, I was just really dehydrated and had some minor burns. My ankles were infected, but I'm taking antibiotics and they're working. I'm good. You, on the other hand . . . fuck, Mia." His eyes went watery; his face crumpled. "I don't know what I would have done if I'd lost you. I don't." He shook his head back and forth fiercely, as if trying to dislodge the thought of it.

"They would have killed us both." They would have had to eventually kill Lucas too. That little arrangement couldn't have lasted much longer, and it wasn't like they would have just let him go.

He tipped his head back to the ceiling, palmed his eyes. He looked wrecked. "I know. You saved my life."

"Don't cry. You'll make me cry, and that will really hurt." I could feel hot tears rolling down toward my ears, and the first tremors of full-out sobs budding in my flayed midsection, threatening to tear me open again. I tried to reach up, hold his face, this face I'd been searching for, but the movement brought a tidal wave of agony. It felt like three hundred pounds had just been set down on my chest.

"I should go get a doctor."

"No, not yet. Just talk to me first." He started to say no, but I cut him off, "Please?"

"Only for a few minutes, OK? But stay still. I won't cry if you promise not to move." His bottom lip stiffened. His hand hovered above my face, like he was looking for an undamaged spot to stroke, then settled for tucking my hair behind my ear.

"Promise." He was thinner, the shine in his blue eyes subdued. Clean-shaven. I hadn't seen his face so hairless in years. I caught glimpses of him at twelve years old, which was probably the last time I'd seen him cry (that's the thing with siblings—you never stop seeing the children you once were floating beneath your grown-up faces). "Thank goodness the flames missed your face." A jab at his vanity.

He patted his smooth cheeks. "I know. This could be even more tragic." He laughed, but it was a forced, hollow chuckle. We stared dumbly at each other for a few seconds.

"The last thing I remember was the bed catching fire, so what happened?"

Lucas pulled his chair in even closer, a miserable-looking scuffle and drag, tugged his gown to make sure nothing was showing, and sat down. "We got out just in time. The whole suite went up, and the fire spread to the first and second floors. The entire building had to be evacuated." I wondered if that had cured the agoraphobe or if she was still there, smoke-blackened, stroking all her ashy gray cats.

"How did the cops know where we were?"

"My caretaker, Russ, told them. The second he woke up, he told a nurse I was in a vacant basement suite. I guess he'd finally noticed his daughter was acting secretive and hanging out a lot in the basement, and decided to have a look-see. Stellar parenting there. When he tried to confront his daughter, I could hear them in the stairwell. She attacked him with her Taser and hit him in the head with a hammer. After Russ saw me and didn't come back . . . I thought I was done. The girls were starting to panic. I don't know how much longer I would have had, Mia. Even before Russ showed, I think they were getting bored with me and starting to decide I wasn't worth the trouble."

"Bailey? Madison?" Suddenly I pictured Madison at the station, nibbling a frosty donut and sipping a chocolate milk as she gave her statement about Lucas kidnapping her, while some social worker nodded enthusiastically, believing every word.

"Alive. Both of them have been arrested. They're facing a number of charges: murder, breaking and entering, assault, forcible confinement, the list goes on. I can't believe anyone could hate her sister that much. I don't know how much time Madison will serve, though. Her lawyer is already tossing around terms like 'intermittent explosive disorder' and claiming she isn't criminally responsible. Your cop friend, Garrett, told me that Bailey could be bumped up to an adult court because she's fifteen years old. Do you know that girl wasn't even in any of my classes?" Lucas shook his head. "I only knew her from around the block. I'd say hi, but I hardly noticed her."

Bailey. All she wanted was to be noticed. I could see her in an interrogation room, pleased that she could finally hold people's interest. She'd be coy about her answers, not wanting it to end. "You've been cleared of all charges?"

"Yes. Thank God. Mia, I really can't tell you . . . you went to hell and back for me. I wouldn't be here if it weren't for you. If you hadn't believed in me." His voice went thick, he gently squeezed my hand without the IV. Tried to laugh because he didn't want to cry. "And now you look like hell."

I gave him a scrappy grin. "Thanks, and yet all this gauze makes me *feel* so pretty. At least one of our faces was spared. Of course I had your back, Lucas. Always. Plus I'm the only one allowed to be MIA."

"I am glad you weren't though—MIA."

"I didn't want to believe it. I knew you wouldn't have a relationship with a student, but then I found the hair and the journal. Still, I knew it was impossible for you to ever kill anyone. How did this happen? Tell me everything."

Lucas took a deep breath, blew out. His lips looked painfully chapped. "I saw an entry in Joanna's journal about a lake house, and something just went off in my head." He snapped his fingers. "I drove out there one day, and I knew I'd been there before. It helped too that Mimi drew a friggin' picture of it. Anyway, I didn't do anything about it at first, but it just sat there, nagging at me, and then I would get so angry that we'd been paying for Mimi's care, that I'm in debt because of it, that I tried to make more money gambling, and I knew you were paying for more than half. I know you tried to hide it, but I knew, and it made me feel like shit. And this whole time we could be related to the family who owns the Harold's chain."

"Why didn't you call and tell me any of this?"

"I was going to, when I knew for sure. I just didn't want to disappoint you if I was wrong. So I started talking to Joanna. I asked a few things about that lake house, who owned it, for how long, did her mom go there too. I guess I started to freak her out, so I just told her I thought I could be her uncle. She was so happy about it. She even thought we had the same nose. We talked about going to St. Roche to do an avuncular test months ago, but it didn't work out. Joanna had a lot of other things going on, so I didn't push it, obviously. Plus we kind of built this nice rapport, like I was the cool uncle she could talk to, y'know? She brought it up again a couple of weeks before she went missing, when it seemed she was starting to feel better after everything she'd gone through. She just asked me, don't you want to know for sure? So I set up an appointment."

"You know you can send away for those kits? You didn't have to go to GenTech."

"The kits don't hold up in court, and if Peter Russo was our father, I wanted to sue for back payments on child support. It's just, when I figured it out and called Peter, and he refused to come to the phone, *refused,* I was just so pissed. I fixated on the money after that. He owed us something. He could at least help us pay for Mimi's care. I just wanted something from him, y'know?"

"I do, but you didn't think that could have been misinterpreted? You and a student, alone in a car, headed out of town?"

"I was used to those kinds of rumors. I didn't take them seriously enough. I mean, there's one every year about me and some student, so I just decided, what the hell." He shrugged. "It was stupid, I know that, but I was sure the test would be positive, so if anyone were to misinterpret it, I could say I was her uncle. It didn't matter anyway because Joanna canceled. She felt so bad about it, she cut off some of her hair and gave it to me. She thought I could use that."

He shook his head again; a sad little burst of air escaped the back of this throat. "She was just like that, y'know? A good, considerate kid. I kept it, the hair, because it felt wrong to throw it out. Plus, who knows, maybe I could have used it if we never got a chance to do a swab test. Which I guess we didn't."

"What about the phone? You should have gotten those kids arrested."

"Joanna had threatened to kill herself if anyone else found out about what the players did to her. She trusted me." He touched his chest. He said this with such conviction; I could tell he'd gotten lost in his own sense of uncle-duty. "I felt it was more important that the players didn't send the pictures around, have it go viral. Even if I did manage to get all the pictures and had the players charged with assault and removed from school and the team, other kids would find out who the girl was and make Joanna's life a living hell. It's happened before. She begged me not to do anything, to keep the phone. I had more power over those kids with the phone and the threat of arrest. When I was put on a leave, I brought it all home to hide it."

"Why didn't you just go to the police when you were put on leave and tell them about all of this?" A nurse came along, flicking at the end of the needle to inject a sedative that I would normally so welcome, startled when she saw I was awake, and said she'd have to get the doctor. "Could you hold off? Just a little while?" I asked. She glanced at Lucas, a flash of a hopeful, flirty smile, though he didn't notice, and said she could give me another few minutes, max, and catwalked out. "So?" I prompted. Lucas chewed his bottom lip. It was something we both did when we were worried or thinking hard.

"So. I didn't go to the police, because the day after Joanna went missing, Madison came to see me. She said she had a message from Joanna, not to worry about her. She just needed a little time to sort things out because she was pregnant. I guessed that was why she canceled St. Roche. I kept thinking, just when it seemed things were turning around for her, this had to happen. I knew all about her bad relationship with her mom. I knew she faked injuries every so often to get out of dancing, and maybe getting pregnant would finally be her way out of whatever pressure Kathy was putting on her. I don't know, it just made sense she'd stay away."

"But Joanna was missing for three weeks." So Kathy wasn't abusing her daughter. I really was just a cruel knife-twister in her eyes. Not a good feeling. I was wrong, but so was she.

"I know. I would obviously have done things differently now. But at the time, Madison kept coming to my classroom between classes, feeding me bits of information like Joanna was about to go back home. She was about to tell her mom she was pregnant, but was afraid Kathy would make her have an abortion. Then something else would happen—Joanna decided herself not to keep it and was going to return after she got an abortion. Then she'd change her mind *again*.

There was something too about how Dylan was going to meet up with Joanna and they were going to live at his mom's house. Then that plan fell through. She was always on the verge of coming back and then something would happen. I was being fed a line of shit, and I *fucking bought it,*" he said, incredulous.

"Didn't you ask where she was?"

"Of course I did. *Sheesh,* Mia are you going to let me tell you or not? I feel like I'm in another police interview."

"OK, sorry."

"I asked Madison over and over, but she wouldn't tell me where Joanna was staying. She'd drop hints, but then say Joanna had moved on to someplace else. Some other friend's house or a cousin. Whenever I pushed Madison to tell her mother or the police or else I would do it for her, she would just shut down. I'm talking a hyperventilating tantrum. Crying, rocking back and forth. She said if I told, then I'd be the one responsible for killing her sister because Joanna would commit suicide for sure—how fucked up is that? But Joanna committing suicide, it really wasn't that far-fetched. I knew Joanna was in a fragile state. She was pregnant. She had a troubled relationship with her mom. This girl was feeling increasingly depressed and trapped. In the meantime my truck was trashed; people were really starting to talk. When I was put on a leave and the police asked me to come in for an interview, I told Madison that was it. I was done. I was telling the police that she knew where her sister was. She begged me to give Joanna the weekend. She looked at me with these big, watery eyes and promised that Joanna would be back on Monday. I never would've thought—" Lucas let his head droop forward, clawed his forehead. I couldn't see his face, but I guessed it was full of self-loathing. "I gave her the weekend."

"It's not your fault." Yes, he should have done things differently, but he couldn't blame himself for what Madison did.

He looked up at me, his cheeks bloodred. "Yes it is. You want to know the most pathetic part?'

"Lucas." I hated how much he was blaming himself. I wanted to stand up and hug him and tell him none of this was his fault.

"I was actually thinking somewhere in the back of my head that when Joanna did resurface, she would probably tell people how I'd protected her from the players, from herself, that I'd helped her get some space from her family before she did something more drastic than fake a twisted ankle. I kept picturing Peter hearing about it, about me, and thinking I was a better man than him. That I was a good guy." Lucas stared at something on the floor. His forehead went veiny. So that was it. That was why his actions were so off. So out of sync.

"That's not pathetic. You felt rejected. Look at me." He did. "You're not pathetic." He gave me a headshake that said he'd need more convincing, but not now. Blew out a gust of air and threaded his hands together loose between his knees.

"Madison already knew I was her uncle, you know. I don't know when Joanna told her, but she knew."

I had a flash of Joanna's last moment. Literally pleading uncle to her sister just before Madison started to tighten the scarf. "What happened next?"

"Next thing I knew, Bailey showed up at my door Sunday afternoon saying Joanna was in the basement and wanted to talk to me. When I got there, it was Madison. *Madison.*" He said her name again, slowly, like it was some foreign word he'd just learned. "I had no idea she had a crush on me. Sometimes she said inappropriate things, wore revealing clothes. I'd find her waiting for me at my car, sitting in my chair, or she'd lean across the desk, trying to be provocative, but she wasn't that different from the other girls in her crew. She's fourteen. Eric said girls that age were test-driving their sexuality and to ignore it—"

"Eric's an idiot."

"I just didn't think . . ." He shuddered. "Fuck, and that whole time that little psycho had killed her."

"They made bracelets out of her hair. Bailey and Madison. I don't know which one is more terrifying; Bailey, who went along with it for the fun and fringe benefits of having a popular, rich friend, or

Madison, who could kill her own sister over an infatuation with someone she could never really have."

"They both scare the shit of me. I didn't even know Joanna was dead until Garrett told me. She was such a bright girl. She reminded me of you. I knew she was going to be OK, once she got out of this town. Away from her mom." He went quiet.

I was starting to need whatever the nurse had in that syringe. "So I met Dad." I said it all breezy, or as breezily as I could manage, like Lucas and I were having lunch in some café. I didn't want us to be sucked into the vortex of whatever PTSD might be on the horizon, not yet.

He looked up. "What a dick, huh?"

"A total dick."

"Well, maybe Peter's not a total ass." He pulled an envelope off the table. "This is for you." He brought it up close so I could watch as he opened it for me. A card with purple flowers coated in a sparkly dust.

GET WELL SOON.

I realize any apology is lacking, especially one made here, but it must be said: I am sorry. I would like to get to know you, if you'll let me.

—Peter Russo

Lucas unfolded the paper that was inside it. A check. Not a set-for-life check but definitely an amount that changed life as we knew it. It was probably hush money, but we'd never have to worry about paying for Mimi's care again. We wouldn't have to worry about a lot of things if we cashed it.

"I got one too." He flashed a hard grin at me.

"Should we accept it?"

"Why wouldn't we?"

So he didn't know. I told Lucas an abbreviated version of my meeting with Peter. He hunched forward, listening, nodded once with a fleeting look of satisfaction that he finally knew the truth about Mimi's accident, but it didn't last and was quickly replaced with wariness. I was suddenly sorry I'd told him; I'd ruined the money for him. But he had to know.

Lucas kept his elbows on his knees, thinking. When he looked at me again, he said, "What would Mimi do?"

It was a rhetorical question. An exit to the moral dilemma of accepting money from the man who had faked our mother's car accident.

"Yeah, what would Mimi do?"

"Keep it," we said at the same time.

"So, what're you going to do with it?" I asked Lucas. "Get that prime real estate in Wayoata you're always going on about?"

"Maybe. If I do, it'll have an impressive guest room. *Even get that new-finagled electricity everyone's talking about?*" He did his hillbilly impression, the one he did when he was trying to call me out for being Chicago-snooty.

"OK, first you're using the word 'finagled' completely wrong, like, totally wrong. You teach English, right?" Lucas laughed. "Or maybe you can get something close to your sister in Chicago."

"That's an idea. Really, it is."

"And don't forget Tom Geller's cut."

"Geller? I owe that guy five hundred bucks, and not until the end of the month. I was stupid. I placed a few bets, lost, and haven't done it again."

"Five hundred? He tried to shake me down for four grand." I told him how I'd thought Geller had smashed in my back window.

"Sounds like Geller. Skeeze-bag. I'm done gambling. Really."

I'd push him later on to make sure he meant it. Send him pamphlets on Gamblers Anonymous programs or whatever. Now wasn't the time. The nurse was back with a vexed-looking doctor, both ordering me to rest.

Lucas stood up again, rearranged his gown. He came in close, pressed his scabby lips to my cheek, saying, "I'll be back later," and started a slow shuffle out of the room, one hand clutching the back of his gown. I watched him go, framed between the crook of the nurse's elbow and the doctor's hip. Noticed just as he reached the door, sparks of cherry-red, dazzling amid the hospital's bile-green color scheme, his high-top LeBrons. He turned back, gave me that chin-up nod that we'd given each other countless times before, a nod that said, *We're OK.*

28

SIX MONTHS LATER . . .

Lucas stood on Mimi's bed and draped a string of Christmas lights around her window. When he finally got them to stay put with some strategically placed Scotch tape, I plugged them in, and the riotous colors beamed into the room. Mimi clapped her hands and jumped up and down. I'd forgotten how much she loved Christmas. Not just as she was now, but always. (This was why Lucas had stuck that old photo to his fridge—it reminded him of Mimi at her best. He always was more sentimental than me.) Tufts of tinsel were draped everywhere, on the TV, her dresser, and unwisely, in her secret ashtray (we'd deal with that before we left). I kept glancing at a pill bottle on her nightstand and fought the urge to check it out to see if it was something I'd like. I hadn't touched anything since my last painkiller (prescribed, by the way) three months ago. I won't lie. It hasn't been easy, going without the fine tweaks that pills offer, but I am doing it. Whenever a craving bites into me, I lift up my shirt and stare in the mirror at the knife scars that stipple my skin. "You lived, don't waste it." I say this to myself out loud. For some reason this works.

Back at work, certain pills no longer made my mouth water. During my time off, while on my "disability leave," I'd realized I missed my job. Missed my quirky, overnight clientele. Helping that sleep-deprived mother who staggered into the pharmacy, blinking under the hard lights like a feral cat, choose the best medicine to quell her child's fever and cough. Or gently explaining to a teenage boy, close to dying of embarrassment, that over-the-counter wart remedies don't work quite the same down there.

There was a pharmacy on every corner for a reason. I was needed.

Mimi insisted we eat our turkey dinners in her room. "You're here to see me, not those wack jobs." So here we were, Christmas in Mimi's room. It was easier this time. Being here. We sat in a little circle, our TV trays angled toward one another. The turkey and instant mashed potatoes and cauliflower and canned beans were all blanketed with the same salted taste, so we kept knocking back the apple cider from our small plastic cups. The Weather Channel (most watched station in Wayoata) was on and playing a steady stream of Christmas carols. Sober Christmas. Almost nice.

The Wilkeses had sent us a Christmas card. A single-sided glossy photograph, with Kathy, Ian, and Ben in matching Christmas sweaters. Ben (wearing stuffed reindeer antlers and maybe an ever-so-slight smear of day-old mascara?) held a framed picture of Joanna. Kathy signed it "The Wilkeses," which I took to mean no longer included Madison. So we were on their Christmas card list. Maybe that meant something, maybe it didn't. Either way, it was a surprising gesture.

I'd talked to Garrett too, a lot, over the last few months. First there were visits in the hospital, then over e-mail, and on the phone. Conversations about the upcoming trials mostly but sometimes about life in Chicago, sometimes about life in Wayoata. Garrett wasn't such an asshole when he wasn't trying to arrest my brother.

He called both of us immediately when the paternity results came in and Joanna's unborn child did not match any DNA samples on file. Paternity would be marked unknown. I felt this was a win for

Joanna, who'd confided in Eric about seeing an older man she didn't want to get in trouble. Whoever he was, he wasn't in trouble.

"Here." Mimi handed us two rolled-up canvases, decorated with Christmas ribbons, made curly by the drag of something contraband-sharp. Two paintings. She gave us each a portrait of ourselves. Lucas received Mimi's rendering of one of the stock photos that was constantly circulating when he was being accused of murder. The one that was taken when he was coaching, in which he had a furrowed, angry glare, and that was meant to intimate this teacher had a dark side. The one of me was clearly from the press conference.

Lucas made a face. "Really, Mimi? This is what you picked to work with?"

Mimi nodded, full of brimming excitement. "It's because you're both so famous. Everyone tells me that."

"These are nice," I managed, nudging Lucas with my elbow. Yes, the choices of images were terrible, but it reminded me, in a way, of that feeling I got years ago when she'd just finished getting me ready and we both kissed the tissue. There was care put into getting me just right.

And the painting of me was not a shabbier, rushed version of Lucas's. It was equal. And I had that thawing feeling again. I wished she hadn't had the accident. I wished all kinds of things had turned out differently for Mimi. But here we were, and I was thawing.

Dessert was microwaved apple pie. After that, Mimi demanded we sit for another portrait and so we spent the next ninety minutes being accused of moving and getting stiff backs until she said she was tired. She walked us to the door, taking the longest possible route through all the various rooms so she could parade us in front of the other residents. We stood outside the LightHouse, waiting for Mimi to get back upstairs and wave us off through her bedroom window. It was a new thing she had to do; Lucas said if we didn't wait, then there could be an issue. So we waited. A heavy wet snow was falling like icy licks on our faces, and we had to keep stepping side to side to stay warm.

Lucas was back at Westfield. When I asked him how he could go back there after the way he'd been treated, he shrugged and said it was the only thing since playing hockey that he felt he was supposed to be doing. I believed him.

Mimi showed in the window. She gave us a queen's wave, while a glow of red and green and blue blinked on and off around her. We waved back.

ACKNOWLEDGMENTS

Thank you to my amazing, talented, incredibly intelligent agent, Beth Phelan, who knows exactly what needs to be done every step of the way. I don't know what I'd do without you!

Thank you to my remarkable, articulate, and wise editor, Amy Stapp, for her razor-sharp eye and for having all the answers on how to make it better. You are a dream to work with!

I also want to extend my gratitude to everyone at Forge for all of your hard work and dedication.

Thank you, Sherry Graham, for being the fastest reader in the west and for catching that someone really shouldn't take their lunch with them into the bathroom.

As well, thanks to my generous neighbor Stacey Hauser for being an early reader, and for all the backyard fires.

I am also so appreciative to Krista Nicholson and Jenna Harrison (aunties extraordinaire) for their babysitting services so I had more time to write. Cheers to the wonderful, caring staff at my Safeway Pharmacy for answering all of my sketchy questions.

Thanks to all my family and friends for chatting up my books to anyone who will listen.

There is not enough space here (or anywhere) to thank you, Tara. In case you don't already know, you are selfless and brilliant and the best thing that has ever happened to me.

Incalculable love to my daughter, Rowan, the other best thing that has ever happened to me. You are the light of my life!